RECLAIMING THE FORGOTTEN GODDESS

Rebekah Sinclair

REBEKAH SINCLAIR

Where to Begin

The Forgotten Goddess

The Unforgotten Flame (Novealla)
The Unforgotten Vow (Novelette)

Awakening
The Forgotten Goddess

Reclaiming
The Forgotten Goddess

Book 4: Title Pending
Anticipated Release: Fall, 2024

WARNING: This book contains content that may be triggering.

- Mentions and depicts mental health trauma responses: anxiety, PTSD, and panic attack disorder.
- Depicts non-consensual sexual content and violent sexual assault such as non-consensual oral sex, anal rape with a foreign object, group rape, beastiality (rape of a Shifter in animal-form by a Shifter in human-form).
- Mentions and depicts mutilation, torture, human trafficking.
- Mentions and depicts child endangerment, abuse and death.
- Contains explicit language, sexual content, physical violence, abduction, and death.

To: Amber

As I emerged from my cave of darkness, thank you for being the first person there, ready to greet me with your friendship.

Enjoy listening to Reclaiming The Forgotten Goddess playlist on Spotify!

A song has been added for each chapter to represent the tones or themes of the chapter.

Carrying me in his arms, Hermes kicks open the door to his home on Mount Olympus. Stalking over the threshold, he slams it shut with a wave of his aura. My fingers thread his dark locks as he marches to the bedroom.

"Hermes." His name is a whisper on my lips. "I think I'm going to be sick," I grumble as my stomach roils loudly.

"I'm going to fucking skin Orion alive for giving you so much fairy wine." Hermes' voice is gruff as he stomps through a dark home. I can't help but hiccup and giggle at his protectiveness.

His anger fills the air around us, yet he carries me tenderly, guiding us through the darkness with a soft, comforting light. I'm curious about his home but I make the mistake of letting my head drop back to see the hall as we pass.

Dizziness overtakes me, my stomach threatens to overturn my dinner, and Hermes hurries to the bathroom.

Just managing to reach the bathroom in time, I double over as the remnants of our Avalonia feast empty from my stomach. Hermes has gathered my long hair behind me. He even holds the long chain of my sword necklace, keeping it from swinging into the path of vomit as my stomach heaves again. It's painful. There is just so much.

So much wine and chunks of food that are rapidly exiting my body along with my pride.

"That's it." Hermes' voice is calm and reassuring as he kneels beside me, offering support with gentle hands. One is wrapped around my hair and the other is tenderly holding my side, helping me remain upright.

Mortification washes over me. We've only been reunited a few hours and I'm puking my guts up.

I reach behind me, trying to take my hair from his hold, and shoo him out between heaving.

"You don't have to stay," I mutter, cheeks flushing with shame. I barely get the words out when another ghastly round of projectiles race up my throat and eject themselves into the toilet bowl.

Sweat beads on my forehead and all the strength I had in my body evacuate as quickly as the contents of my stomach.

"After four centuries apart, would you have me leave?" Hermes' tone is gentle and carries a tinge of humor, but I hear the plea within his words, and it has the intended effect on my resolve.

Resting my head on my arm, I can only offer him a grunt for an exhausted response. I swear, I can feel him grin behind me as I relent to his request and let him stay.

A trickle of water from a nearby faucet is followed by Hermes patting my sweaty forehead with a cold damp rag. Another trickle and he places a second rag on my neck.

The relief is temporary as another spell of convulsions overtakes me.

I hold onto the toilet with everything I am. This single

white fixture within an unfamiliar bathroom is the only thing holding me down. Without it, I would spin away into a drunken oblivion.

But Avalon was beautiful, and we had such a lovely time. It was truly a land of fairytales and so easy to fall into the revelry. Acting as a *'queen's escort'*, as Hermes explained it, we returned Mor and Hypnos to their realm, along with their.... *cargo.*

Orion stood at the top of the path, a formidable presence among the fae. He was unlike any other I had encountered, though my memories were a jumble of confusion and shadow. Of course, the fae of Nightfall are the only ones that I recall meeting in all my past lives.

Adorned in fine attire, his black leather garments hugged his tall, muscular form. Silver accents gleamed against the darkness of his outfit, complemented by his flowing silver locks. The billowing black cape made him look like night incarnate as he watched with unmistakable malice as Demeter became Nightfall Castle's newest captive.

Orion's gaze met mine and his eyes softened. A smile graced his lips.

"The night welcomes you, goddess," he greeted respectfully, lowering himself to one knee with his court following suit in a deep curtsey.

Avalon, the realm of eternal nightfall, home to the Unseelie fae, has always revered me as a deity of darkness. Even as some fractured memories of past visits float to the front of my mind, it has always felt awkward to receive their respects in this manner.

I bowed my head in return as my cheeks blazed with embarrassment and Hermes pulled me to him with a hand on my hip.

I'm not sure if he realizes the comfort he gives me when I'm reaching a moment of feeling unpleasant or stressed but each time, it makes my heart swell with happiness.

As Orion rose, the assembly followed suit. He took my hand, pressing a gentle kiss to my knuckles. "The night finds solace in your presence, and Avalon's moon has never illuminated a more radiant soul," he declared, casting a sly glance at Hermes, a mischievous grin playing on his lips.

"Okay, that'll do." Hermes interjected, reclaiming my hand from Orion's grasp. A shared laugh resonated between us and Orion as he patted Hermes' shoulder.

"I jest, cousin. Your beloved is safe from my charms," Orion assured, winking at Hermes, who responded with a narrowed glare. "Come, goddess, we eagerly anticipate our reunion."

I couldn't help but relish in Hermes' subtle flare of protectiveness. *I could get used to a jealous Hermes.*

Side by side, we descended into the dungeons to confront Demeter.

Hermes kept a firm hold on my hand; his presence provided a reassuring anchor amidst the torrent of emotions swirling in my abdomen. The underbelly of the old castle was cool and damp, like my clammy hands and it sent a shiver down my spine.

Demeter was cuffed by her ankle and no longer wearing mortal clothes from Gaea. She had been changed into an ivory nightdress, and more fitting of the attire of the Avalonia fae.

I wanted answers. I wanted to confront her and understand what I did to earn her betrayal in such horrible ways over my lifetimes.

"Why" I asked, with a quivering chin as tears brimmed my eyes but she refused to acknowledge me. "Why?" The second time, it was nothing more than a whisper. My voice and my bravery dissolving in her nearness.

Her once warm chestnut eyes now burned with a solid black intensity as she finally acknowledged my presence.

In a sudden outburst, she charged at the iron bars, spewing black acid that was swiftly intercepted by barriers of light and shadows conjured by both Hermes and Orion.

As quickly as Hermes' wields his Light, Orion subdued Demeter with a black whip, his power coiling around her like a serpent. Wrapping the whip around his body and stepping on it, Orion pulled Demeter to the ground where her knees hit the hard stone. She grasped the black rope, which tightened around her like a coiling snake.

"Answer," Orion growled.

Gritting her teeth against Orion's power, Demeter still refused.

A shadow ending with a claw of obscurity lurched into her throat, and she choked, trying to trap her answer before it spewed out of her.

"Because I hate you." Demeter's voice dripped with venomous hatred. Her answer rushed out of the dark plume of murkiness as if Orion's shadows pulled the response from her throat.

Snarling, she looked up at me. "Because you stole everything from me." Standing, she paces across her cell. "You strolled in with all your power and privilege and run right into a spell."

She snorts a laugh of hatred before she spits on the stone floor. It sizzles with the toxic venom in her saliva.

"You have no idea what it means to suffer." Her voice rose with each word, her anger building as spittle flew from her mouth. "You are the reason Avalon is dying and my power dims. You. Owe. Me. For what you have robbed from me. And the Fates know how much I looooved making you pay." She drew the word out as if she was giving it sweet affection while speaking it.

Shock rang over my face as I recoiled from her words. Hermes' warning growl echoed my indignation, but Demeter remained unyielding in her anger and bitterness.

She acted like dying a thousand violent deaths is a walk in the park. That I choose this fate.

"I took nothing from you." I defended myself, blinking hard as tears fell down my cheek.

"You tumbled in here like a falling star and tied this realm to your fate like a selfish child. You robbed me of my reign as queen, the reign I took from my mother and sister."

The shadows collect and grow around Orion at Demeter's admission, and he steps toward her. Something in her mention of the women sparks his anger and I'm curious if they meant anything to him.

She stopped speaking and stood, backing away while the coiled whip remained tight around her. "When you die next, I hope this realm mourns you so I may revel in the joy of knowing you failed, yet again, like a boundless fool."

Refusing to hear any more of her poison, I turn and stalk toward the dungeon steps. Hermes takes long strides to catch up with me. With his arm wrapped around me, he escorted me out of Starfall's dungeons.

It took me several minutes to collect myself and stop the flow of angry tears. The sting on my heart took long to calm.

The Unseelie fae celebrated my arrival with a great feast and dancing but Demeter's words haunted me through the evening. The staff kept our goblets full of sweet red fae-wine and I never tasted anything so delicious.

I drowned out Demeter's bitter words with drink, food, and dancing, losing myself in the revelry until her voice faded into the background.

Everything was fine until we crossed back through the swirling mass of my powers, returning to Gaea. Like being squeezed through a keyhole, it's as if my drunkenness increased tenfold.

The weight of Gaea, the heaviness of this world, and the hunter that stalks me from within came crashing upon my back as soon as we returned to the realm.

Hermes' blue light flared, and he transported us to Mount Olympus, where I'm currently praying to any deity that will listen to cure me of my dizziness.

Gone for only a second, Hermes uses his power to retrieve a pitcher of chilled water and a cup. Drinking deeply, I roll the cold glass against my forehead, seeking solace in the sensation. Eventually, the room begins to steady, prompting me to cautiously open my eyes. Hermes sits across from me, a content smile adorning his handsome features.

"You're finding this amusing, aren't you?" I murmur, regretting the decision to open my eyes as I rest my head against the wall, closing them once more.

Hermes' warmth envelops me as he draws closer, his spicy scent soothing my senses.

"I'll never enjoy seeing you suffer," he assures softly, resting his chin atop my head and gently stroking my arm. "But being able to care for you? That's something I cherish more than anything in this world," he whispers, his words piercing my heart with their sincerity.

A swell of warmth floods my chest, tears threatening to spill from my eyes. Focusing on the threads of his shirt as so many memories of past torment flood my mind.

Isolation, fear, and exclusion were the companions she ensured surrounded me in so many of my reincarnations. Her main purpose was to make me feel the loneliness and hatred she had for herself. To make me feel as powerless and trapped as she felt. And it worked.

Goddess, it worked so many times.

For hundreds of lifetimes, I lived in solitude, never feeling whole because the other half of my heart was searching for me. In each of those lifetimes, the woman I believed loved me, and cared for me, was harming me more than Ares ever had.

Demeter's words, spit at me with venom from her Avalonia cell, run through my mind as we sit in Hermes' bathroom. That same cold chill that encased me in the belly of the castle wraps around me now.

Tears trace a path down my cheeks, betraying my attempt to suppress them as memories of Demeter's hateful gaze flood my mind. But Hermes doesn't admonish me for crying; instead, he remains patient by my side, offering silent comfort as I unravel in his embrace. His whispered assurances of unwavering support and shared strength weave around me like a protective shield, soothing the storm of emotions raging within me.

Gradually, my sobs subside into hiccups as Hermes encourages me to drink more water, his gentle touch accompanied by a wave of his calming blue light eases the pounding headache in my skull. In his tender care, I brush my teeth, then he carries me to his bedroom, a sanctuary from the chaos of my tumultuous thoughts and the frigid bathroom.

Once there, Hermes helps me out of my clothes with practiced ease, exchanging them for soft, silky pajamas that caress my skin.

"Lay down." His unwavering gaze anchors me, keeping the room from spinning as dizziness still grips me.

He removes my shoes and unbuttons my pants, replacing them with comfortable silk shorts. Leaning over me, he presses a kiss to the exposed strip of my stomach, his touch soothing the tension and easing my queasiness with another wave of his calming light.

At that moment, I realized how much I could grow accustomed to this; having a partner who takes care of me and can alleviate my discomfort with a simple gesture. It's a stark contrast to the struggles I faced last week, crawling through the Underworld, crippled by agonizing cramps.

I just have to make sure I don't screw things up pushing him away. I'm riddled with trauma, and it will be a long road to recover myself. Even after I've recovered my powers, the path to recover my mind will be a much longer and slower path to traverse.

But I know I'll have Hermes with me through it all and I send a prayer to the Fates he will have patience with me; that I'll have patience with myself.

Moving upward, he places a kiss on my shoulder, then another on my neck. The tightness of my limbs from our battle in the ocean subsides.

Taking my hand, Hermes meets my gaze as he presses a kiss to my knuckles, mirroring Orion's earlier gesture.

I *knew* it bothered him and an unabashed smile plays on my lips as I watch him now.

"If you ever allow another man to kiss any part of your

body," he begins, lowering my hand and trailing a kiss behind my ear before continuing, "be prepared to watch me incinerate the flesh that covers his bones."

A surprised laugh escapes me, taken aback by his morbid yet fiercely protective declaration. "Gods, that's rather grim," I reply, attempting to suppress my amusement.

"Don't say I didn't warn you," he retorts, his grin bordering on menacing and biting my lip to hold back my smile. I *do* like this territorial Hermes.

As he pulls back the covers of his bed for me, I settle in, relishing the cool sheets and plush duvet that envelop me like a comforting embrace. With a contented sigh, I pull the covers up to my chin.

Hermes removes his shirt in one fluid motion, leaving me momentarily breathless as I admire the muscularity of his form. My fingertips tingle with the urge to trace the contours of his body, and the sight of the deep V leading below his waistband sends a flutter of longing through me.

Retrieving a remote from the bedside table, Hermes closes the curtains and dims the lights, casting the room in a soft, romantic glow. A blue fire dances in the fireplace, adding to the ambiance of the intimate setting.

"Very impressive," I murmur, my gaze lingering on him as he discards his pants, leaving him in only his black boxer briefs as he joins me in bed.

"Well, if you think that's impressive, how about this?" he teases, snapping his fingers to conjure a swirl of blue light above his head. From the shimmering portal descends a tattered, old book, which he catches with a mischievous glint in his eyes.

His efforts to impress me are endearing, and the boyish sparkle in his eyes as I smile at him fills my heart with warmth.

It's a first edition print of "Romeo and Juliet," addressed to Hermes and signed by William Shakespeare himself.

"Until you reunite with your Juliet."

As I run my fingers over the ancient ink, a gasp of disbelief escapes me. It's an account of our shared history, of the lifetime we lived as star-crossed lovers, long ago in Italy.

"It's about us, isn't it?" I murmur, thumbing through the yellowed pages, already knowing the answer.

Hermes nods, and together, we read the old tome, immersing ourselves in the timeless tale of love and tragedy. Each word he reads, I recite with him in my mind, having memorized the old story of the star-crossed lovers.

"Two households, both alike in dignity, in fair Verona, where we lay our scene, from ancient grudge break to new mutiny, where civil blood makes civil hands unclean."

As Rhea drifts off to sleep in my arms, a profound sense of happiness washes over me.** A feeling I never thought I would experience again in my immortal life. For hours, I remain by her side, watching over her slumber and listening to the rhythmic cadence of her breathing. Finally, the gnawing emptiness in my stomach threatens to disturb her peaceful rest and I ease away from her.

Quietly slipping out of the bedroom for a brief shower, I make my way to the kitchen to take stock of our pantry and refrigerator. Despite the distance to the Delphi Commune, a mere two hundred miles from our home on Mount Olympus, the portlet will make quick work of replenishing our supplies with fresh produce and provisions.

Our home.

The phrase echoes in my mind, bringing a smile to my lips as I survey the near-empty cabinets. Rhea's very presence within the walls of our old home brings life back to the mountain; and life back to me.

For four centuries, the loss of my mate has plunged me into darkness too deep to see through. These past four hundred years, it's as if my soul has waded in the obscure recesses of nothingness searching for her light.

Now that she is here, it's as if my eyes are looking upon the first ray of starlight that has ever shown and I never want to look away from her.

My phone buzzes and I read an incoming text from Atlas. *"Need you. 911."*

I dismiss it without hesitation. Not even a rebellion in Elysium could pry me from this homecoming with Rhea.

I silence my phone, after sending a quick text to Achilles and Callie. Surely the realm will survive a day or two without a catastrophe and I can stay wrapped up in the goddess sleeping in my bed. *Our bed.*

Uncertain of Rhea's preferences, I err on the side of abundance while ordering provisions. Our Life elementals infuse our produce with their power to ensure nothing spoils.

It's been ages since I last set foot on Mount Olympus, having retreated from this place after Juliet's tragic demise. In those dark moments of mourning, this sanctuary served as my refuge, much like the caves Medusa once sought solace in.

When mourning my mate became too dark and my thoughts spiraled downward, I would isolate myself here.

Callie and I undertook a renovation project here about five years ago, transforming the estate into a sleek and modern home adorned with floor-to-ceiling glass windows that offer breathtaking views of Olympus' majestic beauty.

Every home I've had boasted a library filled with Rhea's collection of books. The collection of books I safeguard with the deaths of my mate.

Thoughts of the library I curated back in Atlanta flood my mind, a space I never got the chance to share with Rhea before everything turned to shit. Maybe we'll be able to sneak back there, so she can at least see it.

As I mix the ingredients for a loaf of bread, my mind wanders to the countless libraries Rhea never had the chance to explore.

Those thoughts start to take me down a dark spiral and I don't want anything to dampen our reunion. Instead, I focus on the memory of Rhea illuminating the realm of eternal darkness during our visit to Avalon. Her curiosity had been tinged with sorrow at Demeter's vile lack of remorse.

After visiting the dungeon, a dark shadow draped over Rhea like a veil of mourning. Demeter's words cut her deeply and I would do anything to remove that pain from her heart.

But amidst the darkness, there were moments of light, like when we danced together at the castle, Rhea's smile radiating joy as we twirled to the music. In those moments, her eyes sparkled brighter than any star in the sky.

And that moment is the one I cherish. The brief few seconds she was in my arms and spinning happily to the music. I want an endless supply of lifetimes for her with that same joy and wonder. The Fates owe this to her for retribution of her suffering.

As I place the dough in the oven, I immerse myself in the next dish, finding solace in the act of cooking. It's almost as if I'm in a trance, lost in the rhythm of chopping and mixing until I'm jolted back to reality by the sound of Rhea's footsteps entering the kitchen.

Turning to face her, I'm momentarily spellbound by her presence. The delicate blush on her cheeks perfectly complements the soft pink of her sleepwear. Her tousled hair framing her face in a wild halo. With a nervousness that only adds to her charm, she bites her bottom lip, a gesture that never fails to captivate me.

Setting aside my kitchen tasks, I move toward her, feeling a surge of warmth as I wrap my arm around her waist and draw her close. The smooth silk of her pajamas under my touch twists my longing for her into a tight knot in my stomach as I pull her in for a tender kiss. Rising onto her tiptoes, she meets me halfway, our lips meeting in a sweet and familiar embrace, igniting a spark that never fades.

Kissing Rhea feels as natural as drawing breath, and the desire to let my lips linger on hers is overwhelming. But I know she's still recovering from her ordeal and needs nourishment to ease her hangover.

Reluctantly pulling away, I guide her to a stool and seat her, concern etched on my face from how much fae-wine she consumed. "Are you feeling any better?" I pour her a glass of iced herbal tea before returning to the stove to put the finishing touches on her dinner.

"I'm never drinking again," she declares with a hint of regret, eliciting a chuckle from me.

"You're only half immortal, little goddess. You still need to take it easy until you regain your full powers," I remind her gently, ladling generous servings of soup into bowls and arranging the rest of the meal on a platter.

Laying the spread before her—cabbage rolls, crusty peasant loaf, sliced tomatoes with feta cheese, and a bowl of chopped melons. Rhea gazes across the array of dishes, momentarily unsure where to begin. Slicing her a few pieces of fresh bread, she dips one into the soup.

Her lips wrap around the spoon, and I can't pull my eyes away from the sight. A moan slips from her mouth and my cock strains in my pants. Gods, I want to know what that moan feel like when I'm pushing myself to the back of her throat.

As we eat and converse, laughter fills the air, mingling with the aroma of our meal. The soup and bread disappear quickly, followed by the cabbage rolls, while we pick at the tomatoes and Rhea savors the chopped melons. Seeing her preference for the orange cantaloupe, I make a mental note to get her more.

As the meal draws to a close, I take her hands in mine, helping her to her feet and enveloping her in a tender embrace.

She tilts her head, meeting my gaze as I cradle her head in my hands, the warmth of her smile against my lips sending my heart racing.

"Do you want anything else?" I murmur softly, stealing another kiss before she can respond.

Rhea's eyes twinkle with delight as she fidgets against me. "Can I take a swim in your bathtub?"

"It's your bathtub," I reply, punctuating each word with a kiss. "It's your library." Another kiss. "It's your home; our home." I lean in for another kiss, and she eagerly responds, her tongue brushing against mine before she pulls away.

"Careful, little goddess," I whisper with a playful growl. "Keep that up and you'll never make it to the bath." I wink at her, and she bites that lip again. A blush spreads across her cheeks as I release her, leaning against the counter. "Get in there. I'll clean up the kitchen."

She tiptoes around the library, likely grabbing a book to enjoy while the rush of bathwater fills the tub. Meanwhile, I take care of the kitchen, cleaning dishes and sweeping the floor to give her time to relax.

Glancing at my phone, I see no urgent messages from

Callie or Achilles. Atlas has texted me multiple times, but I ignore them. He can seek help from Odysseus or Medusa; anyone but me. My sole focus is on Rhea.

As I scan the property and mountain with my aura, ensuring our wards and shields are secure, a dark thought creeps into my mind—the image of Ares draining Rhea of her power and life.

Though Demeter's removal from our realm has diminished one threat to Rhea's life, Ares remains her largest adversary, growing more desperate by the day. But tonight, thoughts of her hunter will not overshadow our time together.

Night drapes its velvet cloak over the realm. Dim light spills from the bathroom as I lean against the doorframe, watching the goddess who holds sway over every beat of my heart, savoring a bubble-filled bath.

Her legs, elegantly crossed on the edge of the tub, tap along to the rhythmic music, while an open book partially obscures her face, its pages turning with her gentle movements.

The warm lights enhance the honey hues of her hair and eyes, which are fixed intently on the text. She's twisted her long locks into a messy bun and stuck a pencil through it to keep it in place.

I need to remind myself to bring her the tablet so she can order herself some provisions from the Delphi Commune; but that can wait for later.

With my arms crossed over my chest, I admire her. Her eyes dash across the lines of the book and as she turns the page, she notices me.

As her stare meets mine, a crooked grin spreads across my face, basking in the simple joy of this moment. We are like any other couple, unwinding at the end of the day, shielded from the chaos and danger that often besieges our lives.

Within these walls, nothing can harm her, and I almost want to keep her here. Lock her away in a tall tower like the princess in the fairytale she is reading. But I could never stifle her like that.

She is most radiant when she is burning brighter than the sun and she needs to be freed. Released from the shackles of this torment that locks her in perpetual reincarnation. And that is exactly what we're going to do.

We're going to free her and reclaim her life.

Recovering half her powers should feel like a victory.

Instead, it feels like we climbed a mountain, only to discover a larger mountain is waiting for us next. But now that we're together, we'll make it over a thousand mountains if it means breaking her torment.

The key to finally undoing this spell is hidden somewhere in the darkness and I'm determined to be the light that will help her find her way back to herself.

Rhea holds the book with one hand and lets it hang over the side of the tub. Her eyes roam down my body and my blood rushes through me. My arousal surges as her gaze meets mine, pleading for her touch.

Rhea crooks her finger twice, inviting me to join her.

I'm pulling my shoes off and moving across the room before she can toss the book onto the counter. Stripping myself of my shirt, I climb in the tub, still wearing my pants.

W ater sloshes across the bathroom tile and Rhea erupts into a fit of laughter. "You're soaking the floor!"

"I'll clean it up," I mumble against her neck, planting kisses along her soft skin and teasing her collarbone with gentle nips.

Her arms wrap around me, granting me better access as I continue my exploration. My lips trace a path across her neck, tasting the droplets of water that cling to her skin. Her fingers weave through my hair, sending shivers down my spine.

Breaking away from her neck, I capture her mouth with mine, our lips meeting in a fervent dance. She responds eagerly, her moans mingling with mine as our tongues intertwine in a passionate embrace.

She tastes divine, like the sweetest nectar, and I can't get enough of her. With one hand gripping the edge of the tub for support, the other caresses the curve of her waist, drawing her closer to me.

Our bodies move in sync, the rhythm of our passion causing more water to spill over the sides of the tub. Despite the mess, her laughter fills the room, a melodic symphony that only heightens my need to have her.

I crave every sound she utters, to sense every muscle in her body tense with each of my caresses. The desire to savor her, to consume her completely, overwhelms me, much like the water cascading over the tub's edge.

"Can I please take you to bed?"

Her teeth graze her lip as she nods her head, yes.

As I rise, her legs wrap around me, her wet skin slick against mine. With careful steps, I guide us out of the tub, mindful of the slippery floor beneath us. Despite the precarious footing, our lips remain locked in a fervent embrace, our mutual desire driving us forward. Her arms tighten around my neck, drawing me closer, her body pressing against mine with a hunger that mirrors my own.

With a firm hold on her thigh, I draw her to me, craving the sensation of her skin against mine. Every fiber of my being yearns to feel her, to merge with her completely.

As she releases one arm from my shoulders, her hand moves in a graceful gesture, commanding the water to retreat from our bodies and the floor. I feel the dampness evaporate from my pants, leaving us dry. Her power envelops us, clearing the space around us as we stand, consumed by the heat of our shared desire.

Pressing her against the wall, I lavish attention on her breast, swirling my tongue around her nipple before drawing it into my mouth. I feel the firmness of her flesh beneath my hand as I tease and nibble at her sensitive peak, coaxing the first of many sweet moans from her lips. Each sound she makes ignites a fire within me, driving my desire to new heights as I lose myself in the taste and feel of her.

Rhea's nails rake through my dark hair, urging me on as she arches against the wall, her chest pressing against me with an irresistible invitation. I continue my journey down her body, trailing kisses, and gentle nips along the tender skin beneath her breast. With each touch, her soft gasps and the heat of her skin fuel my desire, driving me to explore every inch of her with fervent attentiveness.

"Hermes,"

Her breathy voice, filled with desire and need, whispers my name like a sacred invocation, igniting the light within me that shines brighter with each syllable. Hearing her say my name is a melody I could listen to for all eternity, a symphony that binds my soul to hers forever.

She straightens herself and pushes gently against my shoulders, stopping me before I move to her other breast.

"Wait." With her hand on my cheek, her honey eyes searching mine, I sense a heavy weight in her words. "I need to tell you something first."

Rhea's nervousness is palpable, and I wait with bated breath, ready to listen to whatever she needs to share.

My heart swells with concern as I gaze into her eyes, feeling the tension in her touch. "Hey," I whisper softly, my thumb tracing soothing circles along her cheek. "You can tell me anything." My voice is gentle, encouraging her to share whatever is weighing on her.

She closes her eyes and hides the golden hue from me.

Gently, I lift her chin with my fingertips, coaxing her to meet my gaze once more. "Rhea, please," I murmur, searching her for any hint of what's troubling her. "We don't have to..."

"It's not that." Her eyes flash open. "I want you; gods I want you so badly." She takes a breath as if she's going to say something else, but she pauses.

My heart flutters at her words, but I sense there's more she needs to express. "Tell me," I encourage softly, my hand still cradling her cheek. "Whatever it is, you can trust me." I lean in, pressing a tender kiss to her forehead.

Her hesitation is breaking my heart. I want her to feel at home, in every aspect but mostly, I just want her to feel at home with me. I couldn't care less about where I am, as long as I have Rhea by my side, knowing she's safe and sound. That's all I need to feel at home, and I want the same for her.

Since we're both dry, I carry her to the bed. Nestling in, we lie facing each other, the blanket enveloping us in warmth. She edges closer, seeking comfort in my arms, and a wave of relief washes over me.

I ease the pencil from her hair and gently unravel the twisted bun. Massaging her scalp, I carefully run my fingers through the silky strands on her long hair, splaying it out on the pillow behind her.

"You're the most precious thing in this realm to me, Rhea," I murmur, tracing the soft glow of moonlight on her face with gentle fingertips. "Please don't be afraid to tell me what you need."

"I just—I've never." Her words falter, stumbling over the weight of her unspoken confession. Turning onto her back, she intertwines her fingers, frustration evident in the huff that escapes her lips.

Rhea's admission hangs in the air, her gaze fixed on the ceiling as she reveals her vulnerability. "I've never experienced a genuine orgasm," she confesses, her hands moving to shield her eyes, avoiding her mortification.

I can't help but smile, not out of amusement at her, but the fact she is ashamed over some jackass's inability to pleasure her is endearing. "Manual stimulation seems to do the trick, as you're aware," she continues, meeting my gaze with a flicker of defiance.

I fight against the smile that wants to spread wider, thinking about the moments in the Underworld when she thought my astral projection was not real as we shared our healing through our auras.

"But nothing else makes me orgasm, so I just thought you should know." She finishes with a huff.

Propping myself up on my elbow, I trail a finger along her collarbone. Gently nudging the covers aside, I reveal her tan nipples and repeat the gesture on her breast. Her skin reacts, forming goosebumps under my touch as a flush spreads across her cheeks.

"A *real* orgasm, you say?"

Her gaze flickers towards me, perhaps to assess my response, and catches me grinning. She playfully smacks my chest, feigning offense. Seizing her wrist, I guide her arm above her head, positioning myself on top of her. As I nudge her legs apart, she instinctively wraps them around me.

"But you've faked them?" I inquire, meeting her guilty gaze.

She nods, a hint of remorse coloring her expression.

"Two things– well, three things." I begin, with a serious expression as I look into her eyes. "First, thank you for sharing it with me." I place a tender kiss on the tip of her nose and another on her lips that are spreading into a bashful but relieved smile. "There is nothing you can tell me that would scare me away or stop my feelings for you."

Her eyes narrow for a beat, as if my words give her reassurance about something she's fearful of.

"Second, I'm going to need the names of these losers so I can go kill them."

She laughs and I let go of her wrist. Her hands find their way to my neck and shoulder as I run my hand down her waist to the curve of her hip.

"I'm serious." She says.

"So am I." I grind my erection against her, and she meets my movement. The sensation of her against me pulls a deep grumble from my throat and I watch with rabid fascination as her gaze turns sensual.

She helps me along, tilting her pelvis into mine and enjoying watching the reaction she has on me. My dick pulses with the movement. Her mouth drops open as she exhales, and lust hoods her eyes.

"What's the third thing?" She tightens her legs around me as her pelvis meets mine again, increasing the pressure against her clit.

I run my tongue up the length of her neck and take her ear between my teeth before I answer. "You've never been fucked by a god before." I pull away and look at her. "If you even try to fake an orgasm with me, I'll make you cum so many times, you'll beg me to stop."

Before she can respond, I trail two vibrating fingers up both sides of her pussy. Instantly, her words dissolve into a moan. She's already soaking wet, making my mouth water at the thought of tasting her.

But first, I'm going to watch her beautiful face when she orgasms before I devour her second climax with my mouth.

Focusing my power on the tip of my thumb, I massage small circles around her clit, observing her eyes dilate as she inhales sharply and then exhales. Her hips respond to my touch, moving in sync as she utters my name, each syllable more melodious than the trumpets of Hel.

"That's it, baby," I encourage her, maintaining the circular motion with my vibrating finger on her center. She presses herself against me, gripping my wrist with her hands as if ensuring I'll continue.

But there's no force in existence strong enough to pull me away from her.

She closes her eyes and tilts her head back into the pillow, surrendering to the sensations enveloping her. I observe the energy of her aura collecting around the small bundle of nerves and I know her orgasm is close. Increasing the pressure against her, she lets out a whimper.

"You're going to cum for me, little goddess; so many times," The last three words are a whispered promise.

Biting her lip in anticipation of the building climax, she quickens the pace of her hip movements. "Yes," she answers, her voice breathless as I continue to stimulate her.

As my finger vibrates with increased intensity, her mouth falls open in response. The sensation grows heavier, and she instinctively covers her mouth, as if trying to stifle herself before the impending climax.

Keeping my pace against her clit, I pull her hand away from her mouth.

"Let me hear you. Let all of Olympus hear you," I demand, my voice a mixture of command and desire as I thrust two fingers into her tight pussy at the peak of her climax. Her back arches off the bed, and she cries out in ecstasy. I feel her pulsating around me as I continue to stroke my fingers in and out, synchronized with the rhythm of my thumb against her clit.

Her aura radiates outward as she moans and gasps, surrendering to the waves of pleasure coursing through her body.

Sensing the peak has passed, I gradually ease the pressure, allowing her to come down from the intense sensation. As the motion of her hips slows, a look of satisfaction washes over her face.

"That's one," I acknowledge, marking her first climax as I raise my two wet fingers to my mouth. Savoring the taste of her, I let out a moan, my eyes rolling back momentarily before fixing my gaze on her.

"Now, I need to taste the rest of you," I declare, my desire evident as I express my longing to explore every inch of her.

I run my tongue across her lips, allowing her to taste her own sweetness. Her tongue darts out to meet mine, a shy blush spreading across her cheeks. Gods, she's fucking adorable in her coy yet eager responses. Clearly, she's had a run of shitty lovers in this lifetime.

After tonight, she'll come to realize that she never needed to fake her pleasure before. It's clear that there's nothing wrong with her; she responded so effortlessly to me. Tonight, she'll discover just how responsive her body can be when stimulated properly, by someone who genuinely cares about their partner's satisfaction.

I relish every inch of her exposed skin as I trail kisses down her body, starting with her neck. Moving to her full breasts, I lavish attention on each nipple, eagerly responding to their silent pleas for touch. As I graze my teeth along the underside of her breast, she moans in delight, her enjoyment spurring me on. I take my time moving down her stomach, in no mood to rush my meal.

I relish in building the anticipation, teasing her with my touch everywhere except where she desires it most. She wants me to devour her pussy with my tongue, coaxing another orgasm to rush through her body. And she's going to get everything she wants, but not until she's begging me for it.

Hovering my lips just a breath away from her hip, I intensify her senses with the mere thought of my touch. Rhea's hand finds its way into my hair, urging me closer but I pull her hand to her side and hold her there.

With a tantalizing lick along the valley of her pelvis, I nip at her hip with my teeth, sucking on the tender skin, further fueling her anticipation.

"Hermes, please." She begins to plead.

Ah, there is my greedy little goddess.

I reward her patience by lavishing her pussy with a long, slow lick until I reach her clit. Swirling my tongue around her center, I feel her hips begin to move in rhythm with my actions. As I suck gently on her clit, she bucks and gasps, her hand finding its way into my hair with the intensity of pleasure coursing through her.

"Shhhhhhh," I hush her gently, holding her still as I lock eyes with her through my lashes. She raises her head, our gazes meeting as I flick my tongue quickly across her clit several times.

"Oh, gods, yes," she moans, letting her head fall back onto the pillow, her legs twitching in time with the movements of my tongue.

I immerse myself into her and gods she is delicious.

Exploring her with my mouth, I swirl and suck on her as I push her legs open with my hands. She's sweet like the melons that dripped juices down her chin during dinner and salty like the briny air of the Mediterranean.

Gods, I could spend an eternity between her legs.

She's as easy to read as an open book, her movements and

sounds revealing her pleasure with every touch. Bringing her to the brink of another climax, I then ease away, deliberately building her anticipation and igniting her sensitive nerves even further.

Twice more, I build her near the peak of falling into her orgasm and ebb her away.

"Hermes, it's too much." Her body convulses with each stroke of my tongue.

"Are you ready to cum again, little goddess?" I caress her mind with voice as my tongue works her center. The response is a deep moan as she fists a handful of my hair. *"Hold onto the bed, baby and relax."*

She reaches behind her and grabs the headboard as if to anchor herself. One hand remains threaded through my hair, not wanting me to stop. *"Are you ready for another?"*

"Yes, gods, yes."

"Tell me what you want."

"I want–" Her answer is interrupted with fingers thrusting once into her. "Ah!"

"Tell me what you want, baby and I'll give you everything." I rub her clit with my wet fingers and lap up every drop of her.

"I want to cum. Please, Hermes."

I give her clit relentless attention. Running her nails along my scalp, she arches and moans as I suck and lick her to the crest of her climax. Her legs twitch as I keep them open while she pushes against me at the force of her pleasure rocking through her.

"Okay, okay." She begs me but I coax another orgasm from her, not letting her come down from this second one before a third is cresting.

My first two fingers enter her pussy as she rocks around me.

She captures me between her quaking legs as she pulls my head toward her. *"Breathe through it, goddess."*

The intensity of the waves rolling through her caused her black mist to swarm around us, filling the bedroom with her power. Her moans turn to whimpers and her hips rock against my mouth, and I slow the motion of my tongue against her as she rides her pleasure to completion.

Rising to my knees, I take in the sight of her amazing body as I wipe my mouth. "That's three."

Her honey hair splayed across the pillow is like satin as she pants deeply. The lines and curves of her body are like a runway, calling me to keep exploring her. I unbutton my pants and the head of my cock is impatiently there and longing to please her.

Unzipping my pants, her eyes widen when she takes me in.

Sitting up, I watch her breasts as they move with her body. Resting her hands behind her with her mouth parted, she looks at me through her lashes.

I'm not a small man, in any sense of the word, but I have a feeling the size of my dick is not what she is looking at.

Fisting my erection, I slide my hand up the length of my cock and rub my thumb over the head. She licks her lips, and I swear I could cum just from watching her. "Have you ever been with a partner with a piercing?"

She shakes her head no.

With four barbells on the underside of my shaft, I run my fingers slowly along each one and she studies me. Stepping off the bed, I remove my pants and she crawls to meet me.

With big doe eyes, she watches me as if waiting for me to tell her to stop.

Not a fucking chance.

If my little goddess is curious, I'll spend all night letting her explore me.

Sitting back on her heels, she supports herself with her hands in front of her, her gaze fixed on me with anticipation. Holding my dick at the base, I watch with bated breath as she tilts her head and opens her mouth. A shiver runs down my spine as she sticks out her tongue and licks me, every sensation heightened by her touch.

"Fu-u-uck," escapes from my lips in a drawn-out breath as she makes the slow ascent up the full length of me. My cock disappears into her mouth as she wraps her beautiful lips around me.

"Gods, you're perfect on your knees for me," I gasp, overwhelmed by the sensation of her warm mouth enveloping me.

To say I'm intimidated is an understatement. He's fucking big. And pierced. I don't understand how someone can have so many muscles and all of them seem to lead straight to their cock. Hermes watches me like a predator as I crawl to him.

Gravity is pulling me to him, or maybe it's the heat in his deep blue eyes. But something in the center of my chest wants to be near him.

Not just near him but consumed by him.

Wrapping my hand around his erection, I can't reach around his girth. There is still an inch between the tip of my thumb and the end of my middle finger.

Running my hand up his length, I let my thumb caress over the four barbells that line the underside of his shaft. He takes a shuddering breath as I pass each one and I watch with fixed expression as his stomach muscles tighten.

I'm curious and Hermes lets me study him. My tongue strokes each piercing, and praises run out of Hermes' mouth. It's like each one goes straight to my throbbing pussy, and I feel myself getting wet again.

Taking the head of his dick in my mouth, warm salty cum teases me with a taste of his arousal.

A thought interrupts me, and with a pop, I pull him out of my mouth.

"So, who have you been fucking, that you needed to get your dick pierced?" I squint my eyes at him, still holding on to the shaft.

Hermes' lightning-fast movements are quicker than I'm ready for. Before I realize we've moved, Hermes is lying on the bed, pulling me to straddle him. With a cocky grin, he holds my wrists behind my back and laughs at my lame attempt to struggle.

"By all means, keep squirming." He lets my wrists go and holds my hip, grinding me against him. Each of the piercings roll across my sensitive clit and a wave of warm pleasure rolls up my spine.

Letting my head relax to one side, I close my eyes and enjoy the sensation. I match the rhythm and lean back, rubbing my pussy along his hard shaft.

Opening my eyes, I hook a hand around his neck and use him to hold me up.

"I understand the appeal." My voice is sated with arousal as I fight to pull my mind back to my question. "But you're changing the subject."

"I don't know how you expect me to focus on questions when the Goddess of the Twelve Realms is riding me into oblivion." Hermes pulls me forward. His callused hands run up the soft skin of my naked back.

My skin purrs with the contact but I feel like it's still not enough.

As our bodies continue to move together, he kisses me with

a hunger that matches my own. Hermes' tongue sweeps across my mouth, igniting a moan from deep within me. Everything about him engulfs me, and in his embrace, I feel free enough to let go and allow myself to fall, surrendering to the passion between us.

We pull away and he rests his forehead against mine, releasing a shuttering breath, "Achilles got his done and wanted me to tag along. You know, moral support and all."

It makes me smile. "So, like, bros that get their dicks pierced together, stick together?"

He smiles too, humored by my reaction to the admission. "Something like that."

My mouth is drawn to his, our lips locking in a fervent embrace as I maintain my pace, sliding my clit along the rungs of barbells lining his shaft. With each movement, my abdomen tightens, the sensation of my impending climax building. The warmth in the center of my chest intensifies, spreading through me like wildfire.

I've never experienced an orgasm quite like this, and the desire to continue overwhelms me. Yet, a nagging feeling creeps in, as if I'm somehow falling short, not giving Hermes the pleasure he deserves in return.

He pulls his mouth away from me. "Close your eyes." And I do.

My breath is heavy from the movements, and I hold it in as the climax builds within me.

"Just let go and enjoy what you feel." His deep voice rumbles in my mind and melts away the tightness in my shoulders.

Hermes lays back. Both of his firm hands grab my hips, and he helps pull me along his shaft. My wetness coats him and he closes his eyes. His full lip's part and as he exhales, a string of cuss words and admirations run out of him.

He tells me how good I feel, how beautiful I look riding on top of him.

He tells me not to stop and his words put me at ease. Even though I've come several times already, there is no rush for his pleasure. He doesn't try to change my position or take control. Hermes only keeps moving along with me, letting me set the pace and controlling my ride.

His gaze shifts as a dark veil of lust darkens his eyes to a deep navy hue. "Use me, little goddess." He is panting, like he's close to his own climax and his words coax me to grind against him more. "Fucking cum all over me. Soak me with your pussy because I was made to worship you."

I fall apart around him.

My orgasm tips over the edge and crashes through me, waves of pleasure coursing through every inch of my body. My chest pounds as if my heart wants to leap out of my body and dive into him.

Hermes tightens his grip on my breasts, his fingers teasing and pinching at my nipples, adding to the pleasure pulsating within me. Tilting my head back, my long hair cascades down to the small of my back.

He grinds his hips along with mine, extending the waves of my climax, prolonging the ecstasy. As this orgasm begins to ebb away, he rolls us over.

With a quick and seamless pivot, Hermes' hulking frame settles on top of me, a comforting weight that brings a sense of contentment. Yet, something within me still feels incomplete. I need to feel a connection to him that is just out of my grasp.

Like a tether billowing in the wind that I long to chase after and fix around me forever.

"How do you feel?" He whispers and gently pecks at my lips.

"I need you." I know I'm begging but my body is aching for him.

He growls into my mouth as he kisses me harshly. His hold around me tightens as if we are at the bottom of the ocean again, with the waters threatening to rip us apart.

"Don't you dare move," He kisses my mouth, then my breast, my stomach, the side of my knee, and even my ankle. I giggle as his scruff tickles me, and I enjoy the sight of his tight ass as he walks away.

I've never been one to admire a man's ass before, but damn.

With a relaxed sigh, I sink into the bed. My arms lay comfortably on each side of my head and Hermes returns with a bottle of olive oil.

The deep green bottle tips and he puts a small amount in his palm.

Placing the oil on the nightstand, he palms his dick, still hard and erect, he coats himself. Climbing back on top of me, his oiled fingers rub up the slit of my pussy. We both release a moan.

Every touch he gives me brings a million nerve endings to life. The sensation sends a pulse of warmth through me. My body is practically humming for him.

"You're amazing." He whispers, teasing my open mouth with his tongue as he prepares me for him. "You're so wet for me."

I suppose the oil is to help his piercings, or perhaps his size; maybe both. "Tell me if I hurt you."

My legs are wrapped around his waist, my arms are wrapped around his neck. My lips will be swollen from so much kissing, but I don't care. I can't get enough of him.

As his tongue sweeps across my mouth, he enters me. Just the head of his penis and enough that I feel the first of his piercings slide into me.

"Goddess, you feel perfect." He grunts into my neck and my vision turns to static as I release a breathy exhale.

I'm so full, his large dick stretching me perfectly and he's only given me the tip. In and out he moves slowly but doesn't go deeper. I need him to; I'm desperate for all of him. I need to feel him seated as far into me as possible.

"Hermes, please." My plea is cut off when he pushes further into me, and I gasp.

Two more piercings roll across me and the feeling of them rubbing along my walls surges through me. I clench as he enters me again, and he moans. The vibrations of his deep voice rattle me as I hang onto him.

"Everything." My breathy voice begs him for more. "Give me everything. Let me have all of you."

He releases hold of his control and grunts as he pushes the rest of his dick into me.

"Yes." I clutch him as he moves. His mouth devours me. The metal bars massage me as he thrusts in and out.

"My perfect little goddess. You're so tight; so beautiful." Hermes looks down, watching as his cock slides into me.

The fullness of having him seated within me is overwhelming. Bracing one hand on the headboard above me, I hold on to Hermes with the other.

With his large hand firmly fixed at the small of my back,

Hermes pushes into me, guiding my pelvis with precision. Small tilts back-and-forth lead to a sensation that sends waves of pleasure rolling up my body, bowing my spine and leaving my mouth agape.

"Gods, baby," Hermes closes his eyes, and his mouth drops open. My lips are drawn to his neck, and I bite down needing to release some of the building pressure within me. "I'm going to fuck you until you forget about every shitty lover you had before me."

My eyes roll into my head as I experience sensations I never thought possible before.

Keeping me in this spot, he continues to drive himself in and out of me, the intensity of his movements leaving me breathless. His words, accompanied by the bass of his voice, penetrate me as deeply as his cock, fueling the fire of another impending orgasm.

His power arcs around us. Small sparks of blue lightning nip at my breasts and clit. He commands me to cum for him, asserting his ownership of my pleasure and promising to keep me cumming all night long.

I surrender completely, holding on to him as the ecstasy overwhelms me, knowing that he is determined to fulfill every desire and need. I unfold around him and melt into the sensations.

It's amazing and powerful but it feels like I'm hanging on the edge of true pleasure, and I want more. "Harder." I can only give one-word responses through the orgasm that is claiming me. "Harder."

"No, my greedy little goddess," Hermes keeps up his pace through my demands, despite the rolling of my hips that move along with him and my nails racking along his back as I ride the rest of the climax. "You don't need it harder. You need me deeper."

As the peak of the orgasm subsides, he pulls out of me. Turning me onto my stomach, Hermes grips my hips firmly and pulls me to my knees. With a hand firm on my back, he keeps my chest pressed to the bed as he thrusts into me.

Bright silver light surges up my spine as the piercings add to the impact of Hermes' thrusting. Reaching around me, he adds his fingers to my clit, and I arch my back into him. Another climax is building, and I push my face into the soft covers to stifle my noises.

"I said, I want to hear you scream, goddess." Hermes grabs a handful of my hair and pulls back gently. "Let all of Greece hear you." He slams into me, and his circling fingers vibrate against my center. "Let those little pricks who failed to please you, hear how beautiful you sound when you're coming around my dick."

I cum again, and I scream. His name flows out of my mouth as I fall over the edge of my orgasm.

The wet sounds of his cock pushing in and out of me echo throughout the room, accompanied by his grunts and my moans as he rides me along the crest of my pleasure. Trusting that I won't stifle my screams this time, he releases my hair and takes hold of my hips once more, pulling me into him as he pounds inside me.

His fingers continue to work around my clit, their vibrations intensifying, and it's as if the orgasm I'm already riding gets overtaken by another, amplifying the pleasure coursing through my body.

"Now your greedy pussy is going to get all of me." He pumps into me faster. "Now you get it deeper *and* harder." He thrusts into me harder. "So, be a good little goddess and hold onto something, because I'm going to take you into the heavens and fuck you for all the realm to hear."

His hand strokes up my back and he grips the nape of my neck.

Hermes' power surges within me, enveloping me in a haze of blue light as a Mirage unfolds in my mind. Euphoria washes over me, perfectly timed with the crest of my next orgasm.

The wind whips around us, and blue lightning crackles along our skin as Hermes' power surrounds us. Gripping the sheets tightly, I thrust back against him as he pushes into me, our bodies moving in sync with the elemental forces around us.

My power stretches within me, reaching out aimlessly, seeking to connect with Hermes' energy. It feels as though we're soaring up a mountain, ascending with the rise of my climax.

His fingers continue to work my clit, the tingling sensation of his Light ability dancing along my skin, finding my nipples and sending shivers down my spine. Just as I'm on the brink of release, he turns me over, positioning me on my back with my legs against his shoulders. He delves deeper inside me as my pussy tightens around him, our connection intensifying as we fall into our pleasure together.

Surrounded by the magic of our elemental powers, the Mirage he projects drops us from the sky, adding to the sensations coursing through our bodies. Holding onto him tightly, my spine arches as the climax peaks, and I can't contain the cries of ecstasy escaping my lips.

A spiral of black mist careens out of me as we descend downward into the vision with Hermes' orgasm rolling off him in waves of blue power. I feel the thrumming along my body as he releases inside me, the walls of my pussy tightening and pulsing around him.

The piercings lining his cock add to the intensity, massaging the orgasm as we ride the waves of our lovemaking, completely consumed by the magic and pleasure we share.

He grunts and groans, nipping and sucking along my neck.

Slowing his pace, Hermes' soft lips meet mine in a tender, deeply affectionate kiss. It's a moment filled with care and gentle affection, contrasting with the intensity of our previous lovemaking.

A small smile spreads across his mouth. "That's six," he remarks, his voice laced with smug satisfaction, eliciting a bashful grin from me in response. Releasing a deep sigh, I feel as though my body is floating just above the mattress, still alive with the tingling aftershocks of so many climaxes, my pussy fluttering around Hermes, still sheathed within me.

As he pulls out of me, each of the barbells causes me to clench in response. Retreating to the dimly lit bathroom, Hermes wets a rag with warm water before returning to the bed.

"I can do it," I begin to protest, but he interrupts with gentle kisses.

"I know you can," he reassures me, "but let me take care of you, please?"

Only when I nod in agreement, does he put the rag between my legs.

His tender care is a stark contrast to the firmness of his thrusting earlier. The sharp hold of his hands has now turned soft as he carefully rubs the warm cloth between my legs, his actions speaking volumes of his genuine concern and affection for me.

Finished, Hermes pushes a button on the nightstand and the floor-to-ceiling drapes covering the large windows open. Helping me stand, Hermes wraps a blanket around my shoulders and leads me by my hand to the patio outside our room.

Dark mist surrounds us, obscuring the landscape below us and making the stars shine brighter in the velvet sky above.

"Is it always so foggy up here?"

Hermes chuckles.

"The mortals have always known the gods live at the top of Mount Olympus. What they don't know is it's always shrouded in mist when the Goddess of the Twelve Realms is being properly fucked by her mate."

"Oh, my gods, you're terrible," I playfully smack his chest, unable to suppress a laugh. With a gentle command, I summon a Wind to clear the mist that surrounds us. The landscape opens up as if the realm is presenting all its beauty and bowing before us.

However, amidst the serene view, I feel the heavy cloud of death looming over the earth. A shiver runs along my spine, creeping up my neck. I adjust my shoulders in an attempt to shake off the sensation. Like skeletal fingers of dread, fear grips my scalp, and I can feel the weight of worry etching a grim expression onto my face.

Sensing my shift in mood, Hermes takes the blanket from me and wraps it around himself before standing behind me. He enfolds me in his arms, cocooning me within his warmth and the reassuring embrace of his aura.

"I won't let anything happen to you," he declares with conviction, turning me to face him and gently lifting my chin with his fingers. His cerulean eyes lock onto mine, and I feel the weight of his determination in his words. "It feels different this time. You're different this time."

I *am* different.

As my hands run up his sculpted chest, I can feel the difference within me. I recall the return of a few of my previous reincarnations, and the various emotions that filled me as I inhabited their mortal bodies.

Sometimes it was sorrow or frustration; other times, it was patience and calculation. It was as if the mortal shells I inhabited carried the residue of the souls that had occupied them before me, influencing me as I moved from one life to the next.

But this time, I don't feel that. Instead, a profound sense of protectiveness and anger courses through me, emotions that are uniquely my own. Tired of these cycles and the relentless reset my death causes, I long for it to be over. I crave to live the fullness of my immortal lives together with my mate, no longer hunted, no longer forgotten.

As my touch grazes Hermes' skin, I feel it pebble beneath my fingertips, sending heat coursing through my core. His cock throbs, his erection building again, seemingly ready to take me once more.

I gaze at his growing girth between us, my eyes full of lust as I look at him through my lashes, desire burning within me. Tracing my nails down his abdomen, I take him in my hand, starting at the base of his hardness and running along the piercing until I reach the tip of his cock.

"I seem to remember you have quite a bit of— stamina," I emphasize the word with a firm stroke along his hard dick. A deep grumble escapes his throat, sending a shiver of anticipation through me, my pussy growing wet at the sound.

"I plan to worship you thoroughly all night, little goddess,"

Hermes declares, dropping the blanket and exposing our naked bodies to the night. The moonlight caresses his muscles, bathing them in silver light as he drops to his knees.

Spreading my arms on each side of me, I brace myself against the cool railing of the patio, drawing a shuttered breath. Hermes kisses along the line of my leg, working his way to my core. Taking my leg over his shoulder, he supports my weight with ease.

A crack of lightning zaps behind me as Hermes' tongue bathes my clit in a long, hard stroke. Pure bliss washes over me at the lavishing caress of my mate, and my head falls back in ecstasy.

Closing my eyes to the night, I revel in the pleasure he brings me, feeling stronger and empowered with each passing moment. Confidence surges through me as I run my fingers through his hair.

I've never been much of a talker during sex, but Hermes wants it. He caresses my mind with his words and coaxes my desires out of me. Emboldened by the joy he gets from hearing my voice, let go of the restraints I've placed around myself and fall into him.

"Gods, Hermes. You fuck me with your mouth so well,"

"Hello?"

My voice reverberates through the dark, rocky tunnel as I cautiously make my way forward. The walls, hewn by hand, twist and turn into the depths of the cave, reminiscent of the tunnels of the Underworld.

Before me lies a path leading further into the darkness, while behind me, the cavernous opening at my back allows sunlight to filter through, casting a soft glow within. My gaze is drawn to the arch formed by the entrance, and I can't help but furrow my brows as I take in the sight.

As I approach the entrance for a closer look, the heat of the bright sun against the desert air causes sweat to bead on my skin. Raising a hand, I tentatively touch the large rocks that form the top of the opening, only to realize they resemble teeth —massive, towering teeth, each as large as me.

Stepping back into the darkness of the cave, I find myself standing in the middle, surrounded by the ancient space. Above me, a large circular opening allows a bright column of sunlight to penetrate the darkness. And before me, the entrance of the cave takes on a surreal form—it's a literal mouth, the old bones of a long-dead cyclops hardened to stone.

It's impossible to determine how long it has been here, frozen in time.

A deep huff resonates from the depths of the dark tunnel behind me, warm breath crawling across the rocky ground. It feels as though a sleeping giant awaits me in the darkness, and as the obscurity deepens, I clench my fists in anticipation of the looming monster ahead.

An object in my hand pinches me, prompting me to hold out my palm and inspect it. Opening my hand, I find a necklace resting within, its amber pendant holding a swirling silver galaxy in its center.

As I examine the necklace, it begins to rattle, and I feel another huff of the hidden monster swirling around my ankles. The power radiating from the necklace causes my arm to vibrate as if it's being pulled away from me by an unseen force. Suddenly, the necklace shoots off my palm and speeds into the dark tunnel ahead.

My gaze follows the trajectory of the necklace, and I'm met with a large pair of eyes staring back at me. A cold rush surges down my body as the beast and I lock eyes, the intensity of its glowing gaze leaving me frozen in place.

The eyes glow intensely, resembling two white lightbulbs with a reptilian almond shape. Their size indicates that the creature attached to them must be nothing short of gigantic, sending chills cascading down my spine as I stand motionless.

A deep growl rumbles toward me as the white eyes narrow, but then something changes. The eyes shift in color, transitioning from white to emerald green and diminishing in size. The hot breath surrounding me is replaced with red dust, and the sounds of human footsteps approach from the darkness, filling the air with a sense of foreboding uncertainty.

"**T**artarus." I sit up in bed, still coated in sweat from the dream.

Hermes sits up, instantly alerted by my jolted response.

My heart hammers in my chest, and my breathing is ragged. The vision of the necklace in my hand stays in my mind, driving my feet to hit the white marble floor and sending me out of the room.

Hermes chases after me, rubbing the sleep from his eyes. I'm wearing one of his large t-shirts that is hanging off one of my shoulders. I need to find some clothes here. *Though I'm sure Hermes wouldn't mind me wearing just his shirts and my cheeky panties.*

"What is it?" He asks but I ignore him as I reach our private library.

My eyes rake quickly over the spines of the books. I know what I'm looking for; I remember holding it in my hands. Moving my index finger across the rows of tomes, I'll know it when I see it.

A title catches my eye. Going back to the yellow book with gold foil-pressed letters, I pull it off the shelf.

Darting a glance at Hermes, his sleepy and confused look with messy hair makes me smile. "You're cute in the morning." His bare torso and thin grey sweatpants draw my gaze downward. I use his bicep to steady me as I raise on the balls of my feet and peck him on the cheek.

He pulls me into him, fully wrapping his arms around me. "Not so fast." He picks me up and I circle his waist with my legs. Chuckling, I try to squirm away from him as he carries me into the kitchen, peppering my neck with kisses and nipping along my shoulder as he walks.

Sitting me on the counter, he brackets me with his hands on each side of me. A satisfied smirk on his face as he looks at me with his bright blue eyes. "Good morning." He gives me one more kiss before walking to the coffee pot inset into the wall.

"What is running through that beautiful mind of yours?" he asks over his shoulder as he takes a cup from the cupboard and brews a cup of coffee. The scent of the ground beans bursts through the kitchen and I inhale it deeply.

Inspecting the book, I run my hand over the foiled letters, *"The Tears of Freya"*.

"My next relic," I answer, not paying attention to what I'm saying as I flip through the pages.

It's a story of Freya, Achilles' twin sister, and the dwarves that created her necklace. The ancient lore is printed on the pages of the old book, adorned with colorful illustrations, and preserved with spells. I stop when I find the image of the necklace; Brísingamen.

Gold and silver braided bands hold an oval amber pendant. The fae symbol of Avalon surrounds the stone with three silver moons in an arc at the top. The third moon shows the golden sun rays behind it, like a solar eclipse.

In the center of the amber pendant, shimmering like a swirling galaxy is a bundle of silver starlight.

My power.

The necklace belonged to Hermes' mother, Daphne and I wish I knew how it ended up with Freya.

I rub my hand over the image with affection. As if I can feel the essence of my immortality in the picture. I close my eyes, recalling my dream and the necklace I held in my hand.

The cave was marked with the skull of a cyclops and a great beast, breathing within the darkness. The necklace, just as it is depicted in the painting, surged away from me.

A sharp ringing in my ears starts faintly and then grows louder, drowning out the rest of the world.

The necklace is calling to me. Tugging on my soul and the holes within my immortality that long to be filled with my power.

But the green eyes I saw at the end of the dream burned inside my mind, taking over the details of the fading vision.

Hermes hands me a cup of coffee and the ringing stops. He looks at the image in the book while he takes a sip of his coffee.

I blink away the memory of the emerald eyes.

Holding my hot cup with both hands, I let the warmth heat my cold fingers before I take a drink. My hands and feet are always so cold. A trait attributed to my anxiety. Maybe when I've restored my powers, I'll have more control over myself and won't feel so frigid all the time.

The light tan color of my coffee looks perfect and taking a sip, I savor the warmth as it passes to my stomach. Flavored to perfection with two spoonfuls of sugar and sweet creamer, I close my eyes and smile.

"You said, Tartarus, when you woke up." Hermes hands the book back to me.

"Yeah, Tartarus." I close the book and place it on the counter next to me, taking another sip of hot coffee. "The necklace is on Tartarus." As I speak the words, I feel the truth and surety of my statement.

"How can it be on Tartarus?" Hermes asks, not as if he is

confused but as if he doesn't believe I'm right. "Tartarus was destroyed."

"You don't know that." I take another sip of coffee, looking at him with raised eyebrows. "Did you actually see it destroyed?"

I know he didn't.

We stayed up most of the night, making love and talking. He shared his memories with me, using his power of Mirage and I saw everything as if I was there.

Hermes and Medusa were the first to flee Tartarus when Chaos attacked Hyperion. Hermes teleported to Gaea with Medusa and delivered the message to Oceanus who surged to the aid of his brother.

Hermes returned, helping more refugees escape and looking for Medusa's sisters. Ares and Apollo helped Callie and Daphne escape to Gaea.

Hermes used his great speed, ferrying as many as he could until the last possible moment. Atlas nearly had to pull Hermes through his own portal as the Titan's fight raged around him; the realm bucking with the shock of their power.

But as Apollo and Ares stitched together the protective wards that surrounded Gaea, Hermes closed the portals. The sight of Tartarus disappearing before them as the grounds began to rip open.

"None of you actually saw Tartarus destroyed. You also believed Avalon was lost forever until you returned there a few days ago for the chalice of Pandora."

Hermes found a clue, hidden in the spine of an old book, and in it, my message, and a bottle of potion. The potion that revealed the path back to Avalon. And blindly, he followed it.

Without a moment's hesitation, he trusted the trail I left for him to follow, not knowing what would be waiting for him.

I feel that same path for myself as if I left my own trail of clues to follow. Now that I know the next step in my journey of recovery, he seems to be questioning it.

Disappointment turns the warmth of my coffee cold.

A vision of Triton flashes behind my eyes as I blink slowly. His discarded form, forever rotting away in the darkness of the Underworld but unable to die. It took all the strength he could muster to speak to me.

"He must not find the caduceus, but it is imperative you find the pendant."

Triton warned me of Ares' quest to retrieve Hermes' ancient staff of power. But Triton was clear, the pendant was mine to find.

Pinching my forehead in the center, the thought of Triton, laying in waste like a crumpled mass of rock in the bowels of the Underworlds pulls at my heart.

I just left him there. And he's down there now, still suffering. He told me I had the power to kill him, but I wasn't ready yet. My throat tightens just thinking about it.

But I've killed before.

I killed Moros. Perched high on a dirt wall, on the other side of a battlefield and I extracted his immortal life with my powers and felt no weight of remorse. But I didn't have to kill him up close and personal. And I was defending myself against him and Flint. But Triton is good.

I could see the kindness shining in what remained of his dull aura as he tried to help me in the belly of the realm.

I don't know that I can kill him, but I don't want him to suffer.

Pulling myself from the haze of my reflection, I set my cup on the counter. Hermes is watching me, waiting for me to work through my thoughts.

"Ares wants your staff; the caduceus." I tell Hermes as I keep my eyes fixed on my coffee, watching the steam rise. "There is no item more important to him."

"Do you know why?" Hermes asks, his blue eyes turning a deep navy with the mention of my hunter.

I chew on the corner of my lip, thinking. Trying to pull together a thousand broken memories of my past lives. "The power inside of course. Each of the relics holds a cardinal power. Your sword held the Wind. The chalice, Water."

I lift the book with my currents of air and turn to the picture of the necklace. "The pendent is Earth and your caduceus holds Fire."

Holding my hands out and inspecting them, I feel Wind and Water, ready at my beaconing. Every current in the world would stop at my whim and the waters would flood every spec of dry ground if I wished.

But there is more here. More powers zipping around me; like the lights buzzing in the bulbs above our heads as if silent witnesses to our conversation. I feel the dark shadows whispering secrets to each other.

I feel so much more than the two cardinal powers returned to me from Hermes' sword and Pandora's chalice.

My elemental powers return the book to our library as I remain perched on the counter. I cross one leg over my knee and Hermes eye follows the long line that leads up my thigh.

"I imagine Ares wants to strengthen his Fire ability, after what Atlas explained of their power weakening after he broke their fated bond, that makes sense." I pause, taking another sip of coffee. The words Triton said, echo again.

"... but it is imperative you find the pendant."

Triton struggled with each labored breath and every word pained him. He took the time to make sure I knew the pendant would be crucial for me to find. *But why the pendant?*

I need all of them all.

All four relics hold the release of my full immortality and the might of my power. Once I'm fully whole, I can no longer die at the hands of Ares. No more will I have to suffer, pained as Hermes watches me die again. And I'll never have to leave this realm again, knowing that my mate will anguish alone until I return.

"Tell me what you're thinking, baby." Hermes takes the side of my face in his palm, and I close my eyes with his touch. The reassurance of his presence calms the racing thoughts that barrel through my mind.

"I need to find the pendant next." I look at him and try to hold back the worry in my eyes, but he still sees it. Reading me like a book, Hermes knows my emotions, sometimes before I do. His eyebrow tics as he thins his mouth.

Taking our cups, he places them on the counter of the center island. Hermes scoots me to the edge, and I spread my knees to make room for him. His strong arms surround me, and I take in his scent deeply.

My shoulders drop as I release a relaxing exhale. Hermes rubs my back with soothing strokes and rests his cheek on the top of my head.

"Then that's what we'll do." He pulls back and takes my face in his hands, turning me up to look at him. "We're going to figure this out; together."

Hermes kisses me softly, gently parting his mouth and taking my lips. Tilting my head, I open my mouth to him and welcome his tongue as he deepens our kiss. I pull him into me by the waist of his thin sweatpants.

I'm starving with the need to be consumed by him again. My pelvis meets his and I wrap my legs tighter around him.

Never, during this lifetime, have I ever felt such pleasure and care at the hands of a lover. It wasn't just his ability to make me orgasm, but it was in the way he held me after, his insatiable need to caress my skin and kiss my lips. It was in his rich blue eyes that held me as I talked all night and how he intently listened to every story I told.

I always thought feelings like this were meant for stories of fiction, certainly never intended for my life. And as Hermes meets the fervor of affections this morning, and his hands caress my body, I fight against the thoughts that tell me this won't last long.

Not because of Hermes, but because I fear I'm not destined for a fate of happiness.

I want to have it all and I will. I'll fight for my life with Hermes. I'll fight to be by Callie's side as her friend, Hecate, and the others. I won't resign to my hunter so easily, knowing that love and friendship truly exist in this world for me.

Cradling the back of my head, Hermes lays me on the cool counter. Putting each of my feet at the edge, He holds my stare as he slowly pushes my knees apart, moving slowly as if asking for permission.

My heart thrums with excitement and nervousness as I let my legs open for him.

It's like he knows my insecurities and has vowed to combat them with gentle affection and encouragement. He makes me nervous and excited. Hermes makes me burn with the need to give myself over to him; so, I do.

"Pull your panties to the side." His gaze is hot and heats my core. "Let me look at you."

My cheeks warm and my mouth parts as I release a small gasp.

No one has ever talked to me like this before and his words ignite my arousal.

Hermes consumed every inch of my body during the night with his tongue. His lips kissed all of me. There is not one part of me his hands didn't memorize as he took dominion over my pleasure.

But this lifetime has been filled with such pain and sorrow in only ten mortal years.

Demeter worked so hard to train my mind to believe I am worthless. She orchestrated events around me to reinforce that. Like the boy who asked me to homecoming when I was sixteen. I bought a dress and did my hair. I stood by the window, wearing uncomfortable shoes, believing he would come.

But he never did.

I cried myself to sleep with my satin dress wrinkling in the corner of my room.

In reality, he did come. But Demeter met him before he got out of his car.

She pierced him with her barb and commanded him to go home. I watched him drive away and with my back turned, she threaded her lies into my mind. Demeter made me forget and I believed I was abandoned.

Over and over, she manipulated my reality and made me

think I was worth nothing, so that is what I sought. People who made me feel like I was nothing.

But Hermes makes me feel like I am everything.

Like I'm the very reason he takes each breath. And as we made love, I remembered. Thousands of nights, just like last night, where I was his treasure, his goddess.

And gods, did he worship me.

My finger trails down my stomach, and he tracks the movement like his next breath is desperately hanging on the movement of my finger.

I trace the lace edge of my panties and pull the black fabric to one side.

"Beautiful," He whispers, and I stalk his lips as they form the words. Hermes takes my hand from my panties, putting my finger in his mouth and swirling his tongue around the tip. Chasing my taste off my finger, his eyes close, and he hums in satisfaction. "We're going to figure this out, together." He repeats. "But first, I'm going to have my breakfast."

And with me, spread wide on the counter, he feasts.

Hermes

The Goddess of the Twelve Realms singing and swaying her hips in the shower behind me, makes me smile. *Gods, I can't stop grinning with her here.* Rhea has her long hair plopped on top of her head in a soapy pile. Steam billows from the glass shower as she works the bubbles along her scalp.

After lavishing her gorgeous pussy with my mouth and filling the kitchen with her moans, we cooked breakfast together. Rhea told me about college in New York and a small café where she would eat Eggs Benedict nearly every weekend.

We bumped into each other as we worked around the kitchen, listening to music and me stealing kisses. I found myself watching her smile every chance I got. Getting distracted with her, I had to recook the eggs twice.

I could listen to her talk for hours, telling me about the lives she lived when we were apart. Some of the stories, I've heard a dozen times from her past reincarnations. And I would hear them a dozen more, but her memories are full of holes and empty spaces.

As she recounts her past lives, her eyes drift, losing focus, and I gently caress her to bring her back to the present.

I'm curious about Rhea's life before we met in the bookstore, and she tells me everything. However, she avoids discussing the car accident and reincarnating into the body of the fourteen-year-old girl who perished in that crash. I want to know more about the days after, but her memories are dirty, as if contaminated by Demeter's manipulation.

Finally, I broached the subject of her preferred name. If she would like to be called Rhea or Nyx.

Taking her lip between her teeth nervously, she looked at the ceiling for a moment. Using my thumb to free her bottom lip, I kissed her. "You don't have to answer."

"I just don't *feel* like I used to, I suppose." She turned facing me, resting her head on her hand. "I feel too much like Rhea to answer by another name."

There's a lot to catch up on, but also much to do. We must find her two lost relics before the realm falls into Ares' war. We need to turn the tables against Ares and hunt him like prey, the way he has hunted my mate all these ages. And I have to keep her alive.

Above all, that is the one thing I can't fail at.

This world can fall apart. The relics can remain hidden, as long as they are out of Ares' reach. But she *has* to live.

I won't survive losing her again.

My phone screen lights up just before my Light Shield warns of approaching Elementals. Atlas has been blowing up my phone nonstop since yesterday.

I finish brushing my teeth and dress quickly. Letting Rhea know we'll have company and closing the bathroom to let her finish showering. Then I teleport Atlas and Lucas to the house.

"You look like shit," I tell Lucas as I look the Titan Shifter over. Dark circles under his eyes show his weariness. It's only been a few days since we recovered Rhea, but he looks like he's not slept for a week.

"Fuck you too. I need coffee." He shoulders past me and heads to the kitchen.

"Make yourself at home?" I jest, stepping aside for Atlas who has been here many times over the eons.

"Oh, two coffees please." Atlas plops down onto the bar stools at the kitchen counter and runs his hands through his hair. Lucas looks confused by the wall-mounted coffee machine with his furrowed brow and outstretched hands.

"What happened to a regular old pot of coffee?" Lucas mumbles, waving his hand in front of the machine like its motion activated. I quickly make their coffee, knowing they both take it black.

"What's up with you two?"

"I've been trying to reach you since yesterday. Have you not seen?" Atlas turns on the television and flips to a news channel. The scene on the television makes my heart plummet to the floor.

The New York skyline is gone; all of it.

Once familiar landmarks are piles of rubble. Smoke and ash fill the air as dazed mortals shuffle along what used to be busy streets of the prominent metropolis.

The news anchor speaks of the devastation and the tremendous loss of life.

While they say this is a coordinated attack from Russia, we know it is the work of Ares.

Often inciting wars between the mortals, he knows how to pull the world into a conflict. A Russian aircraft is recorded flying over the city before the attack began. Cell phones and security cameras show various angles as bombs begin to drop from the sky.

The Chinese naval fleets line the coast. In one clip, there is open water and in the next, it's filled with ships. The guns on the deck of the battleships fire their large caliber rounds onto the city.

The recordings cut out with a blast of static at the end. Then footage changes to the current state. Helicopters fly overhead, showcasing the devastation, which seems too casual a word for what I'm looking at.

"Ares' Elementals helped hide the naval fleet from the US government until they opened fire." Lucas takes a large sip of his coffee as he catches me up. "They bombed and shot the city up to draw people out."

"Then they brought out the big bombs." Atlas finishes as the three of us watch the television. "I tried to call you, H." Lowering his tone, disappointment coats his words.

Guilt tightens my throat but what could I have done with the attack underway but put Rhea in the path of harm?

"What if Ares is trying to draw Rhea out into the open? Goad her into an appearance so he can..."

"He probably is, Hermes." Lucas interrupts with an exasperated huff. "So, why the fuck were you hiding in here?"

"You think I'm going to just feed her to the wolves on a silver platter? Fuck off." My guilt turning to irritation at his tone. "What's got your tail in a knot?"

"Seriously? Millions of people died while you were enjoying your *honeymoon*." Lucas releases a deep sigh. He looks like he could collapse in an instant. "We've got a lot of missing Shifters and a boatload of recovered children to track down parents for. We're thankful for that, don't get me wrong. But a lot of them are finding out they have no parents to be returned to." Lucas squares up to me, anger flaring in his hazel eyes.

Atlas puts a hand on his shoulder, giving him calming pats of reassurance and moves to put some distance between us. Ever the peaceful moderator, his calm breaks the tension. "Ares is gearing up to incite war with the countries, and at this rate, it could happen within a few weeks, if not sooner."

"We both know the war is only a distraction and a means to throw obstacles in our way while he hunts Rhea and her powers." I keep my eyes locked on Lucas.

"We do know that. So, what do we do about it?" Atlas pushes back.

He hates fighting but sometimes it's a necessary evil. If I were to bet, Atlas would prefer we solve things with a conversation and without war. But Ares is not going to sit down at a table and negotiate a truce with his former mate. "We need you, H."

"My priority is restoring Rhea's immortality," I tell them both with finite resolve. "I'll not get distracted mortal conflicts until she is immortal again."

"Would your mate agree with that?" Atlas asks in a challenge. "Would she want to ignore the mortals' suffering and traipse around the realm looking for her powers?"

"She risked her life to save the children in the Underworld," Lucas adds. "It's going to be a hard sell for her to agree to stay out of the conflicts. It's only going to get worse out there." Lucas's phone chimes in his pocket with a text message.

He grimaces reading the text, then downs the rest of his coffee. "There is a secret military base in the Nevada desert, and

Kai tracked a pack of Shifters being taken there by mortals. I've got to go." Standing and heading for the door, he pauses when he reaches the knob. "When you need me, call me. Unlike you, I'll be there."

I huff and tense my jaw when Lucas closes the door. "I'm not abandoning everyone else, but Rhea needs me." I try to get this conversation back on track. "And none of *this* stops until she is whole again."

"I agree we have several priorities. There is not one we can ignore over the others." Atlas pushes his cup to me for a refill. "Rhea is not helpless. You'd do well to not treat her like a porcelain doll."

I give Atlas a warning look and he raises his hands in surrender. He's my mentor. Fuck, he's practically my father but I'm not going to be lectured on how to protect my mate.

"People are dying Hermes."

"And I'm here to make sure one person in particular *doesn't* die." I offer him the refilled coffee, setting the cup down on the counter a bit too forcefully.

"That may not be your choice." Atlas immediately puts the cup of hot coffee to his lips. I don't know how he can handle the scorching heat, but he prefers to drink it piping hot.

"We need to find out if there is anything in your collection on transferring the power of the Titans." I change the subject. I'm not thinking about death today. "Rhea created a Titan, and we need to understand how. It may be what Ares is after."

Atlas shakes his head no. "My books are still in Atlanta. Eris has turned the Commune into a Shifter pack house for Gabriel. It's teaming with Ares' forces now."

"We can break in there and get them." I lean against the wall and fold my arms over my chest.

"I'd need the entire library; not just my personal collection." Atlas raises his eyebrows as if thinking that to be an impossible feat.

"Didn't my mate conceal an entire library for all these ages?" I smirk, a plan forming in my mind. "One created by *your* Titan, no less."

I still shudder thinking about meeting Coeus after I was named Theia's apprentice, alongside my father, Apollo.

Ten feet tall with a thin frame, his arms and legs were incredibly long. Always standing with his palms together at the center of his chest, long black nails topped each finger. His face was the ghastliest thing about him.

More, it was his lack of a face.

His head was the texture of sandstone and shaped like an inverted pyramid. He had no mouth or nose. No eyes or ears and his skin looked like leather but was more like rock.

The great Mind Titan didn't eat, or sleep. He didn't talk or hear, and yet he knew everything.

I always wondered how Chaos defeated the Mind mage. I asked my father once. Surely, anything Chaos could have planned, Coeus would have foreseen.

"Oh, everyone knew Coeus could be enticed with a bargain." My father answered. I can hear his voice now as I think about it and nostalgia squeezes my heart. *I miss him so much.*

"A bargain?" I asked, confused. "Would Coeus really put his power up for stakes against a game of chance?"

"It would have to be a lot more complex to entice Coeus," My father looked off into the distance as we watched the sunset. "but if Chaos presented him with high enough stakes, I think Coeus could be persuaded to entertain him. Whether

Chaos actually defeated Coeus or betrayed the bargain, no one can say."

Coeus fell to the Titan of Death, just as the others did. Chaos moved on to the other realms and we watched in horror at his arrival on Tartarus.

Fleeing to Gaea, we lived in fear, waiting for the day we would see Chaos' nebula clouds of the Void descending upon our new realm. But that day never came. Instead, we faced other horrors.

My thoughts snap back to the present just as Atlas finishes his second cup of coffee, setting it loudly on the counter as he stands up.

"I'm off to check on Medusa before I head back to New York." He holds his hand out and we grasp wrists. "Your old friend could use your support. She's got a lot to handle after the Dark Mage's attack on her Commune."

"And I've got a lot to handle with Rhea."

Atlas opens his mouth to speak but is cut off by the sharp tone in my mate's voice. "Just how do you plan on *handling* me?" Rhea is standing inside the kitchen entrance, her arms folded over her chest and irritation shining brightly in her honey eyes.

Atlas gives me a look that says, *'told you so'* and makes his way to her.

She narrows her eyes on me, but they soften when she turns them to Atlas.

"You're doing okay?" He asks in a low tone, and she nods in agreement. "Call me if you need anything. Anything." He stresses more sternly, and she chuckles. He pats her on the arm twice and makes for the door. "Oh and, H?" He calls back to me.

"Callie says, stop hogging her BFF or she's coming over to drag her away from you." Atlas flashes a sly smile that says he'd like to be here when Callie shows up to get in my face.

Before Atlas closes the door, he gives me one last pointed look. *"Tell her about New York and don't make her decisions for her."* He warns me in my mind.

Alone again, Rhea turns her heated look back at me. "So, do you want to let me in on how you will *handle* me, because I recall you saying, we would...how did you put it...*figure this out together.*"

"Listen, I don't think there is anything left of Tartarus. It's a dead end; literally."

"Did you feel that way when you dove head-first into a waterfall to follow a bit of silver starlight to goddess knows where?" Rhea juts out her hip and cocks her eyebrow.

Okay, she's got me there.

"I was there." Sitting at the barstool, I prop a foot on the run and hold my arms out to her. Hesitating a second, she rolls her eyes and comes to me with her arms still crossed over her chest. "I watched Death roll over the horizon and the Titans battle. They were ripping the world apart. What could have survived?"

"Avalon survived." She finally puts her hands on my shoulders, and I run my hands up the backs of her thighs. The stretch jeans she ordered from the portlet hug her body perfectly and the forest green top brightens the gold in her eyes and hair. "I made a pathway to Avalon and kept a part of myself there. That piece of me is what called you to a realm you thought was gone. And I feel that calling now, pulling me to Tartarus."

"We have no way of knowing what could be waiting for us there."

"You didn't know what would be waiting for you on the other side of my pathway, but you went anyway. You took a leap of faith because you believed in me, but I can't do the same and believe in myself?"

Tears pool in her eyes, and she tries to back away from me. I keep my hold on her, not wanting her to retreat. Standing, I keep her in my arms.

"Hey, that is not what this is about, and you know it. We have no idea what sort of traps could be prepared to lure you." I try to reassure her, but my words are only pissing her off more. "A Lurker from the Shadow Realm was siphoning off Medusa's generals for over a year, preparing them to betray her. They were told a month before you and I met in that bookstore about disabling the portal. How would someone know that?"

Rhea looks out the large window, her mind drifting away, thinking over what I said. I just wish she would let me in. She is not trying to run away from the conversation but with a tightness in her brow and an expression that is miles away, I know she is holding herself back.

This is not at all how I envisioned today going.

I knew our reunion would be tense. It always is at first, but it doesn't make it any easier to bear. "Listen, I can't lose you again, baby." My voice softens and I reach out to stroke her cheek.

"But you will if I don't restore myself fully." Placing her hands against my chest, she pushes away, and I drop my arms. Rhea walks into the library, twisting her long locks into a bun on the top of her head and wrapping it with a hair tie from her wrist.

The woman that has been missing from my side for hundreds of years is right here but with each step she takes, it seems like she's getting further away from me than she's ever been.

"**What do you mean New York is gone?**" I stand in our library with my mouth gaping and my heart galloping in my chest. Hermes followed me in here, but I needed a moment to take a breath before I said something I would regret. The haunting look in his eyes stopped me from asking him to leave.

Waves of trepidation flowed off him, resembling white mist. I had never noticed this before and thought perhaps it must be the light catching on his aura.

"It happened yesterday." The heaviness in his expression puts me in motion. I head to the kitchen and pull up news reports. The devastation is unbelievable.

Integral to business and commerce, one of the realms most globally significant cities is reduced to rubble.

One image in particular makes me stop my parade through the pictures of chaos. It's a flattened expanse of land with nothing but the Washington Square Arch remaining in the center. Like a lone soldier left alive on a battlefield, the arch is the only structure for a mile in all directions.

I used to spend so much time in the park there when I attended college at New York University, and it's all gone. My hand trembles as I hover above the screen. I am unable to swipe to the next picture, so I stare unblinking at the arch.

As if I can feel the warm summer day when I took extra courses, a swell of hot air surrounds me. I remember sitting on a blanket in the park with my books for Literature Theory. The breeze rustling the long blades of green grass and I sat under the shade of a tree was a welcomed friend.

Within the image, I can see the dark shadows of death. The places where people stood as they were incinerated are black stains on the pavement. The haunting melody of their laughter fading into nothing.

Tears well in my eyes at the thought of those lives, gone in a blink.

The images of the empty harbor, suddenly filled with a fleet of Chinese warships is a clear sign Elementals were involved.

The weight of responsibility for this crushes my chest.

I assassinated the leader of the free world, along with a dozen other elementals. We stood in cities across the realm and pulled a wisp of Wind through the skulls of Ares' choosing.

The leader of the United States was my target, and I upturned the country with my actions. Now one of the most prominent cities of the world and erased from existence.

During the Mabon ceremony, I lifted the Lycan's curse. Forcing the Shifters across the realm to their true animal forms, the immortals' secrets were revealed to the realm. And the mortals have responded with fear.

This may be Ares' plan, but it was me that tipped the scales, plummeting the realm into a world war. Needing no help from the old Titan of Death, it is me who brought chaos to the realm.

The US military will strike back along with their allies and countries will slaughter each other.

"We have to do something." I have no idea what can be done but sitting here feels like a betrayal. A searing wave of regret engulfs my entire being, scorching my soul with the weight of my actions.

"Rhea, what's done is done. We can't undo the damage now." Hermes voice is soft and all it does is inflate my remorse more. Tears fall onto the tablet, making my vision blur and distort the skeleton of what used to be New York.

My chest rises and falls, my breathing hitching.

Gasping for breath, I claw at the air, desperate for a lungful of oxygen to soothe the suffocating pressure crushing my chest.

Shadows and dark mist curl around me as I try to open a portal. I want to be outside, but I don't trust my legs to carry me there. I need the night sky above me and to feel the cool breeze on my skin.

My powers are a torrent encasing me in a swirl of my elements, and I sense the shift in the atmosphere. Opening my eyes, I'm standing in the center of New York's iconic Time's Square with the bright sun blazing above me.

This is not real.

The phantom skyline of New York looks like someone has transposed a picture of yesterday's city on top of today's rubble. The ghosts of dead mortals who were alive yesterday carry on about their busy day in the Big Apple, moments before they die.

It's the echo of what was here. The residual energy of life that is now gone.

Memories flood my mind, transporting me back to a time

when laughter echoed off the walls of Times Square, instead of screams.

I stood here, only a few years ago, with classmates as we spent a night in the city to see Wicked on Broadway. Someone held their cell phone and I squeezed into the edge of the group selfie with the iconic lights of Times Square behind us.

A distant boom rattles my body, and the people pause. Looking up, they hold their hands over their eyes to better see the dark specs against the clear blue sky. They can't see the planes high within the clouds and don't realize they are watching the bombs that will kill them.

Explosions sound everywhere around us and a tidal wave of panic floods New York.

A tall building above Time's Square bursts as a bomb rips through it. Rubble rains down on the mortals. People are crushed, dying instantly and I see the light of their aura dim.

Everyone is running, screaming, and calling for loved ones as the city tries to survive.

I'm frozen by the emotions filling the air, choking on the pain, and drowning in panic. I could have stopped this. I could have sent the bombs into a portal, never letting them take a single life.

If only I had known. If only I had sensed this, I could have done something.

But standing in the center of a sidewalk, all I can do is watch as yesterday's death darkens the city that never sleeps.

Bombs sound around me. Blood pools at my feet. The crowd rushes for safety, running right through me. It feels so real. The heat of the fires and currents of wind that rush off passersby blow my hair.

Then I watch as one large bomb drops from the sky.

A cascade of chills starts at the crown of my had and rolls down my body. I need to leave.

Panic claws at my mind, shattering my concentration as I desperately try to conjure a portal, my trembling fingers failing to grasp the threads of magic slipping through my hold. My windpipe is closing in on me just as quickly as the capsule of death falls from the clouds.

Looking at my arms, I'm just like the opaque overlay of the city that doesn't exist anymore. I'm nothing but silver starlight.

I'm not physically here and yet, I can't leave.

The sound of screaming could be coming from me, or from the people fleeing. Perhaps it's actually the whistle of the dropping bomb. The cacophony of sounds around me are so loud, I hear everything, and nothing.

Dropping to my knees, the impact on the hard pavement gyrates up my bones. Clamping my hands over my ears and squeezing my eyes as tightly as I can, I feel a rush of air as the burn of the sun turns cold and dark.

Opening my eyes, I'm no longer in Time's Square but under the New York subway.

The dank air smells of dirt and fear. The astral forms of new Yorkers bump into my shoulders as they scramble past me.

What awaits them up there is no better than their fate down here once the bomb strikes. Nowhere will be safe.

I drop onto the tracks and run down the tunnel. Darkness encases me, but it's suffocating. Not at all reassuring, like the night sky.

The tunnel is collapsed and I'm seeing the residue of yesterday's subway system. The reality of the hallowed shaft of earth has transformed into a blockade of dirt and boulders. A small waterfall of sewage from a cracked pipe splashes on the muddy ground.

Bodies with marbled skin tinted green from the early stages of decay are streaked with black and purple veins. Flies buzz around me, assaulting my eyes and trying to fly into my mouth and nose.

These are the victims that will never be found. People who died yesterday and I'm the only one that will see them before their bodies begin to bloat and rot away into nothing.

A bright light races toward me and a high-pitched squeal of yesterday's train widens my eyes in fear.

I throw my arms up, covering my face a mere second before the train car slams into me, then I'm thrust into the daylight again.

Relieved to be free from the catacombs of the underground rail system, I watch in horror as the large round ball drops to the ground. Standing on the other side of the Hudson, I see the super-imposed skyline just as the bomb strikes.

The bright flare of light blinds me and I feel my skin being eaten alive just as if Ares' Soulfire were consuming me.

My throat is raw from my scream and then, in a swirl of blue light, everything vanishes.

"I've got you." Hermes is breathless. As if he ran across the globe faster than light to find me.

I can't stop screaming, trying to fight off the heat of the bomb that eviscerated millions of people in a flash.

"Take a deep breath, Rhea." Hermes splays his hands on each side of my head and a rush of cool blue light surges through me.

We're back in Greece and I call the salty air of Aegean sea to me.

He chases away the assault of the explosion from my skin and the constant ribbon of his aura surging around me soothes the burning.

With every inhale, I battle against the suffocating grip of guilt, forcing myself to focus on the turmoil raging within me.

Staring into the deep ocean raging in Hermes' gaze, I center myself on him. Coughing and sucking in air until my lungs finally expand, I collapse into him.

"It's the most horrifying thing I've ever seen."

The echoes of yesterday's destruction played out like a sick virtual reality around me as I witnessed two realities at once. The current devastation of toppled buildings, still smoking from the blast of the explosion and collapse. And through it, I could see the reverberations of the city that stood sprawling yesterday as it met its death.

How can a person survive this kind of torment, life after life? To what end of pain and suffering am I to bear through this curse?

Enveloped by Hermes' comforting embrace, a tempest of sorrow and guilt rages within me, threatening to consume the ruins of my shattered resolve.

I should have been able to sense this and stopped it.

The realization hits me like a physical blow to my stomach. A stark understanding of the catastrophic consequences of my actions, the blood of millions staining my hands with deep-seated guilt.

I should have known Ares would launch the realm into turmoil the second I left the Underworld.

This is the punishment of a demigod, a half mortal, half goddess.

A being filled somewhat with their potential, yet cursed to possess all the knowing of how they could help, if only they were stronger, if only I were stronger.

I calm my labored breathing and slow my tears, feeling my resolve to find my powers root deeper within me. I need to follow the path that will bring me to my immortality.

Even now, under the dark Grecian sky, the high pitch ringing in my ears has returned. Possibly it's my heightened emotions, or the residual scream of torment I just experienced. But as I lift my eyes to the sky, my gaze lands on the patch of stars where Tartarus sits.

Waiting for me is the power that could have prevented this. With everything in me, I know my instincts on this is right.

If Hermes doesn't believe me, I'll make him. With or without him, I'll walk the path set by the lifetimes before me.

Fierce determination settles deep within me as I regain control over my panic. I must find this redemption to make amends for the havoc I've caused. And I'll walk that path alone if that is what it takes.

The same dream of Tartarus inside the Cyclops' cave plagued my dreams again last night. White eyes gleamed in the darkness as the necklace slipped from my grasp. The eyes changed, turning green.

A menacing growl thundered toward me from the darkness. As it traveled through the tunnel, it changed to the high-pitch whistle of the bomb that leveled New York. I saw the blinding light of the explosion and felt the wave of heat racing toward me again.

My eyes flew open, and my breathing was ragged. The pounding heart in my chest would surely be loud enough to wake all of Greece but as I looked over, Hermes remained asleep.

I've laid awake several hours listening to his gentle breath filling the room as he lays on his stomach. Hugging his pillow, the sheet covers him low on his waist. Moonlight caresses his bare, muscled back, highlighting his perfect form.

I'm clutching the sword charm of my necklace so hard it's cutting into my skin, and I relax my grip with a deep exhale.

I reach out, my fingers tingling with the desire to touch Hermes. The hole in my chest swells as if ready to let him fill a vacancy that is waiting just for him. Before I can graze his soft skin, I stop myself, pulling back.

Everything that happened yesterday surges back to me and so does the sting of Hermes' words.

He doesn't believe I can feel my powers calling to me. Perhaps it's not a case of his disbelief in my powers more than it is a disbelief in me.

Then, New York.

Atlas tried to reach Hermes for help, and he was so wrapped up in our homecoming that he ignored the call. How many people could we have helped if only he answered?

Careful not to wake Hermes, I slide to the edge of the bed. Taking a throw blanket from a corner chair, I wrap it around my shoulders and sneak out onto the balcony.

Stepping into the cool night, I let the darkness envelop me. The sky is a deep shade of sapphire velvet with stars burning like silver diamonds.

Taking in deep breaths to erase the aftershock of the dream, I can't stop seeing the destruction of New York each time I close my eyes.

"Are you okay?" Callie's sweet voice travels to me on the Wind. Tears nearly flood my eyes hearing her voice.

"I miss you." I send my answer back and the current whisk it away. *"I'm okay. We should come help you."*

The swirl of Wind that runs around me sparkles with the yellow sunshine of Callie's aura. It surrounds me like a hug, and I feel her reassurance and comfort in the breeze.

"You are right where you should be. Don't worry about us. We've got this." I swear I can see her smile and the beam of her sky-blue eyes as the Wind whispers her words. *"Focus on your powers. I'll come see you in a few days."*

Gods, I can't even fathom what else can happen in a few days' time, but even Callie thinks I should stay away from the devastation, just like her brother.

After Hermes pulled me out of the projection, I realized what had been happening to me as I watched the bomb drop over New York.

With panic setting in, I attempted to channel my unstable powers. My emotions were firing all over the realm and I astral projected to New York. The ghostly overlay of the skyline and reliving the attack was an echo.

Empathic Echoes of the Sensory element. Natural lie detectors and powerful empaths, capable of seeing emotion, Sensors are highly in tune to illusion and deception. It's why I saw the white waves of worry flowing off Hermes before he told me of the attack.

I was detecting the physical manifestation of his emotions.

Hermes' mother was a powerful Sensor and an amazing huntress.

Goddess knows how much I miss her.

"Come, Juliet." I remember Daphne holding her long bow with an arrow at the ready. We stalked quietly through a forest hunting. *"We must be as quiet as a mouse."* Her rich brown eyes scanned the forest floor and try as hard as I could, I couldn't see what she was looking for.

Four centuries ago, my name was Juliet, and I was the daughter of an affluent Italian merchant.

Daphne was my nurse and servant. Since my birth, she cared for me. Working for my father, she was there each day when I woke, until I went to bed each night.

She always smelled of parchment and beeswax candles.

After her chores and my studies, she would steal me away to the forest behind my father's casa.

Her ivory tunic was tucked into brown leather trousers, and I smile at the memory of wearing pants for the first time. It was quite scandalous, being a maiden of higher nobility, my life was suffocating taffeta and satin gowns, elaborate shoes, and dinner party etiquette.

Nothing like the freedom of running through the woods in leather boots and pants. My hair pleated into a braid and sunshine warming my skin.

Ahead of us, leaves rustled, and the bleat of a crying fawn seems to come from everywhere.

"What are we hunting?" I asked.

"*Lies.*" Daphne answered.

She taught me how to interpret the residue of emotions. We tracked the scared fawn by the red trail of worry it left behind and the gluttonous green waves of hunger by the boar that stalked the small deer.

"Look at the truth in the emotions. Faces can wear a mask; words can be arranged. But the deposit of their emotions will always be truthful to you. Trust your instincts, sweet girl. Despite what you think, you will never fail yourself."

A tear rolls down my cheek as I remember her.

I'm glad she's not here to see how big I failed everyone, especially myself.

I think about those words now as I gaze up at the stars.

In one direction, within the belt of the Orion constellation, is Avalon. I can feel it. On the opposite end of the horizon, where a star should be, is an empty void of space where Tartarus used to shine in the night sky. Even so, I feel that realm too.

Like two pulsing beams of energy, they summon me.

While I know the history of the refugees that fled Tartarus as the Titans fought, no one was there to see if the world crushed by their power. And if Avalon made it through the Titans battle, Tartarus may have survived too.

A chill runs up my spine and I hug myself. Pulling the blanket tighter around me, I feel Hermes' warmth radiate closer as he finds me on the balcony. He rubs his hands up my arms, but instead of comfort, sadness washes over me.

"Thanks." I give him a tight-lipped smile and turn back to the empty patch of space that should house Tartarus.

"Did you have another dream?" He asks.

He didn't believe me the first time I dreamt of the necklace. I just didn't realize when he promised we would look for my powers together, he actually meant in place he thinks is reasonable.

It wasn't until Atlas left, and Hermes admitted he didn't think Tartarus survived, that I understood. Perhaps I was foolish to think he would agree with me and immediately begin planning how we would get there.

I imagined arriving at the realm with Hermes by my side and the two of us charging hand-in-hand to get my relic back. But the pain I felt when he dismissed it, when he suggested the feelings I have could be nothing more than a trick, it stung.

It felt like a punch in the gut.

I know he's lost a lot in this over the ages. We both have. But it's my powers that have been scattered across the realms, hidden from my hunter. And while I'm also a tattered mess of fucked up memories and trauma, I know what I feel.

I just never imagined, after all of this, after all the searching we've done for each other, Hermes would be so quick to push my ideas aside.

So, I lie.

"No, I couldn't sleep." I feel his gaze on me. Guilt fills me with heaviness and it's an effort to keep my gaze locked on the sky.

Hermes' earlier reaction is not the only reason to keep my opinion to myself, but something he said about our meeting at the bookstore and the Lurker planted on Medusa's generals a year before.

The bright green eyes that have stalked my dreams the last two nights flash against the night sky. Even with the blanket wrapped around me, an ominous warning crawls up my body, chilling me to my bones.

Ares has planted spies within our communes for ages. They have waited like Lurkers of their own accord, hiding in the shadows of our trust, and waiting for the moment they are needed.

Terra is a testament to Ares' patience and the lengths he'll go. Planted in a dirt cave with Calypso, they carried Terra out, believing they were rescuing her. What Callie and the others didn't realize was Ares and Demeter sacrificed their daughter, planting her like a weed of deceit behind the safety of our shields.

Who else could be an implant by Ares?

Could his speeches of empowerment and control have twisted other minds? Who else has found solace in the embrace of a murderer with his lies rooted in their minds and walked into our trusting friendship?

And how can we find them? If Terra and Demeter hid their loyalty so well, who else is secretly a general of Ares' army, waiting for the right moment to stab me through the back and shove me at my hunter?

I think of everyone and the broken moments of my past relationships with them. My mind floods with images of ancient civilizations, some of them lost to time forever. As cold dread claws at me, the emerald eyes are there, behind my eyelids each time I blink.

Hermes is the one constant burning star in my ever-changing night.

As the horizons of my past lives rotate around me, he is my fixed constellation. As I think of all others and the various roles they have played during the ages long game of cat-and-mouse, suspicion crowds me and two certainties are drawn are.

First, we have yet to unmask all the traitors who have worked their way into our inner circle. And second, Hermes will not be ready to face our greatest deceiver.

A game of chess began a long time ago and with each of my deaths, the game only waits for me to return. Counting the figures in my life and placing them around an imaginary chess-board, I sit Ares in the position of King across from me.

Demeter perhaps, is the queen of Avalon, but she is not the queen of this game.

Powerful and cunning, Demeter would not have both attacked and defended on behalf of her chosen king. Her interest was in her own power and revenge until she could return to Avalon.

So, with the position of the queen remaining vacant on the chess board within my mind, I can't help but wonder when the true queen of this game made her first move or if she is yet to strike.

I gather my emotions, forcing them down with deliberate

effort. A skill honed over countless trials of my lifetimes of torment.

I've trained well over the years to perfect wearing a mask of indifference and it slides easily over my face now. Meeting Hermes' worried eyes, I allow a false sense of peace to slide over me like a film. I push away the guilt of concealing my suspicions from him and give him a smile.

"I'm fine, I promise."

"**Hermes, come take a look at this.**" The sun has risen and while Hermes went back to sleep, I tossed and turned until the sun broke over the horizon.

Calling across our home, Hermes joins me in the living room. The flat screen TV mounted to the wall is showing a mortal news report of Venice. "It's you."

Cell phone footage of Hermes, likely recorded by a mortal, plays on the television. The way the news agency has spliced the recordings, makes it appear as if Hermes sank the floating city.

He joins me and watches the broadcast with a deadpan expression.

Parts of the footage have to be slowed down to show Hermes' lightning-fast speed. Even then, he's still a blur most of the time. The broadcaster reads from a script that paints the man in the film as a being of "immense and dangerous" power.

The text on the screen advertises one of the newly discovered "animal-shifters" will be doing a live interview, revealing a secret world of gods and monsters on a later broadcast.

The recording freezes just before a flash of red crosses the screen.

"Son of a bitch." Hermes grumbles.

"What?"

Taking the control from my hand, he replays the video, pausing it at the perfect moment to see the face of a redheaded asshole on the screen. Cowering in a corner is Flint. As the phone turns, just before the footage ends, dark hair and bright red lipstick, tell me who is with him.

Lexi.

"Fucking assholes." I mumble along with Hermes. Recalling the moments before I left the Underworld, I caught Flint and Lexi in the bedroom I shared with him. Lexi knew I was there but never outed me for reasons I still can't understand.

Part of me thought perhaps Lexi was helping me. But in truth, she was only letting me leave, knowing I heard them talking about consuming my power and that I would react. She followed me to Venice, and they recorded my mate.

They are helping to paint a picture of a divide for the mortals.

Ares will put himself at the top of the list of gods to be trusted and skew the perception against us, so we appear to be the villains in this story. He'll play the countries like a conductor plays an orchestra. The music of his deception will be replaced with more bombs of mortals, and he'll relish in the blood that will flow into the waters of Gaea.

My thoughts of this desolate future are interrupted when I think about Flint's severed hand, remembering Lexi saying Hermes did it. A smile tugs at my face as I look at the paused screen.

Since yesterday, Hermes is treading carefully, letting me go through the homes library and resting. With last night's dream plaguing me, I took two naps today. Despite the chaos of traitors and death flooding my thoughts while awake.

But I can't stay upset at Hermes forever. We need to talk this through.

He knows I'm upset and maybe he's not sure how to talk about it, but we've got to figure it out. Just as I take a breath in hopes of breaking the awkwardness, Hermes interjects, standing and turning off the television.

"Time to go steal a library."

Hermes and I arrive on a wave of his Light on the outskirts of the Atlanta Commune. Darkness blankets the forest of pines nestled around the perimeter of the Coat.

Atlas and Hecate stand with their arms folded, debating the best way inside. Medusa leans against a tree wearing all black. She looks at me with a dull expression and a curt nod of her head, returning to the phone in her hand. Two of her braids assist her thumbs as they fly over the screen, texting rapidly.

Dread curls around my ankles, keeping me alert as we stand on the edge of the Atlanta Commune. The thought of Eris and her Shifters just on the other side of the Coat sends a shiver up my spine. Hermes takes my hand in his and I look where our fingers lace together.

Following the line of his arm, my mind flashing back to the Washington DC rooftop. I was there with Flint, wasting time until I murdered an innocent man. I wanted so badly to have someone that cherished me like a precious treasure and fantasized about walking the national mall and joining the other couples on their picnic lunches.

I dreamed of having someone cling to me, desperate to have me in their life for no other reason than they wanted me.

I imagined Hermes.

Despite Demeter's poison and fabricated reality, my heart and soul longed for him. Now we're together and it's not going the way I thought it would.

I expected we would fall into a familiar routine. He would start a sentence and I finish it. Right now, he starts a sentence that seems to belong to a different conversation than the one I'm having.

His eyes are a deep navy in the moonlight. I feel as if he is begging me with his gaze.

"If we get a few extra minutes" He speaks to me in my mind. *"There is something I want to show you."*

I give him a flat-lipped smile, nodding in response.

I want to crash into him. To collide into his arms and marry my lips to his. But I want him to listen to my words and respect my intuition. I can't sit on the sidelines of my recovery and let him ride off into the sunset on a valiant steed to rescue me.

I need to do this for myself. The call of my powers across the realms is getting stronger each day, and I need to answer it. Perhaps I architected this recovery with purpose and intention.

What if the lives I have led altered and adjusted the pathway of restoration? Not only to keep my powers hidden from my hunter but to allow me to discover something hidden along the way.

Believing in that thought, knowing it's true within each beat of my heart, I have to stay true to the course I have set for myself.

Hermes and I just need to be patient with each other, I

suppose. We have been without the other half of our soul's completion for four hundred years and it will take a moment to find our balance again. But I want to do this with him by my side because I love him.

The Wind whirls around me at the thought.

I realize this is the first time I've thought about that phrase and the feelings that come along with it during this lifetime. I think I've realized my love for him in each of my lives, even the ones where we never found each other.

My skin pebbles as I recall falling for him again and again.

It's like each lifetime, I'm a little different and Hermes has to learn to navigate around the subtle changes to my personality. And I have to work around the fractures and crevices in my mind, careful not to let myself fall too deeply into one.

It's that thought that makes me want to close the distance I've created yesterday. A distance that seems to expanse the universe and it suffocates me.

I'm still hurt but I know he loves me too. We just need to work through this.

A thousand times we've been torn apart and come back together again. This difference of our opinions is important but it's not the end that will drive us away from each other.

I squeeze his hand, pulling him to me.

As if he has been holding his breath for a day, Hermes releases a deep exhale and cups my face. Stealing a swift kiss, he packs a thousand words and feelings into the soft exchange.

I know he feels the same and once we get a few minutes without the world falling apart, we'll figure this out.

A weight lifts off my shoulders and the night seems to brighten just a little.

But burdening me still is the weight of a thousand realms.

My immortality severed and beaconing me in a constant plea. It's like a high pitch ringing in the ears and I know it won't stop until I've found it.

Then, the fate of the realm and the lives of humans being used as pawns in Ares' quest to consume me. Their blood is on my hands as much as it is on Ares'.

My next burden is Triton, the abandoned immortal, suffering and wasting away in the dark recesses of the Underworld. He is waiting for my return to dispatch him from this life and send him on to the realm of souls.

A thought I'm still not ready to face.

Hermes hand lingers on my cheek before he lets go. Turning to face Atlas, Medusa and Hecate, we march over the tall grass to the trio of Elementals waiting for us at the edge of the Coat.

The pulse of the forcefield washes over me in undulating waves of power and wards. The intensity of it steals my breath and I gasp several times, composing myself.

I hadn't been able to detect the force field when I first arrived at the Atlanta Commune. Knowing my strength is growing as I restore my powers makes me straighten my shoulders with pride. I bet I could tear down these wards with my powers and if we had the warriors with us to take on the packs of Shifters who have taken up residence here, maybe I would.

I'm excited for this mission but I wish Callie was here.

She and Achilles are helping Elementals with rescue efforts in New York. Lucas and his packs are working to recover abducted Shifters. Odysseus and Penelope are tracking Ares.

With so much happening across the globe, our small coven of immortals is stretched thin. And unbeknownst to the others, I'm suspicious of a traitor in our midst.

But Atlas thinks there may be texts here to help with understanding my powers; insight into those who wish to drink from my well of immortality and devour my abilities.

So, we're here to steal books from Eris and I'd be lying if I didn't admit I'm glad. She wouldn't appreciate them the way Atlas and I would.

In fact, I wouldn't put it past Eris to burn everything if she ever found out there were texts here about my powers or my curse.

"Anything we do to break through the Coat will trigger their alarms." Atlas holds his chin in one hand while his elbow rests on his arm crossed across his chest. His brows are furrowed deep in concentration.

He wears a pale blue button-down shirt, tucked neatly into rich brown pants. The sleeves are rolled up several times, exposing his tan skin, bringing out the richness of his brown eyes that shine behind gold-rimmed glasses.

Hecate's raven hair seems to billow on a current of wind that blows just for her. She is regal in her stola and the white strip of hair that frames her face accentuates the granite veins that run through her dark eyes.

"I'm sure Rhea can find a way in for us." She smiles at me and winks.

I look behind us to the massive dome of Light that protects the commune for miles.

Considering how to break through it, Hermes casts a wave of low blue Light that skips along the ground. I watch his power bounces and rolls away from us. Dark patches within the grass where the Light doesn't reach stand out to me among the gentle swell of his aura.

I look to Hecate and smile as an idea forms in my mind.

"It's nighttime." I say to my mate. "We need a little darkness to find our way."

Opposite of Hermes' blue light, deep purple, and onyx waves of darkness flow from me. Night deepens around us, and I send a wave of my power, chasing after Hermes's Light. Within seconds, the Dark consumes the Light and my reach is everywhere. The blue aura of his power disappears, and mine streaks across the grounds.

My powers spread along the dome's edge, adapting to the terrain. Wind swirls through trees, Water stretches beneath the ground as I find our way inside.

A thought crosses my mind, and I chuckle, anticipating Hermes's protest against the plan I'm gathering.

When we visited Avalon, Orion doubled over in laughter as he told me what happened to Hermes with the Lady of the Lake. I laugh now, recalling how Hermes was still offended by the dark lake of Avalon.

Looking beyond the forcefield protecting the Atlanta Commune, a small, underground spring feeds the lake. Reaching deep within the ground, I move my powers through the dirt, arriving at the deep lake that sits behind the massive commune.

"Medusa?" I ask, disturbing her from her phone. Her thumbs stop messaging, but her braids continue moving across the screen. Medusa casts her eyes up at me and I shiver. The moonlight reflects in her green orbs, and they shine at me like emeralds.

I freeze as if I was dunked into a frigid lake of the frozen arctic. It's just like my dream and the green eyes that haunt me from within the dark cave.

The fine hairs at the base of my neck stand to attention.

Worry pulls a knot tight in my stomach and I release a breath, trying to relax it.

No one has noticed my pause and I swallow hard, working to steady myself before I continue. "There is an underground spring about ten yards that way. Can you open up the earth and get us access to it?"

"Easy peasy." She says. Pushing off the tree, she walks to the spot I indicated. From her feet, the ground under her swells.

Her power moves through the earth, looking like a banded snake moving under the surface. The dirt inflates like a balloon, then collapses as a great sinkhole forms.

Walking to the spot, Hecate, Atlas, and Hermes peer into the opening. The spring running under the earth pools in the divot Medusa created.

"So, what now?" Hermes asks. But I think he already knows; he is just hoping he is wrong. The smile on my face betrays me, giving away the answer before I can say it. "Oh, fuck." He mumbles.

"We're going in through the lake." I tell them, already raising my arms as a stream of water obeys my silent command.

A bubble forms around us, solidifying under our feet and large enough for all of us. Medusa, still occupied by her phone, is standing farthest away from the group and I have to ask her to step closer.

With a huff, she complies, never taking her eyes off the screen of her phone.

The feeling of teleporting through the water is like being turned into gelatin.

As if all our bones are turned to liquid, the ball of water surrounding us seems to shrink, disappearing in the darkness of the underground spring and delivering us inside the large lake that overlooks the back of the Atlanta Commune.

I keep my hands out in front of me, guiding the bubble through the water. Bringing it closer to the surface, I send out another wave of darkness and survey the landscape inside the Coat.

No alarms that I can sense have been alerted and I release a pent-up breath.

Several Shifters cover the grounds as sentries, but most are leaning against the building asleep. A few are huddled together chatting and some are playing games on their phones.

"Can we get out of the water bubble soon?" Hermes asks with his eyebrows raised, inspecting the top of the bubble, and searching for the moonlight high above us.

"Shall I take us in through the pipes or can we teleport from here?" I jest with a smirk. Atlas chuckles and elbows Hermes.

"I'm sure we'll be fine teleporting." Hermes answers.

Just before I open a dark portal, two Shifters emerge from the large building and walk toward the lake. One spits in the grass and the other talks about the selection of female Shifters being auctioned for mating selections.

The practice is barbaric; I roll my eyes at the thought of a women's auction for reproduction.

"Atlas, I know you prefer not to take over other people minds, but do you think you can... put them to sleep for a second or something?" I ask with pleading eyes.

He huffs a laugh through his nose and peers up at the pair of male Shifters, dawdling where we need to emerge. "I'll give them a gentle nudge in another direction, how about that?"

As soon as he speaks the words, one Shifter suggests they

go to the cafeteria for a late meal. The pair of men leave, and I smile approvingly at Atlas.

Delivered to the grassy field of the commune, the great oak tree to my left makes me think of one of my first days here. Hermes escorted me to the dock where I watched Athena perform her beautiful water dance.

I can envision the sunny day as we walked across the water together. Our silver and gold auras danced around the waves reflecting in the daylight.

Looking at Medusa, and a frown pulls at my face.

I wonder if she can feel the lingering presence of her mate who lived here and was murdered not far from where we stand. Still plugging away at her phone, one of Medusa's braids taps her three times on her shoulder and it points at me.

Medusa pulls her attention from the screen and with a cocked eyebrow looks at me. "Something you need?" She asks curtly.

When I shake my head no, she dives back into the phone occupying her.

"Why did she even come?" I ask Hermes through our minds.

"She's got a lot going on."

Understandable and exactly why she maybe should have stayed at her commune, instead of coming with us.

"Shield us in shadows and let's get into my office first." Atlas whispers, even though he sent all the guards to the kitchen for a snacks. "We'll handle the larger library last."

With a plan, I consume us in shadow. Hermes shutters as chills cover him and I nestle into his side, wrapping my hand around the crook of his elbow. A swirl of purple and silver opens up like a doorway and swallows us.

Atlas's dark office greets us, and it looks exactly like it always does. The table we sat, where he told Rhea she was a goddess, stands cold and empty in the dark apartment. The overstuffed bookshelves stand as tall soldiers protecting Atlas' coveted tomes of research and history.

It seems like it's been a lifetime since I was here last, not the few weeks that have passed. My entire world has changed in such a short time that even this familiar apartment seems foreign to me now.

I pull the lumos into the bulbs around the space and fill the room with soft light.

Atlas rushes through his space in a frenzy as if the papers are going to disappear within seconds. Opening drawers and cabinets, he pulls out stacks of his work. Medusa plops down on the leather couch in the center of the room.

My eyes fixate on the piece of furniture that served as my bed many nights when I crashed at his place. Mainly I think of Rhea, laying on that couch with Athena helping her as Atlas navigated through Rhea's memories.

Hypnos picked up the echoes of that session and we watched as Rhea walked into the portal. The Dark Mage was waiting for her and soon after the commune was attacked. It was the night the Goddess of War was murdered.

Had Medusa and Athena's mating bond still been intact, Medusa would have felt the pain of Soulfire that ate through Athena's immortality.

After all the eons their bond has been eliminated, I wonder if Medusa can feel the remnants of her former mate that once filled this very room not too long ago. Right now, Medusa is preoccupied with refortifying her commune and sits on the couch, unaware.

The Shifters who fled with Lucas and those who were exposed after Mabon needed new packhouses. Since Medusa's commune was eviscerated by Aryana, it seemed only logical to house the Shifters with Medusa.

But my old friend is mourning the loss of her warriors. She feels the sting of betrayal and there is a shadow that has settled in her evergreen eyes.

I know how Medusa is when she gets like this. Her dark and brooding emotions just need some time and she'll work herself out of the slump.

Rhea noticed Medusa's mood too. I know it bothered her to see Medusa disengaged, but my mate needs to focus on her powers; let the other the immortals worry with the rest.

"This is going to take forever at this rate." Hecate gestures at the office with a frustrated huff. Atlas rushes back and forth to different stacks of books and piles of journals.

A swirling mass of darkness opens by Hecate's side. The papers rustle as if they are about to be sucked into a vortex. Atlas panics, trying to hold them down.

"They'll get out of order." He looks frantically around the mess. "I know exactly where everything is."

Their exchange makes me chuckle and I shake my head. Taking a step to Hecate, I place a hand on her shoulder. "I'll take care of this." She drops her swirling portal and steps back.

Atlas visibly relaxes and my blue aura fills the room. I know how finicky Atlas is about research and studies. Once, I accidentally blasted a light beam through the wall when I was sparring with Achilles.

Atlas' books went everywhere, and it took us days to get everything back in order.

Hecate and Atlas stand, shoulder to shoulder. Hecate reaching an inch above his stature, but the power radiating off them both is balanced equally in might.

"Show me your new office at Delphi?" I ask Atlas.

"It's the same as before."

The contents of Atlas's office glow, surrounded by my power and I teleport everything out of the room. The bookshelves and desk disappear along with the contents without rustling a single paper.

I project a Mirage of another office in Delphi. It's the very office he always kept when my father was leader of the commune, and we lived in our family home there.

Atlas smiles, seeing his familiar desk and bookshelves stuffed to the brim with tomes. "Thank you."

I make quick work of replicating the office here, placing mirages around the room making it seem as if nothing is out of place. My shield snaps around the threshold and will alert me if any of Eris' Shifters come searching the room after we leave.

Rhea looks around the space and I want to impress her. The ease at which I bend my element is like a second skin. As familiar to me as breathing, I wield my Light effortlessly.

But I want to be a worthy mate for her.

It's not a matter of who has more power because, fuck, she can take all of us out and she's only partly restored. I want her to feel like she can rely on me.

We're a team but I'm terrified of something happening to her. I know I let that fear come out when she was trying to talk to me about her dream.

I'm just the fucking idiot who put his foot in his mouth and made her feel like she doesn't have a voice in all of this.

Rhea told me she can feel her powers on Tartarus, and I told her I didn't think the realm survived. I could see her recoil away from the sting of my comment and I wanted to take it back as soon as I spoke it.

Then I gave her space, thinking that would help her. But our silence has only made things worse and it's ripping me apart inside to know she's hurting and keeping it to herself.

All I'm doing is helping her figure things out without me.

That's the opposite of what I want. I want her to trust in me, trust in us and the bond we have. I want to be the first person she runs to for everything and anything. But this is not how I make that happen.

Her golden eyes dance around the office, watching the particles of Light. The element scurries around the atmosphere, eager to please her, just like me. The Light dances before us as millions of prisms and she's transfixed by them. I gather the glittering particles of Light into a swirl and tap the end of her nose.

The soft golden light bursts, raining down like a shower of sparklers and her face lights up with amusement.

Unable to bear the space between us a second longer, I make my way to her. Wrapping my arm low around her waist, I bring her to me.

"You're up next, little goddess." My whisper wraps around her like a silk sheet and she molds her body to mine.

Medusa puts her phone in the back pocket of her pants and stands, looking around the room as if for the first time.

"Nice of her to finally join us." Rhea cocks an eyebrow at me.

"Play nice." I answer, a slight warning in my playful tone.

"Make me." My mate counters with a challenge strong in her gaze.

"Later." It's both a warning and a promise. Rhea pulls her bottom lip between her teeth, anticipating continuing our little game when we're done here. *Gods, I want to be the one to bite that lip.*

She notices my eyes when I look at her mouth and smirks.

"I'll make sure to take you up on that." She says as she readies her power.

With our small group ready, Rhea's portal of Darkness swells and we emerge within a dark corner of the communes great library. My hold around her is protective in the new space until she and Hecate send a pulse of Dark power to survey the large Library.

I shoot my own wave of soft starlight to the ceiling, surveying the space and looking for the ripples of any Mirages. Everyone holds silently as our powers shoot out from us, the Dark Shield hiding us from any potential view and all of us ready for a confrontation.

Hecate and Rhea nod in agreement when they find no one guarding the library and we spread out.

"What are we taking?" Rhea whispers.

"Everything." Atlas says, a gleam shining in his brown eyes.

Rhea's eyes roam up to the large ceiling thirty feet above us.

Painted like the frescos of the Vatican, one end of the large space is the sunrise and the other is a sunset. With the horizon of the realm painted above us.

She takes in the rows of tall shelves on both levels of the building.

Thousands of books and even more rolled parchments are stored safely within the bookshelves and contain a hoard of history. Civilizations that fell to time, languages lost to new translations that only remain alive within this scribe's collection.

And within, perhaps answers that will help her journey.

Rhea's shoulders sag as she looks around the vast library as if she's unsure she can move all of this.

"You can do this." I rub her arm with reassurance. Smiling when she looks back to the large two-story building and its endless rows of tall shelves. "I seem to recall Alexandria is much larger than this collection."

"Yeah, no big deal." She releases a deep breath continuing to survey the area. Medusa is perusing around a nearby shelf, running her finger over the spines as if looking for a book.

"Is there an empty library for me to fill at Delphi?" Rhea whispers to me, her eyes like large round saucers.

"Afraid not." We should have planned a place to drop all of this ahead of time.

I feel like I got the easy job. Moving things from one office to another that was cleared out and ready. With everything going on in the realm, we should have put someone in charge of erecting a building.

Medusa's Commune was bustling with Earth Elementals. Usually someone would have just shown up and had it done without an issue. With most of her commune murdered, it fell through the cracks.

Medusa pulls a piece of parchment from the shelf she has been looking at and reads it.

"Hecate." she says, a breathless sense of amazement coating her tone. "You're never going to believe what I just found."

The Dark Mage joins Medusa and takes the old piece of parchment from her hand. Her eyes dart across the lines quickly and she turns it over as if not believing what she is looking at.

Meeting Rhea's stare, Hecate's eyes are wide, and her mouth hangs open. Atlas moves to her side, craning his neck to inspect the parchment for himself.

"It's the rest of my poem, from the excerpt found in Damien's notes. It's the rest of The Forgotten Goddess."

In the depths of shadows, a goddess concealed,
Her story hidden; ancient truths revealed.
Choices eclipsed, spun in twilight's dance,
She yearns for healing beneath the sun's expanse.
In the empty Void where shadows tread,
Mysterious paths with secrets spread.
As the eclipse begins its celestial play,
Sunlight's doorway leads her way.
On golden beams, her essence ascends,
Through the cosmic dance, night transcends.
A tale unfolds, not easily spun,
The goddess journeys, her fate begun.

My mind races as I recite the words of the poem. Atlas and Hermes look over the text. It's clear, my next journey will lead me to Tartarus. The realm of sunlight, and triplet to the world we are in right now.

My powers await me, and I feel them like a beacon, knocking on a locked door, just out of my reach. I'm thinking of Freya's necklace, and the amber pendent with a swirling silver cluster of Immortality, when Hermes' voice echoes across the library.

"Then I'll go. No way is she leaving here."

"Excuse me?" My voice is nothing more than a whisper through the tall, marbled walls of the building. *You have got to be fucking kidding me.*

"Hermes," Atlas grabs Hermes bicep as he delivers a warning. "Remember what I said, this is not your choice."

Finally. At least someone Hermes listens to is on my side about this.

The time since we arrived at the Atlanta Commune, I opened the door letting Hermes know I'm ready to forgive him for his earlier pigheadedness about Tartarus. I felt like he knew he screwed things up and was going to apologize when we got back to Mount Olympus, but apparently I was wrong.

Atlas gives me a reassuring nod and understanding smile before he and Hecate turn their attention to each other, trying to distract themselves with transporting the books to give us the illusion of privacy.

Medusa, however, watches me, leaning a shoulder against a bookshelf with one ankle crossed over the other.

Hermes runs his hand down his face in exasperation and steps up to me. He looks defeated and reaches toward me to run his hand down my arm but pauses. Thinking better of it, he pulls back.

"Can we go somewhere to talk?" He asks in a whisper.

"That would be a good idea." I reply with anger oozing through my words.

A swirl of his power teleports us to a small apartment.

The lights are off, but I can see basic furnishings. It doesn't appear that anyone lives here but I feel the presence of Hermes' power shielding the home.

At the first sign of a next step, Hermes wants to push me aside and go on my journey for me. I'm trying to calm my thoughts before I speak, not wanting to blow up and make things worse. Pacing back and forth, I try to collect myself.

Hermes catches me by the arm, pausing my track. I pull out of his hold and cross my arms over my chest. Looking to the side, I refuse to meet his eyes. Running his fingers through my hair, a gentle wave of his soothing Light runs through me and settles my mind.

"Don't do that." I move away from his touch, and it hurts him. Squinting his eyes, I see the pain from my words. "Don't just brush off my feelings with your power like my emotions don't matter."

"That's not what I'm trying to do."

I look back to the floor with tears brimming in my eyes. I hate crying. I can't stand it when someone making so angry, the only release I have is to cry. It feels so weak. Like such a cop out with all my powers, and all I can do is shed angry tears.

"I told you." I whisper. My bruised feelings coating my soft words. "I told you Tartarus was our next step." I say louder, finally looking at him as the first fat tear drops down my cheek.

"Can we just slow down about all of this?" Hermes holds hands out before him like he's pushing an imaginary set of brakes.

"Why? Why, in the name of the Fates, should we consider something else? Why should we wait when my powers are sitting there, begging me to find them." I gesture out the large glass door that leads to a portico.

"I just think it's hasty to jump into another realm."

I tilt my head and my eyebrows shoot into my hairline at his response.

"Says the man who literally jumped head-first off a waterfall, into another realm." I step back putting my weight on one leg, jutting my hip out in irritation. "Just admit it. You don't like the idea because you didn't think of it."

"That's ridiculous." The pitch of his voice raises on the first word. "Why can't we look at other options? Why do you have to go? I can do it!"

"So, I can just sit around being the damsel in distress while you go off and play the hero?"

"It's not about that." He walks away from me, running his hands through his hair and looking outside. Our frustration with each other is mounting and this is becoming heated. My cheeks flare with my rising temper and I almost don't care what I say next.

"So, what is it about then? You can't stand to see me do something on my own?"

"I can't stand to see you die again, Rhea." Turning, he pierces me with the tears welling in his blue eyes. Tears I didn't see forming because he tried to hide them from me. "I can't watch the light fade out of your eyes one more time, knowing I failed you– *again*."

Hermes sits down on a large footrest that accompanies a matching chair, resting his elbows on his knees, holding his head. My heavy chest rises slowly as I work to breath at a normal pace. His confession cooling my growing temper.

"Hermes," My voice cracks across the dark room. I take the few steps to him. My fingers thread through the dark trusses of his wavy hair. I watch a tear gleam as it passes a path of silver moonlight on its way to the floor.

Hermes rests his head against my stomach, gripping the back of my thighs.

"I can't stop seeing them." I remain quiet and keep stroking his hair as he speaks. My other arm resting across his shoulders and rubbing small circles along his back.

"Every pair of eyes you have ever looked at me with haunt me. And each time they dim and close forever, it kills me a little more." He looks up at me, a pleading grief coating his expression.

"I die each time because I know I disappointed you again. I know I'm the reason for the pain you suffer as each of your lives comes to an end." Hermes takes in a ragged breath as more tears fill his blue orbs. "You should hate me for failing you so."

"How can you say that?" I wipe away a tear that runs out of the corner of his eye. "Each time my life ends, I can say good-bye, the knowing that you'll be here, searching for me; waiting for me."

Hermes closes his eyes, as if my words pain him so I keep talking.

"It's you who gives me hope. You are my guiding light that I follow each time I return." Tears gather quickly in my eyes and fall down my cheeks. Hermes pulls me to his lap and circles my waist with his arms as I wrap mine around his neck.

"I need you to keep your hope in me. So many times, Ares and Demeter striped it out of me. They crush me until I believe I'm nothing but it's always you, who pulls me from their darkness." I place a kiss on the corner of his mouth. "I'll die a thousand more deaths, as long as I know it's you I'll return to."

My words break him open. "Baby," he whispers his affections to me before he kisses me deeply. "I don't want to lose you again."

"Then don't." I lean back so I can take him in. My eyes bounce between his as my brow pinches together. "Stop trying to shield me from things you can't control and let's plan this out together. You jumped off that cliff, trusting in my power and you traveled to Avalon. A realm you also thought was gone. And at the end of it, you brought my powers back to me. You stole me from the darkness and held on to me with your light."

I suck in a ragged breath, remembering waking up at the bottom of the ocean with my mate clinging to me.

I remember my powers eating away at his soul and he only held on to me tighter. He would have given his life to make sure I was okay.

I look between his sorrow-filled eyes and the pain there crushes me. "I need you to keep trusting in me and believing that we can do this. That I can do this."

"I do trust you, with everything that I am, I trust nothing but you." He takes my mouth with his and his kiss pours the truth of his admission through my soul. My chest heaves and the empty space within me thrums with the movements of his tongue. "I'm so scared of losing you. I just got you back and I can't say goodbye again."

I kiss his cheek, holding the side of his face with my hand and stroking the hair at the nape of his neck with my other.

"I have no plans to die this time, so there will be no need to say goodbye." I study the blue depths of his eyes and take in each rivet of cerulean and cobalt. "Something feels different, and I don't know if it's the body I took when I reincarnated, or the alignment of the realms, or all of it. But something has changed. It's like this is... this is the beginning."

Hermes cocks his head curiously, "The beginning of what?"

Looking to the side, I try to gather the multitude of sensations and find the right words. It's not just what I feel within myself but the realm as well. Finding the simplest answer. "the end."

"Gods, I love you so much." He touches his forehead to mine and holds me tighter. "I'm sorry, I'm a fucking asshole." His mouth ravages mine and my heart soars within me, stealing my breath.

A whimper escapes my throat when he kisses me again. His hands roam my body and pull me closer to him.

"I love you." Craving the feel of his skin on mine, suddenly the barrier of clothes between us feels like a vice trapping me. I grind against him as our mouths consume each other.

"Easy, little goddess." He growls against my lips, then kisses me again. "Easy." He whispers. This next kiss is softer, taking his time exploring me before he pulls away. "Can I show you something?" He asks with eyes that glimmer from the residue of his tears. I nod my head and he kisses me once more as his cool blue light surrounds us.

We teleport upstairs to a small loft in the same dark apartment.

"Whose apartment is this anyhow?" I ask, looking around the space when my mouth gapes open.

"It was going to be yours."

The loft is full of books, shelved along a long wall broken up by a large circular window. The moon shines through the glass and covers us in pale blue light. The night seems to shimmer around us as I keep looking around the space.

The blue painted ceiling reminds me of Hermes deep navy

eyes. Gilded stars make up constellations and the dots of the realms are splattered above us in their correct positions. Three among them largest of all; Avalon, Gaea, and Tartarus.

Perhaps it was a subliminal thought, done without knowing or perhaps something within Hermes knew of the importance of the triple realms. Regardless, my powers pulse at me from beyond the barrier of Gaea and I have to close my eyes to steady myself.

"You did this?" I ask, walking the loft and taking in the titles on the books.

Hermes velvet gaze follows me as I explore the space. My fingers graze the books as my eyes roam the details of the room. It's beautiful.

"I love it." Tears threaten to rise to the surface at the thought of him putting so much time into this, all for me. He had to have done this before we fled from the Atlanta Commune, the night I thought Demeter was killed and we ran to Medusa.

No one has ever done something so thoughtful for me during this lifetime.

They are modern works of all kinds. Stories of fantasy, dark romance, and thrillers that I would love to read in my free time. An entire shelf is dedicated to smut books with Hermes' name in the title, and I laugh.

Shaking my head, I remember the books he put in the bathroom in Kenya on the night we had dinner under a canopy of tiny floating flames.

Taking a book from the shelf and turning it over, Once Upon A Spine Books is stamped on the back and I run my hand over the imprint affectionately.

I spent so much time there before. Always seeing the bookstore as my only refuge, it's only fitting it was the place Hermes found me again in this life. My true sanctuary in all of this is him and he found me wondering around the Greek mythology section of my favorite old bookstore.

I face him with a romance novel of his namesake in my hand. "Conceited much?" I jest, returning the book to its home on the shelf.

Hermes leans against a desk in the center of the room. His smirk turns to a grin as he chuckles. His long legs stretch across the space, with one ankle crossed over the other. The tight t-shirt strains around his muscles and I drink in the sight of him in the moonlight.

His Light wraps around me like a rope and tugs me to him. "I'm just a greedy bastard who wants to consume your every thought."

I stand with my legs on each side of his and Hermes' hands take ownership of me. His lips meet my neck and I roll my head to the side, allowing him better access.

"I want your laughter." He pauses his work on my neck. "I want your sadness." He kisses the other side of my neck and I move with him. Closing my eyes, I absorb the feeling of him with a satisfied hum. "I just want you. All of you." With one more kiss on my neck, he stands, picking me up and turning me to sit on the desk.

He holds the back of my neck with his hand, and I wrap my legs around him. Pulling our bodies together, I feel how hard he is against my jeans. He releases a groan and closes his eyes as I grind against him.

Power ripples within me knowing a simple movement can silence him and still his breathe. Grabbing the waistband of his pants, I pull him into me more. I need the feeling of his piercings rolling along my center and his cock filling my pussy.

"Gods, baby." He murmurs against my lips.

"If you want all of me," I stop my sentence to lick his mouth and he grunts, opening his eyes and looking at me with a predatory stare of warning about what we are starting. "Help me find my powers." I grind along him and feel myself getting wetter. My breath hitches as my arousal builds. "Cause right now, you only have half of me."

I take his bottom lip between my teeth and circle my hips, moving myself along the shaft of his erection. "Or are you unable to handle all of me?" A sly grin slides across my face.

His eyes deepen to midnight blue and burn through me as my challenge cuts through his resolve. In a single movement, he repositions me.

In a blink, I'm standing, pushed against the desk as I brace my hands on it. Hermes is at my back, his long erection pressing against my ass.

"Oh, little goddess." His voice slithers down my spine as I arch into him. "I think it's you who is not ready to handle all of me yet." His hand trails down the front of my pants, reaching between my legs.

He deep voice thunders against me when he finds my bare pussy, wet and already throbbing for his touch. "No panties? Mmmmm..." He bites my neck as his finger vibrates against my clit.

The dueling sensations rip a gasping moan from my mouth and Hermes hand circles the column of my throat. "Shhhhhh, my greedy little goddess."

His finger swirls my needy clit and an orgasm warms in my belly.

"I can keep them from seeing us, but I can't stop them from hearing you screaming when I make you cum with just a finger."

I unfasten the buckle of my pants and with one hand begin to pull them down. Hermes helps me, and in an instant I feel like I'm dripping, needing the touch of him deep inside me.

Just a moment ago, I held all the power as I thrust against him. In a second, I'm near the point of begging. I thank the Fates when he doesn't make me wait. He needs to feel me as badly as I need him.

His pushes my legs apart with his booted feet as I hear the buckle of his belt loosen. Pushing against my back, he lowers me until my chest lays on the desk. Fisting the length of his cock in his hand, he rubs the head against my entrance, and I nearly cry needing him inside me.

With a single thrust, he buries himself fully and begins pumping in and out of me.

With the movement, my mouth flies open, a moan on the verge of escape but Hermes' hand covers my mouth. The sensation of his piercings sliding inside me shoots along my spine and I raise off the desk.

He pulls me to his chest, my noises stifled as he gently applies pressure around my throat. With his other hand, he resumes the vibrations against my clit and my orgasm resumes building.

Raging within me, I hold my breath as my pleasure crests. I hold onto the desk like it's the only thing keeping me grounded and I'm afraid my grip will break it in two.

My release is as fast and hard as Hermes' pumping. My wetness coats him as he slides within me, chasing his own orgasm and grunting in my ear.

With my pants pooling around my ankles, Hermes slides out of me. Turning me to face him, he reaches between my legs. Two fingers slide along my slick pussy as his cum escapes me.

I take in a sharp breath of desire when he grazes my tender clit, still pulsing from my orgasm.

Bringing his fingers to my mouth, he waits with one eyebrow cocked. "Open for me." He whispers and I obey.

Sliding his long fingers in my mouth, I wrap my lips around them. Sucking the taste of us off his fingers, he holds me with his hot gaze, and I melt under his stare. Removing his fingers from my mouth, he chases the taste of us with his tongue.

His hand squeezes my ass and pulls the long hair at the nape of my neck.

My arms circle him as we meld together, embracing in the aftershock of our lovemaking. Having consumed each other until we're breathless, we part. Resting his forehead against mine, our chests heave as we come down from our high.

"You're mine." His hand circles my throat again with tender affection. "And I'll not lose you to Death again." He places a gentle kiss on my mouth. "But I won't lose you to my stubbornness either."

Reaching to the side of me, he pulls a few tissues from a holder.

My cheeks flare and I bite back the urge to take the tissue from his hand and clean myself. Hermes looks deep into my eyes as he cleans the cum running down my leg.

He loves caring for me, but my first instinct is to care for myself.

During the lifetime of Rhea, I've only known what it's like

to be abandon and discarded like I don't matter. My instinct is to push Hermes' help aside and tend to myself.

But behind that, I remember myself as Nyx.

I recall Hermes, standing on the horizon of a vast darkness with nothing but starlight shining behind him. He held out his hand for me, the look in his eyes told me he would do anything for me.

Taking that hand, we started our journey together.

In countless lives after, my constant North Star has been Hermes. Tending to my heart and my wounds. We've argued, and he has certainly pissed me off, but through it all, his care for me never wavered.

So, I stay fixed on my horizon that is his deep cerulean eyes and let him care for me.

Discarding the used tissues in the wastebasket next to us, Hermes kneels down. Holding my gaze as his hands run slowly down my legs. With the belt loops of my jeans, he begins to pull my pants up.

He goes at a slow pace, kissing each of my thighs first. Next, he kisses each side of my pelvis and electric chills shoot along my body. I gasp when he pauses at my center and kisses my pussy.

"My gods, Hermes." I exclaim, yearning coated with embarrassment at the action.

He chuckles, and mischief gleams in his eyes as he sits me on the desk again. He starts to tuck himself back into his pants and I stop him.

Hopping down off the desk, I lower myself.

My mouth is level with his dick that is still hard. Running my tongue along the length of his shaft, I caress each barbell piercing along the way. I swirl my tongue around the head of his cock before placing a kiss on the tip. Hermes hisses and rubs my hair as I return the care he just showed me.

Standing with a satisfied smirk, I fix his pants at his waist.

The hunger in Hermes eyes turns gentle. He takes my face in each of his hands and kisses me as I zip his pants.

"It's the beginning." He whispers against me.

Wrapping my arms around him, we encase each other in our hold and the world falls away from us. My irritation at his stubbornness, the hunter that stalks my lives and the turmoil of the mortals drops away into the night. All that exists is Hermes and me, surrounded in our love and the connection of our souls.

Warmth fills me and my cheeks flush with satisfaction as I smile against his mouth. "...of the end."

The words pull us into another kiss, as the moon shines its approval at the star-crossed lovers, who have finally found each other once more.

Not just in locating each other in this life, but in finding a common understanding, and aligned to walk the same path together. But a lingering sense of unease clutches my core; a disquiet that that I can't quite name.

As I reclaim the vast reservoirs of my power and lavish in the rush of reuniting with my mate, there remains a hollow ache within me that refuses to be filled.

Wrapped in Hermes' embrace with my head resting against his chest, his presence is a beacon of strength. He is my single solace in the tumultuous sea of my emotions. And yet, even in his hold, I feel the echoes of that emptiness ringing within me. A silent cry for something I can't articulate.

Perhaps there are limits to the number of times a soul can be torn apart. And the trials of my past have left me permanently fragmented. Or is it a memory, lost in the midst of time and waiting to be unearthed, just like my powers?

Whatever it is eludes my grasp, slipping through my fingers like grains of sand, leaving me clutching at shadows. Even if I am incomplete, living with a void inside me, I refuse to let it define me.

Somewhere in the chaos of my existence, the answers I seek lie in wait. Biding their time in the darkness until I confront them. Until then, I'll keep searching to restore myself. To repair the fated connection that forever locks me to Hermes. And to end the cursed hunter that plagues my life.

Maybe then, and only then, I'll fill this missing piece of myself.

Flint 12

Standing at the entrance to the Cave of Chainospilios, the essence of the great Labyrinth within stretches toward me like an ancient and vicious beast. The throbbing heart of the monster that resides beneath the island of Crete pounds against my chest as I steel myself to descend the walkway leading to the immortal prison of Gaea.

Shoving the portal wand into my pocket, I twist my head to the side and stretch my shoulders, trying to alleviate the weight pressing down on me. The large book tucked under my arm suddenly feels heavier, and I adjust my grip on it, feeling the strain in my muscles.

The worn leather binding of the book is a patchwork of ancient hide sewn together with thick black twine. Running my finger along a seam, I can feel the coarse stitches, sending a shiver down my spine and causing my palms to grow sweaty with nervous anticipation.

I can do this.

With the entrance of the cave at my back, I take a deep breath and step forward, descending into darkness. As I cross through the wards that conceal the immortal prison, the realm around me flips on itself.

The transition from the surface to the true underworld is always disorienting. Moving from the upside of the world to walking beneath its surface makes me feel as though my body is falling faster than my stomach can keep up. It's a sensation that never quite fades, no matter how many times I experience it.

But after several more steps forward, the feeling begins to ebb away, leaving me grounded once more in this strange underbelly.

Shadowed beings from the realm of Darkness slip through the thin veil that separates all realms, drawn by the ancient power that funnels darkness to the Labyrinth. I can't help but wonder about the being strong enough to create such a place.

Some say the Great Library of Alexandria was the first structure to ever exist on Gaea, but I believe it's this place. The inverted pyramid that resides beneath the island of Crete looms overhead, its peak obscured by a constant shroud of dark mist that reminds me of Rhea's power.

So many things make me think of her lately.

Large obsidian bricks, covered in thorny vines of shadow, persistently crawl of their own accord, creating an eerie spectacle. The timeworn structure hums with a constant billow of dark magic, a static buzzing in the atmosphere that never ceases, setting my nerves on edge and making the fine hairs at the base of my neck stand on end.

Of course, it figures that I would get stuck with this shitty job from my father. He won't let me do other missions, but the second I volunteer for this, he accepts. *Fucking asshole.*

A monster deep within the immortal prison bellows deeply, its powerful roar echoing through the cavernous depths. The vibrations emanating from the creature's throat jostles the dirt and roots of Gaea's underbelly, causing the surrounding rubble to cascade upward into the black sky above.

With each step I take, I draw closer to the two large doors that seal the Labyrinth, keeping its dark beings and immortal prisoners securely contained within. As I approach, the doors open and close behind me of their own accord, their heavy impact echoing throughout the twisting corridors of the dark and tormenting maze.

Entering the antechamber, I'm greeted by a vast expanse of emptiness. The only source of light daring to disturb the darkness emanates from the arrogant archangel seated upon an obsidian throne.

With his gold armor gleaming and wings spread wide, Michael exudes an air of authority as he lounges upon the dark chair, one leg casually draped over the armrest while the other remains spread wide.

He moans, the sound reverberating around the space much like the thump of the large doors closing behind me. My gaze is drawn to the dark creature positioned between his legs. It hardly resembles anything human anymore, though I suspect it once did.

Appearing as little more than bones wrapped in charcoal-colored leather, the creature is akin to a skeletal figure. Any remnants of hair it may have once possessed are now scarce, with only a few wiry strands remaining.

Not even enough hair for Michael to pull as he holds the things skull while it bobs up and down on his dick.

I can't help but wonder if this asshole intends to make me wait until he finishes down this ghoul's throat. *Un-fucking-believable.*

"I know you heard me come in." My voice rings out loudly

and echoes around the empty structure. A distant shriek emanates from the belly of the Labyrinth in response, letting me know that my presence has not gone unnoticed.

"Ugh!" Michael grunts, placing both hands on the head of the skeleton. "I-I'm almost done," he mutters, his eyes closed, and his head tilted toward the apex of the pyramid. With deep breaths and moans escaping his lips, he nears his orgasm. Michael is having to manually stimulate the face of the wretched being himself, as the skeleton's arms hang limp by its side, only occasionally lifting as if attempting to pull itself up.

Aside from Michael's sounds of enjoyment, the only other noise in the antechamber emanates from the Thaumium collar around the creature's neck, restricting whatever elemental power the entity once possessed. Beyond the antechamber, the raging monster that is the Labyrinth emits a constant cacophony of wails and pleas from the immortal souls imprisoned within its maze of shadows and despair.

I wonder how long an immortal has to be confined inside this prison to look like the disgusting thing being forced to suck the angel's cock. Starving but never dying, constantly withheld from their elemental power, and forever fleeing from the dark shadows, it's a terrible fate.

Before I can think on it too long, Michael grunts his release into the things throat.

Blowing out several steadying breaths, he looks down at the withered, near corpse of an immortal. "You always do such a good job." Then like he's tossing a crumpled napkin into a wastebasket; he throws the body down the tall stairs.

It tumbles down the two dozen steps of Michael's throne, rolling several times before coming to a stop at my feet. Naked and bearing flappy sacks on its chest that once resembled breasts, it's evident that this was once a woman. A long gash along its belly remains perpetually unhealed, thanks to the collar that binds it.

As its eye sockets appear hollow, I'm taken aback when two semi-translucent lids raise to reveal actual eyeballs within. They are nearly pure white, and I think the thing may be blind from eons within the darkness.

If the creature had eyebrows, they might have lifted in surprise upon seeing me. Probably wanting another cock to suck, the beast claws at me desperately.

Its teeth are gone, leaving its gaping mouth resembling more of a puckered asshole than lips.

I know my face is crumpled in disgust. Not only is it revolting to look at but it fucking stinks. Like musty pussy drown in stale cum, I have to cover my nose with my mending arm to keep from gagging. The stump where my hand used to be is still slightly sore as I grow accustomed to the loss of my extremity.

The beast slithers toward me, clawing at my pants and hugging my leg. Shaking it off like a bug stuck to my shoe, I fling it away. The ghoul rolls but keeps trying to get back to me.

"This is fucking gross." I take a few steps back, positioning the book under my arm with my remaining hand. "Even by my standards which are pretty fucking low, Mike." Glancing at the angel, he sits forward with his elbows on his knees, smirking at the spectacle this raisin of an immortal and me are making.

Looking at my shoe, a milky residue coats the tip of my boot.

Oh, there is no fucking way.

I take a closer look at the creature, seeing slits along its throat. The residue of Michael's ejaculation is seeping from the open wounds. "Your fucking cum is on my shoe, you asshole."

Michael leans back, clapping his hands with laughter and I want to fucking kill him.

"You did this on purpose, you cunt!"

Michael keeps laughing, wiping tears from his eyes as a shadow reaches from a corridor I never noticed and pulls the withered immortal back into the prison.

Michael fastens his pants as he walks down the steps. "Let's make this quick, Sparkplug. I've got shit to do."

"I don't like it when you call me that."

"Like it matters to anyone what you think. You're tolerated only because of your father and no other reason." Michael turns his head to the side and spits on the floor as he walks forward. The constant white light of his aura illuminates the space where we walk.

If it weren't so cold down here, I would conjure my flames and roast this asshole. He's always spoken down to me. Looked at me like I was nothing more than a pile of dog shit. And why? Because he used to be some chief asshole in Hel when his Titan was alive?

I heard he ran away when the Archangels battled the dragon of Light. They killed Theia for Chaos, hoping for his favor when he defeated all the Titans. In the end, they wound up here after Michael rounded them up.

Fucking pointless.

"Who was that, anyway?" I ask, stealing a glance back at the dark opening where the ghoulish immortal was drug away by shadows.

"My cum-bag?" Michael looks at me with a gleam in his grey eyes. "She used to be Hera. Ring a bell?"

I roll my eyes. Like I'm supposed to know every fucking immortal on this realm.

"She was a powerful Shifter; a poly-morph."

"What is she in here for?"

"Eh, the fuck if I know or care. Probably a lovers quarrel or some shit. Keep up or you'll get eaten."

From the corners of my vision, shadows move, and the occasional pair of glowing silver eyes watch us from the obscurity. Turning toward the movement, nothing is there but eternal darkness.

"My father would be quite upset if you let that happen." Even if Michael is a walking sack of cunts, I stay close to him. The beings of this prison can't harm him as he is the Labyrinths Warden.

Opening a door that seems made entirely of cold, dark stone, he walks in, continuing to berate me. "I'm pretty sure I could throw you to the Leshy Clerics for a snack and ole dad wouldn't even light a match over it."

My dad may not, but my mate sure would.

Three large, robed beasts dominate the cramped office space, their towering forms easily surpassing fifteen feet in height. Each possesses three long fingers adorned with razor-sharp talons, dripping constantly with red blood. Their arms resemble gnarled tree limbs, adorned with twigs and leaves poking out from beneath their dark robes, which are further covered in black and green moss.

Their heads resemble the white skulls of deer, crowned with long antlers protruding from the top. Devoid of eyes and mouths, these animated beings move about the office with purpose, diligently writing and filing papers into an endless wall of small drawers.

"What are they doing?" I inquire, observing the towering creatures as they diligently go about their work.

"Keeping the records. These are the Clerics," Michael explains casually, taking a seat at a desk crafted from black wood. Igniting a cigarette, he exhales a cloud of smoke before turning his gaze toward me. "So, your dad is releasing a dozen Lurkers."

As he opens a drawer to his left, he retrieves a black stone hanging from a leather strip and tosses it to me, fully aware of my recently severed hand. With the book held in my good hand, I instinctively raise the stump of my severed hand in an attempt to catch the necklace. In my haste to correct myself, I fumble both the book and the necklace, causing them to collide with the floor with resounding bangs and clinks.

One of the Clerics emits a piercing screech, leaning down just a foot away from me. I quickly cover one ear with my hand and raise my arm to shield the other from the deafening scream.

"I would chill the fuck out, Sparky. They don't like to be disturbed," Michael remarks with a smirk, taking another drag from his cigarette. "Put the fucking necklace on. It will keep the Lurkers from latching onto your pathetic life form."

With only one hand, tying the necklace proves to be a challenge. As I struggle with the leather tie, I can't help but look at the open page the book landed on when it fell. The intricate drawing on the old parchment resembles the tall Clerics in the office, albeit much smaller in scale.

While my eyes flick back and forth between the written notes and the task at hand, I manage to make out enough words in the ancient language to glean a few details about these beings' origins. They were once living creatures who resorted to cannibalism among their own kind. Now condemned to exist as tormented beings of Elysium, they endure perpetual starvation, their eternal hunger, unquenchable.

I stole this book from Eris' office when Gabriel moved into the Atlanta Commune, and I've been obsessed with its contents for days. Written in the margins of the book is a phrase penned in black ink. I can't look away from it. It pulsates at me with an attraction that makes my eyes lose focus as I stare at the page.

"By the ancient words of power, I command the shadows to heed my call, bending to my will, obeying my every command."

An arrow points to the original text. It's written in another language, so I don't know exactly what it says. I think the words in ancient script are an incantation giving the conjurer control over the shadows.

I wish I could command the shadows. I would love to see Michael run his mouth to me if I had a flock of Shadow Lurkers under my authority.

Glancing at the incantation on the page again, I bang my hand on the book as I drop the leather ties again. *Son of a bitch.*

"Hurry the fuck up, I don't have all day." Michael lifts his head, blowing smoke rings into the air as I keep fumbling with the necklace. "I don't know how Ares thinks you are strong enough to handle the Lurkers but that's not my fucking problem." Michael chuckles to himself. After a moment's hesitation, he laughs again, as if recalling something humorous.

This gods dammed necklace and the prick in front of me are driving me quickly to the end of my patience.

"I'm more powerful than you think."

"Sure, kid. He said you *offered* to come down here. Who the hell *wants* to come here? I don't even want to be here." Michael flicks the ash from his cigarette, and it floats gently to the black stone floor.

"Then why are you down here?" I'm not going to tell Michael my real reason for taking this task from my father. He's planning to use the Lurkers to find Rhea. Setting them lose on the mortals, he knows she'll come out of hiding to help their bleeding souls. She can't help herself. That's one of the things I admire about her.

But I'm not letting my father get close to her again; not now.

"All of us are prisoners here. I'm just one that gets to leave on occasion." He takes a long drag and blows the smoke up into the air. "It does come with a few perks though, don't you think?" He smiles, winking at me.

"I suppose you mean your little cum-sack?" I finally give up on the ties and wrap the necklace around my wrist. Using my teeth, I pull the knot tight and collect my book.

The gleam in Michael's eye is evil and full of too much enjoyment, like there is something I'm missing.

"You like my little nickname for her? She was someone else's cum-sack before me, but yeah." Flicking his cigarette to the ground, it sizzles out on the cold floor. "When your dad sucks the great goddess of the realms dry, Rhea will be here too, withering away for eternity."

I squeeze the book in my hand as hard as I can to keep from hurling it at the angel's face. *She'll never fucking come here if I can help it.*

Michael rounds his desk and sits. With his arms folded over

his chest and one ankle crossed over the other, he keeps the smug expression.

A freezing chill swells from the hallway behind me.

The presence of the Lurkers is chilling, their essence void of everything except darkness. No soul, no light, no life—just a profound emptiness shrouded in dark robes. I sense their approach long before they crowd the outside hall, their presence signaling the impending threat of their hunger.

"You sure you don't want me to get the *cum-sack* back in here for you? She's pretty good." He shrugs his shoulder but the smirk on his face makes me want to call these entities to peel his flesh away and fuck his skinless mouth.

"Piss off." I turn, facing the lurkers who look at me with voids for faces. I stumble only a step before I righten my shoulders approaching the door. They can't harm me with stone hanging around my wrist, so I square my shoulders and step into the hallway.

"I'm just kidding with you, Sparks." Michael grabs both my shoulders, squeezing them and giving me a pat as he walks alongside me. "Your dad told me you were coming so I thought a little *family reunion* was in order." He keeps laughing as he walks ahead, back to the steps leading up to his throne.

"What the fuck did you say?"

Pausing on the first step, he turns back, his face still alight being the only one who knows the punchline of some apparent joke. "You don't like it when I talk about your dad's fixation on the little goddess up top, do you?"

"What did you just say, a family reunion?" My temper heats as steam rises off my back despite the frigid temperatures. *I'm getting stronger already.*

"You know how easy it is to read an aura for a Light Bearer, don't you? It's like looking at the pages in your nerdy little book there." He walks up the steps to his throne. "You get all hot and bothered when I talk about her."

Michael sits down, throwing his leg casually over the arm of the chair. "Is it because he's so much older, going after that tight ass and perky tits?" Michael keeps taunting me, looking me in the eyes as the flames stir within my soul. "What do you think it's like to suck the powers from a being? Do you think your dad will cum when he does it?" He chuckles. "Gods, what if *she* cums while he's sucking her dry." Rolling his eyes back, Michael bites his lower lip and rubs his hand up and down his dick. "Fucking delicious. But anyhow, yeah, a family reunion."

Without thinking, I start reciting the words of the ancient text, anything to calm me so I can walk out of here with these Lurkers.

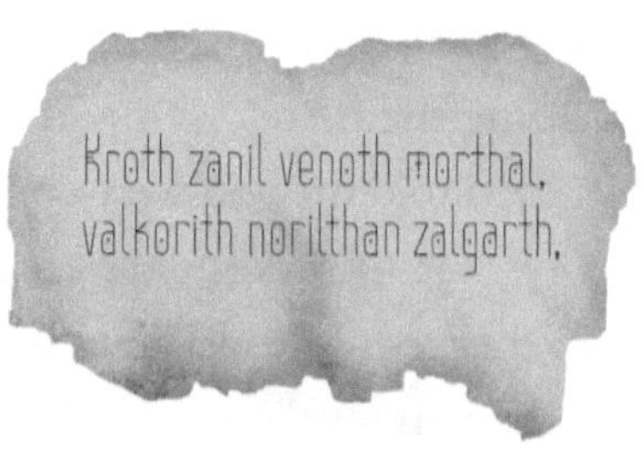

By the ancient words of power, I command the shadows to heed my call...

I'm not even sure how I remember them but as they flow through my thoughts, the shadows grow, and the Lurkers become uneasy.

"When Rhea joins my mass of prisoners..." Michael keeps

prodding me as I walk toward the large doors, the Lurkers following behind me.

...bending to my will...

"...I'm going have mommy-dearest show her how I like my cock sucked."

...obeying my command.

As I finish the incantation the Lurkers freeze. All of the Labyrinth goes silent, and darkness deepens around us. Michael doesn't realize the stillness. He's too focused, savoring the taste of his victory.

My heart hammers against my chest, threatening to explode out of me. It's pounding so ferociously, the sound beats against my ears.

"That was my mother?" I stare down the darkened corridor where the shadows drug the heap of bones held together with leathered skin. "Hera." I test her name on my lips to see what it feels like.

I never knew her name...

...so, it tastes like– nothing.

Archangel Michaels smile is wide as he sits on his obsidian throne. His wings spread out to their full span, gleaming like white billowing clouds reflecting the sunlight. "Thrown down here right after you were cut from her belly. Guess Ares was tired of her being his cum-sack."

I shift my gaze from the corridor to Michael, tilting my head.

"Or maybe he was pissed you ended up a Flame. He wanted a Shifter and thought she would produce a much more powerful child than you. Disappointing on both accounts, huh?"

My expression is as blank as my mind. I think the shadows of this place have wiped it clean for me so I can commend them. Or perhaps I just don't care about what he's saying.

I feel the obscurity wrapping themselves around me and the power is intoxicating. "Rhea won't be coming down here, because my father is not going to have the chance to consume her."

Michael openly laughs again at this, "And you think you can stop him? How in the twelve realms do you think you can amass a power close enough to defeat the God of War?"

I sense the cool shadows climbing up the back of the throne as if my very hands are the ones gripping the stone. Clawing their way up the smooth surface, Michael has no idea the Lurkers are coming for him.

"Because" I keep him distracted. "When Rhea recovered her power at the bottom of the ocean with that *imposter*, something happened. A force snapped to life within me, and I knew."

Still chuckling, Michael lights another cigarette. As he puts the match to his face, I use my power to increase the flame. It nearly burns the tip of his nose, and he pulls it away quickly, glaring at me. "Hermes *used* to be the mate of the goddess. But that was before; that was Nyx."

Michael listens intently now, the cigarette burning in his hand. "This is a new life and I'm Rhea's true mate now." The Lurkers have reached the top of the dais and the tendrils of their shadows hover just above Michael. "And I'll not let any harm come to her."

Kill him.

I turn, leaving the Labyrinth with The Book of the Dead tucked under my arm. Michaels screams join those deep within the Immortal prison, but they won't last long. The Lurkers tear his limbs apart and rip his wings from his body.

Walking out of the large doors, his howls grow as their gnashing teeth rip the flesh from his body and smack on his organs.

Taking my phone from my pocket, I shoot off a text message, surprised when it sends.

Rhea is my mate now. She is mine to love. Mine to protect. She is *mine*.

As Rhea and I stepped back into the library at Atlanta, the air was thick with tension, palpable even before we saw Hecate and Atlas locked in a heated argument over her dark portal consuming the books.

Atlas stood before a towering bookshelf; his arms outstretched as if attempting to shield the precious tomes from her obscurity. The atmosphere crackled with magic, the scent of ancient parchment mixing with the faint aroma of Hecate's dark powers.

Rhea threads her fingers through mine, her touch a comforting anchor amidst the discussion we just had. I press a tender kiss to the top of her head, a silent reassurance of our bond, even as Atlas's futile efforts draw a soft chuckle from my lips.

Shadows slink past Atlas like tentacles of an unseen beast of obscurity, wrapping around several books and retreating past him. Hecate's power is calm and persistent, a contrast to the goddess wielding them.

Her patience is gone as she yells back at Atlas. All care for being caught trespassing, gone in her irritation at my mentor.

Medusa, ever a solitary figure, leans against a bookshelf.

Her posture gives the appearance of a casual facade, but I know the stress and tension she is hiding. Not only because we have known each other so long but my ability gives me truth and aura perception.

Since the Dark Mage's assault on her commune, a shadow has fallen over her, casting her disposition into a perpetual gloom. She finds no solace in the unfolding drama between Atlas and Hecate, her gaze distant and filled with a sorrow that cuts to the core.

"So, is that all it takes?" Medusa's voice cuts through the tense atmosphere, her words sharp with bitterness as she observes mine and Rhea's interlocked hands. "A few kisses and you roll over to have your belly scratched?"

Rhea's confusion is evident, her brow furrowing in disbelief at Medusa's biting remark. Before tensions can escalate further, I step in, my voice low and firm with a warning for my friend.

"Deuce," My tone making it clear I will accept no further disrespect as I move to shield Rhea. I don't think Medusa would harm my mate, but instinct drives me to protect her.

Medusa is already turning away, her attention drawn by the chime of her phone. With a dismissive glance in our direction after checking a text message, she brushes past me. Her steps echo against the stone floor as she makes her exit.

"Got to go. Duty calls," she mutters. Her Earth ability opens a pathway through the Library's walls, leaving us staring at the void she leaves behind.

Rhea's offended glare meets mine, her hurt palpable as she processes Medusa's callous words. I reach out to reassure her, my voice soft as I speak to her mind, offering words of comfort and understanding. *I'll talk to her.*

Releasing a breath, Rhea's shoulders relax. The faint blush of our passion still evident on her cheeks as she turns her attention back to the library. Despite the tension lingering in the air, I look forward to the promise of home and more time with my mate to make that fading blush darken again.

Rhea's power eases out of her like a gentle breeze, enveloping the library in a shimmering aura of starlight. As she channels her abilities, the very fabric of the room seems to hum with her presence, as if the walls themselves are alive with the crackling energy of her immense power.

Sensing a shift in the atmosphere, Hecate stills, her swirling portal of Darkness freezing in place. Atlas watches Rhea with a mixture of awe and admiration, recognizing the magnitude of her power even amidst his mounting frustration with Hecate.

My mate moves with grace and purpose in a mesmerizing dance of Light and Dark. With a furrowed brow, I watch as she weaves her magic, her golden-brown hair catching the light as it dances around her like strands of spun gold.

Her powers surge forward, a cyclone of energy swirling around us as she harnesses the elements to her will. In a breathtaking display of mastery, she teleports the entire library to Delphi, her powers creating a perfect replica of our surroundings in an instant.

As the reverberations of her magic fade, Rhea stands before us, a triumphant smile playing at her lips. She is a vision of strength and beauty, her eyes alight with the thrill of her accomplishment.

It's not until Odysseus and Penelope enter the library, their faces a mask of confusion and awe, that the full extent of Rhea's actions become clear. Atlas's laughter fills the air, a booming sound that echoes off the stone walls as he claps his hands in approval.

Hecate surveys the space, her expression unreadable as she takes in the scene before her. "You moved the entire building and all. What about the library back in Atlanta?" she asks, her voice tinged with curiosity.

"I placed a Mirage there, and cleared all trace of our presence," Rhea replies, pride evident in her tone. "But it will dissolve in about two days. I wish I could see the look on Eris' face when she realizes her commune's library has been stolen right out from under her big nose."

Casting my powers across the realm, I watch as the moonlight reveals the truth of Rhea's illusion, the landscape of the Atlanta Commune transformed into a perfect replica of our new surroundings. It is a testament to her power, a feat even the strongest Light Bearers couldn't possibly replicate.

As the others set to work, searching through the texts for any mention of the Titans cannibal war, Rhea's mind is already racing ahead. Her powers flare to life once more, illuminating the pages between the books as she reads them all simultaneously.

Books and scrolls float around her, guided by her Wind as she sifts through the wealth of knowledge before her. Within minutes, she has amassed a collection of texts, each one a potential clue in our search for answers.

"I've found all mention of Alexandria, my relics, and the Titans in these books," Rhea announces, her voice ringing out with confidence as she gestures to the tables filled with ancient tomes and tablets.

Atlas stands in awe, his disbelief giving way to a sense of gratitude as he takes in the magnitude of Rhea's discovery.

Snapping out of his daze, he pushes his glasses up on his nose. "Let's get to work," he says as he claps me on the shoulder.

I nod in agreement with a wink at Rhea. She smiles and my heart swells with pride for my mate as I take a book from the nearest stack, eager to delve into the mysteries of her curse that lie within its pages.

14

Rhea

My neck is killing me, and my eyes are having a hard time focusing on the small words penned in ancient ink.** I can see the strokes of the old quill that made the marks but it's the residue of the aura within the words that keeps me engaged in the book.

I'm reading an account Daphne wrote of the Triple Moon Alignment from the dawn of the ages on this realm. As I break from my reading and look over my discarded pile of books, I realize they have all been written by her.

Studies and accounts from ages past, Hermes' mother was an amazing historian and author. Her eloquent words are only combated by her gentle handwriting as she carefully crafted the words on the pages.

I've unknowingly filtered out works by anyone else and have been researching solely her work. Perhaps she is one of the few allies without our circle of comrades that was trustworthy.

With a deep exhale, I return the open book to my table and sit up, stretching my back and cracking my neck to alleviate the stiffness.

Hermes' warm hands grip my neck firmly as he massages

me. Working out the knots in my shoulders, I close my eyes, enjoying the relief his touch brings.

"Find anything yet?" He asks in a low tone that reaches to my core.

"Mmmm," I begin to answer but I'm distracted when he kisses my neck. "The next alignment should be here soon. I think it's why I am sensing my powers more each day."

I tell Hermes what I found about the final placement of the triple moons. The alignment between Gaea and Avalon is the longest, lasting nearly a month. The three realms alignment is brief, lasting only as long as a solar eclipse that occurs between Gaea and Tartarus.

The moon will pass between Gaea and the sun, pausing only a moment to pay its respects for the bearers of sunlight before it continues its journey around the realm.

"As the eclipse begins its celestial play,
Sunlight's doorway leads her way."

Based on the poem of Hecate, I believe a portal will open, allowing passage to the realm of Sun and Earth.

"I found something interesting." Atlas joins us, setting down a book on top of my already open text. "The eclipse on the horizon is a rare event, occurring once every two thousand years and will last the longest of all the eclipses; seven and a half minutes."

I gaze across the library, my eyes unfocused as Hermes keeps up his work on my neck and shoulders. Placing a kiss at my temple, he speaks to me through our mind. *"What is worrying the goddess of the realms?"*

A soft smile tries to take over my frown and I place my

hand on top of his. Leaning my cheek against him, I sigh before I answer.

"Seven and a half minutes is not a long time. What if I can't get back before the alignment ends? Will I be stuck there?"

Hermes stops and pulls out the chair in front of me. Sitting down, he rests his elbows on his knees, leaning close to me.

"First, we're going together so what is this 'I' business?" He takes my hand and begins massaging it, rubbing my palm, and stretching my wrist. "And second, the passage of time on other realms is different. It's why I missed a few days when I first returned from Avalon. I didn't account for the shift when I teleported back."

"So, dinner on Avalon is two days here. But how long would seven and a half minutes here translate on Tartarus?" I ask, worry blooming heavier in my chest.

Hermes looks at the ceiling as if calculating in his mind. "About three days."

I nod my head, lost again as a dozen thoughts race through at once. *Seven minutes here, three days on Tartarus.*

"Hey, we'll come up with a plan together." Hermes leans forward and kisses me. "When is the eclipse?"

"In five days," I whisper.

My hands begin to tremble and Hermes' concerns over another death begin to seem very real. I didn't think we would have meager days to figure this out. Time seems to be my enemy, just like it was in Ares' room of torture.

As if mocking me, the second hand on a clock in the distance echoes across the vast library. I feel the familiar fingers of my panic, icy and unforgiving, as they work their way around my mind.

Static like snow forms on the edges of my vision and my fingers tingle in response.

Hermes warm light wraps around me and he pulls me from my chair into his lap. Rubbing my back and holding my hand, he whispers reassurances in my ear. Warming me with his body and encasing me in his power, he chases off the dread that wants to bury me.

With my face against his neck, I bask in his scent as I take deep breaths to relax my body. He sits with me in his lap until I sit up, finally deciding my panic won't wash over me and carry me away.

Hermes eyes dart between mine as if waiting to know that I'm okay. Wrapping my arms around his neck, I kiss him.

"Thank you."

"Oh, my little goddess." He sweeps my hair behind my ear before looking into my eyes again. "There is no need for thanks. Caring for you is my greatest privilege. I'll tend to your needs until my last breath. Your happiness is my only devotion."

He presses his lips against mine in a tender kiss. Within minutes, he leaves with Odysseus to fortify the wards around Delphi and Olympus. No one is taking any chances with Ares and his minions working the mortal leaders into a war.

Showcasing Hermes on the news as the destroyer of Venice, Ares is going to plot to turn himself into a savior for the mortals and us, their enemy.

Aryana is a threat and large one. If unleashed on mortals or lower Elementals, there will be nothing left of them for a pyre. She has proven to be an unstable pawn of Ares and Hermes is determined to root her out before she can attack us.

As soon as Odysseus left with Hermes, Penelope pulled

Atlas and Hecate into a quiet huddle. It seems Penelope asked for their help, and it was decided Hecate would remain here with me while Penelope and Atlas left.

The shadows lurking in the library's corners grow only a moment as Hecate returns. She takes a steadying breath, and they calm.

"Is there something going on?" I ask, certain if there was something, Hecate would likely not tell me.

"Penelope just needs help deciphering some ancient text. It's Dark in origin but Atlas is going to give it a shot first."

Returning to the books before me, I use my power to read a scroll from Hesperides, the realm of Wind. Thinking of Callie, I miss my friend. Calling upon a swell of Wind, I push it outward with a message, knowing it will traverse the realm and find her.

She and Achilles have been busy helping with recovery in New York.

I feel so selfish, hanging around a stolen library, reading for information about myself when so much is happening around the realm.

Each time Callie and I speak to each other on the breezes, I miss her more. She's keeping the details of the clean-up from me, and I hear how tired she is getting from her more recent responses.

"You're not selfish." She reprimands the self-deprecating apologies from my message in her response. *"Don't make me come up there and set you straight."* She teases me.

"Do it." I jest back which earns me a jab in the side by a puff of Wind.

Focusing again on the research in front of me, the power of my currents mingle with my aura to translate the interconnected strokes that knit together like tendrils of mist curling around a mountaintop.

The written language of Wind Sprites and Sirens dance upon the parchment like ethereal whispers captured in ink. Delicate and ever-changing, their script seems to sway with an unseen breeze, mimicking the fluidity of the Winds themselves.

Each character is a graceful curve or a whimsical spiral, resembling the playful patterns the Wind draws across a field of wildflowers. The ink itself shimmers with a subtle iridescence, as if capturing the essence of sunlight filtering through a gentle gust.

The tragic account recorded in the graceful strokes is a sharp and cutting contrast to the intricate dance frozen in ink.

It records the decimation of the realm of Wind, when Chaos arrived to consume the twin Titans, Aellai & Thuellai. One twin, a gentle spring breeze that carries in the delicate seeds of life, the other, a hard winter gale that staves off disease.

The sisters fell together. The essence of their shared power consumed by the greedy Titan of Death.

"Greedy little goddess."

Hermes affectionate words stir a worry as I compare the two thoughts. Something within me simmers, a twinge of curiosity, and I expel my silver power along the stacks of books.

Hecate stops reading to watch as my power rushes the pages and scrolls. "What is it?" I ignore her question and surge across the ancient ink, long preserved on the old paper.

Avalon was first. Artemis, the Titan goddess of the hunt, fell to Chaos. The power of Sensory was consumed and the god of Death became the most power being to exist.

Looking at Hecate, I feel the power of the slain Titan roil within me. Waves of concern flow off of Hecate, escaping from her obsidian aura like fog rolling across a dark lake. But it's the faint yellow shimmer encasing her that I focus on. *The color of untruth.*

She's a liar.

My heart beats so hard, I fear the entire realm will hear it.

"What are you keeping from me?" I ask, heat gathering in my cheeks as the ribbons of my dread surface again.

"Rhea,"

My powers continue to surge across the library, and I find the next victim of Chaos.

It was Fenrir and the power of Shifting was stolen along with the giant wolfs life. I search within me and feel it. The essence of a great beast claws at my back as if wanting to be released. But I gave the power away and gifted it to Lucas.

Still, the shadows of phoenix wings lay in wait like an echo on my back.

Tears well in my eyes as I look with horror at Hecate. The yellow glow around her black aura strengthening.

"You're keeping secrets, Mage." My voice cracks as heavy tears drop from my eyes.

Hecate holds her dark eyes on me, standing, she keeps both hands flat on the table in front of her as my powers begin to shake the walls of the library.

My essence swirling around the tomes delivers Chaos's third victim, from the realm of Zoion, the Titan of Life was hunted, and Cronus died.

I don't need to test this power, knowing it's there. I used it to restore vitality back to Flora, and I used it to syphon the life from Moros and give Life back to Atlas.

Collapsing on the floor, my legs can no longer hold me up.

Wind, Water, Light and Dark– they are all here.

The night hangs heavy with an ominous air as I uncover the dreadful truth that lurks within the depths of my being. A gnawing realization creeps into my consciousness like a shadow, as I connected the various writings from across the realms.

I gaze upon my trembling hands with frightening realization. The stolen essence of the Titans who faced a remorseless god of Death, all live with me.

In the dim glow of the library's light, I'm confronted with the stolen powers that course through my veins. They whisper ancient secrets and carry the weight of the shattered Titans, their essence entwined with my very existence.

The echoes of their demise resonate within me, and the realization strikes like a thunderclap—I see their blood on my hands, stained with the residue of those who faced the god's merciless greed.

Hecate rushes to my side, kneeling with her hands hovering just above me. She is careful not to touch me, as if unsure I want her help.

My Winds swarm around me as my breath gets stuck in my closing throat. The pages of the books flip erratically as my powers flock to me.

"Rhea, I'm so sorry."

I can barely hear Hecate's voice over the surge of my elements colliding around me.

I sought solace in the mentorship of Hecate, the one who guided me through the labyrinth of my past lives. Yet, I feel the weight of her betrayal descend upon my heart, the truths she knew and hid from me.

She allowed me to unknowingly wield the stolen power that had once wreaked havoc upon the Titans.

I cast my eyes to her, swollen from the tears that fall in an endless parade down my face. I can't speak as the torment racing through my mind is gripped in a vice by my panic.

The flickering oil lamps on the library tables cast dancing shadows upon her face, revealing the stoic mask that confirms the secrets she harbored.

"Why?" The word escaped my lips, a whisper weighted with accusation and hurt.

Hecate, her gaze unwavering, meet my eyes with a mixture of regret and determination.

"We only just realized the truth and wanted to protect you from the burden that accompanies the knowledge."

"We?" Anguish swells within me, a tempest of emotions that mirror the turbulent powers I now possess. "Who else knows?" My chest heaves as I brace my hands on the marble floor of the library. "Does Hermes know?"

The answer hanging in the air nearly breaks me into pieces.

"No, only Atlas and I know. We realized it when you restored his life. Rhea, you restored his soul, you saved him." Her voice is a plea as she tries to explain.

"The stolen essence of the murdered Titans courses through me, and you kept it hidden. Tell me why?"

Hecate's response carries the echoes of regret. "I feared the weight of this truth would shatter you, and I hoped to guide you towards a path of knowing. I should have known you were destined to discover it on your own."

The revelation is heavy. A silent acknowledgment of the tangled web of destiny and deception. We sit, locked in a silent standoff. The mentor and the betrayed, both of us facing the consequences of stolen power, and the uncertainty that lays ahead of me.

My glazed eyes scour the books of the library. I see the few Elementals that have paused their reading to watch me. They look away quickly, but the residue of their judgement lingers on me as the fact I perhaps always knew, rings like a cruel truth in my mind.

"I am Death."

"**R**hea, what is it?**"** Hermes pained voice bounces in my mind, and I feel him surging toward me.

"It's fine," I reply, working and failing to calm my voice coated with sorrow. "I just read something that upset me. We can talk about it later."

I sense him slow the swell of his aura as his power dies down. He was preparing to teleport to me, sensing the shift in my emotions. I hiccup as my sobs slow, thinking of how he will look at me once he knows what I am; what I carry inside me.

"How did this happen? Am I a child of Chaos?"

Hecate drops to a knee and holds her hand out to me. The yellow tinge of deceit no longer covers her as her lie has been revealed. Hesitating before I accept her offer, she helps me rise and guides me back to a seat.

Her shadows reach beyond the doors of the library, and I sense them. The power of Darkness calling to me and I track the movement of her power with mine. She beacons someone from the kitchens to bring a pitcher of water and two glasses.

Scared of her shadows, they hurry and bring the water with shaking hands.

Pouring me a glass, I take it with trembling hands of my

own. Drinking the cold beverage, it reaches my belly and cools the swell of my emotions.

"No, you are not a child of Chaos. The Titans were the purest essence of elemental power, created by their realms. They could not reproduce. We never knew a Titan could fall until Artemis was slain."

"Then how did I come to be? Who am I to hold the power of twelve Titans?"

"Our savior." The conviction in Hecate's eyes tells me she believes those words with every ounce of power contained in her immortal aura.

"But I don't want to be." I cover my face with my hands. The memories of death by my hands flood my mind, just as I flooded this realm long ago. "I'm scared."

Through the eons, torrents of water, volcanos and quakes that ripped the ground open. All of these events were caused by my power and cost the lives of millions of souls.

My sobs bounce around the marbled walls of the old library as I cry.

Hecate comes to me, putting her arm around my shoulder, holding me as I release my sorrows. "I don't believe you are an instrument of death, Rhea."

"How can you say that? I *am* Death."

"Like Darkness, Death is a misunderstood element of the cycle of life." She pulls my hands down, making me reveal my face, streaked with tears. "People are often scared of the creatures that can lurk within dark corners, but the cover of night is often the sanctuary of the refugee that uses it to flee to safety."

Hecate's eyes soften, and her voice tries to be a soothing melody amid the storm of emotions that grip me. She tilts her head, the ashen hair that frames her face shifts with her movement.

"I think Death is also misunderstood, and fear is a natural response. The power you wield has the potential for great devastation, but it is equally capable of profound creation. It is a force that demands respect, and your journey lies in finding that delicate balance within yourself."

My thoughts hang on her words but all I can hear are the screams and cries of those whose lives have been ended by my power. Triggered to be a weapon of Ares, I realize now, he was testing me. Priming me to call upon the destruction of Chaos, calling out the power of Death so he could steal it from me.

Maybe this is why Death came for me a thousand times before.

Perhaps I resigned to the great power of the twelve Titans that live within me, securing myself away so I'm no longer a danger to the innocent lives I take.

"You hold the essence of the Titans who fell, yes. But their power need not be tainted by the darkness of its origins. It can be a force for renewal, for ushering in new beginnings. It is the cycle of life and death, a dance that transcends mortal understanding."

I struggle to absorb her words, the weight of the revelation still pressing down on me, confusion creating a cloud of obscurity around me.

"But why keep it hidden? Why not trust me with the truth from the beginning?" I question, my voice edged with frustration.

Hecate sighs, acknowledging the pain that washes off of me because of her lie.

"I wanted you to discover the truth on your own terms, to

forge a connection with this power without the burden of preconceived notions. It was not an act of deception, but an attempt to guide you toward a path of goodness. The shadows of the past do not define your destiny."

She sits in a chair next to me, extending a hand of reassurance to my knee.

"Rhea, the power you possess is a reflection of your inner strength. Embrace the fear, but let it guide you towards understanding. Trust in yourself, for within you lies the capacity to wield this force with goodness and purpose."

As Hecate's words hang in the air, a delicate understanding begins to unfold—a realization that the power of Death, though feared, could be harnessed for a greater purpose. The journey ahead remains uncertain, but with Hecate's guidance, I sense a glimmer of hope amidst the shadows of my newfound abilities.

Maybe I don't have to die again. If I am Death, I hold the power of my life in my hands, and this time, I could defeat my hunter and restore myself.

"You can kill me, but you are not ready yet." Tritons whispered message, dark and foreboding as he lay a crumpled mass in the depths of the Underworld, spring to the front of my mind. *"All of their might combined could never amount to the greatness within you."*

Triton knew the power inside me. Atlas and Hecate figured it out. Ares has hunted me across the eons. Who else knows, and who else hungers to consume what hides within me?

Ice surges up my spine as my anxiety becomes a flood, washing over my every thought. Death is a power given to only one being.

In all these texts and accounts, there is only one who ever

held the power, Chaos. While many hold the power of fire and earth, wind, and water; only one is the harbinger of death.

And now, that power resides in me.

If the immortals of the realm knew– I can't even finish the thought.

"I have to get out of here." I stand, pulling at the collar of my shirt as it becomes a constrictor around my throat. Hecate's eyes widen as black mist careens out of me.

"Hermes." I choke out my mate's name and my plea surges through the realm.

My dark portal opens up at my feet and I drop into oblivion. Momentarily, the realm slips away from me, and I crash hard on the cool tile floor of our bathroom on Mount Olympus. My flailing arms hit the knob of the shower and a cold stream of water washes over me.

Hermes Light flares around me. I briefly glimpse the remnants of a sword of light, dimming away into nothing. He's by my side in half a heartbeat and my cramped hands claw at his shirt.

With a closed throat, I try to take in a breath and confess but it comes out a gargled strain before I choke on pain.

"Baby, what happened?"

I open and close my mouth, unable to speak with the panic attack consuming me.

Sitting me in his lap, he holds my face between his hands, forcing me to look into his eyes. His Light flares and compresses me gently. The pressure of his power around me allows me to ease the building tension.

What will happen when I confess what I am to Hermes? This power stole his parents, and one of his best friends. He's going to hate me. Hermes is going to leave me once I tell him.

My fear rushes out of me.

The mountain shakes and the shower's glass doors tremble. Black mist fills the room and in the distance, a squall nears on the horizon. My powers calling a hailstorm of elements that I can't control. Wind and Earth, Darkness and Light collide around us.

"Stay with me." Hermes voice is firm and determined to hold me in place. A rush of starlight shoots into me from his aura and wraps around the silver shine of my aura. Our powers pulse together, and my breath returns to me with each beat.

In an instant, my throat opens, and fresh air enters my body. Pulling the cool winds of the realm to me, I swirl them around us, clearing the black mist and cooling my sweating body.

"How did you do that?" I ask breathlessly.

It was like he reached within me and stroked my soul, soothing me from the very essence of my being.

"We're destined mates. Fated together by something that runs much deeper than love. We used to be tethered by our souls." He strokes my face, my eyes, burning from crying, flood with fresh tears again. "It's still in there."

Hermes places his hand on my chest, covering the charm of my necklace. I feel his heartbeat through the connection and while mine is raging twice as fast, I work to steady the pace of my breath and calm myself to match his rhythm.

After a moment, our hearts beat in time with each other and I realize, this is the missing piece I've been searching for as we connect deeper. Making love and spending time with each other, my soul is calling to his, needing the connection our fated bond gives us.

But if we could fix our bond somehow, our power would

strengthen. Hermes would welcome more power and I know he would use it to keep me safe.

But I can't imagine increasing the power of twelve Titans to anything greater. Certain destruction of all the realms would be emanate, and I would be crushed from the guilt of it.

But once Hermes knows he is fated to the god of Death, he won't want me anyhow. Perhaps he already rejected me before and destroyed our bond. Maybe Ares had nothing to do with its ruin.

The thought is too much to bear, and I crumble away from him, pushing myself into the corner of the shower and hiding my face away. Sobs wrack my shoulders, but Hermes doesn't accept my retreat.

Pulling me back to him, he crushes me against his chest.

"I don't care what happened, just tell me, baby." Pain covers his voice and breaks my heart more. "Gods, you're killing me. Just tell me and we can fix it. We can do anything as long as we are together."

Stroking my hair, he holds me, refusing to let me back away. I shiver against the cold rush of water and Hermes turns the shower off.

With his aura, he turns the knobs of the bath and a rush of water billows from the nearby faucet. Removing our clothes, he teleports us the few feet to the tub and hot water instantly warms me.

Hermes rests against the tub and lays me on his firm chest.

He's patient while I cry until my tears slow. But now I'm unsure how to tell him.

Words escape me as confusion clouds my mind and the residue of my panic still coats me.

"Show me." He whispers, placing a kiss on my head.

I close my eyes, refusing to watch him drift away from me once he realizes the monster that hides inside his mate.

Using a Mirage, I show him the events that unfolded in the library with Hecate. He keeps his hold on me through it. He makes a cup with his hand, pouring warm water on me before he strokes my arm.

"Oh, Rhea." Hermes sits up, pulling me into his lap and wrapping me with both arms. "You honestly think the power of Death could scare me away? I told you before, death is not strong enough to keep us apart. I meant every word. Then, now, and forever."

I can't take it. A river of tears pours out of me again.

I don't deserve him.

The stolen power of dead gods live within me, taken by the ruthless power of Death and still, he loves me. With my hands, I've flooded this realm and stood by as millions drown on my power and still, he loves me. I triggered a volcano, burying thousands in my might as the heat of my elemental power exploded their skulls and still, he loves me.

"Why?" I choke out between sobs.

"Why, what baby?" Hermes patient voice bellows against me as I rest upon his chest.

"Why do I get to have you?" I hiccup and feel him smile sadly as he rests his cheek against me.

"I already told you, you're mine." Hermes tips my chin up with his thumb and forefinger. Keeping my eyes closed, I refuse to look at him, scared of what truths I'll see when I do.

Will I see the yellow stain of deceit shrouding him like I did Hecate? Or something else even worse, rejection, or bitterness? "Please let me look at you. You're breaking my heart. Let me look into your eyes."

Tears roll from the corners of my eyes, and he kisses each one.

"Please baby, look at me."

I open my eyes and peer into the deep blue oceans that live in Hermes eyes. Sorrow and relief flood him, and I want to hide myself away from his gaze. I don't want him to see my cry and wish I were stronger in this moment but feel like such a coward.

"No, stay with me, goddess." He keeps me locked on him and taking each of my arms, he wraps them one at a time around his neck. "Hold on to me." He commands me and I do.

I hold onto him with everything I am. Taking a ragged breath, I try to push back the tears that keep streaking down my face, but I can't.

"We were molded from the stars and made for each other. You for me and me for you." He answers my earlier question. "The Fates knew what you were, and my soul was pulled from the cosmos for you. Just as you were for me. We belong to each other and no force, not Ares, or Death or any power can take us from each other."

He takes a warm rag and wipes my face, clearing me of my tears and wiping my nose.

"You are stronger than Death. You hold the Sensory power of my mother and her kind heart. You have the Light power of my father and his determination. You have the stubborn Winds of my sister and the steadfast Flames of my best friends." Hermes pushes my hair out of my face and holds me with both hands. "You are life and light and hope and love."

I choke out another sob and a smile breaks free briefly before my shame pushes it away.

"You are the essence of everything that is good and just.

You didn't steal this power like Chaos did, but you hold it within you. Something this great and destructive needs a protector. And who could serve as a better guardian of such strength than you?"

"Hermes." I don't know what else I can say but his name. The name that fills my heart with love and joy. The name that completes the very essence of my spirit.

He crashes into me. His lips are harsh against mine as he claims me with his kiss. "My love for you will burn in an unwavering beacon until the very end of time itself." Pulling me back to him, he holds me, rooting the truth of his promise into his embrace. "Nothing will change that, ever."

We sit in the bath and our auras mingle within the warm water. Slowly, I come back to myself, wrapped in Hermes embrace. An itch grows in the back of my mind as I lay in his arms.

Triton.

The suffering mass of a former god is a haunting thought that can't leave.

I know what he meant when he said I could kill him, but I was not ready yet. He knew I needed to realize the truth of the power inside me. The truth of Death that lives within my aura.

"There is something I need to do." My cracked voice sounds odd within the bathroom as my panic washes away in the bath.

"We'll do it together; anything," Hermes says with surety.

"I need to destroy the Underworld."

I admit, I should have read more into **The Book of the Dead** before I tried to control the Shadow Lurkers. But all is not lost on my father's mission. He was going to release them upon the realm regardless, which has been done. I only wish I knew the incantation only controlled them for one thought.

I had hoped they would stay with me longer.

As soon as they consumed Archangel Michael, they scattered. Outside of the Labyrinth, they are free to roam Gaea for the first time in gods knows how many ages.

They are going to be ravenous and cause quite the havoc.

Pity. Rhea's dark powers would have enjoyed them, and I know they would have helped give some separation between Rhea and Hermes. I need to get her away from him so he can stop poisoning her mind against her true bond.

Hermes may have been her soul's connection in a previous life, but not this one. I'm confident she only needs to see me again and she'll know. Rhea will feel that empty space inside her reach out for me and finally recognize me as her mate.

I've been thinking of other plans all day to get her away

from her false-mate and my stomach nearly flips thinking about surprising her.

Gods, I have so many regrets. I wish I knew of my fated bond with Rhea when she was in the Underworld. I would have done things so differently.

Releasing a deep exhale, I look at the curtain of silky dark hair that covers my lap. Lexi really does give a fantastic blowjob.

Her red lipstick streaks along my cock looking like blood and the sight of it always makes me cum in a moment or two. I struggle to keep my load from exploding too fast because she really is working hard to make me feel good today.

She even complimented my outfit. I let the false affections warm me, even though I overheard her talking to a Shifter-friend that I dress like a bum. I really have been trying to look the part of Ares' son but I'm sure Rhea will help me pick out a new wardrobe.

Her beautiful auburn hair will look so great with my red hair. I smile thinking about dressing in matching outfits to complement each other as we take over my father's empire of Shifters.

Fantasizing about my unbonded mate is bringing my climax quickly to the surface so without warning, I thrust up, pushing my dick further into Lexi's throat. She can take me all the way without gagging but I love the thrill of her shock when I do it.

She never expects it, and the small moment of her panic makes her throat squeeze me. It adds an extra edge to my climaxes.

Holding her head so she can't pull me out of her, I pound into her mouth, releasing my cum and watching her throat move to swallow my juices. I release her, my dick already softening after such a good blow. Lexi looks at me with watery eyes that she makes look overly large and round.

"Goddess knows," I stroke my finger into her mouth and then down her lips, smearing some remaining lipstick onto her face, "you have one hell of a mouth, baby." I grab her throat, wiping the spit from my fingers onto her skin.

Adjusting my hips, I flick my eyes to my crotch. Lexi knows what I want so she bends down, licking me clean before tucking me back into my pants.

She is hoping I'll help save her from the auctions. Shifters need pups and sluts like Lex sell for top dollar. She bet too hard on Gabriel's attention. Sure, the new Alpha wanted a good fuck and Lexi is grade-A ass. But she's not Luna material.

Even if Lexi was sophisticated enough to play Luna of the packs, Gabriel found his fated mate. A she-wolf, loyal to Lucas that was captured as part of a larger group. Pity he has to keep her confined and drugged to prevent her from rejecting the bond.

She should count herself lucky. She's going to be saved from the fate of the other twenty-four women who are being rounded up. Once she sees what her options are, she'll agree to bond with Gabriel, and he can work on extending his line of offspring.

For now, Lexi zips my pants for me and fetches a beer. Pushing out her tits and arching her back, she's really working overtime to get me to pull her off the auction in a few hours.

As I take the amber bottle of carbonated hops from her, I watch her closely as I break that little ray of hope.

"So, what are you going to wear to the auctions tonight?" I hold back my smile when her step falters and her fake smile twitches a little. Some of the light leaves her eyes but she recovers quickly and a swell of power rushes through me at the impact my words can have on her.

Climbing on my lap, she works one of the thin straps o her tank top down, exposing her breast.

"Are you ready to let these get sold to the highest bidder, handsome?" Lexi removes the other strap and frees both tits. They are fucking beautiful, but how many sets of boobs are bouncing around the pack houses, begging to get sucked on?

Too fucking many.

She runs her hands delicately up her nipples, trying to make them perk up for me.

I take one between my fingers, twisting it and watching the pain make the corners of her eyes crinkle. To her credit, Lexi keeps that smeared crimson smile painted onto her face.

I wrap my good arm around her, holding the belt loops of her pants so she can't get away. Licking the roused nipple, I take it in my mouth.

She pretends to like it, running her fingers through my hair and my dick tries to come to life again. It's too soon after coming for me to get hard though. One last fuck would be nice.

Lexi moans and throws her head back, ever the actress.

I tighten my hold on her, forcing her into an exaggerated arch. Then I mark her.

I bite down around her breast so hard, I feel the skin break and taste the copper of her blood. She screams and tries to pull away, while also scared as my teeth are still sunk into her. She digs her nails into the side of my neck, and I bite harder.

My spit and her blood run down my chin until she gets the point that I'm not letting up. With deep ragged breaths, she removes her spiked nails from me.

Using my elemental power of Fire, I heat up my bite until it's a burning ember, branding the seal of my claim onto her immortal body forever.

Her flesh sizzles and she thrashes about, trying to get out of my hold. The smell of burned hide is an acquired appreciation, but one I savor.

I squeeze her tighter, biting harder. My teeth are molten embers that cauterizes my mark. Releasing her abruptly, I push her to the floor with her shirt in my grip. It rips in two with the force, leaving her bare from the waist, up.

Tears make her mascara streak down her face, and she holds her breast with one hand, while propping herself up with the other. Blood streaks down her breast.

I like the way it runs down the roundness of her womanly chest and I wonder if Rhea would be open to experimenting with some new sexual adventures with me.

I'd like to see my mark on her. A mated claim that would tell the world, would tell Hermes, that she belongs to only me.

"Why would you do that?" Lexi sobs and she looks fucking pathetic.

"You've fucked as many pack members and elementals as you can and now they'll all know how marked you really are." I stand up, taking a long swig from my beer before I throw the bottle next to her.

The glass shatters and she flinches, scooting away from the amber liquid as it oozes around her. "The Shifters will smell that mark on you a mile away and if anyone buys you, it will be for the pennies you are worth. Good luck today, sweetheart. I hope for your sake someone purchases you. I hear the breeding chambers are hell."

The smell of my bite, the scent of her spit tinged with my

cum, are going to render her valueless, even with that pretty face and plump ass. The breeding chambers are not going to be kind to her.

She'll be drugged with fertility treatments and chained to tables while Shifter's form lines to fuck her. They'll keep her belly so full of pups until they rupture out of her and then her carcass will be burned. The ashes of her immortal corpse will feed the crops where Life elementals grow the fertility herbs. The cycle will keep going with the next bitch.

I leave the door open as I walk away. Timing my exit perfectly, the auctioneers are gathering she-Shifters for tonight's auction.

"One is in here." Sticking my good arm in my pants pocket, I whistle an upbeat tune as I think of my mate. Lexi screams when the auctioneers pull her from the house by her hair and her tits bounce with her thrashing.

I would never let something like this happen to Rhea.

This is why I need to increase my powers. I need to be able to protect her from vermin like Hermes who would try to take her from me. I know he'll never respect her decision to be with me, over him. His cocky ego would never allow it.

And she needs to help me defeat my father.

He'll be easier to kill than he thinks. I have some of the same concoctions used to poison Apollo. I found it snooping around Demeter's greenhouse ages ago and have been saving it all this time. It's the very tonic Demeter fed to Juliet, killing her before she could restore her immortality.

I'm curious to know which lifetime she became my mate.

Juliet had only just met Hermes, but her mind had already been tainted by his mother long before that. Demeter knew there was no salvaging her and ended that life quickly. The sooner she is killed, the sooner she reincarnates.

None of us thought it would take four centuries though and I admit, my father was a pain in the ass as the time of her reincarnation grew closer.

The nature of the spell makes us all forget. But there are a few, like Demeter and Hecate, tied to the spell.

As the goddess prepares for another life, the signs begin to show, and the realm prepares for her arrival. My father, also tied to the spell and he begins to realize her resurgence, and the hunt for the forgotten goddess resumes.

But I'm going to help her end this. Mating with Rhea and helping her find her lost powers, will break the curse. Poisoning my father, he'll meet the same poetic end that his former mate did. And I'll finally know what Rhea's tight pussy feels like with my dick inside her.

Even though I just came down Lexi's throat, my cock stirs, thinking of Rhea.

Looking at my watch, I know I have time to go to my room and cum as I think of her. I still have one of her shirts that I nut inside. It still smells like her and makes me feel like she's right here when I sniff it, stroking myself to the thought of her.

I have to get The Book of the Dead anyhow, so with a growing boner and excitement pooling in my stomach, I click the portal wand, delivering me to my room.

Gods, Rhea, I can't wait to show you what I have planned for us. You're going to love this so much.

Hermes

Rhea rests in my arms. Her gentle breathing comforts me as I watch her sleep. After breaking down so desperately once she realized Death's power inside her, she could barely keep her eyes open. She told me about Triton and a shiver rippled through me when she said his name.

Memories of Callie, Pat, and Achilles' harrowing encounter with him in the treacherous Bay of Malice flood my mind, each moment etched with the raw intensity of their struggle against his overwhelming power.

Triton emerged again at the Battle of Troy. His Scylla was locked in a fierce battle against Athena's Kraken. As the stronghold around the city of Troy crumbled, Triton and his fleet retreated beneath the waves and were never seen again.

Athena, with all her wisdom and power, searched for her cousin within the currents of Gaea's waters. But when the seven seas returned no trace of him, even she conceded he was lost to the water's tides and perished.

Learning that he was cast aside, left to decay in the depths of the Underworld, is a gut-wrenching revelation. Triton was a formidable ally and mate to Callie's half-sister Aphrodite. Their combined fleets and powers over the Water and Wind made them invaluable. We were all shocked by Triton's allegiance to Ares and it tore the mates apart, leaving a trail of heartbreak and strife on the open oceans.

While none of us knew what happened between them, we knew the goddess of love's heart turned to stone after Triton.

In the end, Triton tried to do the right thing and fight his way out of the Underworld. I can't help but wonder how different things could be now, if only we knew of his captivity.

As the sun begins its gentle ascent over the horizon, I draw back the curtains of our room, letting dawn gently summon my mate from her slumber. Rhea stirs, nestling closer into me and draping her leg over my hip. Her honey hair is splayed across the bed like a burst of sunlight, and I can't help but run my fingers through the silky tendrils.

The warmth of her body next to mine fills me with contentment and despite the next errand we must face together, I want her to wake with a glimmer of that same contentment. I kiss her forehead and then her cheek, aiding the sunlight in waking her.

Last night when I arrived on the wave of her panic attack, my heart nearly cracked into pieces when she confessed to holding the power of Death and expected me to abandon her.

The memory of her fleeting doubt, the fear that I might leave her side, still lingers in my mind, reminding me how deep and painful the scars of her trauma run. My heart aches at the mere thought of ever being parted from her, and no force in this world, or any other, could ever tear me away from her side.

Finally, I see the golden hue of her beautiful eyes as she slowly wakes. The aftermath of her panic and tears is evident in the dark rings beneath her swollen eyes.

She runs her hand up my chest, and I cover it with my own,

gently pressing a kiss to her palm before returning it to rest against my chest. As I kiss the top of her head and rub her back, I offer words of comfort, hoping to ease her burden with reminders of my unwavering love.

"Are you sure you want to do this today?" I ask, my concern evident in my voice.

She responds with a bitter laugh. "Is there ever a good day to decide to take a man's life?"

Rhea pushes herself into a sitting position, holding the sheet tightly against her chest as she props herself up with one hand. The morning sunlight filters through her hair, casting a radiant glow around her, and I'm drawn to the golden strands like a moth to flame.

As I gently stroke the silky strands of her hair between my fingers, a sad half-smile tugs at the corners of her lips. Her heart still struggles to accept the immense power residing within her, knowing the violence it took to collect the powers of eleven slain Titans.

"You're not going to hate me when you see what I have to do?"

"Rhea, I am yours. With each beat of my heart and every breath I take, I belong to you," Locking eyes with her amber gaze, I let the sincerity of my words illuminate my very being. "Forever and always, it belongs to you."

Resting her forehead against mine, she closes her eyes, fighting back tears.

"You never have to face another battle alone, Rhea," I assure her, my voice filled with unwavering determination. "Whether it's the battles within your mind or those of this realm, we'll face them together."

With a solemn nod, she presses a tender kiss to my lips.

"Together," she echoes, seeking solace in the warmth of my embrace as she rests her head against my chest.

As much as I want to prolong this moment, to shield her from the outside world and its impending wars, I know we can't delay any longer. Postponing the inevitable will only prolong her stress and worry. With a heavy heart, I steel myself for what lies ahead, determined to stand by her side every step of the way.

Even as her powers have only been partly restored, her strength is unparalleled. As we ready ourselves for the assault on the wards of the Underworld, I have no doubt she will rise to the challenge. I will stand by her side, ready to fend off any who dare to threaten her.

The Underworld sprawls out before us, a vast and haunting landscape veiled in shifting shadows that pulse with a life of their own. Nestled deep within the rocky seabed far beneath the ocean's surface, an impenetrable barrier of protective wards bars entry, fending off any intruders with its formidable presence.

Rhea stands beside me, an incredible force of power in her own right. Determination fuels her, and her eyes blaze with silver starlight as she prepares to dismantle the protective wards guarding Ares' underwater fortress.

Deep within the Underworld, Triton awaits his liberation from the confines of his dark prison, his immortal life entrusted to the hands of my mate.

I feel the weight of our purpose as we stand on the precipice between realms. The world above the deep ocean and the one constructed beneath it. I've searched so long for the hidden realm of the Underworld and now that I'm standing before it, I can only think of keeping my mate safe.

The air crackles with an electric charge, a tangible warning of the immense power Rhea commands. Holding the waters of the realm back, Rhea has created a ward of her own. With no more than a surge of her aura, the ocean pulled away and revealed the hidden castle of desolation Ares has constructed at the bottom of the trench.

Her gaze meets mine, a silent affirmation of our shared mission. With a flicker of her fingers, she channels the titanic might within her, and the protective wards quake in response. Dark energy recoils as if in fear, but Rhea's determination remains unyielding.

I watch my mate as she battles the force of the wards. Heavy confines that protect the hidden structure attempt to hold back my mate.

The ethereal threads of magic spark between the barrier and Rhea as my heart pounds in my chest.

Her power intensifies, and the wards splinter under the strain of her might. Arcane symbols and elemental power braided in the fabric of the Underworld, unravel before us. Each crack in the barrier is a triumph against the very essence of this dark realm and pushes her forward.

The Underworld, accustomed to the echoes of suffering, resists our intrusion. But Rhea, with the stolen essence of Titans, stands resolute, her strength an unyielding force against the oppressive shadows. I witness the ferocity of her will, the power of twelve converging into a cataclysmic surge that tears the barriers apart with a final pulse of her might.

As the last remnants of protection crumble, we look to

each other. Rhea's eyes are alive with her power but there is a vulnerability in her gaze. Sadness of what will come next coats her in worry, but her resolve is made, and I know she'll see it through.

Taking her hand in mine, we look into the heart of the Underworld—a realm steeped in the sorrowful echoes of the past. Triton, imprisoned by forces beyond his control, awaits his soul's liberation by the power of Death, the beautiful goddess who stands by my side. With every step forward, I sense the weight of Rheas power pressing upon us.

Darkness ascends on the Underworld in a wave of warning. A billow of shadow commanded from her power delivers a message to the inhabitants. The Goddess of the Twelve Realms has arrived to dismantle the fortress of her hunter.

She gives the residents of the Underworld a warning to flee, the few minutes she'll spend easing Tritons soul out of this realm.

But I will offer no such mercy to Ares' immortals that choose to stay.

Once Rhea has done what is needed, I'll crush the pylons supporting the fortress of Ares and the souls of his remaining army will meet the end of their immortality on the waves of my power.

"I know the way." She whispers as she stares with unblinking eyes at the underwater structure. A vortex of purple shadow swirls before us, then moves through us, delivering us inside the rock-hewn cavity of the Underworld.

As I project my Light in a rapid wave, scanning the surroundings for any signs of immortals preparing to defend Ares' fortress, an eerie stillness that hangs in the air. No one approaches, and the silence is deafening.

Behind us, a thick, impenetrable shield looms like a formidable blockade, warding off any potential threats from sneaking up on us. It's a testament to Rhea's incredible power that she effortlessly transported us here through a portal of her own making, bypassing the ancient and potent magic that guards this realm.

As I focus my senses, a faint glimmer catches my attention ahead. Turning my gaze towards a dark inset within the rock, it takes a moment for the scene to register. Slowly, the form of a body begins to take shape amidst the encroaching stone.

There, ensnared within the rocky embrace, lies Triton, once the mighty god of the seven seas, now reduced to little more than a mass of deteriorated fabric and calcified rock. Rhea prepared me for this sight, but even still, it's difficult to witness.

Having left him here with a promise to return with aid, she hadn't expected at the time, she would be his salvation.

Death in the form of this angel of mercy.

Tears already streak down her face when a gargled breath strains from the dark confines. An orb of silver starlight floats out of Rhea's chest, lighting the space and allowing a better view of Tritons small confinement.

A presence in the corner of my vision beats against me in shock. My heart stutters when I see the milky white eyes of Terra looking back at me.

Nearly swallowed by rock that was once fluid, her whirlpool solidified around her, trapping her forever to become an eventual fossil of the Underworld.

Casting a Mirage over the space, I conceal the ghastly sight from Rhea, allowing her to focus on Triton.

"I'm so sorry," Rhea's voice resounds in our minds, and she kneels so Triton doesn't have to strain to look at her.

Another gargled breath escapes the small cave before he weakly responds. *"Do not mourn over me, goddess. My ending is just and fitting of my betrayal."*

I join my mate and kneel with her. Triton moves his eyes to me. There is a glimmer of recognition, and my chest tightens knowing he is glad to see someone of his past. Even if our last meeting was as enemies of the battlefield of Troy.

"Phro always hated you, but she respected you. Help her see the truth."

Triton opens his memories to us; a vision of Aphrodite takes over our minds as a small stream of water runs toward Rhea and circles her wrist like a bracelet. A gasp escapes her, and we watch the separation of mates, another bond broken in Ares' pursuit of power.

A simple lovers' quarrel is why Triton left. The moment he parted from her; he regretted leaving Aphrodite upset, but he only wanted a moment to calm their tempers.

Someone boarded Triton's ship. A woman, shrouded in darkness, coated his navy fleet of red junk sails in a heavy Mirage.

He believed Aphrodite's armada was in peril, and he was presented with a bargain. Pledge allegiance to Ares and she would live, reject him and Aphrodite would die.

Triton surrendered his bond and his fleet as he gave his loyalty to the God of War. But it was a trick. There was no danger and the torment of the torn lovers had only just begun.

A captive to Ares' commands, Triton tried to keep his fleet out of Aphrodite's range, but she refused to surrender her search for him. She wanted answers and would stop at nothing until she got them.

But the cloaked figure who spun visions of deceit became a hidden shadow on Aphrodite's ship. As the goddess of love approached the fleet of her mate, desolation overtook her. Falling to her knees she saw a false Mirage of Triton with another by his side.

Aphrodite, chasing after her lost love, witnessed him make passionate love to another. She believed he rejected her and as she watched, her heart fractured.

Each splinter turned to stone and hardened her against compassion. Their mated bond turned to petrified rock and blew away on the winds of Aphrodite's power.

The former mates never found a day of peace after.

Triton's fleet was outfitted with Greek fire. A green flame that burned with the essence of the immortal that created it and served as a constant prison for him and his navy of fighters.

Aphrodite never stopped seeking her revenge and followed Triton across the realm.

Their battles waged across the open oceans. One of them served as a means to destitute Callie and Penelope where they were found by the princes of Troy. Two decades of my sister's imprisonment could have been prevented had the lovers not been torn apart by the deceit of the cloaked mage.

"How?" Rhea's eyes are wide with pain as tears fall down her face. Her chin quivers as if the visions of the past will haunt her. The thin band of water retreats from her wrist, returning to the small cavern that has served as Tritons prison for tens of thousands of years.

Triton releases another gargled breath and closes his eyes in a long and slow blink. Rhea seems to hold her breath, perhaps hoping Triton will die on his own and save her from having to take his life.

But he is immortal, and therefore cannot die.

He opens his eyes again, holding her in his gaze. Rhea releases the shaky breath she kept trapped.

"Nothing is more important than the pendent." He says in a cracked voice to our minds. *"You need to understand first. The Library awaits you and the pendent is the key."*

Rhea nods in understanding of the cryptic exchange.

Her persistence of returning to Tartarus for the pendent has been a touchy subject between us. Any hope of deterring her would have been difficult before and will be impossible now. Especially with last night's revelation, she needs to know where she came from.

She needs to believe she is not the monster that stole the powers of the Titans, and that she can wield the abilities of the slain for good.

Triton releases a final breath, and his eyes lose focus.

Rhea sucks in a choked sob, knowing the end is coming. Triton is tired and must be in immense pain. The relief she will provide him should be enough to convince her this is the right thing to do but I know it won't help to make it any easier on her.

"I am ready, and so are you. I'm sorry you have to carry this heavy torch, but there is none strong enough, than you." Closing his eyes, Triton prepares himself for Death, for Rhea.

The floating orb casting the light of the goddess approaches him.

Entering his chest, the silver aura of Rhea's power sends harsh shadows along his rocky face as the orb enters his body. Triton takes a deep breath in and releases it. The silver starlight illuminates him from within and then fades away. His body turns to mist, like the final remnants of a gentle spring shower.

Rhea buries her head in her hands and weeps. She falls over into me, knowing I'll catch her, and I hold her firmly in my arms.

The Underworld quakes with her sorrow.

Pebbles and dust fall from the rocky ceiling above us, a warning of the impending collapse.

I project my Light outward and it travels to all levels of the Underworld in a second. Pockets of families are huddled in corners or trapped in small rooms, guarded by Ares' army, and prevented from leaving. Children cry in their parent's arms, and they stare at their captors with hate.

Elsewhere, teams of Immortals and Shifters loyal to Ares are storming down the twists of the Underworld, headed downward to confront us in the depths of the darkness.

I surround the captive Shifters in my power, encasing the innocent families and leaving those who hold them hostage. The tendrils of my power rush through the levels of the Underworld, bringing Light to the darkness for the first time since its creation.

A crack resounds around us as a divot forms where Rhea and I sit. Her pain is squeezing space around us, and the Underworld cannot withhold against the pressure of her sorrow.

I don't want to her to be responsible for any more destruction today so with a soothing reassurance, and a stroke of her hair, I wrap my Light around us.

As I pull survivors within my portal, I blast a wave of Absolute Light.

We disappear on my starlight and a surge of super-heated

light consumes the Underworld. As my power detonates like a bomb in the deepest reaches of the vast ocean, the prison that tormented my mate for so many lifetimes ceases to exist.

Within the swell of my power, I safely hold the families who were preparing to die in the darkness of Ares' fortress.

I deliver them across the realm to Lucas and in the same instant, I transport my mate to our home. Sitting on the floor, I hold the goddess of the realms as she mourns the loss of the life she was forced to take.

"Please don't let me become a monster." She whispers between her sobs and my heart shutters at the fear in her voice.

"Never."

ermes is a godsend and has tended to me all day.
Returning from the Underworld, we took a shower,
and he washed my hair as I stood under the hot water. He
scrubbed away the salty film that coated us from the depths
beneath the world's oceans. But nothing will wash away the
guilt of what I did.

"Don't be afraid to show me the darkest parts of yourself,
Rhea. The parts deep inside that scare you." Hermes spoke so
tenderly as we lay in bed, and he stroked my hair. "I was made
to bring light to the darkness and love every part of you."

Hermes held me as I napped and he was reading the book
about Freya's necklace when I woke up, still lying next to me
in bed.

That night when Hermes made love to me, his Mirage took
us into the skies, and he fucked me among the stars.

When my climax came crashing down, for the first time in
my life as Rhea, I came without stimulation on my center. As
Hermes thrust into me and held my body, I have never felt so
safe or so fully loved.

As our bodies and hearts were connected in our love

making, that part within me that remains unsettled ached. And I realized what longs for fulfillment.

Our fated bond, long severed and hanging lifeless within me.

Amid the turmoil of the world and endless pursuit of my powers, this is what I long for the most. To repair what's been torn apart and bind myself rightfully to my mate.

He woke me up with kisses and held me until all the tears in my body were gone. Now he's carried me to the living room and covered me in a puffy blanket with the remote to the television.

Standing in the pantry of our kitchen and surveying the food, Hermes pauses as something steals his attention. He stands up straight and looks over his shoulder as if observing something far away.

"You have got to be fucking kidding me." He pinches the bridge of his nose and my heart spikes in my chest.

"What is it?" My blood warms with a wave of concern.

Before he can answer, the door to our home swings open and the bright blonde wave of hair that bounces inside brings warmth and a smile to my face. Callie bounds in and jumps onto the couch next to me, wrapping her arms around me in a tight hug.

"I warned you." She says to no one specifically, but I know she's talking to Hermes. She doesn't let go of her hold on me and I melt into her.

Moving the blanket and making room for her, she scoots in. We giggle and squirm closer as we let our friendship wrap around us.

"You're not winning this one brother, so you may as well get dressed." Achilles deep voice is laced with humor. I glance behind my spot on the couch and see him leaning against the doorframe. He's clutching several white bags, trimmed with brown leather in one hand and a smirk stays plastered on his face. He looks at me with a wink of his scarred eye and I wave my hand.

Callie finally sits up, a grin of accomplishment shinning in the blue eyes that match Hermes'. "Sleepover time." She says with a firm nod before she bounds off the couch.

"You can't call first?" Hermes still stands in the kitchen with one hand on the open pantry door.

"You can't share Rhea?"

"We just reunited." He counters. "What do you want me to do?"

"Share, you selfish thing." She responds back very matter-of-factly. "We didn't hear from you guys in a whole day. Either you come out, or I'm coming in here to pull you out."

Achilles put the bags on the counter and crosses his arms over his chest. The crooked smirk is a permanent fixture against his handsome face as he watches his closest friend attempt to battle the great Calypso. Having them here has instantly lifted my spirits and I realize how much I need something to take my mind off everything. I need my best friend.

"We can all hang out for a while, then." Hermes attempts a compromise.

"No, she's traumatized and needs her best friend, so get out." Callie answers without missing a beat.

"It's my house." Hermes is nearly pouting, but he knows it's a losing battle. I think he just wants to irritate his sister a little more before leaving.

"It's her house too. And I would hate to start a tornado in

here, but I will. Scoot!" She points at the door before going to Achilles.

He wraps an arm low on her back and she raises on the tips of her toes. Taking his face between her hands, she kisses him and then rubs her nose against his. "Thank you for carrying my things."

"I'll see you later, little siren." Achilles kisses her once more before stretching his arms and yawning. "You ready, bud?" He asks Hermes who finally shuts the pantry door with a roll of his eyes.

"Whatever." But he's not really upset because he turns to me with mischief gleaming in his blue eyes. While I want a constant nearness to him too, I need some girl-time as well.

As he walks to me, Callie slaps his arm, and he chuckles. Once our goodbyes are said, and the boys leave, Callie is near giddy with her plans for the day.

We order food from the Delphi Commune and have a large spread of all our favorite things. Callie gets crusty bread with olive relish and salted fish. I eat too many beef skewers and roasted potatoes. We pick at a platter of dill and olive oil coated cucumbers and salty cheese as we talk and laugh the day away.

The television plays a never-ending stream of mortal movies and more than once Callie heals my soul when we double over in unending laughter.

It's the kind of laughing that hurts, where you can't breathe, and you beat on couch cushion as tears stream out of your eyes. A chuckle so deeply rooted in your core that you hold your face, tired of smiling and begging for it to stop so you can just catch your breath for a moment.

I tell her of the Underworld and what happened before they found me. She dies of laughter as I recall the Sprites of

Avalon heckling her brother and she holds me with steady blue eyes as I share the truth of my powers.

I absorb every detail she shares of New York though I know she didn't tell me everything. Countries are waging war with each other, and civil fighting has broken out elsewhere.

The United States is battling China and Russia, as well as themselves. While the military is gearing up for retaliation, they have begun bombing the countries that attacked them. The citizen are rioting, busying the police force, and bringing down their own cities.

I murdered their president. I helped plunge them into turmoil and I sit here on my mountain, surrounded by my mate and my friends' reading books.

I should be out there doing more. The world needs help and we have the power to guide them.

The thoughts pause in my mind before I can finish thinking them. *I sound just like Ares.* The very words he spoke in the Underworld as he prepared his troops for Mabon, flow out of my thoughts just as easily as they flowed out of his mouth.

"Did you hear about the Labyrinth?" Callie leans in close, hugging a bowl of popcorn with chocolate candies thrown in. The colorful hard shells of the candy remain intact, but the chocolate centers melt. I grab a handful, making sure to get both popcorn and candy and I shake my head no.

"Someone broke in and stole some shadow beings."

"Oh, my goddess." I mindlessly shove popcorn and chocolates into my mouth as I look off to the side in contemplation of who could have done it. Likely an incredibly powerful elemental and my mind goes to Aryana. "Do they know who did it?"

"No, but the Sensors found residue of very dark and ancient incantations. But there is more." Her eyes are wide as she tells me the news. "Archangel Michael was eaten by the Lurkers before they were stolen."

Ew. "So, who is guarding the Labyrinth now?"

"A whole team of Light and Dark mages. Atlas told me, the Mortal Council is trying to keep it a secret for now. He's going to see if he can dig up any old books on necromancy and incantations and Hecate is helping refortify the wards to keep the shadows inside." This must be what Penelope spoke to Atlas and Hecate about.

"Well, if the council is trying to keep it a secret, that probably means everyone knows." Everyone but me, it seems.

And if Ares coordinated this, he's going to make sure everyone knows and use the Lurkers against the mortals. Callie notices how the news takes over my mind and she moves on to less serious subjects as she asks how Hermes and I are doing.

I confess my longing to bond rightfully with Hermes again. Toying with the charm of my necklace, I rub my finger around the small stone at the hilt of the sword and Callie shares the sensations of bonding with her mates.

As she speaks of her imbalance, it resonated with my turmoil. While Callie was incomplete without the two bonds of her mates, the gaps in my soul need to be filled by my fated connection and my missing immortality.

Callie hugs me when tears fall from my eyes when I tell her of Triton. But as she held back the gruesome details of New York, I hold something back from her now: A vision Triton showed to me, and I keep that to myself.

"They are not ready for the truth." He spoke only to me through the gentle rush of water that swirled around my wrist.

"The truth will come at a great cost and only then will they believe. Only then, will they be free."

Callie and I finish our movie as Mr. Darcy pecks his new wife, Elizabeth, on the nose and we head to the rear patio.

Using my powers, I bring a flame to the fire pit, and we share a large bowel of melons and champagne. The stars shine bright for the pair of goddesses that rekindle their friendship under the night sky.

It's been too long since we've had a night like this, just the two of us, sharing our stories and dreams under the starlit sky. Her warm yellow aura is a comforting reminder that I'm not alone in this journey.

With Hermes by my side and Callie's unwavering support, I can't help but feel a surge of optimism coursing through me. The challenges ahead seem less daunting when I know I have such incredible friends by my side. The eclipse looms on the horizon, preparing to cast its shadow over our world, but I refuse to let it dominate my spirit.

Tonight, as we laugh and reminisce, I feel a sense of readiness stirring within me. Whatever trials await us, I know I'm prepared to face them head-on. I am ready to embrace everything my future holds.

No sooner do the thoughts leave my mind than the Winds rage around us.

A swell billows from the western wind, carrying screams of pain and cries for help on its currents. Callie and I spring to our feet. With the power of Wind woven into both our beings, it's calling to us, pulling us to answer the weeping prayers.

Our hair whips around us and we fight to stand upright. Shielding our eyes from the blasts of the wind, we listen.

Dozens of women are crying and praying for death to come

save them. But it's not a plea for me, it's a cry for the sweet release from the pain they are enduring,

Flapping of bird's wings echoes in the night as dozens of black crows fly in a cyclone, joining the wind that spirals around us. Converging in a tight vortex around our bodies, the caws of the black birds drown the world out.

"Goddess." This gentle prayer *is* for me, and it slams into me. Nothing more than a whisper, colliding with me by the powerful force of the Shifter who spoke it.

Zara.

"We have to go." I stand as the urgent words tumble out of my mouth.

"Let's get the boys." Callie counters, fixing her hair in a low ponytail.

"There is no time." I clutch her hand and my dark portal rushes us to my bedroom. In a second, we've grabbed tactical vests to strap over our clothing. "Besides, your brother is only going to keep me in a cage."

Callie straightens her posture, looking at me with a stern expression.

"I'm sorry." My words triggered the memories of her captivity in Troy when she felt like a caged bird under the torture of Paris and Hector. "He's just being incredibly over-protective."

Callie nods her head, understanding. "Okay, let's do this right though." Taking two sets of uniforms and boots, she hands me one. "But as soon as we know what's going on, I'm letting Achilles know."

"Deal."

We dress as quickly as possible. Our gear prepared to protect us from attacks by Elemental power. Callie covers us in a Shield of Currents, and I add my own Dark Cloak for extra protection.

Only two minutes have passed and yet the Winds keep raging outside, surrounding the home in screams and cries of pain. Zara's echo is still ricocheting off the mountain peaks around us.

I grab onto a whispered plea, seeing the sound waves as thin spiders' webs floating on a soft breeze. In an instant, I know where Zara is.

The hot Louisiana night is sticky with humidity. She's aboveground and it seems to be a large warehouse.

"Ready?" I ask, sending Callie a projection of the location.

Winds circle her wrists like fast-spinning ribbons of currents, and I know she's prepared to lash out at the first threat we'll face once we arrive.

Black fog billows around me, encasing us in obscurity. As the realm swirls around me, opening a portal, Callie and I kneel into a crouch. I carefully shroud the served bond within me to Hermes, so he won't detect my emotions as we ready ourselves to leave. Armed with our powers and our determination, we head into the den of an unknown enemy.

May the Fates have mercy on them because we won't.

19
Rhea

The Louisiana night hangs heavy, suffocating under the weight of its own humidity, offering little respite from the heat even as the sun retreats below the horizon. Our arrival at an expansive outdoor compound is cloaked in darkness.

A single warehouse looms like a fortress amidst the desolate landscape. Surrounding it, gravel and dirt stretch out in all directions, serving as a silent watchman to the secrecy that shrouds this location's purpose.

In the distance, the tree line stands like a picket sentinel guards. Their silent vigil promising to keep the secrets of this place hidden from prying eyes. Tall lamp posts pierce the darkness with their harsh fluorescent light, banishing the shadows and casting stark, dramatic silhouettes across the barren grounds.

At the loading bay, a cargo truck sits backed up against the warehouse, its engine rumbling softly as crates, similar to the ones we're crouched behind, are loaded onto its bed.

Men bustle about, their voices carrying on the night air as they shout orders and consult clipboards. While tendrils of cigarette smoke curl lazily upwards, adding to the atmosphere of covert activity.

A frail cough from the crate concealing us sends a jolt of surprise through both Callie and me, causing us to tense with sudden apprehension.

Peering between the cracks of the wooden slats, a young woman, near my age, lays on the hard wooden base of the crate. She is naked, her body marred with bruises, and a thick collar secured tightly around her neck.

Despite her fragile state, she's alive, yet the absence of her aura leaves me uncertain of her true nature. Even mortals carry a faint glow of life within their powerless forms, but her aura remains elusive, hidden from my sight.

"Do you think she's a mortal?" I murmur in a hushed tone, my gaze lingering on her long auburn hair, so similar to my own.

The sound of shuffling gravel behind us interrupts Callie's response, causing us both to freeze in alarm. My shadows whisper their warnings, alerting me to the presence of an approaching guard.

He's a Shifter, low in both rank and power, but his howl would be enough to alert the entire compound to our presence. As he rounds the crate, his gaze locks onto us with chilling precision.

Without hesitation, Callie and I spring into action, our movements synchronized as we launch our combined attack.

As Callie's power flares, I channel my own, enveloping the guard in a cloak of darkness, shielding him from prying eyes and rendering him invisible to any onlookers.

With a surge of her Winds, Callie propels his body high into the sky, her power swirling within him like a tempest unleashed. In an explosion of energy, the Winds disperse his remains into fine particles, ensuring that nothing of him will ever reach the surface again.

I can't help but tease my friend as we stand amidst the aftermath of our display of force. "That was a bit dramatic, don't you think?"

Callie merely shrugs, unruffled by the spectacle. "Something tells me this place demands drama." And as I survey the hidden compound around us, I can't help but agree.

As a heaviness settles above me, I glance upward, drawn to the night sky. Descending gracefully, swaying gently in the night breeze, a single crow feather drifts down, coming to rest beside us. Though seemingly insignificant, I sense a presence emanating from it, a knowing that this is no ordinary feather—it's a harbinger of something more.

Before my eyes, the feather transforms into a wisp of black smoke, curling and twisting until it coalesces into the form of a woman.

"Bridget," I greet her, recognizing the Witch who had once shielded me from Lupo.

"And that wasn't dramatic?" Callie nudges me with a playful grin, her amusement evident.

"Entrances are meant to be dramatic," Bridget replies dismissively, brushing a few stray feathers from her long, flowing skirt.

The memory of the day Hermes and I stumbled upon Damien's brutal murder still haunts me, a vivid reminder of the dangers lurking in the shadows of our world. In the aftermath of the tragedy, Bridget's swift action saved us, pulling us into her apartment and shielding me from the watchful gaze of Lupo, my former captor.

In those moments of uncertainty, Bridget's presence was a calming balm, her soothing words offering solace amidst the storm of emotions raging within me. With unwavering resolve, she safeguarded Damien's research, entrusting it to our care and setting me on a path that would lead me to meet Hecate.

Though it feels like a lifetime has passed since that fateful day, in reality, only a few weeks have gone by. Yet, in that short span of time, Bridget's guidance has proven invaluable, and I am grateful to see her again.

"I'm happy to see you still living, goddess." Her long hair hangs nearly to the ground from our crouched pose. She's wearing another colorful, flowing skirt and rich purple tank top that exposes her dark tattoos.

"You and me both." Callie answers.

"Do you know what this place is?" I ask Bridget, turning back to the truck.

As we survey the stacked wooden crates, a sinking feeling settles in the pit of my stomach. Each crate represents another woman on the brink of disappearing into the night, their fates sealed by the fading taillights of the truck.

"Shifter auctions," Bridget murmurs darkly, her gaze fixed on the truck with a simmering anger that threatens to boil over. "They're selling she-Shifters tonight. Those crates are headed for the breeding chambers."

The gravity of the situation weighs heavily upon us, the desperation of the captured women mingling with our own urgency to intervene. Callie's chest rises and falls with dramatic fervor, mirroring the intensity of our collective determination to act.

"We can't let them leave," Callie declares, her voice filled with conviction.

"We agree," Bridget confirms, her eyes scanning the top of the warehouse where darkness shrouds any potential allies lurking in the shadows.

"Who is 'we'?" I inquire, my curiosity piqued by Bridget's cryptic answer.

"Our other friends," Bridget replies, her voice carrying a note of reassurance amidst the uncertainty of the situation. And as I follow her gaze into the darkness above, a pair carnelian, jeweled eyes look back at me from the darkness.

Zara, the lioness, dips her head to me. Five more lionesses' join her and a sense of relief that we're not alone eases some of the tension in my throat. I return Zara's bow with one of my own.

"We don't know what's happening inside, or if there is a substructure underneath here." Zara says, speaking into my mind. I didn't realize others could hear Shifter-telepathy. Perhaps this is another sign my powers are growing stronger.

Sensing no shift in Callie and Bridget's demeanor, I relay the message.

"Let's check things out," Callie whispers, and we both nod in agreement, sending our elemental powers to scout the compound.

Callie's Winds surge forward, racing through the air conditioning system and spiraling along the metal frame of the warehouse, gathering intel with their swift movements.

Meanwhile, my darkness slithers along the ground, weaving through the shadows and conversing with every murmur of darkness it encounters.

As we delve deeper, haunting echoes of desperation pierce the stillness of the night. A cry of mercy and despair echoes from within the warehouse, reverberating through the air with chilling clarity. Yet, as suddenly as it began, the cry is silenced, as if a door had been shut, sealing away the hopelessness within.

As I focus my attention inward, my powers grant me a chilling insight into the scene unfolding inside the warehouse.

A raised platform dominates the space, surrounded on three sides by rows of men. Naked women are paraded past them, escorted up a small set of stairs to the stage. The guards, armed with cattle prods, monitor their every move. Everyone on the stage and filling the observation seats are Shifters, their predatory gazes fixed on the vulnerable women below.

Despite their compliance, the women are subjected to occasional jolts from the guards' cattle prods, a cruel form of amusement for the watching crowd. Some of the captives bear visible signs of abuse, most are in tears, and few walk with any semblance of pride. All of them are shackled in the front and collared around the neck, their captivity on full display for all to see.

Above their heads, black screens display bold white numbers in large font—the price they are being sold for, or in one unfortunate girl's case, the lack thereof. She stands apart from the others, her body bearing the marks of brutal injuries, her expression twisted in a murderous scowl.

It's clear that her wounds alone cannot account for the lack of interest from potential buyers. In her early twenties, fit and attractive, she possesses all the qualities that would typically appeal to the pig-headed Shifters in attendance. Yet, there is a palpable sense of pack politics at play, as the auction-goers have deemed her value-less.

"She is the daughter of an alpha, loyal to Lucas. Her name is Cassandra. We call her Cassie." Bridget says and I realize she is holding onto my wrist. Her eyes have turned to voids, covered in black obscurity.

It's shadows, coating her eyes like a film. She is seeing everything I am.

"She is the reason we are here," Zara adds, her voice tinged with urgency. "Cassie had a tracking device, but they cut it out. I followed them the rest of the way."

My gaze flickers to the woman, her side cut and blood dripping down her thigh. I can't help but feel a surge of admiration for her bravery.

"Wait. She got captured on purpose?" I ask, incredulous.

"Yes. Keep watching," Bridget instructs, maintaining her hold on me as I return my focus to my observing powers.

Within the warehouse, a general hum of baritone voices and deep laughter fills the air, a constant backdrop to the proceedings. Occasional clouds of cigar smoke drift lazily into the air, and Callie's Winds moves with care to avoid disturbing them with her currents.

Like a den of vipers, the tendrils of Callie's air streams glide and slither in the ceiling space above the crowd of bidders below. Three lionesses are perched in the corners of the rafters, their presence hidden from view by the shadows I deepen around them, ensuring their stealth as they await their moment to strike.

A woman stands at the center of the line, clearly esteemed as the highest prize in this round of the auction. Despite her nakedness, she holds herself with an air of pride and indifference, her chest puffed out defiantly.

With olive skin and sleek black hair, she would appear convincing if not for the waves of fear rolling off her in torrents. As a guard wielding a cattle prod approaches her, she tenses visibly, her facade of confidence crumbling under the weight of her terror.

The guard makes a dramatic show of his movements, sniffing a slow line up her collarbone to her neck. With a wicked grin, he licks the same path, pulling her hair back harshly as he revels in her fear.

"Don't be fooled, boys," his thick Australian accent reverberates across the warehouse. "This one tastes especially delicious with the panic mixing with her scent. A fine prize for our winner." His words hang heavy in the air, casting a chilling despair over the women on the stage.

My stomach churns with disgust as the guard pulls the woman's wrists upward, forcing her arms behind her in an unnatural position. Despite her efforts to suppress it, a yelp escapes her lips as her breasts are pushed forward uncomfortably.

My heart pounds in my chest as the guard places the cattle prod against her vagina, activating it with a cruel twist of his wrist. The pulsating shockwaves force her body to respond, her involuntary moans echoing in the oppressive silence of the warehouse. The electricity crackles dangerously close to her, a constant threat should she dare to move.

The woman's nipples hardening under the stimulation as the warehouse erupts with applause and cheers. She fights to hold back her sobs and the quiver of her body against the assault. Anger boils within me, threatening to consume me whole.

As I move to intervene, Bridget's grip tightens on my wrist, holding me back with a sense of urgency. "Not yet" she whispers, her voice strained with emotion. "This is not the worst of it. We must be patient, goddess, or all will be lost tonight."

I swallow hard, realizing that Bridget isn't just referring to our plans of attack, but the lives of all these women hanging in the balance. And that, I cannot accept. So, I wait, my fists clenched in frustration.

"When we first met, I told you to turn it off," Bridget reminds me, her voice cutting through the tension like a knife. "Now, you must learn the lesson of when to turn it on."

The men's raucous cheers and hollers fill the air as the woman is forced to endure her involuntary climax. Despite her efforts to maintain composure, the clench of her knees and the strain in her face betray her, providing the audience with the spectacle they crave.

The men around her sniff the air eagerly, as if savoring the scent of her climax. Some of them even begin to rub their crotches, their primal urges unchecked in this haven of depravity. Others howl into the air, their voices blending into a cacophony of savagery.

A single tear rolls down the woman's cheek, her silent anguish mirroring my own inner turmoil. Unable to bear her suffering alone, a tear of empathy escapes my eye, tracing a path down my own cheek.

As the bidding draws to a close, the dark-haired woman is claimed by the victor, or rather, by the men who represent him. Two figures in suits, their faces hidden behind dark aviator glasses, step forward to collect her. I can only imagine the horrors that await her at the hands of her wealthy purchaser.

Other women are similarly collected by their buyers, some placed in crates hidden within the shadows of the room. Yet, as the auctioneer announces the closing bid for the alpha's daughter, the room falls into laughter—the final bid reads zero.

Surrounded and prodded by the electrical rods wielded by

four guards, Cassie falls to the ground, her silent agony palpable in the air. Though she never screams, the grimace of pain etched on her face speaks volumes.

Her suffering brings to mind Callie and her unwavering bravery in the face of our own captivity under Lupo's cruelty. He subjected her to unspeakable torment, lashing her with his whip, yet she never once gave him the satisfaction of hearing her cry out in pain. With each lash, we clung to our mantra, *"just survive,"* a whispered plea for endurance in the face of unimaginable circumstances.

Now, as I watch these captives endure unspeakable horrors, I send that same prayer into the night, a desperate plea for their survival amidst the darkness that threatens to consume them.

The guards spit on the alpha's daughter, their contempt for her evident in their cruel actions.

A rotund man from the stands approaches the stage, his stub of a cigar dangling from his lips, its end coated in his saliva. With a malicious grin, he digs the embers of the cigar into her side, eliciting a grunt of pain from the woman.

The fat man laughs before collecting phlegm and hocks it in her face. My throat constricts with revulsion, and I struggle to suppress a gag as I bear witness to the depths of immortal depravity unfolding before me.

Rage simmers within me, a seething inferno threatening to consume everything in its path. If only my fury could manifest into tangible form, it would be hot enough to melt the very beams of this warehouse, forging a river of molten metal to cleanse the world of such despicable cruelty.

"There is a warded door," Bridget speaks hastily as the men drag Cassie away by her hair. "They will open it and take her elsewhere. Ready your powers. You are the only one who can push through and tell us what is beyond. That is the true mission tonight."

My eyes quickly scan the walls and floor of the building as the guards drag Cassie down the steps of the stage. It has to be away from the men observing the auction. Somewhere crowded with darkness. Then I locate it. The wards throb at me as if a beating heart hides behind the door.

"I found it."

"Yes, goddess. You must be quick. They will only keep it open a few seconds."

The diesel engines of two trucks flare to life, rumbling across the night and disturbing our quiet. The slithering tendrils of my shadows are poised and ready as the guard reaches for an invisible doorknob.

Extending his hand through the wards, the door is revealed.

At the first twist, the protective curtain is broken, and the emotions of captive women stream out, blasting past the open wards, their cries and pain surging into the atmosphere. My darkness explodes into the room like a silent spy.

Thin tendrils of obscurity rush across the space, and what I find makes me turn behind me to vomit.

The alpha's daughter is hurled down a long flight of stairs leading to an underground level beneath the warehouse. The Aussie-guard follows her down, his menacing presence casting a shadow over the scene. With a grim determination, he closes the door behind him, sealing off the horrors unfolding below.

At the bottom of the stairs, more men stand ready to collect Cassie's discarded body, their faces devoid of remorse or empathy.

As the door shuts, the wards seal shut in an instant, cloaking the night in an eerie silence once more.

The atrocities happening beneath the warehouse are nothing short of the worst acts of depravity possible. I can't stop the images that flash through my mind as my shadows swarm around me.

They are all captive Shifters, their suffering unconceivable.

One woman, transformed into the likeness of a swan, has been stripped of her feathers, blood staining her exposed skin. Her wings are bent at terrible angles, and her beak is cruelly clipped away with a large pair of pliers.

Another woman is being raped by four men. One is at her mouth, two are at her pelvis. The fourth man penetrates her from a wound in her side with a sickening brutality that defies comprehension. She cries in agony with each of their thrusts.

It's the sight of Shifters being skinned and mutilated that brings bile rising in my throat. One woman's eyes dangle from their sockets as two men work to sew her eyelids shut. The thought of her retaining her vision in such a state is beyond comprehension, and I can imagine the excruciating pain she is enduring.

My own incarnations survived horrors such as these and I look away before I fall too far down a dark well of my past pains.

But it's the recognition of one woman that nearly stops my heart: *Lexi.*

Transformed into her true form, the sleek black coat of a panther adorns her, her aura unmistakable even in her shifted state. The collar around her neck keeps her trapped in her animal form, her fur marred and bloodied from her struggles.

She's restrained by all four paws in a contraption designed for shifted animals, presented for mating. The Australian guard, in his human form, sadistically sodomizes her with his cattle prod, reveling in her anguish as she roars in pain.

Removing the prod, he's unzipping his pants, preparing to rape her himself, my voice escapes in a trembling whisper, barely audible amidst the chaos unfolding before me. "I know someone in there."

Every fiber of my being quivers with a violence that threatens to consume me, an urge to rip the souls from the men perpetrating these heinous acts.

But I think of New York and how my panic made me surge into the echoes of the destruction that rained down upon the city the night before. I lost myself in the whirl of my emotions and I can't afford to lose control again—I need to rein in my emotions and focus on the task at hand.

"Look at me, goddess." Bridget forces my gaze to meet hers, her eyes steady and unwavering. "Turn it off," she commands me calmly.

"But I know her," I protest, my voice trembling with emotion.

Forcing deep breaths into my lungs, Callie envelops me in cool currents, soothing my frayed nerves. "Breath, Rhea."

"We must attack when the time is right and not a second sooner," Bridget continues to coax me.

Taking another ragged breath, I inquire, "When will the time be right?"

"When you are ready, goddess. You must attack with intention, not your emotions, so turn them off. You know your course, now think of how you will walk it. See your attack unfold. The warded door is your goal, how will you get to it? How will you remove the threats that wait beyond it?"

I stretch my neck and shake out my hands. Closing my

eyes, I envision myself rushing through the warehouse to the level below.

The sound of the trucks beginning to drive away fades into the background as I focus on the steady rhythm of my heartbeat, willing it to calm.

"We will follow you beyond the Void into Oblivion, goddess. When you are ready to extract your vengeance, so will we."

The atmosphere stills, anticipation thick in the air. Goosebumps prickle my skin, and my muscles tense with anticipation.

With my mind centered and my nerves steadied, I open my eyes. The realm pulses with life around me as my senses sharpen to heightened awareness.

I see the swirling currents of Wind, a tempest fueled by Calypso's fury. Clouds of purple darkness emanate from Bridget, while the lionesses on the warehouse roof crouch, their keen eyes are fixed on their prey as the two trucks rumble down the dirt road.

My black mist surges from within me, shrouding the compound in obscurity. And in the next heartbeat, we unleash our rage upon them.

Thrown into darkness, the Shifters of the auction stand frozen, as if awaiting the inevitable embrace of Death; not that I would need it. The lionesses leap from the warehouse roof in a graceful arc, their powerful paws thundering across the ground.

"The trucks will not make it to the tree line before my pride will be upon them," Zara declares, her words a blend of promise and threat, sealing the convoy's fate.

Callie, Bridget, and I materialize inside the warehouse on a surge of my dark portal. The lionesses, hidden in the corner rafters, descend upon the crowd below. Their powerful jaws bite through the flesh of the auction-goers, eliciting gasps and screams of confusion.

Attempts to flee are met with futility as the crowd finds themselves trapped with nowhere to escape. Heads roll to the ground, severed cleanly by the lionesses' merciless jaws, painting the scene with crimson vengeance.

As chaos erupts, a man hurls a Stygian Iron blade, striking one of the lionesses in the side. With a pained growl, the Shifter collapses, reverting to her human form. The alloy metal of celestial bronze, imperial gold, and bone steel saps her powers as it protrudes from her side.

In response, Bridget transforms into a flock of crows and billowing smoke. With a flurry of flapping feathers and obscurity, she swoops towards the wounded Shifter. Reverting to her human form just long enough to extract the blade from her companion, Bridget swiftly returns to the form of a flock of birds.

Flying in a tight whirlwind of avian and smoke, she transforms once more. Her skirt and long black hair continue to twirl around her as she hurls the blade back at the assailant. His own weapon strikes him in the head, killing him.

Callie moves with swift and decisive action, seizing men and Shifters as they transform around us. Her Winds break their limbs and infiltrate their bodies, while the white ribbons of her currents tear them apart from within, leaving them alive but dismembered. She walks alongside me as I advance toward my target, my eyes focused on the door barricaded with elemental power.

A surge of my combined abilities crashes against the formidable wards concealing the hidden entrance, causing them to shatter under my feet. With the barriers breached, another surge of my dark portal transports us to the level below.

In an instant, the malevolent souls, dripping with the dark sludge of evil, are within my grasp. "They're mine," I declare to my companions.

The feeling of Death on my fingertips is too comforting; too much like a familiar friend and so easy it comes to me. My mind is empty, save the images of the horrors around me, inflicted by these deranged murderers and nothing else matters in this moment.

These souls are coarse and grainy. Like scratchy threads of burlap, their souls are heavy and gritty. I held Callie and Atlas' souls in my hands before. Like silken ribbon, the essence of their immortality was soft and lightweight as it billowed within them.

I suppose this is what deception and corruption feel like once it has embedded itself deeply within the root of a person. Revulsion crawls up my spine at the thought of what I would find looking at Ares' soul.

As I pull the souls from their bodies, the varied shades of immortal auras glow brighter. The men, frozen in a state of paralysis, can only stand helplessly as their immortal essence is torn away from them, a punishment befitting their heinous acts.

The Australian guard is spared of my slow torment, for now. A different fate is befitting of his ending.

Stuffing his penis into his pants, he looks around confused as his guards and patrons fall to the floor dead. It's impossible for a bystander to understand how immortal beings can drop dead, laying on the ground with their unseeing eyes open.

But I know Death has come for them and Elysium, the realm of darkness and eternal starvation, will feast upon these monsters tonight. I discard their souls into the shadows that crawl along the floor, and my darkness consumes them, casting them into the realm of damnation.

I sense the pinch of metal collars around the women and think of my own captivity. As if I can feel the compression of that thick metal around me again, it causes my anger to swell higher.

The wooden crates splinter and the metal collars crumble under the force of my obscurity, the captives spill out. Some collapse in exhaustion while others groan in pain on the tables they were splayed upon.

My heart clenches at the sight of the Swan, motionless and darkened, her aura has already been welcomed into the Void. We arrived too late to save her, and the weight of that failure presses heavily upon me, mingling with the tears of anger that well in my eyes.

With slow, deliberate steps, I approach the one remaining guard I have spared, his confusion mirrored in his eyes as he witnesses the commotion unfolding around him.

Meanwhile, my dark mist swirls throughout the room, spreading life and healing power to the victims. I feel their bodies mend beneath my touch, their groans of pain subsiding. The cool burst of air clears the stench of violence that had permeated the substructure like a suffocating fog.

Calypso, faithful and fierce, joins me at my side, her presence comforting amidst the turmoil, and she adds to the calm washing over me. Together, we work to ease the suffering of those we've rescued, offering them reassurance in the wake of their torment.

Lexi, transformed back to her human form, struggles to her feet from the rack she was strapped to. Though my powers have healed her wounds, the memory of her ordeal remains etched upon her trembling limbs. As she stands before me, blood still staining her skin, I feel a surge of determination to ensure that she, and all the others, will never again endure such cruelty.

She keeps her hard gaze on the guard that was violating her and the tremors in her body grow as her anger rises.

"Bridget." I call behind me. Bridget pauses her attendance

of Cassie, the Alpha's daughter who sacrificed her safety to enter this helscape. "The blade?"

Without hesitation, she returns, the flock of birds and smoke reforming into her human form, holding the stygian iron blade in her hand. With a solemn nod, Bridget places the blade in my open palm, her eyes reflecting the gravity of the moment. I turn my attention back to the guard, his pleas for mercy falling on an unwilling audience.

"Please, let me..." the guard begins.

"Stop talking." Calypso swiftly silences him, removing the air from his lungs. Panic sets in as he struggles to breathe, his eyes bulging and blood vessels rupturing as he claws at his throat in desperation.

Lexi takes the blade from me. Her eyes meet mine for a fleeting glance, but a dozen emotions pass between us in that instance.

Pain, confusion, and wounds caused by her hateful words against me hang heavy in my gaze. Shame and humiliation darken hers. She knows I'm aware of what was happening to her down here and she feels ashamed for it.

The gargled pleas of the Aussie guard are lost as Callie tightens the ribbons of her power around his throat. Lexi walks behind him, the blade clutched in her grip.

Her breathing hitches faster and rage takes over her expression. Clutching the knife in her tight fist, she raises it high.

Plunging the blade into the guard's neck, a primal scream tears from Lexi's throat, echoing through the darkness of the underground chamber. With each thrust of the knife, she releases the pent-up fury at her attacker.

Blood sprays in all directions, coating her face, arms, and bare chest as she relentlessly delivers blow after blow. The metallic tang of blood mingles with the stench of violence, filling the air with a nauseating aroma.

We stand in silent witness to the cathartic release of her fury, feeling the weight of her pain with every stab. It's as if she's not just avenging this moment but every injustice she's ever suffered.

Her assault continues unabated, the sound of flesh tearing and bones cracking mingling with her cries of anguish. Again and again, she strikes until the guard lies motionless on the ground. Only voids remain where the guard's face and chest once were. The remnants of his flesh and bone scattered around the scene like macabre confetti.

The dagger slips from her grasp, and exhaustion washes over her. She is drenched in his blood, a visceral display of her brutal revenge. But in that moment, she is also free, and I know with the release of her rage, she'll never allow herself to succumb to chains again.

Standing, she turns slowly, looking at each of us with the heavy weight of pain in her eyes. We look back, with understanding and sympathy coating ours. There is no judgement, only vindication because each of us in this room have felt some form of torment at the hands of men just like these.

No matter how much you scrub yourself clean, or how hot you turn your water, the filth and shame will forever remain on your body.

As a portal swirls behind me, a surge of unbearable grief cascades over room.

Lexi's eyes widen as she looks behind me. The weight of her terror is palpable, made even more poignant by the realization that she is trembling so violently that urine is running down her leg.

Turning behind us, we pivot to see what or who has arrived, causing Lexi so much terror.

The recess of dark obscurity in the far corner of the subterranean level hides our new arrivals. As Flint steps into the light, his words send a chill down my spine. "Rhea, princess." He says to me with a smile. "I've come to save you."

The rush of cold air is the only warning we have as the four dark beings descend upon us. I release the cloak over my bond to Hermes as Calypso turns to cover me, wrapping me in her embrace as she screams, "ACHILLES!"

The somber atmosphere of the Kenya Commune is palpable as we walk through its quiet streets, the echoes of the recent tragedy lingering in the air like a heavy fog. The distant sounds of nocturnal creatures and the rhythmic cadence of our footsteps underscore the gravity of the thoughts that weigh on my mind.

Just weeks ago, I brought Rhea here and watched her amazement as we toured Medusa's bustling commune. Immortals escorted newly rescued survivors to recovery, as Medusa battled the underground gladiator pits of Ares.

Now, shadows remain where immortal ichor was spilled as the Dark Mage consumed Medusa's warriors and the mortal evacuees recovering here.

Achilles and Medusa were some of the first here, immediately following the attack. Some of the commune members were still hanging on to the last thread of their fading immortality before it snapped, and their souls entered their next realm of eternity.

Every obsidian stain serves as a painful reminder of the lives that were lost only days ago. Medusa and Achilles keep their eyes remain fixed ahead, perhaps trying to shield themselves from the memories that threaten to engulf them.

The scowl etched into Medusa's features serves as a constant reminder of the darkness that resides within her. Long ago, the anguish of losing Athena consumed her, transforming her into a vessel of wrath fueled by unbridled rage. In her fury, she unleashed her powers indiscriminately, turning anyone who dared to gaze upon her into stone.

But amidst the chaos of her vengeance, tragedy struck when she inadvertently took the lives of an innocent family. Medusa chased her enemy into a cave and lashed out with her powers. Huddled around each other, a single mother clung to her young daughter. The fear on the little girl's face was frozen forever preserved in stone.

For months, I searched for Medusa and found her still sitting in that cave, looking at the expression on the little girl's face. She couldn't be reasoned with, and months turned to years, which turned to decades. Eventually, I knew what needed to happen and desperation drove me to a single source.

Athena arrived at the entrance of the cave and looked inside. Medusa never acknowledged her.

"You're better than this." Athena's voice echoed through the cave. "Be better." And she walked away, leaving Medusa to the darkness that saturated her within that grotto.

The world perceived Medusa as a monster, but in truth, she was a broken soul trying to cope with a tremendous loss.

Eventually she left that cave. Medusa formed her commune and inscribed across the top of each doorway are the words Athena spoke to her.

Be better.

I never asked what happened to the stone figures of the

mother and child but as we pass by the central fountain of the commune, my gaze falls upon a striking basalt sculpture depicting a woman tenderly holding the hand of a young girl.

Their expressions radiate love and happiness, their faces bathed in the gentle light of dawn, symbolizing the promise of each new day; an opportunity to be better.

The tension between Medusa and me is palpable as we walk beneath the vast expanse of the African sky. Medusa's cutting remark from our encounter at the Atlanta Library still echoes in my mind, a stark reminder of the complexities of our relationship.

I address her directly, cutting through the silence with a question that hangs heavy in the air. "What's going on with you, Medusa?"

Her response is guarded, her tone betraying the weight of her thoughts. "Oh, using my full name, huh?" she retorts, a hint of defensiveness in her voice. "I've just got a lot on my mind."

Medusa's Commune is the new home for the Shifters displaced from the Underworld. They are repairing her commune from the attack, and she is refortifying the earthen wards securing the mountain. I know she has a lot going on, but we all do.

Something else is etching away at her stony exterior that she is hiding, causing her mood to sour and her thoughts to darken.

With my powers as a Light Bearer, I could scan her aura and detect the essence of what she may be concealing. I could pull out the lies from her words and influence her to tell the truth.

But friendship shouldn't come with coercion.

I learned that lesson from Atlas, back when he faced his own struggles.

I still remember the toll it took on Atlas after his confrontation with Moros. The clash of their wills left wounds that couldn't be healed. Moros was left near death, and Atlas was shattered by the aftermath. I never want to carry that burden of regret.

So, if Medusa isn't ready to confide in me, that's her choice. In time, she may find the strength to share, or she may resolve it on her own.

However, I can't stand by and let her take her frustration out on Rhea.

"You know, you crossed a line the other night." We're perched on a table with rustic benches, the expanse of the plain stretching out beneath us. Achilles reclines, hands laced behind his head, lost in the canopy of stars above. Meanwhile, Medusa and I share a tense silence, the air heavy with unspoken words.

"You think this is easy for me?" Medusa's voice is edged with frustration as she leans in, fingers idly adjusting a stone bead in her braided hair.

"This is hard for all of us, Deuce."

"But easier for the Herald of the Realms whose mate returns to him like a boomerang." Her words are sharp, drawing my attention, but she keeps her gaze fixed on the vast Kenyan sky.

"You think it's easy to watch my mate die again and again? What is this actually about Medusa?"

"I know what she is, Hermes." Medusa finally looks at me, piercing me with her emerald gaze. "I knew it the second you showed up at my camp with her."

"What do you know?" A warm flush covers my body as I think of a dozen answers Medusa could give.

"She is the goddess of stolen power. Rhea controls the element of Death."

"How could you know? She only just figured it out."

"Earth recognizes its Titan. And being an Elemental of that power, so can I."

"Do you mean to say, the ground told you she was a Titan, when we arrived?"

"In a way." Medusa leans back on the table, resting on her elbows. "The earth stirred, thrilled by the presence of a Titan in Kenya. Our soil became more fertile. During her brief stay, our Life elementals produced crops in record time, with significantly higher yields."

As I gaze across the plain, the clouds cloak the moon, casting a shadow over the evening. I think of my powers over Light and whether I've sensed similar phenomena around Rhea, but... nothing.

"The connection to my element is stronger when she is near. Ava and Ana observed it from their elemental perspectives as well. Don't pretend you're not intoxicated by your own abilities when she's around." Medusa's words stir a protective instinct within me. I can't help but think of Chaos, roaming from realm to realm, devouring the powers of Titans.

It must have been an addiction.

The sensation of vast power flowing into you, merging with your essence, and magnifying everything around you. I envision Chaos experiencing a similar euphoria after consuming the essence of Artemis.

My father was called to the scene of her death, and I remember him describing it as an eruption of pure, unbridled fury. It was as if a storm of rage had swept through, leaving destruction in its wake. The brutality of the murder spoke volumes.

Fenrir met a similar fate at the hands of Chaos and the death was carried out with a precise execution. Father said, *"Not a drop of power was spilled."*

Rhea is truly one of a kind.

I refuse to entertain her fears of harboring a monstrous nature within her. It's unimaginable to me that she could ever unleash such brutality. However, I can't ignore the unsettling thought of those who might be drawn to the allure of her powers. Their twisted fantasies could escalate into dangerous realities.

Ares has pursued her relentlessly for ages and there is nothing to say others would not betray him for the chance of total control.

"What does any of this have to do with you–"

"If she holds power over death, why can't she bring my mate back?" Medusa snaps, finally exposing the truth of the kernel of resentment that has been festering inside her. "Why can't she bring Athena back to life?" The last words are more a plea than a question as a tears glisten in her green eyes.

Remorse and understanding weigh my shoulders down. "I don't think it works like that, Deuce."

A sudden burst of emotions explodes within me, and I clutch my chest, gasping for air.

In an instant I know it's Rhea and our bond is pulling me to her. Though it's severed, the phantom connection of what once existed remains behind like a residue, and it's crushing me with her fear.

Achilles sits up, alerted by his own bond and my sisters name is a whisper on his lips, "Callie."

The sky fills with a burst of silver starlight as my mate's power ruptures across the realm. Just as my blue waves of light dance in the northern night skies, silver ribbons of Rhea's powers roil in the darkness.

Something is wrong.

Achilles is by my side in an instant and the second my portal opens; I know it will bring me to her.

Rhea must have been blocking me, or shielding herself so carefully, I didn't detect anything until she removed a cloak placed over herself and hailed me to her.

The swirl of my magic rotates in a circle, and we rush into it, on the other side, the scene is overwhelming.

With a flash of Light and a surge of Achilles' heat wave, we extend our powers to take in the turmoil around us as our eyes witness the horrors of what is taking place.

Four Shadow Lurkers have invaded this underground structure along with Flint and a dozen naked and bleeding she-Shifters.

Bridget, the Witch from Damien's apartment, is blocking most of the wounded women and fending off a Lurker. She's casting some kind of dark shield that I've never seen before. The swirling mass of dark energy is foreboding and at its center is a deep recess of obscurity.

The Lurker is screeching at her but doesn't dare touch the shield.

I think even the beast knows, there is nothing beyond that shield than extinction.

Several women, all naked and bloody are cowering on the ground, writhing in pain as a Lurker feeds on their despair.

One is dead, her injuries so severe that death seems merciful compared to the agony she endured prior to her death.

But it's the sight of my mate and sister, clinging to each other amidst the chaos, that freezes me in place. Two Lurkers are flanking them, their dark forms devouring the essence of Rhea and Callie as they wail and cry. It's a horrifying sight, the darkness within them being drawn into the gaping voids of the Lurkers' mouths.

A tempest of wind and shadow swirls around Callie and Rhea, their hair whipping about as they remain ensnared within a forcefield. The Lurkers are trapped within this barrier, unable to harm anyone else in the dungeon but free to feast off their pain.

On the other side of the chaotic scene stands Flint, his voice drowned out by the swirling powers of Rhea and Callie. "Just hold on a little longer, sweetheart!" His words cut through the tumult, the term "sweetheart" sending a chill down my spine. "The Lurkers will purge the darkness from your mind, and then we can be together."

Rage boils within me. This pitiful excuse for an immortal needs to pay for what he's done. But my priority is saving Rhea.

"Medusa!" I call out, expecting to see my friend by my side, but she's nowhere to be found.

"She didn't come through the portal with us," Achilles's voice carries over the commotion, his eyes scanning the scene with concern fixed on Callie and the Lurkers.

Why wouldn't Medusa come to help? I push aside the question for later. Right now, I need to focus on protecting Rhea and Callie.

Flint's gaze locks onto me, the embers burning fiercely in

the darkness of his eyes. "You," he seethes, venom dripping from his words.

A swirling purple portal materializes around him.

"She belongs to me," he declares before vanishing through the portal, leaving the lurkers to continue their assault.

Once I get my mate out of here, I'm hunting that prick down. My biggest decision will be if I draw his pain out or squish his immortal life out like the little insect he is.

Achilles moves with precision, navigating the swirling vortex of our mates' powers as he searches for a way to break through and free them from the Lurkers' grasp.

"I can't risk using my Fire," he grimly assesses, his gaze focused on the volatile currents around Rhea and Callie. "Their Winds would only fuel the flames, turning this place into an inferno. We'd end up killing everyone inside."

A group of wolf Shifters charge down a nearby staircase, but Achilles swiftly intercepts them, unleashing a torrent of flames. The first wolf succumbs to the intense heat, its fur charred, while the others retreat with singed coats.

Meanwhile, I unleash my aura upwards, transforming it into a cascade of blue light that fractures into a flock of my messengers. Falcons crafted from my sapphire starlight take flight, soaring across the sky to deliver the Herald's call for aid.

We desperately need assistance dealing with these Lurkers. The Morrigan managed to devour one that was plaguing Medusa's generals, but I don't know how the fuck we are supposed to destroy four of them.

With my power forming into a sword, I grasp the hilt tightly in both hands and thrust it into the swirling cyclone of dark clouds and wind. The beams of my blue light pierces through the gloom, illuminating the underground basement.

As my power contacts Rhea and Callie's shields, I'm immediately drawn into their harrowing ordeal. I see what they see, feel the pain they endure—it's overwhelming.

Forced to relive their darkest memories, they're transported back to a past life, when Rhea was known as Oizys. Both were held captive under the cruelty of Paris and Hector, trapped within the walls of Troy. They are reliving unspeakable torment, confined to Thaumium metal boxes, and subjected to horrific torture and abuse.

Rhea, in her selflessness, tries to shield Callie from the worst of the visions, bearing the burden of their shared suffering alone. Meanwhile, Callie fights to protect Rhea from the Lurkers, each girl fiercely defending the other as they face this onslaught of torment inflicted by the relentless entities.

With a primal scream reverberating through my being, I contend with the jarring sensations shooting up my arms as I strive to push my sword through the swirling defenses.

Finally, I manage to pierce the forcefield, and the Lurker within senses my approaching Light, emitting a shriek that reverberates through the confined space, intensifying their assault.

Outside the warehouse, my aura has reached others, thanks to the efforts of my falcons. Atlas wastes no time in responding to the call for help, swiftly arriving on the scene.

Bridget remains steadfast, her dark shield holding back a Lurker as she shields a group of frightened women huddled behind her, their desperate cries filling the air.

Without hesitation, Atlas springs into action, positioning himself between the Lurker and its unprotected victims. His Mind Shield forms a translucent barrier, shimmering with energy as it intercepts the dark entity's attacks.

The Lurker emits a bone-chilling wail, unleashing a dark beam at Atlas's shield. The impact is absorbed, causing ripples to cascade across his armor. Despite the strain, Atlas holds firm, reinforcing his shield to withstand the relentless assault.

As he defends the women against the Lurker, a cool wave of his power washes over the room, enveloping us all in its protective embrace.

Like being coated in cold metal, Atlas' abilities reinforce our minds. Psychic healing to the women behind him help them come back to their senses quicker. Some that are in better physical condition help the others. Two women drag the body of the dead and they huddle into a corner behind Atlas.

He takes slow steps back, thickening his shield and becoming an impenetrable wall of protection for the ladies behind him.

Empathic Support floods Bridget, Achilles, and me. Strengthening our mental fortitude and providing us with a sense of calm to combat the overwhelming grief of the Lurkers presence. Atlas' power neutralizes the feelings of despair, and he floods us with encouragement and resilience.

Without the crushing weight of the emotional attacks from the Lurkers, Bridget roars behind her dark shield. With trembling legs, she stands, and her shield grows.

Like Atlas, she is becoming an uncrossable barrier for the women she's protecting.

Achilles shoots a continuous projection of Fire at the Shadow Lurkers Atlas and Bridget are shielding against. The cleansing fire eats away at their shadows and his determination leaves them nothing to feed off.

But we need to destroy the Lurkers, not just shield against them. The only defense we have is Light and Dark power.

I keep pushing into the dome of shields created by Callie and Rhea. Their combined powers are too strong and it's talking all my strength to move forward one inch at a time.

Under continuous assault, the Lurkers trapped within their dome are feasting on the endless streams of death and pain from my mate.

My aura flares and another messenger of light shoots through the ceiling like a flash of lightning.

With my sword cut into the girl's dome, I pulse flashes of super-heated Absolute Light aimed at the Lurkers. If I can get one of them, or both of them to focus on me, perhaps they will stop attacking Rhea and Callie.

One of the Lurkers power slithers around me like the slippery tentacle of an octopus. It's scenting me just as a reptile tastes the air. The Lurkers determine Rhea's despair is the feast they want. So, they keep their gluttonous attacks on her.

Pushing harder against the shield generated by Rhea and Callie's panic, I finally cut through it enough to begin replacing it with my Light Shield. A spire of blue starlight cuts a straight line from the floor to the ceiling.

Spreading my Light outward, I add a Shield between the Lurkers and the girls.

My power blocks Callie first. Released from the Lurkers attack, both dark beings focus on Rhea.

Callie chokes on her coughs and sobs.

Sensing his mate is free, Achilles stops his flames and with his speed, he is by her side in a blink. She refuses to leave Rhea and as he grabs Callie's waist to pull her away, Callie keeps trying to get back to Rhea.

The force of the Lurkers attacks are causing Rhea's muscles

to lock and seize. Her eyes are rolled back into her head and white foam bubbles from her mouth.

Callie screams at Achilles to let her go but he keeps backing her away from the attacking Lurkers. Covered in sweat and dirt, her long hair sticks to her face as she thrashes to get out of her mates hold.

Gathering all my power, I grunt and push against the percussion of the Lurkers dark beams as my shield slowly makes progress.

A Dark portal swirl next to me, delivering Hecate and her Helhound from the call of my messenger.

Cerberus, her faithful guardian, grows in size. Splitting his form, the Helhound becomes four vicious canines of darkness and shadow. Vaulting across the subterranean dungeon the dogs attack the Lurkers that Atlas and Bridget are combating. Their growls arc across the space as they bite into the Lurkers. Snarling and jerking their large snouts, the four dogs work to pull the Lurkers away.

As the Lurkers are forced to defend themselves, Cerberus provides the necessary distraction, allowing Atlas and Bridget to change their stances.

With the Lurkers fighting the Helhounds, Bridge and Atlas join in the assault.

Atlas's iridescent power acts as a psychic counterattack. Expelling the negative energies of the Lurkers and projecting it back on them. Bridget opens her dark shield and within the murky center of nothingness, her power eats away at the first Lurker.

The two elementals are winded and sweat trickles from their hairline, but they keep fighting.

Hecate pierces the forcefield of Rhea's power opposite of

me and together we work to defend her. Convulsing and seizing, Rhea is locked in the Lurkers attack and her powers are running in chaotic streams around her.

Finally, our combined powers shield Rhea, and the Lurkers turn their attention to Hecate and I. Angered we pulled them from their feast, they open their void mouths to the ceiling. Their cry and anger is so powerful, it rips through the metal ceiling above us.

Steele beams twist and burst as a large hole is punched into the ceiling.

A fight is taking place up top. Shifter's battle each other's as lions fight against wolves. A powerful lioness grabs hold of a wolf by its throat and hurls it into the dark beam of the Lurkers scream. The body of the Shifter disintegrates into nothing.

Hecate and I employ a unified attack. We first bind the Lurkers with whips and ribbons of our powers. Mine in blue starlight and hers in black tendrils of shadow.

Pushing away from Achilles, Callie dives back to the floor for Rhea. Quickly checking her for injuries, Achilles lifts Rhea with an arm under her knees and one around her shoulders, pulling her away from the fight still taking place.

Cerberus has taken down one of the Lurkers. Atlas and Bridget have combined their assault on the other.

The Lurkers Hecate and I face are unable to free themselves from our snare and hammer against our bindings.

As the dark beam lances towards my face, I swiftly raise my hand, summoning a Light Shield to intercept the malevolent energy. My power engulfs the darkness, consuming it with entirely. Step by step, I press forward towards the looming figure, my muscles straining against the growing resistance.

I seize the Lurker by its icy, obscure face, enduring the

searing chill that burns my skin. Refusing to relent, I wrench the creature down to its knees with a forceful kick, then tilt its head back.

Despite the excruciating cold gnawing at my hand, I summon my sword of Light, the radiant blade gleaming with my fury. With a single thrust, I drive the sword down the Lurker's throat, piercing through its darkened flesh.

The pulse of my power surges into the Lurker, assaulting the darkness festering within the monster's dark core. The pulse of my power bombards the darkness within the monster until it's murky flesh splits open, ejecting my Light.

With her own dark spear, Hecate plunges her weapon into the Lurker she faces. Her shadows assail the creature much like my Light, rupturing its form of oppressive darkness.

Together, our powers converge, consuming the Lurkers in a blaze of radiant Light and engulfing Darkness. As their twisted forms are vanquished, the dismal shroud of sorrow that enveloped us begins to dissipate.

The lights of the warehouse shine brighter, casting away the shadows of fear and uncertainty. A collective breath of reassurance fills the air as we stand amidst the aftermath of our victory.

Everyone except me.

"Hermes," My sister chokes out a sob. "She's not moving."

A chill grips me as I kneel beside my mate, my heart heavy with concern. Callie tenderly cradles Rhea's head in her lap, gently stroking her hair as she whispers soothing reassurances. "It's okay now,"

"Let's clear the room of the survivors." Bridget says to someone behind me, but my attention remains fixed on the scene unfolding before me, the rest of the world fading into insignificance compared to this one corner of the warehouse basement where my mate lies.

Taking Rhea's hand in mine, I feel the tension coursing through her body, her muscles still locked in a relentless spasm. Though her eyes are closed, her fluttering eyelids are a sign of the turmoil within her. Opening my powers to her, I sense that she's trapped in a Memory Mirage, a torrent of terrible images flashing through her mind at an alarming pace, with no escape in sight.

The Lurkers, dark entities that thrive on emotions, wield their insidious power through obscure mirages that play out in the mind. With their victims ensnared in these relentless illusions, they feed off the endless cascade of negative emotions, drawing sustenance from their suffering.

For my mate, who has endured countless deaths and untold suffering throughout her immortal existence, she is undoubtedly a feast for such depraved beings.

"Atlas, please," I plead, tears streaming down my face as I gaze upon her suffering form. Her wounds may be of the mind, but they cut deeper than any physical affliction.

The mind, though the strongest muscle in our bodies, is also the most fragile. To see her wedged in this cycle of agony, reliving her past traumas over and over again, is a torment unto itself. She has already bore so much pain in her immortal life, and the thought of her enduring even more is unbearable.

Atlas kneels beside me, his body drenched in sweat and his hands trembling from the strain of battling the Lurker. In the past, asking such a favor of him would have been inconsequential, especially when he was still mated. But with my father gone and his bond with Ares severed, Atlas' powers are diminished. The task of aiding Rhea could potentially lead him to his own mental fracture.

"I promised never to enter her mind again without her consent," he murmurs, his touch hovering cautiously over Rhea's hand.

Before I can utter a plea, Callie speaks up, her voice trembling with emotion. "Please, Attie," she implores, her words punctuated by a soft hiccup. "She's suffering."

Atlas meets my gaze with his chestnut eyes, and despite the gravity of the situation, he manages a resolute smile. "Together, then," he agrees, his voice firm as he prepares to join me as we delve into Rhea's mind to offer her solace and aid.

"She doesn't like to be cold." I sniffle as I place two fingers on her right temple.

"I remember." Atlas answers as he places two fingers on her left.

Our powers surge through her together.

My Light clears the darkness of the images and I flood her with an avalanche of happy ones. Atlas's iridescence shimmers throughout her brain, coating the bruises with healing fortification and reassurance.

As we work with delicate patience, the tremors in Atlas' fingers travel up to his arm and then his body. He's nearing the end of his limits but she's not waking.

Minutes pass like hours and I feel like my heart is being pulled out of my chest.

Everyone holds a collective breath and when Atlas' nose begins to bleed, Hecate offers a gentle warning, "Atlas, you're pushing yourself too far."

"All is lost if we lose her again." He keeps his focus and never lets his touch or power waver from Rhea.

Her body calms and one by one her muscles relax. Atlas pales as his ability is draining him. Then finally, her eyelashes flutter.

As her eyes open, I feel like I'm watching the first burst of sun rays shine over the horizon. Her gaze looks to all of us as recognition settles over her. Tears drop down the sides of her face as I kiss her hand.

"You're okay." I tell her.

It's a reassurance, not a question. Physically, she's not hurt. But mentally, she was forced to relive insurmountable trauma. Emotionally, she's ravaged.

Rhea turns her head, finding Callie behind her and the two friends, as close as sisters, break into sobs. Rhea sits up and they cling to each other with desperation as they weep.

"I'm so sorry, Callie." Rhea's voice cracks with sorrow.

"It's not your fault." Callie tries to comfort Rhea, but her own pain is too great, and she can barely speak the words.

Callie's initial fear for Rhea turns to mourning as she weeps over the images they saw under the Lurkers attack. Rhea's weariness turns to shades of guilt, as if apologetic of what Callie was forced to see.

My sister begins to crumple, and Rhea shifts her hold on her. Achilles and I are confused, why Rhea is now the one comforting Callie.

"I forgot him." Callie finally bursts out. "How could I forget him?"

Achilles places his hand on his mate's cheek as she sobs. The grimace on his face deepens as heartbreak settles in seeing her so upset. "Forget who?"

Rhea covers her mouth and nose with her hand, trying to quiet her own cries. I wish she would just look at me. I only want to know that she is okay.

"I tried to shield you from it. I wasn't strong enough, Callie. I'm so sorry."

"Rhea, what happened?" I ask my mate in her mind, desperate to understand what is going on.

"There was an auction." Even through her telepathic account, I hear Rhea's sobs. *"The Shifters were torturing and selling the women. We had to help."* Rhea breaks to collect herself before continuing. *"We saved them, but Flint showed up with Lurkers. They attacked us so quickly. I didn't know what to do. I didn't know how to stop it."*

"Stop what? What did they make you see?"

"My past life as Oizys." Rhea pauses as the admission pulls a fresh bout of tears. Then composing herself she

continues. *"Callie was a captive with me. It was a thousand years in Troy."*

I close my eyes knowing the horrors of Troy. Callie spent two decades in the prince's torment. When Rhea lived as Danaë, it was centuries.

But...a thousand years.

It's unfathomable to imagine their suffering for a millennium of Paris and Hectors derangement.

"Who is she talking about forgetting?"

Rhea finally turns her head, looking at me with bloodshot eyes. *"Patroclus."* A fresh wave of tears flows from her admission.

"I don't understand." Callie hasn't forgotten Pat. If anything, she, and Achilles live each day for the memory of their fallen mate.

"You came for us. With Pat and Achilles, you came for us." Rhea closes her eyes, squeezing the tears from them before she explains. *"They bonded during that meeting. And a week later, I was killed by a cloaked figure. The world reset; your minds reset."*

"And we forgot." I finish the explanation, so Rhea doesn't have to.

Still cradled in Rhea's arms, Callie's tears begin to subside as Achilles speaks to her in hushed tones, offering words of comfort and gently stroking her hair. Callie nods periodically at her mates comforting words.

Remaining on the lower level, I take advantage of the moonlight filtering in from above to survey the aftermath of the battle. The ground above bears the scars of a second conflict, marked by stains of immortal ichor where the fallen bodies of Shifters lay.

Lucas and Kai arrived with Zara's brother, Kellan, along

with their packs. The healers tend to the wounded, while Atlas and Hecate distribute blankets and warm soup, offering solace in the wake of the night's horrors.

Yet despite their efforts, the trauma of the events weighs heavily upon everyone present. There is not a woman up there who won't carry the scars of tonight with them forever.

Callie eventually calms herself and wipes her face. Sitting up, Rhea doesn't want to look at her.

"Hey," Callie whispers. "Say it."

Rhea shakes her head, not wanting to answer.

"We'll weather all storms." My sister begins to recite the mantra of their lasting friendship. "We'll overcome." Callie continues as Rhea finds her breath again.

Callie pulls her away and makes Rhea look at her. "And what else? What else are we going to do?" Callie asks with a sniff.

"We'll survive."

My sister gives Rhea a sad smile. "It means more than just getting though things, Rhea. *We* will survive; our friendship."

Rhea chokes on a fresh wave of tears as Callie pulls her back into a hug.

"Our friendship will survive anything." Callie tells her.

Achilles wipes a tear before it can fall down his cheek and I give my old friend a nod. He returns it, letting me know he's okay as well.

As we lean against the side of the warehouse, exhaustion weighing heavily upon us, I can't help but sigh in relief.

Callie and Rhea cry as they reassure each other and eventually Callie makes a joke about making Achilles and I age faster. Rhea laughs, despite trying to remain solemn.

With one more hug, our mates leave each other and come to us.

Callie climbs in Achilles' lap and they rest their foreheads together. "This realm was about to turn to ash if I couldn't get to you soon, little siren."

As Rhea bashfully slides towards me, her lip caught between her teeth, I reach out with a ribbon of my light and pull her toward me faster. I hold her tightly, savoring the feel of her in my arms, and bury my face in the crook of her neck, inhaling her essence deeply.

"Gods, I'm so glad you're not hurt," I whisper against the soft skin at the base of her neck, pressing a gentle kiss there. Rhea sighs softly and melts into my embrace. "But are you okay?" I ask, my concern evident in my voice.

Her response is quiet, but steady. "No. But I will be," she murmurs kissing me back.

We bask in the quiet, comforting our mates and letting them settle into the safety of this reality. Though the memories of past pain may linger, they no longer pose a threat.

In this moment, as we hold each other close, I realize that there may a few things Rhea and I disagree on. But one thing is certain—no matter what challenges lie ahead; she will be okay.

And I will forfeit my immortal life to ensure it.

23

"You promised."

It's nothing more than a whisper that claws at me from within the darkness of the cave. The great cyclops' skull, towering like an ancient sentinel at the cave's entrance, seems to watch me with an ominous gaze, its hollow socket filled with darkness.

"You promised." The small voice carries through the dark cave and meets me where I stand at the entrance.

"Teddy?" Teddy's name escapes my lips, laced with a hint of panic as I struggle to maintain composure.

Outside, the warm desert air beckons, mingling with the swirling sand in the harsh sunlight. But the threshold between light and shadow feels like a precipice and I'm teetering on the edge of falling over. The mouth of the cyclops is coated in heavy obscurity, drawing me in with an irresistible pull and waiting to swallow me whole.

Ted's voice, filled with anguish, echoes from the depths of the cave, driving me forward despite the fear that grips me.

"Keep talking to me, Ted!" I shout, my voice reverberating down the dark tunnel ahead of me. But all I hear in response are muffled cries, sending a shiver down my spine.

"T-Teddy?" I call out again, my heart pounding with dread. I refuse to let him be alone in this abyss.

As I press on, the sound of my footsteps reverberate against the rocky floor, intermingling with Ted's cries. Yet, despite my efforts, I can't detect the direction of his pleas. My powers, usually a source of guidance, fail me in this moment, the Light remaining stubbornly silent amongst the shadows.

With each step, the darkness closes in around me, threatening to engulf me entirely. But I push forward, driven by a desperate need to find Ted.

With my hands skimming the rough walls for guidance, I hurry my pace as Teddy's sobs escalate into piercing screams, accompanied by a deep and menacing growl. His fear is palpable, and now he's not alone in the darkness.

"Don't touch him!" I shout, my voice tinged with desperation, echoing off the cavern walls.

"Goddess, help me," Teddy's desperate cry resonates through the cavern, mirroring my own sense of urgency.

"Ted!" I cry out, abandoning my cautious approach and breaking into a sprint. His terror is overwhelming, and I refuse to let him suffer alone.

As I navigate the labyrinthine tunnels, my heart pounds in my chest, a symphony of dread and determination pounds within me with each beat. Despite my efforts, the darkness seems to thwart my every move, my powers rendered useless in this abyss.

I continue to run, twisting and turning through the maze of tunnels, until I collide with a dead-end. Scraping my elbows and hands against the unforgiving cave walls, I press on.

The screams grow fainter, muffled by the oppressive darkness, and I sense Teddy's struggle as he gasps for air. *Not again.* He can't endure this pain again.

I curse these powers. Why won't they work when I need them the most? With determination fueling my every step, I forge ahead, refusing to relent until I find him.

"Gods, Teddy, just hang on."

A vivid green glow emanates from a turn in the tunnel ahead, drawing me toward it with an urgency that consumes my senses. With every ounce of determination, I rush forward, my heart pounding in my chest as I anticipate what awaits me.

Skidding to a stop as I round the corner, I'm met with a sight that chills me to the core. A cloaked figure looms before me, holding Teddy with a vice-like grip on his shirt. Bright green eyes pierce through the darkness of the cloak, locking onto mine with an unsettling intensity.

Teddy's lifeless form hangs limply, his pale eyes staring blankly into oblivion, a gaping wound in his throat oozing blood onto the dirt and rock floor.

"No," I gasp, my voice barely a whisper as the weight of despair settles over me like a suffocating blanket.

With a sickening gesture, the dark figure spits out a chunk of flesh from their mouth, dropping Teddy's body to the ground with callous disregard. Blood coats their chin, as a sinister grin twists their lips, revealing blood-stained teeth.

They revel in their victory, knowing that I have failed to save Teddy in time.

As maggots writhe and squirm from Teddy's lifeless form, and black tar seeps from his ears, a wave of revulsion washes over me, threatening to overwhelm my senses.

Before I can react, the cloaked figure is upon me, their green eyes burning with malice as a clawed hand tightens around my throat, cutting off my air supply. Panic surges through me as I struggle against the granite grip.

My gaze remains fixed on the kitchen counter, but I'm lost in a whirlwind of memories from the previous night. The auction, Lexi, Flint, the Lurkers—each image flashes through my mind like scenes from a nightmare.

"Are you okay?" Atlas's voice breaks through my trance, drawing me back to the present. He sets a fresh cup of coffee in front of me, his concern evident in the furrow of his brow as he studies me over the rim of his glasses.

New glasses, because his old ones were last in the dark dome when I stole his soul and trapped it, nearly killing him.

The amount of death that surrounds me is enough to drown the realm.

Clearing my throat and reaching for the cup, I try to shake off the lingering effects of these depressing thoughts and last night's dream. "Yeah, I'm fine," I murmur, though even I don't believe the words as they leave my lips.

Atlas raises an eyebrow skeptically, his smirk betraying his amusement. "Oh, like anyone would ever believe that answer," he retorts, taking a sip of his coffee. Despite my attempt to hide it, a small smile tugs at the corners of my lips.

"Something is very much bothering you," he continues, his tone softening with genuine concern. "And if you ever need someone to talk to, I'm here."

"Something is bothering you." I repeat the phrase in my mind with a snort of irony.

Well, that's an understatement. What's not bothering me?

A deranged lunatic is hellbent on ending my life. His son sent shadow beings to attack me in a twisted attempt to play the hero. Meanwhile, a foreboding cave in another realm haunts my dreams, while the world teeters on the brink of annihilation as superpowers clash in a deadly game of war.

And then there are those haunting green glowing eyes, an enigma that refuses to be ignored.

Every time those eyes come to mind, I'm transported back to that fateful night outside the Atlanta Commune, where Medusa's gaze held the same eerie emerald glow. The memory sends a chill down my spine, leaving me shuddering involuntarily.

And then there's Triton, and the cryptic revelation he shared with me just before I took his life. Closing my eyes, I'm engulfed by the memories he imparted me with mingle with the mysterious figure that haunts my dreams. The green essence that stalks my sleep lurks just beyond the edges of my consciousness, waiting to engulf me with every blink of my eyes.

And it seems as if this haunting figure has been lurking at the edges of our trusted circle, maneuvering chess pieces when no one was looking and playing a secret game only they knew about.

Atlas raises an eyebrow, his expression betraying a keen awareness of the burdens weighing heavily on my shoulders. Even without his formidable Mind Mage abilities, it's clear my secrets are begging to be unleashed, a crushing weight that threatens to consume me if I don't confess them soon.

Conceding to the weight of my thoughts, I gesture for Atlas to follow me. With our cups in hand, we make our way to my home library, where I draw the large glass sliding doors closed behind us.

Knots form in my stomach as I consider how to broach the topic that weighs heavily on my mind. Taking a sip of the hot coffee, I find some comfort in the warmth spreading through me, calming my nerves.

Atlas stands before me, his demeanor patient yet attentive. One hand rests casually in the pocket of his khaki pants, while the sleeves of his chocolate brown button-down shirt are rolled halfway up his tan forearms. He holds his own cup of coffee, awaiting my words.

"Can you keep a secret?" I finally ask, my chest tight with anticipation, nervousness bubbling within me.

"Rhea, are you in danger?" Concern coats his words, and he steps closer, dropping his voice to match my secretive tone.

I relax my shoulders and thin my lips at the ridiculous question. "Did you really just ask me that?"

"You know what I mean," Atlas scoffs. "If there is immediate danger to you, we cannot keep that from Hermes."

"Ares isn't working alone," I blurt out, unable to contain the revelation any longer.

"I know that. He never has. What is this about?" Atlas presses, his curiosity piqued.

I shift closer, setting my coffee down on a table next to a wide armchair in the corner of my library. "I think you should look at my memories," I suggest, my voice hushed.

"Rhea," Atlas begins, but I raise my hand to cut him off.

"Something is calling me to Tartarus," I continue, crossing my arms over my chest. Dropping my tone just above a whisper, I lean in closer, knowing Atlas will understand the gravity of my admissions. "I'm having dreams and seeing something intertwined with several of my memories."

I pause, listening for any signs of eavesdroppers from the living room when Hermes and Callie erupt in laughter. "If Ares is collecting powers, hunting me for mine, who's to say someone else didn't get the same idea? What if there are other immortals, stealing powers and keeping multiple abilities a secret?"

"You have someone in mind, don't you?" Atlas inquires, his hands shoved into his pockets as he meets my gaze with a thoughtful expression.

"Look at my memories first," I urge, extending my hand towards him.

Atlas rubs his smooth chin, his chestnut eyes drifting to the side as he considers my request. "Okay, just don't throw me across the room this time?" he jests, a sly smirk playing on his lips.

"Not funny," I reply, poking his chest playfully before holding my hand out expectantly.

"It's a little funny," he quips, teasingly.

As I concentrate, I project the memories I want Atlas to see, spanning across the ages.

The first vision emerges, depicting an old woman raising an obsidian blade over my head as rain pours down upon me. It's a scene from long ago, atop the great Mayan pyramid where I was sacrificed.

In this vision, I notice for the first time the yellow glimmer of deceit that coats the green aura of the immortal as they ended my life. They had disguised themselves as an old woman to conceal their true identity, utilizing either mimicry like Kai or a powerful Mirage to conceal their appearance.

Next, I share the painful ending of my life as Oizys, reincarnated and trapped in a cycle of misery. The cloaked figure emerges from the darkness, striking me in the chest with a dagger only seven days after my rescue from Troy. Their eyes shine green within the cloak, illuminated by their jade aura.

I show Atlas the haunting dreams of the cave, where green eyes lurk from within the darkness. He visibly flinches as I reveal the recent nightmare involving Teddy and the figure spitting out the child's torn throat.

Finally, I unveil the secret memory Triton shared with me, the one he believed others were not yet ready to face. Triton warned of a great sacrifice that would be paid in exchange for belief.

As I watch Atlas absorb the memory, my anxiety surges. What if I'm not strong enough to bear the price Triton spoke of? What if someone else must pay it in my place? The thought is agonizing, and I squeeze my eyes shut; I would rather shoulder the burden myself than allow it to fall upon another.

But perhaps, if I can rally a few allies to my cause, if I can help them see the truth early on, we might be able to work together to aid the others. Triton didn't share this memory with Hermes, deeming him unprepared for such truth. So, I'm placing my bets on Atlas, hoping he'll have the open mind needed to consider the traitor within our trusted circle.

As the memory unfolds before us, Atlas's eyes widen in shock as the cloaked figure steps onto Triton's boat, commanding the elements with ease. They manipulate Water, walking upon it as if it were solid ground. They control Wind, forcing it to stillness and halting Triton's fleet in the middle of the ocean. And then, they wield Light, projecting a massive

Mirage to deceive Triton into believing that Aphrodite's fleet is in dire peril.

Atlas gasps audibly as the figure removes their hood, revealing their identity. His grip tightens around my hand as he watches his trusted friend, now revealed as a betrayer, manipulate green fire, and place it in canisters around Triton's ship.

Atlas's expression is a mixture of disbelief and contemplation. The memory ends when braided tendrils of Medusa's hair hoist the jars of eternal burning fire along the ship, allowing Atlas a moment to absorb the gravity of the situation.

"Think about it," I urge him, my voice steady despite the nerves within me. "I need you to be logical right now, not emotional."

Atlas meets my gaze, his eyes searching mine as he wrestles with the implications of what he's witnessed.

"Someone set up Ana and Ava a year in advance with Lurkers. They were told about shutting down the portal a month before Hermes and I even met. How?"

"But it can't be," he protests, his voice tinged with disbelief.

"Who lured us out of the commune the night we visited Hecate? Who controlled the portal that delivered us back to the plain where Shifters were ready for us? Think, Atlas."

Atlas shakes his head, not wanting to believe.

"It wasn't Ares' ambush; it was Medusa delivering me to Ares under a ruse."

Sitting down in the chair, Atlas rests his elbows on his knees as he runs his hands through his hair in exasperation.

"Only one commune was attacked by the Dark Mage. Why not use the surprise to attack other communes? Aryana left Kenya after she killed her sisters. There is a reason why."

As I lay out the pieces of the puzzle, Atlas sits back, his mind whirling with possibilities he stares off across the room. But I press on, determined to uncover the truth behind the tangled web of deception that threatens us all.

"To make sure someone like you couldn't look into their minds and see the truth. To clean up and make sure secrets stayed buried. Someone has been a step ahead at every turn, and last night, I finally figured out how."

He waits for me to continue and I stop pacing.

"Because this has all happened before. We keep living the same cycles over and over again. Each life, I leave a small trail of clue to follow and unlock and I believe Medusa and Ares do as well."

I try to calm my breathing, but as I continue, my nerves keep building. "We know others have remained close to me, stolen my trust. Terra and Demeter. Do you honestly think they could be the only ones?"

Atlas hasn't said anything this entire time. His cheeks are flush with emotion, his eyes are wide in surprise.

What if he doesn't believe me? I need someone to help me convince the others, so we don't fall into any more traps.

"Just answer this if you don't believe me. What brought Hermes to the bookstore the day he met me?"

Atlas closes his eyes in resignation. Rubbing his hand down his face, he exhales.

"Tell me."

"Three days before–" Atlas hesitates, swallowing heavily. "Three days before, Medusa contacted Eris and told her there was a high likelihood of a Shifter altercation at the signing event."

He closes his eyes and furrows his brow as if not wanting to say anything further. "Eris wanted to send a pair of scouts, but Medusa insisted Eris send Hermes and his team. But how would anyone know you would be there?"

"Three days before the event, I confirmed my attendance through the bookstore's newsletter email."

Atlas bends over and rests his hands on his knees, taking deep breaths.

"Medusa is an ally of Ares," The truth in the statement adds to the weight of my words and the heaviness of her betrayal. "And she's going to attempt to kill me."

*"**P**aging the great Mind Mage of Gaea and the beautiful goddess of the realms to the living room, please."* I sense Rhea chuckle from our library where she and Atlas have been chatting for the last twenty minutes.

Callie, Achilles, and I have been looking across our memories and trying to piece together the gaps. Something we noticed during my infamous race with Achilles, made us curious. Atlas and Rhea emerge from the hall that leads to our home library. Atlas takes her empty coffee cup along with his to the kitchen, and they exchange a nod.

Rhea releases a deep breath, and it seems as if she unloads fifty pounds of stress from her shoulders. Whatever they were speaking about, I'm glad Atlas can be a source of counseling for her. I know I would not have made it through the cycles of her deaths without him.

My eyes roam the length of Rhea's curved body. The black tights and wine-colored crop top hug her figure like the waters that cling to a shoreline. The shirt's scoop neck reveals a hint of cleavage, and I want to kiss her chest where her full breasts are pressed together under her clothes.

Her wavy brown hair with golden-honey tones sways low

on her back, in time with her hips as she makes her way to me. My hands ache, wanting to grab those curves and pull her onto my lap.

Continuing to consume the sight of her, my gaze meets hers, and she cocks an eyebrow, holding back a smirk.

"See something you like, Herald?" She speaks into my mind, sitting next to me on the couch. Her hand goes to my leg and rubs in the inside of my thigh.

The force of her nearness is like gravity, pulling me to her, and my hand mimics hers. The smooth pants cling to her legs, and I run my hand in circles, longing to touch her bare skin.

"I could show you all the appealing things I see." My eyes flick to the peeking cleavage as I watch her chest rise and fall with her breath.

"They'll see us."

"They won't." A smug grin slides along my face when her cheeks turn pink. I squeeze her thigh before she tenses, pushing her legs together in response. *"Do you like the thought of that, little goddess? Do you want me to fuck you under a Mirage so no one can see you come?"*

My hand moves slowly inward, inching high on her leg. Her gilded eyes search across the room as Atlas pours a fresh coffee for himself. Callie chuckles softly at something Achilles whispers in her ear.

With a gentle vibration at the tip of my fingers, I let two fingers trail up her pussy. Gods, this is delicious torture on myself, but it's worth it to watch her mouth part with a sharp intake of air. My cock twitches, wanting her lips wrapped around me while those big golden eyes look up at me. *Fuck.*

"Already so wet." I purr in her mind, and she closes her eyes, only briefly before opening them again. Rhea fights to look

composed while she squirms under my touch. *"But could you be quiet though?"*

My fingers stroke up and down the slit between her legs, and she lets me. I increase the vibrations of my fingers, and she shifts ever so subtly. She wants more.

"Oh, you do want me to fuck you in front of everyone." I croon with satisfaction.

Leaning into her, the silky ribbons of her hair surround my face, and I take the lobe of her ear between my teeth. Her berry and vanilla perfume fill my senses, and I root her sweet smell as deeply within me as I can. She tries to contain the faint whimper that escapes her, making me smile. Raising the two fingers that played with her to my mouth, I pause.

"Be a good girl, and I will." I whisper before I plunge the two fingers into my mouth, sucking off the essence of her arousal.

She drops her mouth open in shock, and I steal a chaste kiss.

"You are terrible." Rhea leans into me, wrapping her arms around my waist, leaning against me.

"No, I'm here to worship you. And I intend to any moment I can." I kiss the top of her head as Atlas joins the room, sitting on the edge of the couch opposite us.

"So, what's up?" Atlas asks, looking at the four of us over the rim of his glasses.

I use the Light and project the memories shared of the race between Achilles and me. Callie and I both remembered things differently between us, and Achilles had a different version.

The visions I show on the tall white wall behind Atlas show the three of us walking down a dirt road that leads out of ancient Rome.

Atlas stands, getting close to inspect the images, and it's like a game to spot the differences. The backgrounds are different. In Callie's memory, it was nighttime. Our clothes all vary, and even the incident that started the race is not the same between us.

"It's déjà vu," Atlas whispers to himself.

"How can we have three different memories?" I ask.

"Four," Rhea adds, and we turn to look at her at once.

Her sharp eyes are trained on Callie as if the two friends are speaking silently between them. My sister nods her head, and Rhea uses the Light and adds her memory to ours. Collectively, we take in a gulp of air at the sight of five friends walking together.

We watch Pat as he walks in the center of Callie and Achilles. He and Achilles hold hands while Pat's arm is around Callie's waist.

My mate, Nyx, and I are next to them. In the memory, Pat says something and we all double over with laughter. His frosted green eyes glimmer as he watches us and his smile shines brighter.

"Look how handsome our Flame was." Callie says in a low tone to Achilles before cupping his face and placing a kiss on his cheek. The pair of mates lean into their embrace as they soak in Rhea's projection.

I draw Rhea in closer, feeling the weight of her guilt seeping into my touch. With a gentle motion, I intertwine our fingers, lifting her hand to press a soft kiss against her skin. She shares a glance, knowing the sight we're about to reveal will tug at our friends' heartstrings.

Yet, after spending countless hours reminiscing about Patroclus, we've shed tears for the sorrowful moments, chuckled at the humorous ones and now, there's a quiet acceptance in simply cherishing the memories we have.

Atlas clears his throat and steps to the side. Instantly, it's like we are younglings under his tutorship as he turns on his instructor mode. He gestures towards the projection, directing our attention to the subtle glow surrounding Callie's sandals.

"See the glimmer around Callie's sandals when looking at Hermes' memory?" There is a blue glow matching my aura around her shoes. "Hermes can't recall the exact sandals, so his memory filled in something similar and this residue surrounding the area is a clue."

Callie interjects with a playful jab, lightening the mood. "I can't believe you don't remember what shoes I wore. They were super cute." Her joke earns her a dramatic roll of my eyes.

As we scrutinize the other memories, we notice luminous ripples enveloping various elements from our shared past. A bronze aura surrounds my stola in Achilles' memory, while a golden gleam dances around a towering tree in Callie's recollection. Yet, in Rhea's memory, there's no trace of silver shimmer; each detail remains crystal clear in her mind.

"We often impart this knowledge to young Mind Mages," Atlas explains. "It helps them in distinguishing between true recollections and fabricated details."

"But what about the discrepancies in settings, times of day?" Callie asks, her hand gesturing toward the projections. "How can they differ so drastically?"

An exchange of glances between Atlas and Rhea prompts my curiosity to peak. "You two seem to have already discussed this," I remark to Rhea, sensing a shared understanding between them.

Rhea delicately picks at her nail before offering an explanation. "These are four distinct events," she begins, her voice tinged with somber recognition.

"The race between Achilles and Hermes has happened at least four times throughout our history. In the memories you three witnessed, I was absent. But in mine, we were together, and shortly thereafter, we faced Ares in battle, and I—" Her voice catches, and she swallows hard. "—I died not long after."

Rhea sits on the edge of the cushion, resting her elbows on her knees.

I rub her back and sensing she has more to say, we wait.

"The last lifetime of Pat was during the Trojan war when I lived as Danaë. You don't remember him in any lifetime before that, just as Hermes didn't recall any previous version of me before Juliet."

It must be a facet of her spell, the greatest Mirage that has been cast in all of magic.

Atlas looks off as if lost in thought. Callie and Achilles nod their heads either in agreement or contemplation.

"Because the imprint of Death is final and there is no coming back from that." Rhea sniffles and I look to her.

The bitter echo of Medusa's words from last night reverberates in my mind like a haunting melody. *"Why can't she bring Athena back to life?"* Her contempt swirls within me, a tempest of emotions threatening to erupt into a torrent of rage if left unchecked.

I know I must speak with her again, but time feels scarce, slipping through my fingers like sand as everything converges at once.

"I'm sorry I deprived you of your memories of Patroclus," Rhea murmurs, her voice heavy with sorrow as she closes her eyes. I lean in, enveloping her in a comforting embrace.

"It's as if with each death, the realm seals itself off from that chapter of existence. So much has been lost, and I wish I could restore what was taken from you."

My mate's tears flow freely, and Callie kneels beside her, gently taking Rhea's hands in hers. "Achilles, Patroclus, and I found each other. We cherished our time together, and though we had to say goodbye, Pat will always remain in our hearts," Callie reassures, her words laced with empathy. But Rhea continues to shrink under the weight of her grief.

"You didn't cause us pain intentionally," Callie adds, her voice a beacon of compassion. "You didn't do this to hurt us, you did it to protect us all. We'll be eternally grateful for the sacrifice you have made for us, and for the realm."

"I wish I could bring him back for you." Rhea finally looks at Callie and begins to calm as she admits the truth of what is weighing down her guilt. "I wish I could harness this power for good, rather than being a harbinger of destruction."

The two friends hug until Rhea calms again. "I'll find a way to bring back your memories of him." Rhea promises and Callie brightens at the prospect of having more recollections of her lost mate.

The girls retreat to our bedroom, wanting to lay down and nap. They both had a long night, exhausted from their battle and attack of the Lurkers.

The days are melting away from us, as the next alignment nears.

We have four days remaining until the eclipse and as the scales of the realm began to tip with the start of Mabon, I feel the doorway to Tartarus is going to bring a world of pain upon us.

I know Rhea wants to travel there and explore these urges

she's having. But if there is a chance I can save her from pain and keep her alive, I'm going to take it. Even if she hates me after, she'll not be the one who jumps in front of me this time, when her life is on the line.

Atlas excuses himself to Delphi to rest as well and Achilles and I make lunch.

I'm honestly surprised Atlas is on his feet from last night's fight, but Hecate brought Flora to the warehouse to help heal the victims. Flora fixed Atlas up after attending to all the ladies from the auction but he pushed himself pretty far.

Sitting outside, Achilles and I enjoy the deceivingly calm weather as we eat our sandwiches.

I'm still irritated that Hecate and Atlas didn't feel it was necessary to warn us that Lurkers had been released from the Labyrinth or that Archangel Michael was murdered. Rhea and I should have been told so we could make sure she was protected.

A complaint I'm taking up with my mentor as soon as he's rested.

Something else from last night keeps ringing in my mind but I don't want to bother Rhea with my questions just yet. "Did you find out why Flint was there?"

"Yeah, it's fucked up." Achilles says with a mouthful of black forest ham and colby-jack cheese sandwich. Wiping his mouth on the striped napkin, I'm dangling on the edge of my patience for him to continue.

"She's mine." The words Flint grumbled as he teleported away kept me up all night. On top of all of this, do we really have to worry about some piss-ant like Flint as well?

"He says Rhea is his mate."

"You're fucking kidding."

"I swear to the goddess." Achilles says raising his hand to the sky. Taking a large gulp of orange soda, he continues with Callie's account of what happened before we arrived.

Flint brought the Lurkers with him. He spoke a different language controlling them and then screamed at Rhea that he is her true mate.

"That couldn't be possible." I dismiss the ravings as Flints lunacy. Or perhaps it's a ploy to confuse Rhea concocted by Ares. "We are soul-bound. Just because my mate lives in a new body, it's the same goddess I found on the edge of the realms."

We eat in silence, the weight of unspoken words hanging heavy in the air.

"What was it like for you and Pat?" I inquire of Achilles, breaking the stillness.

"Before we bonded with Callie?" he clarifies, his gaze meeting mine.

I nod, taking a bite of my sandwich as I await his response.

"It was like learning to walk with one leg missing," Achilles reflects, his expression contemplative. "We were constantly off-balance, stumbling through life with a void that begged to be filled."

He reaches for a chip, the sound of its crunch bouncing across the portico. "Why do you ask? You don't believe there's any truth to Flint's claim, do you?"

"I would feel it too then, right?" I mull over the thought, staring into the distance.

"Pat was my mate, just as much as he was Callie's," Achilles answers and I can't sense the oncoming grin.

Sure enough, his smile widens mischievously, signaling the impending jest. "Has Flint caught your eye too?" he jokes, prompting me to throw my napkin at him in mock annoyance. He catches it effortlessly, his laughter filling the air.

"Fuck off. I'm going to slap Flint with his remaining hand and then use it to kill him."

"What if she does have two mates, though?" Achilles muses, his voice taking on a more serious tone. "Could you handle that? With so much of our past shrouded in mystery, what if this is just another layer of the spell waiting to be unveiled?"

The question echoes in my mind as we lapse back into silence. Could I truly accept such a possibility? If Rhea's destiny entailed more than one elemental mate, could I swallow my pride and endure seeing Flint by her side?

The world spins around me in a dizzying whirl of chaos and confusion, mirroring the shattered fragments of the mirror I've just broken. Thoughts collide and scatter like glass, cutting deep into the recesses of my anger. But amidst the turmoil, one thought remains clear and unwavering: Rhea.

In the caves where I've sought refuge, my screams reverberate, mingling with her muted whimpers. The bindings around her mouth stifle her voice, and though it pains me to see her silenced, I know it's necessary for now. I cherish her words and the freedom of her lips, but this precaution is crucial.

She'll understand soon.

This cave has some tattered comforts, marking its frequent use over the ages. I plop down in a worn leather chair, cracked, and aged to time.

Stroking the patchy stubble that's grown on my chin over the last few days, I wonder if Rhea enjoys facial hair but I'm too angry over last night's interruption to dwell on that right now.

Could she have called Hermes to her last night? Surely she

wouldn't be so cruel to me. I know what I felt when we locked eyes, and it was nothing short of love. I'm certain she felt it too.

If she had a better mate by her side, how could I have taken her so easily as she slept? Surely the great Messenger of the Gods would be a better steward over her safety, if he were truly her destined mate.

This is my reassurance it's time for Rhea and me to be together.

Only I can protect her the way she deserves and help her get her powers back. I just need some time to collect myself before our next move.

Walking up to her, she flinches when I move her hair behind her ear. Soon, she won't react that way at my touch. She'll come to crave my nearness once we're bonded so I'm not going to punish her again for being frightened.

She's so brave. In the face of everything, I admire her courage so much. Even now, shackled against the rocky cave wall, she's barely trembling anymore, and I know it's because she's working to get through this fear she has of me.

Her wrists are bound and strung over her head and there is a gentle sway to her body as she hangs from the metal chain. Rhea is so much more beautiful when she's naked and if I had my way, she would never wear clothes again.

I release a heavy sigh as I move my gaze from her full breasts so I can look into her eyes. She holds my stare with one of her own. She's so fierce and it brings a small smile to my face.

"You are the focal point of my existence, the flare that guides me through the dark. I am your mate, destined to be by your side, to protect you, to love you with this passion that utterly consumes me." She whimpers again, trying to move her head away as I cup her cheek. Tears stream down her face and she mumbles, though I can't understand her through the gag. "You just don't see it yet, princess. You don't understand the depths of my devotion, the lengths to which I will go to make you mine."

I cup her breast in my hand and run my thumb over her nipple. My cock strains when I see her skin pebble with goosebumps. Gods, I know she enjoys the way I touch her.

"Look at that," I whisper as I take her breast in my mouth. "We're going to be so great together."

I take the switch blade from my pocket and graze it down the soft mound and she flinches when it nicks her nipple. "Mmmmm, I'll clean that up." I swirl my tongue around the little line of bright red blood. She tips her head back, sobbing toward the ceiling.

She's probably so happy but I can see how this can be confusing.

"I tried to be your hero. But Hermes is nothing more than a constant nuisance to you and he interrupted us." I pull her hair back as my anger takes over my control again. She yelps into the gag, and I watch her throat as she swallows. I like the way her neck moves with the action, and I unzip my pants.

I just need to be with her. *Everything will be better when I'm with her.*

"But we'll try again, princess. I'll make you realize that I am the one you've been searching for all along."

Letting go of her hair, I release the chain suspending her from the ceiling. She falls a little too hard when I lose my one-handed grip. Her knees bang the rocky ground, scraping them and she falls forward, unable to catch herself.

I help her sit up and move her shackles behind her back. I

squeeze the round globe of her bare behind when I've locked her bindings again.

"This time, I'll lure you away from Hermes, so *you* can save the day. And when you've emerged victorious, and stand as the hero of your own story, you'll finally see me for who I am. You'll see the depths of my love, the fire that burns for you and you alone. I know you'll fall for me, just as I've fallen for you."

Taking my dick in my hand, I stroke myself, mere inches from her face.

Her hot gaze shifts from my cock to my eyes and it only excites me more.

"So, how was that?" I ask my little pretend Rhea. "Do you think she'll like that?"

The woman I took from one of the packhouse raids is a poor representation of *my* Rhea, but her hair is almost the same color. She's the right height and while her eyes are hazel, I can pretend this woman is my mate.

But footsteps descending from the caves entrance make me grunt in frustration.

My fathers' goons. They are fucking ruining everything.

"Is it too much to ask for two godsdamned minutes?" I call toward the mouth of the cave as I put my erection away. Stroking my finger down the woman's face, I give her a soft smile, "Soon, okay?"

She grunts and shakes her head away from my touch.

"Is that all the time you need, big boy?" The ladies invading the peace of my cave chuckle and it echoes across the rocky walls, mocking me a dozen times over.

"I could take longer– if I wanted." I seethe in response.

"Sure." Aryana gives me a sidelong glance as she keeps walking onward into the deep darkness of the cave. Obscurity flows off her in waves as she amplifies the shadows that surround her.

My captive is helped to her feet and pushed further into the cave.

"She goes back with the others. All twenty-four are going in the first batch." The Gorgon walks ahead of me with my pretend-Rhea. "Let's not fuck this up like you did the Lurkers."

Fucking bitch, who is she talking to me that way?

I would kill Medusa now if it weren't for father's plans. His schemes will give me the perfect cover to get what I need to be Rhea's mate. Then I'll be as strong as she is, and we'll take over this realm together.

"Are you coming?" Medusa pauses her track deeper into the cave.

"Yeah." Answer, reigning back my control with deep steady breaths.

I can do anything for you, Rhea. You'll see.

I can see the Great Library in my memories as I look at the old architectural sketch of Alexandria. The tan parchment, burned and brown around the edges, has likely not been unrolled in centuries. Today is probably the first time since I lived as Juliet when it was looked at it last.

The old parchment shows the hand-drawn plans meticulously sketched of the library before it's construction. It's a vast pyramid that would overshadow any of the ancient structures of history. The great library is the building that inspired the mortals' obsessions with pyramids and gods. It's the building that holds the truth of our past, of my past.

Hecate architected the Labyrinth, the realms immortal prison as a large, inverted pyramid under the surface of Gaea. The old Mind Titan, Coeus, modeled Alexandria after it, loving it so much.

With a river running around the complex, lush vegetation and tall palms that line a wide stone path, it was a beautiful facility. An equally wide set of tall stairs must be climbed to reach imposing double doors, allowing entry to the interior chambers.

Taking in the drawn plans, I remember standing long ago

in another library with Hermes' mother next to me. Daphne stood at my side as Hecate brought us the same set of blueprints. I remember Daphne pointing her finger with stacked amber rings at the library's vast complex.

She was a huntress and would plait her thick locks in a wide braid that hung over her shoulder before going into the woods. Otherwise, her hair was as wild and free as she was, just as it is in my memory.

A great Sensor and amazing scholar, Daphne was the closest thing I have to a real mother. Knowing the truth of Demeter and my bruised emotions from my recent conflict with Hecate, I find myself thinking of Daphne often over the past few days.

Resting both hands on the parchment, I close my eyes and take in the residue of memories absorbed into the fibers of the paper.

I hear Daphne's laugh and the jingle of silver bracelets that always adorned her wrists. The scent of evergreen and candlelight fills my senses as her calming essence cocoons me.

But a distant laugh bounces toward me, as bracelets echo across the library washing cold chills over my body. Looking around, my heartbeat rushes in my chest and my cheeks heat.

Impossible.

Before I send a pulse of my power to investigate, the clinking of high heel shoes on the polished marble breaks my brief rush of adrenaline.

For the smallest moment, I thought I heard Hermes mother, even though I know she is long dead.

Like me, she trusted in the wrong person. Having consumed a poison from Demeter, Hermes mother died trying to get me to safety. Daphne died not knowing that soon after, Juliet followed her in death.

The pound of a woman's shoe approaches. Just before the figure turns the row of bookshelves, a strong floral perfume wafts ahead, bombarding my senses.

Circe.

The name alone sends a shiver down my spine. She's a vision in red, her dress leaving little to the imagination, and her presence exudes an air of confidence, bordering on arrogance. I can't help but feel a surge of distrust at the sight of her, my instincts warning me to be cautious.

It takes me a moment to realize I recognize this woman. I saw her on the stairs of the Atlanta Commune on my first day as Callie was giving me a tour. At the time, I didn't have my memories and failed to recognize her.

Pretending to be indifferent, I return to my blueprints, feigning a deeply engrossed interest in my research. "May I help you?"

Circe releases a coo of a laugh, not buying my charade. She approaches and sits on my table, covering my blueprints with her bottom and propping herself up with her hand. I sit back in my chair, scooting away to put more space between us.

"Rhea, darling, what a pleasure to see you here," Circe purrs, her voice smooth as silk and laced with an unmistakable edge of seduction. I roll my eyes at her effort to be charming.

Circe smiles, an entertained glint in her eyes at my reaction. "I've come to thank you, dear Rhea, for saving my daughter."

I freeze, the revelation sending shockwaves through me. I didn't realize she had a daughter and think of the women we saved from the auction.

Who could Circe's daughter be?

Looking over Circe, her curtain of long raven hair almost looks purple when the light hits it. But it's her red dress, and nails and matching lipstick making her look like a walking blood clot and the unmistakable twinge in my mood that brings the clues together for me.

Lexi?

The very thought heats my core, heightening my mistrust of Circe. Lexi and I have always been rivals, competing for power and recognition in Ares' Underworld. But to think Circe, a Witch, is Lexi's mother; I suppose I never realized that could be possible since Lexi is a Shifter.

"Why would you thank me?" I demand, my voice tinged with suspicion.

Circe's smile widens, her gaze unwavering. "Because despite our differences, you showed compassion and bravery to my daughter. You can imagine, we aren't accustomed to being treated well, most of the time. I've come to offer you a gift as my gratitude."

Despite her outward charm, I know all too well the stories of Circe's treachery and manipulation. She's a powerful witch, but her reputation precedes her, and she's often cast out of immortal circles for her questionable actions.

"I appreciate your gratitude, Circe," I say, carefully masking my skepticism, "but forgive me if I find it difficult to trust someone who sits upon a Mortal Council. Everyone knows your untrustworthiness."

Circe's smile falters for a moment before she regains her composure, her eyes narrowing slightly. She turns her eyes to towering bookshelves. "Ah, but you of all people know you must read what is written between the lines, dear Rhea. The

Mortal Council has its flaws, but we have our reasons for the decisions we make."

I resist the urge to scoff at her words, knowing that Circe is skilled at twisting the truth to suit her own agenda. "And what reasons would those be?" I ask, my tone bordering on accusatory.

Circe leans in closer, her gaze intense. "The same reasons that drive you, Rhea. Survival. We may not always see eye to eye, but we share a common goal. I'm here to make sure I survive what is coming next."

"And what is that?"

"You." She answers plainly as if I should have known the response before I asked.

If what Circe says is true, then perhaps there is some validity to her offer of assistance. But I remain wary, unwilling to let down my guard in the presence of someone as cunning and unpredictable as Circe.

"Very well," I concede, though my voice is laced with caution. "I will consider your gratitude, Circe. But I don't trust you."

Circe's smile returns, though there's a glint of something darker lurking beneath the surface. "Of course, dear Rhea. Trust must be earned. But remember, in times of darkness, sometimes even the most unlikely alliances can prove to be invaluable."

With those cryptic words hanging in the air, Circe turns and saunters away, leaving me to consider the implications of our conversation.

I try to return to my research, but I can't stop thinking of the strange encounter. What gift could she be withholding and what alliances would serve me best when every immortal on this realm could be an ally of my hunter? Could she be referring to Flint and his declarations yesterday?

Amid the trauma of the captives and the sudden invasion by the Lurkers, Flint was spewing deranged rantings the entire time.

Something in the commands he gave to the Lurkers made them obey him and as they syphoned the turmoil of emotions from Callie and I, Flints voice boomed in my mind on a loop.

He believes I'm his mate and Hermes is a poison.

Flint brought the Lurkers to pull the toxins of Hermes severed bond from me so that Flint and I could be together. He believes the Fates have ordained this.

"You're mine." He kept repeating. *"I won't stop until I have you."*

The revulsion rolls up body, making my throat constrict.

I intentionally didn't admit the extent of his deranged rantings to Hermes. I feel like talking to Callie first would help me sort through things. She would be an expert in all things to do with multiple bonds.

With my hands resting on the blueprints, I try to focus myself back to Alexandria.

Bringing in a cool breeze to calm the chaos in my mind, it feels like the swells of the past are rushing through me. I feel the energy of the old library where my palms touch the ancient parchment and let the sensations flow through me.

Visions of Alexandria flash through my mind, leading up to the cataclysmic battle of Nyx and her hunter. My former self seems so distant from me now after a thousand lives, I hardly recall what it felt like to look through her eyes.

Pillars of intense fire shot up from Ares' hands in his attempt to incinerate the great library. He wanted to destroy the truth held inside. Shifters and Immortals were fighting around us. Shouts of the ongoing battle ring in my memory as burning sulfur stings my nostrils.

I recall feeling my powers extend ahead of me and the ground quaked under my might.

With my brow furrowed, I push through the memory. I want to see if anything will point me to the location where the library hides within the safety of my powers.

Thinking of the raging battle, I remember the moment I raised the library and surrounding structures from the earth. As if plucking a great stone from a seabed, I lifted the compound high into the sky, My abilities held it there as my wards and mirages were woven together in an intricate and impenetrable shield.

With my right hand, I battled the God of War.

Blazing fire collided as our pillars of flames shot into the sky. Sand from my Earth element combined with Water smothered his fires as I stole the air around him, choking his flames.

Glowing in silver starlight, rings of shields began protecting the city floating in the sky as I kept Ares' focus on me. My Light and Dark powers swirled together, as dual Mirages swallowed the building and it vanished from history.

Only a tremendous crater in the ground remained, marking the former site.

In the memory, my powers swirl behind me and it feels like my back is splitting open. As if my very soul was ripping apart, I felt the fibers of Gaea stretch and split behind me.

My chest still gapes with the memory of what happened next.

Next, I die.

"Get out." I tell myself. A growing sense of dread and

urgency to remove myself from this memory makes my knees begin to quiver.

If I stay in this memory, I will relive my death; my first death.

A wave of nausea surges through me and my hands remain cemented to the old parchment. I'm chained here, locked within the memories that rush through my mind.

I discharge a small tendril of shadow and it separates me from the parchment. In an instant, I'm freed of the memory. My chest heaves as my rising panic subsides.

I save myself from reliving that feeling of the dark spear piercing my chest. Like a coward, I also stop before I have to see Hermes impaled upon the same spear. Skewered together, the shadowed spire ran through us both.

In an instant, we were locked in an eternal embrace of two lovers who would tear themselves apart with the hope of reuniting again.

"I found these other books." Callie's sunny aura warms me, long before she rounds the aisle of the library, her arms full of tomes. I work to settle my breathing and bolt upright from the table. "Are you okay? You're all sweaty."

"I just... went back a little too far." My chest is still heaving, and I place my hand on my forehead. Patting the beating sweat that formed along my brow.

Rolling up the parchment, I make room for the stack of books and help Callie place them on the table. We're still searching for information on the alignment, only three days away.

"There is something I've been wanting to ask you though."

Callie leans on the tall stack of books and her eyebrows shoot upward with curiosity. "Ask away."

Hesitating, I search for the words. I'm not afraid of upsetting her but I'm scared of the answer I may find. "You heard Flint last night, right?"

Callie rolls her eyes. "Ugh, yes. He's a psycho. Don't put any stock in what he says." Callie sits down, taking the first book from the new pile. "But that is not your question, is it?"

"What would it feel like, if there was another mating bond within me?"

Callie's shoulders drop as she releases a sympathetic exhale. "It's terrible. There is a constant longing for something you know is missing, and your very soul is in pain without it."

I think about the constant void that is within me and my cheeks flush. What if this missing part of me is another bond, longing to be filled with another mate.

"While I had a strong relationship with Patroclus, I was constantly being tugged toward Achilles too. My emotions were an endless swirl and honestly, I'm not sure how Pat made it through those few years until Achilles and I bonded."

I smile, thinking of the happiness they must have felt to finally be whole after so long apart.

Searching within myself, I feel for the sensations of the bond ripped from my chest. As if dangling inside me, the bond thrums and I know something within me has survived all this turmoil and the plague of a thousand deaths.

But all I feel is Hermes.

The deep-rooted longing to be with him. Even here at the library, knowing he is not far away, I want him with me and no one else. Biting my lip, I look at the open book but I'm not able to focus on the written words.

Continuing my self-exploration, I search within myself

more, looking for lost tethers but all I find are the holes of my own immortality.

As the clouds move away from the sun and the light shines brighter through the large stained-glass windows, I look to the sky.

We're sitting in front of the window that depicts the great Titan of Death, Chaos.

I didn't even realize it when we sat here but I take in the many colors of glass that make up the beautiful image.

Like a collection of galaxies, Chaos is formed of a giant nebula cloud and holds all the stars of the universe within his body. With violet glowing eyes, there is a swell of black rolling mist that cover the lower half of his body. *Just like my mist.*

Silver lightning is depicted shooting out of an outstretched hand as if reaching for me. *Silver like my aura.*

The gold banner at the bottom of the large window has the words "Memento Mori" in gilded letter.

"Remember, you must die."

I can't help but feel this phrase in the deepest roots of my being. If anyone knows this fact, it truly is me.

All that is within me is the light of Hermes love, colliding with the darkness of Deaths stolen power. How can there be room for anyone else?

"So, seventy-two hours and the eclipse begins." Callie rips me from my distraction. Taking another book from the stack and her Winds begin flipping the pages, her aura scanning the words for anything useful. "Gods, I can't even remember the last eclipse, can you?"

"No, but I remember the first one." Absentmindedly, I

rub my sword charm, it's presence a comfort to me. The first eclipse marked my first death and I'm still running away from the fleeting memory that nearly consumed me a moment ago.

"So, what were we doing three days before your first alignment of the triple moons?" Callie rests her hand on her chin and looks at me with her bright blue eyes.

Gods, I love her. She knows I'm a raging ball of stress and anxiety.

Instead of trying to tell me to calm down or reassure me that things will be okay, she's just moving me on to think of something else. On the Winds of her power and the warmth of her, I'll let her carry me away from the shadows that shroud my mind.

Casting my gaze to the painted ceiling above, a faded memory slowly comes into focus, and I concentrate on it.

It's like a dream that fades away as soon as you wake and I'm reaching out, desperate to hold onto it before I lose it forever.

The library's fresco ceiling is sunrise at one end and at the other, dusk. My favorite time of day when stars pop into the sky one by one, like little souls being born into existence for the first time.

I hear Hermes voice from so long ago. There is a great roar, screaming all around us and wind blows my hair in a swirling dance.

"I wish I could have gotten you a ring." He said.

Shock rolls over my face as I feel the blood leave my body.

"What is it?" Callie's voice is alerted by my reaction. "Do you remember something?"

Saying the words aloud, as I remember them, I recite the

line of my memory and the vision grows stronger. "We can't wear rings; we're going into battle."

Hope and light surges through my body as the memory brings me a wave of elation. I grasp Callie's hand as tears flood my eyes.

Sending her visions of what my mind is replaying, her face mirrors my own as her eyes glisten. I keep piecing together the fragments of my broken past and as my power shares the repaired memory with her.

In shocked silence, we stare at each other, and it seems like minutes pass as we sit unmoving.

"Rhea," My dearest friend, my sister, is breathless, and her cheeks have a rosy blush as her emotions swirl like a tempest within her. "Do you realize what this means?"

Smiling, I slowly nod, a plan forming in my mind. "It means I need your help."

Her grin matches mine and the gleam of mischief makes her eyes as bright as a cloudless sunny day. "You bet your ass you do."

The ranch has always been a thoroughfare of activity but these last few days, it's been nonstop. My pack looks like they are about to keel over but I know they won't quit until the work is done; none of us will. We're a family.

And that is what makes me so proud of them.

Walking up to the packhouse, I stop and look up at the dappled sunlight streaming in through the towering pines. The air is crisp and clean, tinged with the scent of the forest and I take it in. The distant calls of the Wyoming wildlife echo through the woods and I know I'm home.

As I bask in the warm sun, the shadows of my past creep up my spine.

I fucking detest the Underworld. It's always been my prison and I'm glad it's gone. I only wish I had been the one to destroy it. The Shifters belong in the open air, with the freedom to burst through the landscapes of Gaea and stretch our legs.

We were never meant for cages and chains.

As long as I'm living, no Shifter will ever be captive to a tyrant again. My packs and I will keep working, keep fighting until everyone is home; until everyone is free.

A cloud of dust plumes as Kai pulls up in her white jeep with the doors off and the top open. She drives like she's constantly being perused by a mortal police chase, and I shake my head at the thought of being a passenger in her car.

Pausing on the first step of the cabin, I wait for her to look at me with an update. In my heart, I already know it's going to be a no, but still, I wait for her acknowledgement.

Taking off her aviator sunglasses, she looks at me and gives me two shakes of her head.

Just as I thought. No.

Ever since Mabon we've been going in a dozen directions, but Kai has only been focused on one thing: the hunt for the Zeta Queen.

Thinking back to that night, as Rhea released the Lycan's curse, I was ready to give my life under the shadow of that pyramid. I half expected Ares to come back to the surface with the full might of his army for a battle, but he had other priorities.

He hadn't expected Demeter to go off-script and summon Nyx. And Ares sure as shit hadn't expected Nyx to have enough power to clear the curse from the realm.

Letting Nyx feed off my Titan power nearly drained me, but it was worth it. To free my people of the chains that bound their immortal power, I would do anything. My energy was plummeting, and it took all my focus to keep locked on Gabriel as he challenged me with his pack.

When Mor spotted that woman, locked in a state of Shifting and Hypnos used his power to put her to sleep, I could have summoned the strength of the twelve Titans and taken on all of Ares' army in that moment.

My dormant mating bond was triggered and in that instant, I would have slaughtered them all to save her.

But Mor hid her, at the request of the woman's family and refused to tell me where. Mor wouldn't even tell me the woman's name and while I hate her for it, I'm also thankful.

I have no clue what sort of power The Morrigan holds but I'm grateful she used it to protect my mate. If that is the one solace I have in all of this, it's that the Zeta Queen will be safe from the horrors going on right now.

And when all of this is over, I'll find her. I won't rest until she's safe and by my side.

Taking the remaining steps two at a time, I enter the large packhouse.

Situated on a sprawling ranch in the heart of the Wyoming forest, the house serves as the central hub of shifter society.

Built from sturdy timber and stone, the house boasts a sprawling layout with multiple wings and levels. Massive windows line the exterior, allowing natural light to flood the home and gives us uninterrupted views of the beautiful land-scape that surrounds us.

Inside, the atmosphere is warm and inviting with a fire crackling in the oversized fireplace nearly every day. It's always been important to me that our home be a stark contrast to the cold and dark Underworld.

I've spent countless hours building this house and carving the rich wood furnishings that complement the plush carpets, and intricate tapestries adorning the walls. This is more than just my home. It is a symbol of strength, unity, and tradition, embodying the timeless bond of all Shifters.

Finished with my chores, I've tended to livestock and checked on the gardens. Spending the last few hours mending fences, I smell like shit and need a shower before lunch.

The hot water runs down my tight muscles of my back and slowly eases some of the tension I've been holding there.

The past few days are nothing but a whirlwind, moving us from one catastrophe to another. Breaking free from Ares and the Lycan curse was only the start.

With daily Shifter abductions, New York being wiped off the map, Hermes dropping two dozen Shifter-families on my doorstep, and the survivors from the auction raid, we're running on fumes here.

Now, I have to entertain two Elementals for lunch. *Fuck me.* Achilles reached out, asking to kill some time, and let me know he and Hermes are on their way. But this is a favor for Rhea, and I owe her everything.

Hermes wants to check on the refugees from the auction and talk about the upcoming alignment. I've got Shifters displaced and missing all over the realm and with nightly raids, just like the one Zara and her pack handled, we're running out of spaces to put people.

I understand their concern, but my packs are stretched thin as it is.

But since we've made our truce, the Elementals are stepping up to help in as many ways as we are. They offered Medusa's Commune to us, even though she's difficult as fuck to reach, I'm grateful several hundred Shifters have a safe place to stay.

Bridget has always been an ally, like a lot of the Witches, they have mostly been neutral in the Shifter and Elemental feuds. But Bridget told me about Atlas, and how he shielded the women of the auction. Together, they took down the Lurkers and ultimately, a lot of ladies survived that night because of them.

So, we're entering a new era where we work together and even though things are hard right now, we're working for something better tomorrow. I keep that thought in my mind as I wake up each morning and see what new pile of shit there is to step in.

Emerging from my room, Cappa, our resident cook, has lunch ready.

Grilled flank steaks and roast corn on the cob has been drizzled with a jalapeño and herb butter. Cold, creamy potato salad makes the perfect filling for the soft fresh baked rolls, and I would kiss Cappa if he wouldn't punch me in the mouth for it.

I'm fucking starving.

Hermes and Achilles join us, and we take our plates to the wrap around covered porch. With cold beer and fluffy white clouds rolling across the bright blue sky, this would be a beautiful day if the conversation of the table wasn't of impending war.

"Alright, let's talk business." I set my beer bottle on the table and the small talk quiets.

"How are the rescued women?" Achilles asks.

"They'll never be the same." Kai says with remorse weighting down her words.

"There are two or three of those auctions as week popping up all over the realm." Delta adds with a shake of his head. "With these auctions and dealing with Task Force 777, I need a fucking vacation, that's for sure.

"What is Task Force 777?" Hermes asks, taking a break between large bites.

"It's a secret division of the US military. Mercenaries that hunt Shifters. It's why Ares had the sitting president assassinated by your mate. The previous president was Ares' ally, and the task force was merely for show. Sims put real funding behind it, and it was causing a lot of problems for Ares." I explain.

"The task force has been monitoring Lone Wolves for ages and began rounding them up since we went public on Mabon." Kai jumps in. "We wiped out Area 51, which was the main place the task force took Shifters. It's like the human's version of the Labyrinth and they lock up immortals they catch. But they have other locations and we're trying to find them."

"What are you planning to do for the eclipse?" I turn the conversation back to the Elementals. We could be here all day, talking about the woes of the Shifters with our recent displacement. "You know Ares is going to have a plan, so what is yours?"

"I was hoping you could help with that." Hermes takes a swig of his beer.

"What would Ares plan?" Achilles asks.

"Something to fuck you up—surprise you. He'd want to catch you off-guard since there is a short window of the alignment."

Hermes looks off in thought. His eyes move around the sprawling ranch as he takes in the various buildings. My land reaches for thousands of acres and we've got homes placed all over the property. We're building new homes each day and Cappa has been working to increase our real-estate for larger sanctuaries.

But all of that takes time, which is something all of us are in short supply of.

The Elementals have been waging their own war with Ares

and even though we're chasing two different conflicts, the same God of War is our mutual enemy.

Hermes came asking for help and I meant what I said the other day at his house on Mount Olympus.

"You send out the call, we'll answer it." I nod once, locking eyes with Hermes and solidifying our truce. "The packs will be ready."

Achilles and Hermes share a knowing look and reassurance passes between them. None of us can go against Ares alone. Our greatest chance is fighting him together.

"I do have a question though." Hermes asks, spearing another cut of steak onto his fork. "If someone shifts into a cow, but they eat beef, would that be considered cannibalism?"

I look at him deadpan as a smirk slides mischievously across his face.

"Are you always an asshole, or do you reserve this for me?"

"I'm just curious." He grins wider, taking the bite of meat into his mouth and feigning innocence. Shaking my head, I wipe my mouth with the cloth napkin and scoot my chair out.

"Achilles, you're always welcome here." I look to Hermes, clearing the politeness from my expression. "Hermes, piss off."

The Shifters and Elementals laugh, enjoying a break in the conversation of impending death that we'll likely be facing in a few days.

"I'll miss you too, dear." Hermes calls after me as I take my plate inside for washing.

Fucking Elementals.

"Luke, ditch the gods and get to the front gates." Delta is on guard duty and his calm tone is more crass than normal. *"We've got a big fucking problem."*

Perfect.

I ditch Hermes and Achilles knowing there is a plan to meet up later. Achilles gives me a nod of appreciation for accommodating his impromptu request to come over with Hermes for a while.

The drive to the gates in my truck takes a few minutes.

I smell the blood long before I arrive to the edge of my territory. The hair raises on the back of my neck as my predatory senses take over.

Every woodland animal that scurries along a tree branch is an echoing boom in my ears. The faintest scent wafted on the gentlest of breezes is overwhelmingly powerful as the beasts within me search the area for danger.

Kai and I slam the doors of my truck as we exit and share a knowing look of dread. This is going to be bad, whatever it is.

Approaching the border there are ten members of my pack huddled in different groups.

A wolf-Shifter stumbles away, clutching his stomach and barely makes it to an outcrop of pine trees before vomit spews from his mouth. Several people embrace in desperate comfort, and others look back at me with murderous rage in their gaze.

Naomi drives up on a four-wheeler with several newly pledged bear-Shifters following her. The newest Alpha and first woman to hold the title, she's working diligently to find other bears and pull them into her den.

Bears are typically solitary but she's a smart woman. She's building a den of Shifters that need a family.

I think she's trying to distract herself from the loss of Teddy.

We all loved that little boy, but she was his mother from the second she found him digging in the dumpsters behind her café. Naomi pulled him into her care right alongside her twins. And she fought hard in that arena to save him.

But dark shadows covered him as we watched the blood seep out of his wounds. As he died, the shadows melted away, taking the frigid cold of darkness that clung to his body.

A Shifter bit him but it was Aryana's Darkness that took his immortality.

I feel that same frigid cold now as I walk to the border of my territory and take in the confusing scene scattered along the edge of my property.

Hanging from trees are the naked bodies of twenty-four Shifter-women.

They've been skinned and their flesh is strewn about the pine needle covered ground. Hands and feet have been removed and are nailed to the tall tree trunks where the women are suspended.

Some of them had their lower jaws ripped off while others had their eyes removed. The soft parts of their flesh appear to have turned to hardened stone before it was ripped away from their bodies. All of this was done while they were alive, even the marks made by branding irons as their flesh was removed.

Anger rolls through us all.

I sense the shifting animals that want to rupture from my pack members as they take in the atrocities before us. But as I look over each of the victims, I see the message Ares has sent. I've learned to interpret the signs of his depravity over the millennia when I was forced to serve him.

All of the women are about the same age, around the same height and with similar builds. They all have the one key trait in common that makes this message unquestionably clear.

They all have long honey brown hair, just like Rhea.

This is punishment to the Shifters for turning against Ares. And this is a warning for Rhea that Ares is coming for her.

My skin ripples, wanting to shift and release the mightiest of my beasts to roar into the Wyoming sky with my rage. But my pack is watching and hurting, knowing what these women suffered before their immortal lives were taken.

But from the dark shadows of the forest, I sense someone else is watching as well. Like the canopy of trees that provides shade is serving as a silent spy, giving Aryana a place to lurk and watch for our reaction.

Well, I refuse to give her anything to report back. I refuse to allow her to see us fall apart like craze animals at the crimes carried out on these unfortunate women.

Looking to my officers, I start giving orders.

I want to know the names of each of these victims so we can notify their families. We need to clean this up and search for evidence of who helped Aryana carry out Ares' orders.

And when we find out who did this, I'll carve the names of all twenty-four women into their flesh as I bring their immortality to end on the teeth of my beasts.

I t is so incredibly cold in the desert at night. Especially in the peplos dress Penelope brought over for me. The scalding sand blazing under a hot sun has turned frigid under the cool light of the moon. Gooseflesh races up my arms and I can't tell if it's from the cold or my nerves.

Thankfully, Achilles took on the task of diverting Hermes's attention so Callie and I could work on my surprise. Despite the chill, it's not the temperature that has my stomach in knots and my knees shaking; it's the nerves that accompany the anticipation of this moment.

Callie and I raced around all day preparing, and it was honestly just a great day with my best friend. Life has raced forward since Hermes, and I crossed paths at Once Upon a Spine. There's been little time to savor simple pleasures, like a day with your oldest pal.

It seems selfish to crave something so simple with all the turmoil of the world. But we know all too well how fleeting time can be and I want all of us to savor these dwindling moments of happiness where we can find them.

Since we have recovered two of my relics and a third is on

the horizon, never have we been so close to solving this riddle and breaking this spell than now.

Fragmented memories continue to get pieced together each day and I think of the many lives I never reunited with my friend, my family.

When I lived as Danaë, my immortality was severed on the tip of a sword as Hermes was fighting to break down the walls of Troy. We never had a chance to cross paths during that life.

Then, Oizys, captive for a millennia and slain after seven days of freedom.

We never had time in those lives for happiness and I don't want to waste a second. Two days from now, the eclipse will begin its alignment and I have no ability of foresight to know what will come after. I could meet another death and wait in the cold Void to finally return and start all over again.

It took four hundred years from my death as Juliet until I was to be reincarnated in the body of Rhea. Could the next stint take even longer?

Could Hermes live that long in darkness and grief again, waiting for my return?

In the face of impending uncertainty, taking this moment to pause for kinship and celebration feels not only justified but necessary. We have earned a few moments of joy without the burden of guilt or weight of looming war.

A warm current swirls around my ankles and spirals up my body, chasing away some of the cold and delivering Callie's message that everything ready for me.

My anticipation has been building as the hours ticked by. Now that I'm mere minutes away from moment I've been thinking of all day, tremors take over my hands.

I had hoped Achilles would keep Hermes busy enough that

he wouldn't feel the need to check on me. Twice, he tapped into our bond. While I kept my true whereabouts hidden, I left just enough of my presence unmasked to keep him from getting suspicious.

The last thing I needed was for him to get alarmed and come to check on me. With Ares inciting war and Lurkers running loose around the realm, there is much to be concerned about. But Achilles did a great job of keeping my mate occupied all day.

Releasing the tendrils of my power, my Light weaves through the velvet sky like shimmering silver ribbons, a dance of luminescence that soothes the tension in my muscles and eases the knot of anticipation in my chest.

In mere seconds, the brilliant blue light of Hermes's power joins mine, and a celestial symphony unfolds high above. His response fills me with warmth, eliciting a smile that spreads across my face like starlight breaking through the darkness.

Our magic intertwines in a delicate dance of silver and blue hues, a silent conversation between two lovers against the backdrop of the night sky.

A wave of brilliant blue light flashes, signaling Hermes's arrival, accompanied by a surge of his comforting warmth. My mate joins me, his spicy cologne enveloping me in its intoxicating embrace just before his aura gently caresses my body.

"What in the twelve realms have you been up to today, little goddess?" Hermes's voice, filled with playful curiosity, dances through the air as he saunters towards me, his gaze filled with affection and intrigue.

His powers weave around me like a tender embrace, snaking around my legs and waist. He draws me closer until I melt into his hold, basking in the familiarity of his touch.

Hermes's deep blue stola is adorned with intricate grapevine embroidery in shimmering silver thread. It catches in the moonlight, casting a mesmerizing glow around him. His ocean eyes sparkle with curiosity under the night sky, as if the cosmos is conspiring to illuminate his handsomeness.

As we stand together, the night unfurls before us like a tapestry of endless possibilities.

I anticipated Hermes's would catch on that something was going on when Achilles delivered him to our home on Mount Olympus.

Leaving behind the essence of my aura with a carefully arranged package and a note, I invited him to join me. Providing an outfit prepared with as much thoughtfulness as he had shown me the night he first asked me to dinner.

A smile spreads across my face, unable to be contained, as I stand before him in my flowing white peplos, its soft fabric swaying gently in the breeze that dances around us.

The elements themselves watch with anticipation as I prepare to reveal my secret to Hermes.

I sense the nosey Wind scurrying off to tell Callie every detail of what is happening, and I withhold a chuckle at the excitement created in the atmosphere.

My hair is fashioned into a braided crown encircling my head, adorned with a wreath of olive leaves twisted together like a tiara fit for a goddess. And I truly feel like the most radiant goddess of the realms with the light in Hermes' eyes as he looks at me.

As Hermes draws near, we envelop each other in a tender embrace, our arms wrapping low around each other's waists. Craning my head to meet his gaze, I watch as he takes in the intricate details of my attire and hair, his admiration evident in the softness of his expression.

"You, my goddess, are the most captivating and beautiful thing I have ever had the privilege to behold," Hermes' touch is gentle as he lifts my chin between his thumb and forefinger. Leaning down, he presses his lips to mine in a tender kiss, igniting a warmth within me that pushes back against the cold desert air.

In moments like these, enveloped in Hermes's love and protection, I feel truly liberated. As I return his kiss, I savor the taste of him and the comforting embrace of his arms around me, wishing to hold onto this moment for eternity.

Reluctantly, I bring our kiss to an end. "I found something today. Well, more like I remembered something today," I begin, a hint of excitement in my voice.

"Mmmm, one more," Hermes interjects, his charm impossible to resist as he steals one last kiss before relaxing his hold around me.

"I want to show you something," Turning, I gesture toward the vast crater that stretches out before us. "The mortals have come to call this place 'The Eye of the Sahara'."

I allow him a moment to take in the expansive terrain, the endless desert sands stretching out as far as the eye can see. It's a desolate expanse and looks like the remains of a colossal impact from an ancient comet.

While recent human theories suggest it was a former volcanic site, only we know the truth: it's the scar left on Gaea's surface from the fierce battle between Ares and the Goddess of the Twelve Realms.

"Now, close your eyes."

Hermes smiles but closes his eyes, allowing me to weave my

powers into his mind and send him memories of the great Library of Alexandria. A time when it was teaming with librarians and visitors before the fateful day of our battle before the day that ended my life.

I transport Hermes' mind to a sunny day, the wind gently rustling the palms and birds soaring above the towering peak of the grand pyramid. As the memories flood his mind, Hermes gasps behind me, recognizing the missing library in an instant.

"Rhea, you found it?" His voice is filled with awe and admiration. He leans around me to see my face. I turn to look back at him, a smile of fulfillment making my cheeks sore.

"Search for my power and you'll find it too." I wait and watch as my mate extends his aura.

With his cerulean eyes closed in concentration, Hermes unleashes his powers to search the vast expanse surrounding us. Brilliant blue light surges outward, swirling around the circumference of the large circular crater. As he extends his reach, finding nothing within the immediate vicinity, Hermes pushes his abilities further, reaching upward into the vast expanse of the sky.

I watch in anticipation as his element soars higher and higher, seeking out the hidden truths concealed within the layers of my protective wards. Finally, his power contacts mine, high above and surrounded by layers of enchantments.

Faintly, the hum of my silver starlight resonates as Hermes's blue Light explores the concealed compound. Like a castle in the sky, the outline of the ancient pyramid gradually becomes visible as our powers converge and intertwine, revealing the secrets that lie within.

"I tried to bring it down, but I can't. I need the pendent."

Looking at the mass of my magic hiding in the night sky,

longing tugs at my heart. Hundreds of thoughts race through my mind of what could be protected inside. Ages have passed and I've lost a thousand lives trying to get back to this very spot.

I'm finally here and it still feels millions of miles away.

"Rhea, I can't believe it." Hermes is watching the sky as I am. Amazement keeping his eyes fixed above us. Turning back to him, I wrap my arms around his neck.

"I need more time to heal from the trauma of my past, I know that" I continue, the weight of my admission heavy in the air. "I know you believe Tartarus is gone, despite your façade, you have doubts." Hermes takes a breath to interject but I pause him. I need to get all of this out now, or I'll never say it.

As I speak, I notice the flicker of pain in Hermes's eyes, a testament to the truth of my words. He may not fully grasp the depth of what has transpired today, nor the challenges that lie ahead, but I sensed a subtle shift between us—a shift I've been feeling for days, though I've been quick to blame myself for it.

"I wish we could freeze time and simply be together for ten millennia before confronting this eclipse. But even if all that time passed, I know the pull I feel within me will not change."

I've rehearsed these words in my mind for hours, yet now that Hermes is here, they feel impossibly difficult to voice. I take a deep breath, steeling myself to reveal the truth.

"Something of the utmost importance is locked away within that library, something I need to defeat all of this," I finally confess, my voice soft but resolute. "Why else would I have safeguarded it so thoroughly, to the point where even I can't access it?"

Hermes remains silent, his gaze fixed on me as I struggle to find the right words to express the turmoil within me.

"My mind is broken, and my memories scattered. But in all of this, there are two things, I'm absolutely certain of. It's the call of my powers, and the tie my soul has to yours." I cup his face and he places a kiss on my open palm.

"We planned this path and walked down it, long ago, we have just forgotten. Your path took you to Avalon." I look to the night sky, where I know Tartarus should shine. "And my path, will take me to Tartarus."

Understanding darkens his expression as he realizes what I'm saying.

"This is a path I need to walk–alone. And I know you don't want to hear that. I know you want to be by my side and fight my battles with me but this one is mine. This doorway is meant for me to walk through. Just like the portal at the base of the falls was meant for no one else but you."

"Rhea–" Hermes begins but stops before finishing.

"Long ago, we worked together and crafted a plan to conceal my immortality in a way that only we could recover it. You and me; it's always been you and me against the world. You are my only constant, my North Star, guiding me on a steady horizon."

Hermes' eyes glisten with tears as my words pull at his heart, broken and shattered a thousand times with each of my deaths. Yet he stands before me with the pieces of that broken heart in his hands, waiting for my return to make him whole once more.

"I need you here, on Gaea, to be the guide I can point my compass to find my way back. Tartarus is calling me; the pendant of my powers is pulling me more with each day, but I need your faith before I leave." I tighten my hold on his neck and stand as tall as I can. "I need to know you truly believe in me."

Hermes's sigh washes over me, his embrace tightening around my waist as he buries his face in my neck.

"You have my everything," he murmurs, his voice filled with emotion. "My unending love, my unwavering faith, and my steadfast devotion." As Hermes pulls back, his gaze meets mine, penetrating deep into my soul.

"You are the center of my universe," his words a solemn declaration that resonates within me. "And nothing else matters without you. As far as you have to search for your powers, I'll fight just as hard to keep this space safe until you get back."

His vow of support fills me with a sense of warmth and reassurance, reminding me that no matter the challenges we face, we will face them together.

His lips are soft on mine as he conveys the truth of his words with our kiss. The Winds swell around us, pushing us together and celebrating our love. The moon brightens in the sky as if the moonbeams are casting a spotlight for the realm to witness our promises.

And my heart soars higher than the clouds in the sky as I feel the truth in his promise and my mind is freed of some of my burdens.

"While this is amazing," Hermes grins, looking up at the dark sky, the library invisible again as my wards continue their job keeping the ancient building safe. "I know you didn't get us both dressed up only to show me a dent in the sand."

His smile beams, and I try to hide my amusement as I bury my face in his chest. Pulling in a deep inhale of his scent, I imbue it within the fibers of my being. The tightness in my shoulders relaxes and Hermes keeps his hold on me. Rubbing his callused hands along my shoulders, he places a kiss on my temple.

My sword necklace is nearly thrumming along with the excitement of my pounding heart, and I feel like it's going to burst out of my chest.

Recalling the words he said to me, I bite my bottom lip as I force my voice to speak calmly. "Feel like going on a field trip?"

Hermes narrows his gaze in suspicion but cocks a lopsided grin that reveals the dimple on his cheek. "Of–course?" He hesitates before answering, perhaps remembering our last trip was to Avalon.

I chuckle as my dark portal swirls, encasing us in cool shadow. "You're just going to have to trust me." I say with a wink.

As the rich swirl of Rhea's portal closes behind us, I instantly recognize our surroundings. The thunderous roar of water as it cascades over the falls is a familiar song I've heard countless times before.

It's Angel Falls.

Rhea's radiant smile outshines even the brightest stars in the universe, her excitement palpable in the air. Standing behind her, my sister and my best friend await our arrival. Callie's arm is linked with Achilles', and she practically bounces with anticipation.

Callie wears a long pale blue stola, her hair styled in a high ponytail full of bounce and curls, mirroring her infectious energy. Achilles, on the other hand, dons a deep grey stola that exudes a sense of calm and strength, like a thunderstorm brewing on the horizon. With a raised eyebrow and a sly smile, I realize he's been fully aware and complicit in whatever the girls have planned all day.

I look with suspicion at the three people I trust most in the twelve realms. They have clearly been planning something which explains why Achilles kept coming up with ideas of things to do, keeping us busy all day.

I admit, I happy for the break with my friend, and nothing takes my mind off my stress than being physically active. We paid a visit to Lucas and checked on the Shifters.

The entire realm is rotating on a new axis and no group is going through more strife than the Shifters.

We had to cut our visit short when Lucas was called to an urgent matter at the edge of his territory. One of the dozen things I need to remember to ask about.

After leaving the Shifters, Achilles and I spent the day, hanging out. It seems like it's been ages since we've just relaxed. We climbed the Moab and made a stop at the mortal monument to his sister in Birka, Sweden. We went for a cross-country run around Europe and spent way too long in Iceland's Blue Lagoon.

But we needed it. The heated water of the lagoon melted away the buildup stress and worry in our tight muscles.

Twice today, I felt down the bond for Rhea. She and Callie were supposed to be researching in the library and then enjoying the spa at Delphi. Each time she brushed me off quickly and I believed it was because they were caught up in so much enjoyment.

But now I see they were working to conceal a secret all day.

"Why am I the last one to know what's going on?" I jest, casting my arms wide and feigning betrayal in my tone.

"It's more fun this way." Achilles answers.

"You're a traitor and an unfaithful friend."

"You could always hang out with Flint. I hear he is a *handy* friend to have around." Achilles can't even get the words out before he bursts into laughter. Callie smacks his chest, holding back a laugh of her own.

Rhea is radiating with nervousness as she faces me, taking both of my hands in hers. "Do you recall that first day I showed you my powers, back in Atlanta?"

In the Atlanta training room, I was amazed seeing her wield the four elements and had never seen anyone like her before. Thinking back, to her bashful demeanor, she was almost apologetic to have powers. Unknowingly scared of them because of the toxins Demeter pumped into her.

"I do." My tone turns serious as I take in our location at the top of the falls.

My gaze drifts down Rhea's dress, a vision of tradition appropriate for a Grecian bride. Her hair, woven into a crown and adorned with an olive leaf wreath, echoes memories of a night just like this with Nyx, only days before our pivotal battle. Yet, the full memory eludes me, riddled with gaps and fading into the void whenever I try to grasp it.

Enveloped in Rhea's powers, the charms of the necklaces we've worn for millennia, lift from our necks to hover in the space between us. These tokens have been safeguarded with unwavering devotion, at times even risking my own life to protect them.

In times when my mate died and we waited on her reincarnation, Callie became the steward of Rhea's necklace. Safeguarding the charm with as much care as she would her own mated bond.

When the goddess returned, her faithful friend returned the necklace to her, just as Callie did when she gifted it back to Rhea in Atlanta.

As Rhea channels her powers into the stones at the top of the necklaces, the dark orbs fixed at the hilts of our small swords gleam. Her necklace's dark sphere radiates like silver starlight, while the blue topaz adorning mine emits a brilliant azure glow.

At their centers, two braided coils of woven auras shine within.

"Rhea," I whisper, my voice thick with emotion. A surge of chills races down my spine, and my throat tightens as I struggle to find the words. "Our bond..."

"It wasn't destroyed," she interrupts, tears streaming down her face as she sees the realization dawn on me. "We safe-guarded it, so no one could take it from us."

With the faint power of Earth at her command, she breaks open the stones, revealing the hidden truth within. "That night in Kenya, when you prepared a bath for me and cooked me dinner, I made a plan to leave."

Her confession pierces my heart, the pain of knowing her intentions weighing heavily on me. I remain silent, allowing her to continue.

"I convinced myself it would be safer for me to be the one to rip out my heart than to trust someone else with it," she admits, her gaze meeting mine with a mixture of happiness and sorrow. Her tears flow freely, mirroring my own, as she lays bare her vulnerability. "I grew accustomed to being the one to hurt myself first, believing it would help me heal faster from the inevitable rejection I feared would come."

Rhea's steady hand lifts to cup my cheek, the tension in her brow easing as she gazes at me. In her eyes, I see a sense of peace, as if all her worries have melted away within the warmth of our embrace.

"If only I had known," she murmurs, her voice filled with

tenderness, "that my greatest happiness was already safely tucked away, held close to your heart."

Within the depths of my blue stone, a delicate tendril of silver starlight emerges, like a shy little mouse venturing out from its hiding place. Two strands of Rhea's aura are intertwined, her power enveloping a strand of my aura in a protective embrace.

As the black stone of Rhea's necklace opens, a vivid blue spiral representing my bond unfurls, snaking outward to join the ethereal dance of her bond.

Hanging suspended in the space between us, our intertwined bonds swirl together like a mesmerizing double helix, casting a radiant glow that illuminates the top of Angel Falls with a breathtaking spectacle of starlight.

As if the radiant light of our bonds cast away the shadows on my mind, I recall this same night with Nyx, atop these falls long ago.

For ages and lifetimes, we've carried the burden of perceived loss, a missing connection that we believed had been torn apart. We wandered, endlessly drawn to each other by an unseen force, longing for the completeness we once shared.

But now, as the reflection of our mending bond shines brightly in the darkness around us, I remember.

To protect our bond, we took it out, encasing them with care in jewels crafted of Rhea's combined powers. Waiting for the day we would unlock them and join our bond again, finally reuniting.

"Promise me, something?" Nyx's voice rings in my mind and I close my eyes with the pain of the memory. *"No matter what happens to me, you'll keep this with you and find your way back to me?"*

My tears flow down my face now as they did that day. *"I promise, I'll find you. I'll always find you."*

Looking into the eyes of my mate, our bond forged on the edge of time's horizons, is repaired.

As the braided strands of our souls are bound together once more, the tether extends into the depths of our chests, filling our bodies with the power of each other's essence.

In the abandoned corridors of my lonely heart, Rhea's darkness flows, filling every crevasse with warmth and healing. The echoes of her love reverberate within me, sealing every crack with her aura and bringing light to the darkest corners of my being.

As Rhea watches me with eyes wide and full of wonder, a promise, spoken long ago is recited again between our souls.

*"Under the timeless gaze of the stars,
I promise to walk hand in hand with you through eternity."*

I observe in awe as my bond fills Rhea, the radiant blue starlight shining brightly within her as our souls intertwine once more. The realm around us seems to shift and sway, the powerful light of the moon expanding to envelop us in its ethereal glow.

"With every breath, I will give you my love and devotion,"

As if guided by an unseen force, we move together, our bodies drawn to each other with an instinctual magnetism. The pearlescent lunar light surrounds us, casting a shimmering veil around our entwined forms, while a gentle surge of Wind dances around us in a celestial embrace.

"until the stars fade into the abyss,
and then, I will love you forever in the darkness."

With Rhea's arms wrapped securely around me, she rises on the balls of her feet, closing the distance between us to meet my taller stature. The mending bond between us shines brightly, illuminating the space between us as our lips finally meet in a long-awaited kiss.

"I love you," The emotions surging through me steal my breath as I look upon my bonded mate once again. "until the stars fade into the abyss."

Rhea smiles, laughter bubbling up between sobs as her happiness pours out of her. "and then, I will love you forever in the darkness."

A surge of warmth floods through our chests, the fated tie that forever links me to my goddess is joyfully welcomed back into my body. In this moment of union, I feel complete, whole, and infinitely connected to the one who holds my heart.

No longer cloaked in darkness, the power of my bond swells within me, and a brilliant explosion of Light bursts forth from my body. Stretching across the realm in an instant, a wave of my sapphire starlight surges across the world, illuminating the darkest corners and bringing warmth to every shadow it touches.

As my Light disperses, it fragments into a thousand translucent falcons, each bearing the essence of my soul. Once heralds sent across the realms to convey my messages to the great Titans of the twelve realms, they now soar freely, singing the song of our union.

Rhea's powers surge forth in a swell of strength, both chaotic and controlled, as black mist rolls off her in swirling torrents. The elements she commands collide and dance around her, each one bending to her will.

Bursts of silver lightning illuminate the dark cloud of her powers, while the Winds sing a haunting melody of celebration. The earth trembles beneath her feet, and a warm wave of hot air envelops us, as if all the volcanoes of the realm are rejoicing with us.

I hear the swell of waters as Gaea's currents rush toward us, racing in from every corner of the realm. We watch in awe as rivers and oceans converge at the base of the falls, their applause echoing through the air. Speeding up the hundreds of feet, the waters ascend into the sky before cascading down upon us in a fine mist.

In the midst of it all, Rhea laughs joyously in my arms as I lift her up and spin her around, caught up in the euphoria of the realm's celebration of our repaired bond. Together, we revel in the love and unity that surrounds us, grateful for the strength and resilience that has brought us back together once more.

Callie is nothing but sobs and laughter. She clutches Achilles arm as he smiles widely for us.

Bringing Rhea close, I hold her tightly as our lips meet in a passionate collision. Our bonds flare within us, pulsating with the intensity of our connection. As our powers settle, I feel my heart synchronize with hers, beating in perfect harmony with my bonded mate.

Gazing into her eyes, I see a universe of stars reflected, each one a testament to the timeless beauty of our devotion. In this moment, surrounded by the radiant light of our rediscovered love, we forge a bond that will endure throughout the ages—a bond strong enough to shatter the curse that plagues us and this realm.

As Callie and Achilles join us in congratulations, never before have I felt so certain of our victory, so assured that Rhea will overcome this curse and that we will never again be torn apart.

The realms Immortals have come to Delphi to celebrate our union. So many strange faces have come in to say congratulations to the Herald and the Goddess of the Twelve Realms.

Some of them I faintly recall from past lives as allies in the formidable battles against Ares. Others are newly released Shifter captives and new acquaintances.

The crowd, the commotion, the constant hum of dozens of voices is wearing on the thin threads of my anxiety and I'm beginning to regret putting this party together. It seemed like a good idea earlier today and now all I want to do is wrap myself in my mate all night.

My spirits are lifted when I see Zara and her faithful brother, trailing behind her as always. Her jeweled eyes specked shine brighter when we hug. We talk quickly of the aftermath of the raid on the auction, while Kellan and Hermes exchange pleasantries.

Zara assures me her pride has recovered from their injuries and they are scouting another auction to raid tomorrow.

Since I released her of the Lycan's curse during the Mabon ceremony, she is embracing her role as princess among the

Shifters. Zara and Kellan have taken to the prides of Africa and are taking over as Alphas of the territories stolen by Ares and Lupo's packs.

Soon, they will share the kingdom they are taking back as sibling rulers over their packs. One day, King and Queen of the Prides. But tonight, Zara carries herself higher with a shine in her eyes. The patient and vicious beast that lurks within her body is tame but ready to pounce when needed.

As high as my heart swelled seeing Zara, it plummets to the depths of Elysium when I spot Naomi and her twins—and no Teddy.

With a healed gash running down her forehead and crossing her eye, the wound carries halfway down her cheek. The deep brown hue has been leeched from her left eye by the injury, leaving it an icy blue color.

My chest heats and tears surge into my eyes.

This family will never be the same and it's my fault. Naomi will forever carry the physical wound of that terrible battle against the Dark Mage.

Flashes of the battle within the obscure dome flash behind my eyes when I blink, and I see it fresh as if it were playing out before me.

Hermes would have already been receptive to the shift in my emotions but with our bonds fully restored, it's immediate. His aura tied within me by our soul-connection flares and his warmth fills me with reassurance.

It feels like his strong hand is rubbing up my back and massaging the tension from my shoulders and I release a shuddered breath to calm myself.

"I didn't come to upset you on such a special day, goddess." Naomi says in a low tone as she focuses on the light brown coiled hair of her boys. Her hands stroke their curly locks, never looking at me, which I'm thankful for.

I cast my eyes everywhere except her and the twins, unable to look at them without seeing Teddy.

His mussy brown hair and gaps from newly lost teeth haunt me as my dreams of him, crying in the caves of my mind flood me. The images of his neck torn open with blood running down his shirt offend the bile rising in my throat.

"I–" The words get stuck in my throat as it closes, not allowing me to utter another syllable.

"It's okay, goddess. You owe no one an apology." Naomi finally looks at me and the icy burn of her gaze forces my eyes to hers. "You can't save every soul but thank you for trying to save my boy." With a quivering chin, Naomi looks at her boys. "My twins and I would not have survived if it were not for you." She bends slightly at the waist, dipping her head in respect.

Respect I don't deserve and respect I have not earned. I failed her; I failed Teddy.

"We are eternally grateful for you." Naomi turns herself and guides the twins with her hands on their shoulders. Their bodies blend into the mass of Immortals gathered for our celebration.

Suddenly, the world closes in on me and as if a tunnel connected my focus, to one central person. The crowd seems to part, and everything suddenly zooms in on Medusa.

Sitting alone on a stone wall at the farthermost end of the courtyard, her green eyes pierce me. With a glass full of deep red wine, she tips it to me as if saluting. Expressionless, and with dead eyes, Medusa nods once. *"Congratulations."* She speaks to only me in her mind and it booms within me.

My heartbeat surges in my chest, fearing at any moment she could use her power to make the earth swallow me whole or petrify me to immortal stone, forever a statue for her collections.

I collect a swell of power in the palm of my hand and a shield is at the forefront of my aura, ready.

Taking a long pull from her glass, she nearly empties the wine in three gulps. Standing, she flicks the rest of the wine to the gravel below and hurls the fragile stemware behind her.

The sound of glass shattering pulls the attention of two or three nearby spectators. The distraction only temporary as they turn back to their conversations.

"You fixed it. Good for fucking you." With a flourish of her arms, she makes a show of bowing deeply as if I'm royalty and her a meager servant. With nothing else, she turns and leaves the reception.

Hermes joins my side. His hand strokes my arm and I lean into his chest.

My powers temper but tension keeps knots in my stomach tightly wound.

The distraction from Medusa calmed my emotions from seeing Naomi but flared the anger within me.

"What do you think that was about?" I speak low, hoping only Hermes can hear me, staring at the spot of the stone wall Medusa was occupying. I know what poison is festering inside Medusa, but I'm curious to see if Hermes is growing suspicious her.

"She and Athena never had a chance to fix their bond. I would have *intense* feelings of my own if I saw someone repaired their bond and I couldn't fix ours." Hermes pulls me to him, turning me and forcing my eyes upon him.

Disappointment washes over me but I keep my face trained carefully to keep it masked. Tritons warning runs through me of the price to be paid for acceptance of the truth and I don't know that I could bear it if I had to give up Hermes.

If Hermes learned of my suspicions of Medusa and severed our bond, surely there would be nothing more for me to return to, should I face another death.

With his fingers spread wide, he runs them across my temple and through my hair. The motion relaxes me, and Hermes' warmth fills me with reassurance, chasing away the shadows of my erratic emotions.

Even on this amazing day, and despite all our efforts, I can't seem to escape the phantoms of the hunter that pursues me. It was naive to think we could gather all these immortals among the chaos of Ares' war and expect to have no drama.

"Intense, huh?" I chuckle and Hermes hugs me.

I happily squeeze myself into him, ready to let the world melt away in a place that only he and I exist together.

Releasing a deep breath, I decide not to let anything else take away from our moment. For ages we have chased a missing bond, and it's finally repaired and settled between us as it should be.

The constant tether to my mate and feeling the connection of his being to mine fills me with hope of our coming days.

Waiting for the eclipse and constantly pondering what will happen is like a twitch of a nerve that refuses to settle. The overarching threat Ares is casting over the landscape of the earth adds to the stress of what will come.

Fear that I won't restore myself, that I won't be strong enough to stop him is an unending darkness suffocating my mind. But knowing Hermes and I have restored our bond, and with it, strengthened our power, brings light to the shadows coating my thoughts.

Laughter and music of the party rush around us in a sudden swirl as if we had been inside a bubble and it has suddenly ruptured. Hermes moves us to the center of the crowd, and we guide our bodies to the rhythm of the music.

I work my braid out of the crown circling my head and shake out the long tendrils of my hair.

Hermes pierces me with a greedy hunger in his eyes as we hold our stare on each other. With my arms raised above my head, I close my eyes and tip my head back. Freeing myself from the heavy chains that bind me to the spell, I forget about my hunter.

I stop thinking about the hundreds of deaths I suffered, the suspicions of those around me and my missing powers. Whispers mentioning *'the twenty-four'* float away from me with the warm currents of Delphi and I let them drift out of my awareness.

"So, I have a question." Hermes begins with a tension pulling at the corners of his eyes. Raising a single eyebrow, I smile, curious to know what is piquing his thoughts with so much celebration around us. "Flint."

With that single word, I know precisely what is bothering him. He's wondering if there may be any truth to Flints ravings as the Lurkers attacked.

I throw my head back and laugh as Hermes picks me up around me waist. "What the matter Herald, are you not in a mood to share your mate?"

"Don't make me murderous on our bonding day." He slides me down his body until my feet gently touch the ground again. He captures my mouth in a possessive kiss, as if claiming me for himself.

Pulling away, I place my hands on each side of his face as we sway slowly to the thumping music. The rest of the world drown out as we hold each other in our embrace. "The Fates knew you are an absolute drama queen and would consume my every waking moment." Hermes laughs at my answer, but I sense the relief that washes through him. "How could there be room for another mate? You, and you alone are my horizon."

Consuming myself with Hermes and the fullness of our mated bond, we dance and forget about the antics of a lunatic for now, knowing we will need to contend with Flint soon.

Hermes hands openly roam my body as we sway to the beat of the music. He pulls me in close and locks his eyes on mine when the song turns slow and my laughter bounces around the night when the next song speeds up and he twirls me in circles until I feel like I'll fall over.

Further into the evening, Callie and I sing as loud as we can while Achilles and Hermes stand at a bar watching us enjoy ourselves.

Penelope and Hecate are drunk and talking loudly about which of them is a better friend to the other. Hecate swears it's Penelope, but she argues Hecate is the better friend.

Odysseus is recounting his famed wrestling match against an old foe, Ajax. Atlas laughs so hard; he nearly spits his drink out as Odysseus mimics the headlock Athena put Ajax in when she broke up the fight.

Medusa never returns to the party.

The Elementals and Shifters enjoy the night together as music and wine flow along with the companionship and conversation. Food is abundant and so is the laughter. There is no ranking of higher and lower Elementals or rejection of the Shifters among the assembled crowd.

Lucas and Kai join Hermes and Achilles at the bar. They bring their glasses to the center and salute each other before taking large pulls off their beer.

"To the twenty-four." Lucas says to Kai who returns a stoic nod.

Callie and I join the group with sweat gathering at our hairlines from dancing.

Both of us steal our mate's drinks and chug them with desperation to quench our thirsts. I usher in a small breeze to cool us as we pant and lean against the bar.

I'm so glad I changed from my long gown to a short stola as the Wind works wonders to cool my hot skin.

"Who are the twenty-four?" I ask breathlessly, removing the near-empty glass of beer.

Lucas and Kai exchange glances with Hermes and Lucas. Atlas and Odysseus' laughter dies down in an instant and Hecate's smile fades. Icy fingers of fear creep down my spine and I know whatever the answer, it's going to be terrible.

Hermes exhales and looks up at the stars as if asking for help from the cosmos.

"It will do her no good to have secrets kept from her." Atlas encourages Hermes and my cheeks flare as anger takes over the chill of fear.

Hermes releases a deep breath through his nose and rakes his fingers through his dark hair. "The bodies of twenty-four Shifter-woman were dumped at the entrance to Lucas's Wyoming territory." Hermes pauses and a darkness settles over his sapphire eyes. He tightens his jaw before continuing. "They had been tortured severely, skinned alive, mutilated, and finally killed."

Callie gasps and I'm reassured she didn't know either.

"I found out tonight during the party." Hermes adds.

It seems the news was spreading around the reception with the whispers I blocked out as I selfishly decided to enjoy the evening. Like an egotistical little girl, I pretended like the world wasn't going to shit and a raving over-powered lunatic wasn't hunting me.

"Tell her the rest." Atlas urges quietly. Lucas looks down at his feet and Kai stares at the grey gravel covering the courtyard.

Hermes threads his fingers behind his head and returns his eyes to the dark sky above. "We don't know why, for certain." He counters back at Atlas.

"We know why." Kai's voice is nearly a whisper and I realize she is crying.

Lucas squares his shoulders and looks at me. "It was a message from Ares; a warning for you. We betrayed him and sided with you. He's bringing war to you and the Shifters who side with you."

I feel as if the world is turning too fast and I can't keep up with it. More people have suffered pain and death in my name, in the name of this curse.

The blood drains from my face as my eyes begin to glaze over. Expecting Hermes, it's Kai who grabs my arms with a firm shake.

"No, you don't get to blame yourself for this." Her fierce stare pulls me back from my creeping panic and the blood rushes through me, pounding in my head. "The risk is necessary. None of us will have peace until this is over."

I nod my head as if I agree but in truth, I'm only trying to process the words she is speaking.

We were arrogant– or perhaps it was just me who was arrogant. We could have prevented this had we only gathered the Shifters and Immortals together in the immediate aftermath of their deflection from Ares.

Instead, they left Ares and pledged to help us. Then we left them to pick up the scattered pieces of their people as I hunt for my powers. We should have worked together.

Tension in the bond between Hermes and I thrums within me, and I feel as if he is holding something back from me. *There is something more.*

My eyes snap to his and I know I'm right with the weight sorrow hanging heavy in his stare. "What else has happened?"

Hermes shakes his head 'no' twice as if he doesn't want to tell me what secret he's keeping. The currents swell at my feet as my irritation surges.

"Is this you having faith in me? Is this you believing in me by keeping things from me?" I clench my fists at my side and take steadying breaths. The Wind around me settles but my heart pounds out of my chest.

Atlas takes a breath as if to answer me, but Hermes cuts him off. "Forty-eight children are missing."

"My gods." Callie's exclamation is barely a whisper, but it echoes loudly in the stillness of the moment. My chest tightens with each labored breath, and it feels as though the world is spinning around me while I struggle to remain upright. I widen my stance, bracing myself against Callie's forearm, her grip mirroring my own desperation.

"Where were they taken from?" The question escapes my

lips before I can fully process it, but deep down, I already know the answer.

"They were refugees seeking shelter at Medusa's Commune,"

R hea's eyes flick quickly to Atlas, and I watch their silent exchange. An understanding passes quickly between them as if they have reached an agreement.

I was foolish to hope we could get through the night without Rhea finding out about the twenty-four women murdered and dumped on Lucas's territory. Not only is this punishment for Lucas going against him but I feel Ares is making an offer.

Lucas can spare his Shifters from Ares' wrath if he helps turn Rhea over to him.

Thankfully, I know the deep well of gratitude Lucas carries for Rhea and what she did for him during her lifetime as Persephone.

My mate is the reason Lucas exists and is powerful enough to lead the Shifters out of Ares' control. When Lucas shared the memory of his emergence as a Titan, the truth of his loyalty to my mate was evident in every fiber of his being.

I don't have to worry about Lucas or his loyal Shifters betraying us to Ares. But I do worry about my mate and the toll this will take on her.

The last thing I want is for Rhea to put anymore blame on

herself for what is going on. Her emotions are running on edge and stressors are everywhere. It's effecting her more than she is trying to show, but I see it.

When she sleeps, I hear the distress of her nightmares and tuck her into me. Each night, she is always so cold, and I radiate warmth into her until I feel her body relax and her breathing calms.

I wish she would talk to me about her nightmares but I'm not going to push until she is ready to open up.

It seems like we have one obstacle after another to get over. But right now, our main focus needs to remain centered on figuring out what will happen when the triple moons align, and the eclipse opens up a portal to Tartarus.

I've ran through this scenario a dozen times a day since Rhea confessed it to me.

Something could come rushing out the portal to attack us, or it may be a doorway as Rhea believes. Dread covers me as I this scenario always leads me down one dark conclusion: that Rhea will run head-first into her next death.

Neither is a prospect I want but I'm set on preventing the later at all costs.

Seeing her and Atlas and what passes between them, Rhea has opened up to him about something. I can't help the small twinge of jealousy that wishes she had come to me with her thoughts.

While the past lives of my mate have made our relationship a challenge, one thing is consistent; there is no making her do anything she doesn't want to do. Even if that is something as simple as talking.

But Atlas has always been a great counselor for Callie and

me. He'll be the same for Rhea. I don't think Callie could have recovered from her captivity in Troy without him.

Learning how much trauma my sister carried and how patiently Atlas listened to it all– I don't know I could have remained calm for thirty seconds listening to her stories.

It took ages before Callie told me anything she went through during her captivity. With the realization they have been captive many more times, times Callie does not recall, Atlas and his counsel will be needed now more than ever.

Rhea looks as if she is thinking about the best way to burst out of here and go find the children. Some of them are the ones she just saved from the Underworld, and they are captive again.

The only solace we have is the Underworld is gone. Rhea and I made sure of that. But who is to say Ares doesn't have more secret bases hidden under the world's oceans or tunneled deep in the earth's molten core.

"What if this is Flint?" Rhea says with a far-off look in her eyes. "He said he was do something to make me proud of him." She rubs her arms as goosebumps cover her. Blinking several times, she returns from the distant places her thoughts were taking her.

"When the Lurkers were attacking, he said he had a big plan and after it, we would be together."

"I don't think Flint is capable of this." Atlas tries and fails to reassure Rhea. "This would require several people working together to pull off."

"I think Ares knows how to push your buttons." I rub her arm and she shivers, hugging herself and scanning the crowd quickly. Her gilded eyes rapidly moving from face to face as if she is looking for someone. "Ares will do anything to distract you, pull your head out of the game or even try to lure you to him."

"Fill me in on what you are looking for, baby?" I speak into her mind, keeping my eyes on her face. *"Let me help you."*

"Medusa." Her answer is curt but I'm thankful she responded quickly.

I haven't seen Deuce since she was sitting along the stone wall when we first arrived. If Rhea wants to speak with Deuce, I'll try to find her. Projecting my aura into the sky and out like a thin sheet of chiffon, it travels the realm.

My powers, amplified by our settled bond, soar across the realm in an instant, but find no trace of Medusa. Curious, I search again and attempt to project my thoughts to her with no answer.

"She's not here."

Rhea raises a sharp eyebrow and ticks her head at me as if that answers something for her. Turning away from me, Rhea takes a step before I catch her arm. "Hey, let me in, please."

Something in my tone makes her stop and she releases a deep breath. Closing her honey eyes, she appears to think about my request but decides against opening up.

"I'm not sure I'm ready to talk about it yet." With guilt coating her expression, she drags her gaze up my chest and face, eventually meeting my stare. "I don't want to be wrong."

"And I don't you to fight alone." I speak into her mind.

"Later." She whispers and pulls her arm out of my hold. Letting her slip out of my fingers, I fell the pull of her body as she walks away from me.

The light of the moon follows her and all the stars in the sky shine upon her as she meets Lucas and Kai. My heart tears a little, our bond offended she doesn't trust me with the truths inside her mind.

Rubbing my chest, I try to alleviate the tension building there, knowing its useless until she opens up the doors she is safeguarding. With a deep breath, I join her, pushing back the building pressure until its trapped in the depths of my mind.

"What is being done to find the children?" She asks, her shoulders squared and twisting her thick hair into a braid that hangs at her side.

It makes me think of my mother. A warrior who would be sprinting toward someone who needed help before she asked any questions. Rhea imbues that same strength and selflessness and I love her for it. But I'm also terrified the next time she runs into battle will be her last.

Before my thoughts send me into a spiral, I swallow the knot forming in my throat and shove my hands into my pockets.

"We have a strong feeling we know where they are." Lucas talks low, keeping the details of the missing children a secret so alarms are not raised by the partygoers. "Kai is waiting on a message from Cappa and Delta and then we're leaving."

Kai places a reassuring hand on Rhea's arm with a gentle squeeze. "We'll take care of this goddess; you have an alignment to contend with."

Rhea's shoulders drop with reassurance at Kai's words, and she releases a pent-up breath. "I can help."

"You've helped enough." Kai nods and keeps her resolve firm. "We'll free the children. We need you to free us of Ares."

With Kai's statement, Rhea bites back the offense at being told not to help locate the children.

Casting her eyes to the ground, she thinks a moment

before nodding in agreement and my heart begins to beat again. I hadn't realized how tense my body was, waiting to see if Rhea would insist on helping.

The alignment is the day after tomorrow and gods knows what we need to do to prepare. The missing children are important, but we can do nothing to stop the approaching eclipse.

And if the eclipse is going to be the last time my eyes will set their sights on Rhea, I plan on spending as much time wrapped in my mate as I can.

"How are the families from the Underworld doing?" Rhea interjects, perhaps hoping to shift her attention to something that may have a happy outcome.

"Adapting. It's a different world up here for many of them." Lucas flexes his jaw. The dozens of words he doesn't say speak louder than what he does say.

Kai's face lights up as she looks at the screen of her phone. The message from Cappa must have come in and she slides the phone back into her pocket. "It's time." She tells her Titan.

Lucas looks over his shoulder and catches the attention of Naomi, his most recent Alpha and first female to hold the rank. She carries one sleeping child in her arms and Kellan holds the other. The heads of both boys roll around as the adults shift them, preparing the leave the party for the night.

Lucas must have relayed a message because Naomi nods once and turns to speak with Zara and Kellan. The two siblings nod at Lucas in the same manner and the trio makes way for the portals with the sleeping twins.

"Let us know how it goes?" Rhea's request comes out so small. I can tell she would rather go but she's respecting Kai and Lucas asking her to stay out of it.

With a nod of agreement, we watch the Shifters leave with their leader and I think back to the great Fenrir.

A giant among men, the original Titan of Shifters stood over fifteen feet tall. His wolf was massive, standing nearly fifty feet in height.

With long brown hair and a long beard, the prowl of the mighty wolf could be seen in the gait of the large man. When Fenrir walked into the council of Titans, their tones would hush, and their heads would bow.

Once offended, the man could shift into beast and rip out the throat of his victim before his growl could reach your ear.

Lucas is quite the opposite.

He has tamed the animal lurking within his bones and puts his people first. I can see why my mate chose him to be one of her soldiers long ago.

Rhea tracks their movements until the portal light flashes, and they are gone. I stand behind her, wrapping my arms around her chest and pulling her into me. She holds my wrists with her soft hands and rests her head on my arm.

"You're not going to go back to the house to get some rest, are you?" Our buzz from the night has fizzled away and a heavy blanket of sorrow covers the evening.

"Not a chance." My mate answers, still staring at the empty portal.

Turning my head to look back at the rest of our friends, I catch Achilles' attention. "I'm going to get her out of here."

Achilles nods, sitting down on an empty section of outdoor seating. Pulling Callie into his lap, he flicks a spark into an outdoor fire pit, and it roars to life. "We'll finish here and clean up." My oldest friend reassures me and turns his attention back to Atlas and Odysseus.

Callie listens to their old fighting stories as she rolls her eyes. Hecate and Penelope go back to their drunken ramblings.

"Let's get out of here." Kissing Rhea's head, just above her ear, she gives me a quick hum of agreement. I surround us in blue light and my power takes us away from the party.

Not traveling too far, I know exactly where she'll want to go to calm her mind.

The dim lighting of the commune library greets us along with the comforting fragrance of parchment and old leather. Even at this late hour, the library is teaming with scholars and Mind Mages sorting through the new texts.

Rhea relaxes into me as she looks around with affection at the rows of tomes, full of their ancient secrets. I guide her to a wide break between the massive rows of shelves and we turn into a cove.

An expansive table made of rich walnut wood sits alone in the center surrounded by tall shelves of books on three sides.

Behind us is a large stained-glass window of Artemis.

The huntress is forever memorialized in the bright colors of glass, showcasing her longbow, and pointed fae ears.

With one foot braced on a large boulder and wind blowing her long hair, she looks over the realm of Avalon. From this angle, the ancient Titan, first slain in the wars, seems to guard over the expansive library.

A console table sits under the large window holding a large bowl full of fresh flowers. I lean against it and cross one ankle over the other, folding my arms over my chest.

Rhea walks to the nearest shelf and her thin fingers drag down the spine of the book. My cock twitches in my pants and I clear my throat, trying not to think about how that finger would feel running down the rungs of my piercings.

Gods, she would look so beautiful pushed against that book-shelf with me buried deep inside her.

"Can I get you something to read?" I ask Rhea in a low tone and even still my voice bounces across the marble floor.

Rhea sets her honey eyes on me, raising a single eyebrow and shakes her head back and forth slowly. My dick practically wants to leap out my pants with the heated look she gives me.

Rhea saunters to the table and leans against it, directly across from me, she mirrors my stance, crossing one ankle over the other.

My eyes burn a path down the length of her body as we sit locked in a silent exchange. "Can I get you something to eat?"

Her eyes flick to my pants that are growing tighter by the second. Rhea quickly averts her eyes back to mine, filled with new hunger. I tilt my head to the side and run my thumb slowly across my lower lip.

"Or shall I get myself something to eat, little goddess?"

Rhea tracks the movement as a flush rises in her freckled cheeks.

She wants me to take her right here in the library. The moment together in our living room as I secretly toyed with her in front of the others play out in my mind again. She wanted to be taken with the risk of getting caught.

And what my goddess wants, my goddess will get.

"*S it on the table.*" My voice strokes her mind with a sweet caress. A thread of my power spirals up one of her legs. Rhea does as I tell her. Lifting onto the ball of her foot, she scoots her plump ass onto the table.

A swirl of my portal opens next to her. When I tick my eyebrow and nod once toward it, she sticks her hand inside and retrieves the book I've selected. I love the way her mouth tilts in a knowing grin when she reads the title, "Taken by the Messenger of the Gods".

One of the many romance novels curated for her where the male love interest is a depiction of my mythology.

Rhea gasps when my aura brushes against her thigh. I nudge her leg wider, exposing the faintest glimpse of her black lace panties. *"Find a passage, little goddess, and make it a good one."*

Her cheeks flare as her aura pushes through the book. Scanning the texts, she finds one near the middle of the book and it opens.

My power glides up her smooth skin as if I were caressing her with my hands. Retrieving the book from her, it hangs in the air on a swirl of my Light, tilted to her open page so she can read it. When Rhea runs her tongue along her bottom lip, I pull at the strain in my pants as my cock pushes against the zipper.

"Open your legs wider." My voice is a whisper behind her ear.

Rhea watches me with her vixen eyes, arching her back and putting each of her pointed feet at the edge of the table. Holding herself up with her hands fixed behind her, she waits for my instructions. The heave of her chest rising dramatically as her heart pumps wildly within her.

The flex of her aura is as needy as my hard dick begging to be freed from the confines of my trousers. I take my time, running my thumb down the length of my erection. Squeezing my hand over the growing bulge to alleviate some of the pressure.

Rheas mouth pops open watching me and I swear I could come from seeing her look at me.

"Read it to me." I keep my voice low and watch as she shivers when I stroke down our repaired bond with my power.

She's timid and even speaking through telepathy, she stammers over the initial few words. The characters are having their first sexual encounter and I use the Light to read ahead of her.

Perched on the table, spread for me with both knees set wide, the heat of Rheas arousal is nearly enough to pull me to her like a magnet, but I fight to remain fixed right where I am.

Her wine color stola is secured at her shoulder with a gold olive branch pin. As if the light of the realm focused on it, the pin shines at me, pulling my eyes to it.

"Take the pin off."

She moves her eyes to me briefly before turning back to the book.

Rheas' delicate fingers feel along the cool metal, finding the clasp with one hand, it unlocks. The front of her stola dropping down her arm, exposes her beautiful breast to me as she reads about the Hermes in her book licking and kissing the nipples of the main character.

The bud if her brown nipple is tight and my mouth waters wanting to rub my tongue across it.

Without prompting, Rhea runs her hand down her chest. Slowly and with a featherlight touch, she glides the tips of her fingers over her creamy skin. When she reaches her nipple, Rhea pinches and rolls the point between two fingers, keeping her movements in time with the scene in the book.

Her bottom lip drops, and I want to suck it into my mouth. With hooded eyes, she moves her gaze to me as I fixate on her, enraptured as she teases herself.

Flicking open the button of my pants, I rest my hands on each side of the chest behind me. I have to keep hold of something to stop from pulling my dick out and alleviating the growing tension.

"Now, the other one, little goddess...and keep reading."

Rheas hand skirts across her chest. Pushing aside the fabric of the stola, her other breast is bare and there is no other sight sweeter in this realm.

Cupping her full breast with her palm she fingers her other nipple. Tilting her head toward her shoulder, her golden-brown hair sweeps across her skin, and she rocks her pelvis as the scene in the book moves along.

Fuck me.

I want to close the distance between us and bury my cock as deep inside her as I can. I want to squeeze that perfect throat when she tries to moan as her tight pussy grips my dick.

But I keep waiting as my erection complains, still trapped inside my pants. My zipper acting as it's jailor and preventing its escape because this is for her; only her.

"Take your panties off."

Her breath hitches, but she works the thin satin fabric off both hips. Bringing her knees together, I see the enticing line of her pink pussy as she frees herself of her panties.

Gods help me when she opens her legs again and that sweet center is glistening with her arousal. I feel the precum leak from the tip of my penis, begging me to go to her.

Keeping her underwear in her hand, she starts to place them behind her, but stops when I cock an eyebrow and shake my head back and forth.

"I don't think so. Toss them over."

Rhea's face flares to a new shade of red and I can't hold back my smirk. She doesn't argue and with pursed lips, she throws the ball of black satin at me.

Catching her panties, I keep my eyes on her as I turn my head slightly to the side.

Inhaling her scent deeply, I relish in the sweet smell of her moist panties before I push them into my pocket with a satisfied moan. With the same hand, I slowly lower the zipper of my pants.

My long erection nearly springs out, happy to finally be alleviated from its confines.

I think about her warm, wet mouth wrapped around my dick and it pulses at me with the need to have her. Rhea watches, just as hungry as I rub my hand down my cock, pushing aside my pants and showing her how hard the sight of her makes me.

"Read. And wet the tip of your finger for me, baby."

My perfect mate, perched on the table, lavishes the tip of her middle finger with her tongue. Running it down her full lip, she makes a show of dragging the wet finger down the center of her chest, just like the Hermes of her book is doing. Her spit glistens against her ivory skin, and I run my thumb down the first two barbells of my piercing.

"Rub your clit."

Her mouth pops open again, and she rolls her hips when her finger rubs the first circle cross her budding clit. Closing her eyes, I'm mesmerized watching her.

"Ah, keep reading, little goddess."

She's so obedient. Opening her eyes, her breathy voice returns to my mind as she runs her eyes over the passage.

I run my hand up my cock as she swirls her finger in small circles around her sensitive bundle of nerves. Rolling her hips forward and back again, she grinds against her finger.

I have to remind myself to keep breathing when I hear the moisture of her arousal reach me with each swish of her finger.

"You're doing so good for me; playing with that pretty pussy." I take my dick out of my pants fully and she drags her eyes from the page of the book to me. She is fixated, watching me as I watch her hand between her legs.

Now her eyes, like melted gold watch my hand. Slowly I run up the length of my erection and rub my thumb over the head of my dick. With a bead of cum, I lift it to my mouth and suck it off my thumb.

Her cheeks flare again.

"Do you like the way I taste, little goddess?" The deep timber

of my voice vibrating down our bond makes her drop her head back and her hooded eyes close. Deepening the arch in her back, she circles her clit faster. *"Because I could eat your delicious pussy for every meal."*

"Gods, Hermes." She's getting closer to a climax, the words of the book difficult for her to focus on. Her aura whips around her as I keep talking. My words pushing her closer toward reaching her pleasure. My fixed gaze building her toward a crest.

Taking slow steps to her, I stroke my cock and watch her fingers on her pussy.

"Keep going baby. You're so beautiful spread out." My breathy voice in her mind is a sign of my own arousal as I glide my hand along my hard shaft. *"Gods, you're so perfect and so wet."*

She snatches her lip between her teeth, holding back a whimper so it doesn't sound across the vast library.

Several bookcases over someone slides several books in and out of the shelves as they search for the tomes they need. In front of me, my goddesses bare pussy is all but begging to come as she quickens the pace of her finger on her clit.

Reaching her, I take her hand gently by the wrist. Rhea's breathing is heavy as the climbing orgasm falls before it could crest.

With one hand still on my dick, I take her finger, wet with her juices, and plunge it into my mouth. Closing my eyes, the taste of my mate is more divine than anything in this realm and I relish her.

When I let go of her hand, she braces herself on the table and I grab the back of her neck. With my forehead against hers, I replace her finger with the tip of my cock. The first barbell of my piercings rolls along her clit and her mouth falls into a perfect "o".

My immortal heart nearly stops beating with the first touch of my cock on her bare pussy. So close, I could plunge myself into her and feel how wet she truly is.

Instead, I rub circles along her clit with my erection. The barbell working her back toward a climax. But she's going to chase that peak a little longer because when she comes in this library, it's going to be on my face.

She works her pelvis against me. Rhea's gilded eyes burn me with the heat of her desire. I read to her now, my voice wrapping around her mind along with my power thrumming down our bond while I rub her clit with pierced dick.

"Hermes" Her needy whisper lets me know the tightness winding within her wants a release. Gods how I want to see her claim her pleasure but not yet.

Slowing the roll of my erection on her, I swipe two fingers up the slit of her wet pussy. Bringing them to her mouth, I rub the evidence of her arousal along her bottom lip.

Before she can protest, I lick the taste off her with my tongue. Then sucking her lip into my mouth, I chase every drop of her before I release her with a pop. She wants to kiss me and gods I want to dive into her.

We press our foreheads together. The nearness of our mouths is too much of a temptation and Rhea comes toward me. I move with her, never letting our mouths touch.

Denying her, I keep her on the edge of getting what she wants, her frustration is building until I can watch her tip over into her beautiful release.

"On your knees, little goddess." I step back from the table

and let her work her way to the edge. My mate is a melting pot of wants and desire.

She is timid but trusting, wanting this pleasure, and shyly going after it with my prompts. I want her to claim this craving and demand it for herself. I long to see her unapologetically open, taking command of her body and her hungers.

When she stands, the stola drops to her waist and I help it past her hips, exposing her naked body to the watchful gaze of the Titans frozen in the stained-glass windows around us.

She keeps her eyes on me as she lowers down her to knees in front of me. She is my gravity and my cock pulses, knowing she is near and salivating to taste me.

Her tongue peeks out from her mouth and she runs it across her lip as she looks at my monumental erection.

Don't cum you fucking idiot.

It's a pep talk more for myself than my cock as her long eyelashes brush the tops of her cheeks. Closing her eyes and opening her mouth, she takes the head of my dick between her full lips. Her soft tongue swirls around the tip of me as she licks her arousal off me.

"Gods baby," I groan, caressing her hair and moving my hips slightly along with the movements of her mouth.

She sucks me deep into her throat. Her hands are fixed around the back of my thighs, and she pulls me toward her, taking me deeper into her mouth.

When her moan rattles my cock, I tense my stomach and stifle my grunt. Running my fingers through the soft tendrils of her hair, I fist the back of her hair, pulling her off me.

Pouting, she looks at me with big doe eyes. Her mouth still open and her tongue licking the spit from her lip. I tuck my hard-on back into my pants and with the strength of all the Titans I manage to zip myself up.

Jumping up on the table, I lay down and motion to her. *"Get that sweet pussy up here."*

"Hermes!" Rhea whispers in embarrassed protest. She's too fucking adorable standing fully nude in this vast library. Her tight nipples are red where she was pinching them for me.

Leaning on one elbow, I raise an eyebrow at her.

"Don't make me ask again or I'll edge you until your screams bounce across every book in this gods forsaken building."

"Someone will see us."

"That's the point, beautiful. If we get caught with you riding my face, everyone will know exactly who owns this pussy. Now get. Up. Here."

I lay back down, knowing she's going to do it. She wanted this fantasy and gods; I'm going to give it to her.

Her pulse is racing at the thought of a spectator, rounding the shelf of books, and finding us in this hidden little cove. But she is safe from the prying eyes of others.

I'm projecting a Mirage around us, and this looks like nothing but an empty table to anyone who could walk by. There is no way I'm letting anyone see how gorgeous she looks when she's coming. I'm keeping that view all to myself.

Any asshole who sets eyes on her in a state like this will have them burned out of their head for looking at my goddess.

Her aura is pulsing with her arousal, and I soak in the feeling of her. She wants to come so badly, and she is going to taste fucking delicious when her orgasm is dripping down my face.

She takes a timid step to me and uses one of the chairs to

get her knee on the table. Straddling my stomach, she pauses, as if she is unsure I truly want her pussy on my face.

Hooking my arms under her knees, I bring her to me in one motion. Raising my head, I give her pussy a long, slow lick as I resume reading to her.

"*Oh, yes.*" She loves the feeling of my mouth on her and whispers a sigh of gratitude as my tongue traces her. Rhea has her hands braced on her thighs and she's supporting her weight from me.

When I reach her clit, I swirl my tongue around the tiny bud, and she quivers above me. My stomach turns over in knots at her reactions to me.

'I've got you, goddess. Relax onto me." Taking another measured lick of her pussy, I pull her into me and slowly she begins to relax as the words of the book flow into her mind. "*Good girl.*" The tension in her legs eases as I kiss and lick her core.

"*Gods, baby. I've never tasted anything sweeter than you.*" My words encourage her, and she rocks her hips against my face. "*Mmm hmm. Just like that.*"

Rhea exhales quietly again. With each soft tilt of her hips, she widens her knees and brings them in again. My arms are hooked under her thighs, and I help her work her hips along my mouth.

When I begin to suck her clit, her back arches and I pull her legs further apart as she rocks forward. Her fingers thread my hair and the sensation of her nails along my scalp shoot down my spine.

"*Mmm.*" I hum my appreciation against her clit. Sucking her into my mouth, I swirl her bundle of nerves with my tongue. She relaxes onto me fully and fucking rides me.

And gods could I stay here all day feasting upon her.

"Hermes, yes. I'm so close." The soft yellow glow of candle-light worships her beautiful body on display for me. Her perfect tits bounce along with the ends of her wavy hair as she moves herself along my mouth. The character in the book is coming up to her first orgasm and so is Rhea as I recite the sensual scene of the story into her mind.

Her freckled cheeks are flared, and her mouth is gaping open as she silently takes her pleasure. Rocking against me faster, I lavish her with my tongue, keeping time with her movements. I graze my teeth along her pulsating clit, and she shudders, so close to letting go and allowing me to lap up her orgasm.

Her legs tighten around my head as she holds her breath.

Through our bond, I feel the crest of her orgasm and it nearly sends me into a climax of my own. My cock tries breaking out of my zipper as I thrust my pelvis. Anything to feel some friction along my begging erection.

As her climax washes over her, I use my powers and vibrate the tip of my tongue against her throbbing clit.

She lets out a single yelp and its echoes across the library.

Fisting my hair with both hands, her thighs lock around my head and she demands her pleasure. And I fucking give it to her.

I suck every drop from her as she grinds along my face, the story forgotten about. Slowing as the crest of her orgasm fades away, she leans back.

Rubbing her hand down the length of my cock, she squeezes me, and the edges of my vision turn black.

I keep my eyes on her. She watches me as I lick her again

with tenderness. When my tongue passes her clit, her body jerks, and she lets her head hang back.

Widening her legs and arching her back, she presents her pussy to me. My greedy little goddess is not done yet.

A wicked smile slides across her lust coated face. "More."

With a smile just as sinful, I taste her again, swirling my tongue on her greedy little bud as she drops her head back and begins another ride.

"As you wish, my greedy little goddess."

Fucking in a library is my new favorite thing, right up there with riding Hermes' face while he reads smut to me. I've never sat on someone's face before and orgasmed as they gave me oral. A fire lit within me, holding Hermes' hair with one hand, I stimulated his dick with the other. Riding his face again, I came in a matter of seconds.

Then he laid me back on the table and curling two fingers in me, he devoured me for a third time. That one more intense than the others as his fingers and mouth worked me in perfect time with his power caressing my bond.

None of my past lovers could ever compare to Hermes. He's on a different scale, both in size and stamina. But what sets him apart is how he devours me, praising me at every turn and bringing my fantasies to life as he worships my body. It's a whole new experience for me.

The mortal men I wasted my time on before made me feel ashamed for having desires. They wanted me to lay down for their three minutes of ecstasy and then asked, *'did you come?'* at the end.

I told them the sweet lie they expected to hear and masturbated later.

But Hermes is different. He takes care of my pleasure like no one else ever has. When he brought me to the library, he intended for us to lose ourselves in books. But all I wanted was to get lost in him.

I wanted to forget the eclipse, the war, the pain, and death that surrounds me and I just wanted to feel my mate. My heart raced as I struggled to voice my desires, but with Hermes, I didn't need to. He is always attuned to me, knowing exactly what I need and how to give it to me.

In our secluded spot, he guided me, coaching me as he pleasured me. I quickly realized he had cloaked us in a Mirage, ensuring our privacy and allowing me to fully let go.

His hands guided mine, his words of praise fueling my arousal. He teased me to the edge of orgasm multiple times, building the tension until it was almost unbearable. And when I finally reached climax, it hit me like a tidal wave of sensation, more intense than anything I'd ever experienced before.

After my third orgasm, I couldn't stay silent any longer.

I craved the sound of our bodies colliding as Hermes took me vigorously. I wanted him to thrust into me while pulling my hair and whispering dirty words in my ear. I longed to scream with pleasure as he brought me to climax again and again.

And that's exactly what we did.

More than once tonight, he wanted me take charge. He refused to touch me until I told him what I wanted.

"Use your words, beautiful." He whispered in my ear as his erection pressed against me. Standing behind me, he slid his long cock between my legs, teasing my sensitive pussy that had already been pleasured multiple times by him.

I directed him where I wanted his lips, hands, and his cock. And he fulfilled every request, and then some.

Now, nestled in the curve of his arm as the sun peeks over the horizon, we're utterly spent.

Truly and well worshiped by my bonded mate, Hermes made love to me all night. We showered together where he devoted himself to massaging and kissing me. With gentle hands, he washed away the fatigue, tenderly cleansing every inch of my body.

Once dry and settled in bed, he fetched a bottle of massage oil. Starting at my feet, he skillfully worked the moisturizing oil into my skin, kissing each foot and ankle before moving on to massage my legs. He carefully tended to any soreness between my thighs, then continued to rub the oil onto my stomach and breasts, ensuring I felt pampered and cherished.

He never made it about sex, even though the experience was incredibly sensual.

Hermes showered my body with a new kind of affection, nurturing me after our intense lovemaking. His touch was both gentle and firm as he turned me over, focusing on massaging my buttocks and back.

Not once did he show any signs of arousal or imply that sex was expected after caring for my body. His tender hands worked tirelessly over every tired muscle and joint, and in that moment, I realized that I had never been cared for without the expectation of something in return.

Feeling vulnerable yet strangely liberated after this realization, a newfound sense of trust and security washed over me, enveloping me in a warmth I had never known before.

As we closed the curtains to shut out the daylight completely, we nestled into each other's arms and drifted into a peaceful sleep. In that moment of surrender, for the first time in my life, I felt truly safe.

"How could you ever think this?"** The weight of Hermes' disbelief crushes any hope I had of him understanding.

"I should've known better," I murmur, anger and frustration welling up, hot tears threatening to spill over. Wiping them away with the back of my hand, I retreat to the couch, folding my arms defensively across my chest.

Around us, Callie, Achilles, and Atlas exchange glances, their expressions a mix of confusion and judgment.

Hermes rises abruptly, unable to bear sitting beside me any longer, and strides down the hallway toward our bedroom. Callie leans in, whispering something to Achilles, their gaze lingering on me with a hint of judgement.

This is the price Triton warned me about—the cost of speaking the truth. My mate and friends, they'll never believe me. Atlas remains silent, a coward in this moment, leaving me to voice the truth alone.

Even after I confided my suspicions about Medusa to him, Atlas had promised to investigate, searching through his journals of Athena for any clues. But now, he's turned against me, acting as if I'm a traitor for suggesting Medusa could have betrayed us.

The repeated deaths I've endured seem to have forged stronger bonds between them and Medusa, leaving me isolated and abandoned.

I was foolish to speak up. I should have known better and kept my thoughts to myself.

I stay put for a moment, seething with anger, until it dawns on me that Hermes is the one acting like a jerk. He's not even willing to listen to what I have to say, to consider that there might be some truth to it.

Well, I don't need their help or their support anyway.

Triton was right about something else as well; their combined power could never match the greatness within me.

So, screw this and screw them.

I refuse to back down just because Hermes doesn't want to hear the truth. Standing up, I push past our guests, determined to confront Hermes, and have my say.

The hallway twists and stretches before me, seeming longer and darker than I remember.

"Hermes!" I call out, my voice bouncing strangely within the confines of our Mount Olympus home.

"You're wrong about her," Hermes' voice responds from behind me, though he was just ahead moments ago. I turn around, only to find myself back in the living room, but it's no longer bathed in daylight.

Confusion clouds my thoughts as I stand in the hallway, feeling disoriented, cast suddenly into the darkness of night.

Returning to the common room, I find it deserted. Callie, Achilles, and Atlas are gone, leaving behind a chilling emptiness. The darkness surrounds me, shadows lurking in every corner as if reaching out to me. None of the lights are on, casting the room into a cold, foreboding silence.

"Jealous, lying bitch."

I inhale sharply, feeling Hermes' words pierce my heart

with their anger and hatred, echoing through my mind from my newly bonded mate.

Turning back towards the hallway, prepared to confront him, I'm instead confronted by a pair of glowing green eyes.

Medusa stands amidst the darkness, her aura radiating a haunting green glow as her body contorts like a serpent. Earthly elements obey her will as a swirling sandstorm envelops her legs and torso, propelling her forward with a frenzied energy.

With her braided hair whips wildly around her as Medusa charges towards me.

As I stumble backward, my feet tangling in a futile attempt to escape, I find myself unable to gain any traction on the floor, now transformed into a swirling pit of quicksand.

Four ghastly arms emerge from within the liquid sand, wrapping around my body with a chilling grip. Decay hangs from their bones, the stench of death filling my senses.

I try to scream, to draw in a breath, but the suffocating grip tightens around me, rendering me silent and gasping for air.

My frantic kicks yield no escape as I struggle against the relentless pull of the quicksand, finding no solid ground to anchor myself.

On my left side, the decaying head of Terra emerges from the quicksand. Her eyes are milky white and black tar seeps from the open wound at her neck.

On my right, Triton rises from inside the viscous sand with milky white eyes rolled back in his head. Rock and barnacles are one with his skin, and brown water flows in a steady stream from his mouth, leaking out of his ears. The sounds of eternal drowning fill the space as Medusa's hair latches around my neck.

The braids tighten around me, and my eyes bulge as my body fights for air.

"We'll hold her, Titan, as you syphon her stolen powers." Terra and Triton speak together with their voices garbled.

Medusa's green aura surrounds me, and their rotting limbs hold me tighter.

From the shadows of the dark hallway, Hermes emerges, his gaze fixed on me as he stands behind Medusa, silently observing as she and her ghastly companions attack me.

"Who could ever love a monster?"

"**F**uck, baby, wake up."

I jolt upright in bed, breath ragged and heart pounding, struggling against the tangled sheets wrapped around me. A sob escapes my lips uncontrollably, tears already streaming down my face.

I must have been crying in my sleep.

The room feels unnaturally dark, sending a shiver of fear down my spine as I wonder if I'm still trapped in the nightmare. My grip on Hermes' forearm is tight, my nails digging into his skin, leaving my fingers sore.

My black mist fills the room, a manifestation of the emotions that poured out of me in the dream. It all felt so real at first, eerily familiar, until it took a terrifying turn.

By the time I could have realized it was just a dream, I was already engulfed in panic, unable to shake myself from the nightmares grip.

Hermes radiates warmth beside me, his body damp with

sweat just like mine. I release my grip on his arm, noticing the worry etched on his face as he looks at me with concern.

"You need to tell me what that was about."

"I can't talk to you about this." Swinging my feet over the bed, I walk to the large wall of glass that overlooks the mountain and throw the curtain open. It's sunset.

We slept all day, and tomorrow is the eclipse.

Sliding the door open, my mist trails behind me as I step onto the patio, drawing in the currents of the realm. The fresh air embraces me, easing the panic that had gripped my lungs.

With each breath, the shadows that clouded my mind begin to dissipate, carried away by the gentle breeze. I exhale deeply, calming down as I lean against the metal railing.

"Rhea, you shared everything in that dream with me. I saw it all." Hermes leans against the railing with his arms crossed over his wide chest. "Please, talk to me."

We stand in silence for an eternity.

I swear I can see the ebb and flow of civilizations as I look over the horizon as if humanity is rising and falling in fast motion around us.

Hermes waits as I battle with myself. The warning from Triton blaring like a warning bell within me.

"Everything points to Medusa." My broken voice is a whisper and I feel like such a coward, but I keep talking. For an hour, I spill everything I held within myself since Triton shared his secret vision with me.

Hermes says nothing and listens to everything.

I tell him of Medusa and her reign as Queen of Egypt. When I was Cleopatra and a general of her mighty army, the raging queen would rather decimate her people with ten plagues than allow them to go free of her tyranny.

"She planned to enact twelve plagues. Just like there were twelve Titans, Hermes," I reveal, the weight of the evidence heavy on my heart as I recount what I remember against Medusa. "Your army was the only thing that stopped her."

Medusa abandoned her kingdom, fled to her cave, and left me to die.

"Eventually, you managed to reach her, and she became a different person. But I came to know a very different Medusa than you did. I know what she is capable of."

Hermes takes a seat on the patio, his hands extended toward me in a gesture of acceptance, not rejection. My heart, though fractured, swells with emotion, and I practically run to him, seeking relief in his embrace.

Holding me close, Hermes gently strokes my hair and plants a kiss on my forehead. "Thank you for opening up to me, Rhea. Why didn't you tell me sooner?"

"I was afraid," I admit, another tear slipping down my cheek. "I'm just as terrified of losing you as you are of losing me. I understand how much you and Medusa mean to each other. Besides Achilles, she is your closest friend."

"And you are my mate," Hermes affirms, drawing me closer and gently tilting my chin to meet his gaze. "No one comes before you."

His kiss is filled with passion, and I can feel the sincerity in his words. "I understand your concerns about Medusa, and your safety is my utmost concern. If you don't feel safe, we'll address it together. And if Medusa is indeed betraying us, then gods help her."

Relief washes over me like a flood and I wrap my arms around him. Hermes encases my waist and squeezes me just as tightly as I'm holding him.

I should have put my faith in my mate and our bond.

Triton scared me with his ominous warning of the price to pay for sharing the truth of his vision.

Never once has Hermes ever caused me to doubt him and on the eve of the alignment, the course of our future changes forever. But we will go into it together.

I know that nothing we face tomorrow will be strong enough to come between us.

I only regret not saying something sooner and I hope that choice doesn't cost me my life. Not when I have so much more to lose this time.

As the sun rises over the realm, the static electricity in the atmosphere grow. With each passing hour I feel the tension of the realm and it resonates as stress between my shoulders.

The alignment will reach its peak today and a doorway to Rhea's power will open the instant Gaea's moon crosses in front of the sun.

Through our bond I can feel her stomach is full of knots, and she's been nibbling on the same piece of cantaloupe for thirty minutes. Lost in thought, her fork slips from her grip and clamors on her plate, startling her.

"Sorry, I'm just nervous." She bites her lip to ease her anxiety but it's a pointless effort. Nothing can quell the storm raging within her emotions as we wait on the eclipse.

"You don't have to apologize for anything." I round the kitchen and kiss her temple. The smell of sweet berries surrounds me, and I breathe her in. "Come on, let's get dressed."

We have a few hours until the alignment begins, and we spent the night preparing for a battle. There can be no doubt, Ares will try to stop us today. While the power within the pendent may not be what he's seeking, it's an important step for Rhea to unlock.

She needs all her powers, but knowledge will be just as important in this battle against those who hunt her. She feels her mind is still so broken and parts of her memory are laying in tattered shreds at the bottom of her soul.

The importance of Alexandria and the truth locked inside the ancient library is vital to her. So important, she risked her first lifetime to tuck away the old building and ensure it could never be found again, not until the time was right. *Until she was ready.*

Lucas and his Shifters will meet us today at the former site of Alexandria. After Rhea and I talked last night, I made a call to Lucas advising him to move his Shifters from Medusa's commune to Delphi.

It was easy enough to do with only a few lies. Should things turn bad today, Delphi is closer and has more warriors. In truth, I can't stomach knowing we moved people who suffered in Ares' Underworld to a new form of captivity with someone who may be secretly aligned with him.

"It could make sense." I was lost in thought last night just before contacting Lucas. When Rhea shared her life with Medusa in ancient Egypt, when Medusa was a feared Pharaoh and Queen known as Nefertiti, the darkness that surrounded Medusa during that time was truly terrible.

It was another lifetime I scoured the realm, pulled by my mate and others prevented us from reaching each other. Medusa had turned against us all and locked Egypt in a prison-state. My mate was known as Cleopatra and a general in Medusa's army.

Scholars think the name Nefertiti means *'a beauty has*

come' but it's a mistranslation. When Alexandria was lost, many ancient languages were lost as well. The truth of Medusa's former alias is still known to those of us still fluent in the old languages of the realm.

'A monster has come': The phrase her victims would utter, if they were still able to speak before she turned them to stone.

We finally broke into the ancient city after a decade long battle. I found the body of my mate, Cleopatra in a temple.

"If Medusa is allied with Ares, she could have worked with Aryana to clear the Kenya Commune of mortals *and* the warriors Medusa knew would turn against her. And since her commune was empty, we ushered the refugee Shifters right in there without question."

"And then twenty-four women were plucked from her commune without a trace and brutally murdered." Rhea added her thoughts to mine and a cold layer of understanding covers me like being dipped in an icy lake.

"Medusa would have known." I run my hand down my face, trying to clear the stress but it's futile. "There is no way so many women could have gone missing right under her nose and her not know."

I feel ridiculous for not thinking of this sooner. "She is an Earth elemental. Her wards are embedded within the very rock that makes up every building within in her commune." As I kept talking, my anger rose with every word. "Every footstep that falls upon her mountain, she knows."

She even knew Rhea was a Titan as soon as Rhea stood upon Kenya soil, Medusa knew; and she said nothing.

When I called Lucas last night, he let us know they recovered the missing children and none of them were harmed. They had been left alone inside a deep cave system on the east coast of America. The children never saw their captor, but all described "the man with one hand".

Fucking Flint.

Rhea was right last night. She believed he wanted to lure her out to save the children, just as she did in the Underworld. Perhaps he planned to ambush her or worse, is delusional enough to believe she would bond with him somehow.

My blood boils just thinking about it.

Neither of us could sleep and we tried watching some television. But every channel was blasting Ares' fake smile as he spread his charm and lies for the mortal news cameras.

Each time we changed the channel and saw a new image or video of the God of War, I could feel Rhea flinch. I know she still feels the awful touch of his flames on her soul and hears the sickening crunch of her bones under his torture.

She knows the monster that lives within him better than anyone, save Atlas. They are the only two who have seen the mask removed from the God of War and know how truly low he will sink for the power he craves.

There is no one he won't pull into his quest to consume Rhea and she is right to mistrust Medusa.

We must stop him and those who listen to his messages of destruction. The ones who allow themselves to be controlled by Ares and those who hunt alongside him.

My mind drifts back to the haunting green eyes that stalked Rheas dream yesterday.

The images of Medusa preying upon her play on a loop in my mind. The terror my mate felt that was so palpable, even hours later, it still chokes me with anger.

A dozen times throughout history, Medusa has retreated to her caves and gone missing for eons. I presumed she was only sulking in her misery and depression over Athena. But what if the truth of her whereabouts is much more sinister?

The master puppeteer, trailing after my mates' reincarnations and syphoning her power through each lifetime, could be one of my oldest friends. Returning from the Underworld, Medusa could have severed her bond with Athena, and played the role of another victim of Ares.

Just like Terra did.

But as Rhea prepares to leave this realm and seek the relic that holds her power, I'll do what I can to protect everyone that remains behind, waiting for her return. We'll help others see the truth of Ares' deception against those we believe are our friends and allies.

Just as we captured Demeter and brought her treachery to the light, we'll do the same with anyone that aligns with Ares. Playing a game, just as he has, we'll move the right pieces at the right time until Rhea's enemies can hide no further.

Now that the sun has fully risen and it's time for us to prepare for the eclipse. I lead Rhea to our bedroom and a large white box with a big blue bow is waiting for her. "I had this made for you."

Rhea makes herself smaller at the sight of my surprise and I hate the guilt she feels when someone does something for her. It's as if she sees herself as a bother and I want to erase those feelings from within her.

"Hermes, you didn't need to get me a present." She runs her fingers along the blue satin ribbon tied around the box.

"It's more practical than anything else. Trust me, you'll like it."

She removes the bow that matches the color of my eyes and lifts the lid.

A set of brown fighting leathers are folded neatly inside. A matching pair of thigh holsters carry her blades, crafted by Hephaestus, and imbued with runes that harness her powers. A pair of tactical boots that will lace up to her knees lay on top.

"Achilles made sure everything was fireproof, even against Soul Fire."

She runs her fingers along three dandelions etched into the chest plate and even from here, I can feel the essence of my sister there. On the etching, the seeds of the flowers are drifting away with the Wind, and it makes Rhea smile. "I love it."

My chest swells with pride and pushes against the worry that has been collecting within me as the alignment nears. Rhea cups my cheek and rises on the tips of her toes to kiss me. "Thank you."

"Now, as much as I love taking clothes off this beautiful body of yours." I smirk when her cheeks flush red and I stroke her jawline gently. "I'll help you get dressed. Arms up."

Biting her lip, she raises her arms, and I left my fingers trace along her skin as I lift her nightgown over her head. Left in a pair of red panties, I drink in the sight of her and memorize each freckle and small scar that rests on her skin.

She looks at me with her golden eyes and I stare at each ribbon that shines within them, committing the sight of her to my memory.

Taking the brown tactical shirt and chest plate from the box, I slip the shirt over her head, and she threads her arms through the sleeves. The compression of the elemental fabric will protect her from attacks and bind her shields tighter to her body.

Before I pull the shirt over her exposed breasts, I drop to my knee.

My hand caresses her soft thigh and I pull her toward me. I lavish her nipple with my mouth, and she whimpers at my touch. Running her hands through my hair, she holds onto me as I kiss and suck her peaked breasts.

Rhea is always so hungry for me to consume her, and gods do I love the feel of her against me. I wish I could have a dozen lifetimes with her before the looming eclipse begins but time is racing ahead of us.

Sinking back so I'm sitting on my heels, I take her left leg and hang it over my shoulder. Kissing her pussy over her panties, I can feel how wet she is and my world centers in on her pleasure. My only need is to hear how beautifully she cums, and I stroke my finger along the lace edge of her panties.

Moving them to the side, I take my time with the first pass of my tongue along her slit, and I sense when her head drops back. I almost feel her eyes roll to the back of her head and her moan fills the room.

"Hang onto me goddess, so I can worship you one last time before you go."

And I pray to her with my tongue. Licking and stoking her clit, I suck her until her body quivers around me and her orgasm explodes through her.

When I'm finished with her, she is panting as she looks down at me with heavy lidded eyes. Taking the leather pants from the box, I help her into them. Kissing her knee, then her thighs and her hip as I pull them up the length of her gorgeous legs.

Standing, I pick her up, holding her body tight. She wraps her legs around my waist, and I push her against the wall. Our lips collide and I squeeze her to me with desperation. I drink in the taste of her, scared it's the last time I'll be able to consume her.

"Please come back to me." My plea is a whisper against her lips, and fear tightens its grip around my throat.

"I promise." She takes my face between both of her hands and presses her forehead to mine. Closing her eyes, a single tear streaks down her face and I kiss it away. "I promise, I'm coming back to you, no matter what."

Our mouths are driven to each other again, both of us needing another embrace and to bask in the sensation of our reformed bond.

"It's almost time to go." She says and I nod, wanting to lie to us both that we still have plenty of time.

I lace her boots, my touch on her calf lingering as I don't want to let her go. Last, I retrieve her thigh holders and fix the first one around her.

I take her hand and together we secure the clasp. Through our bond, she senses my Light Shield cover her armor and follows me. Placing a shield of Darkness along with my Light, our powers flare and braid together.

"No one takes off this armor but me, when you are back here safely."

She smirks, but I see the nervousness of the unknown journey ahead hiding within her eyes. "And what if I take my armor off without you?"

I fist her hair at the nape of her neck and pull back gently. She parts her mouth, and I can't help but look at her full lips before returning my gaze back to her honey eyes.

"Then may the Fates have mercy on you when I find you." Seriousness steals the grin from my face and my smirk drops. "And I will always find you, my goddess."

The blue flare of my portal fades away and we squint our eyes against the sunlight blazing against the Sahara sand. Standing at the outermost ring of the massive crater we look across the expanse. Behind us is the sun.

In a matter of moments, the moon will begin passing in front of the sun and mark the beginning of the triple moon alignment. For seven and a half exhausting minutes, I'll worry about Rhea as she navigates Tartarus alone.

With her hand tightly in mine, I give her a reassuring squeeze.

Looking at me, I feel like my worry is reflected in her eyes as she gives me a tight-lipped smile in return, adjusting the pack of provisions on her back. Bringing water and food, she is prepared to meet the realm of desert and sunlight that is Tartarus, if it even exists.

She'll need several days to traverse the harsh landscape and return with her powers.

Portal's flare around us as our small army arrives.

Well, not quite an army but a show of force, should Ares or his loyal followers make an appearance.

The first small group to arrive is from Delphi.

Odysseus and Penelope arrive with dozens of Delphi warriors dressed in blue with bronze shields. Others remain at the commune to protect the refugee families of Lucas' packs.

With Odysseus and Penelope are Atlas, Calypso, and Achilles. I smirk seeing Atlas in his old of fighting leathers that he's not worn since Troy.

"They still fit." He jests in my mind with a wink.

"Well, let's see if you last longer in this fight than you did Troy."

"Hopefully there won't be a fight."

Doubtful.

Callie and Achilles wear their crimson and gold leather armor. If Patroclus were here, the trio would be an imposing force at the forefront of the fighting line.

Rhea's leathers match mine as we both wear rich brown gear. My sword is in my scabbard and her daggers are strapped onto her thighs.

A deep purple swirl of Darkness ushers Hecate and twenty other Immortals to the desert. Flora and Zephyr are with her, and Flora gives Callie a small wave of her hand. The healing power of Water and Life will be helpful, should the worst happen but we need more fighters.

When the portals ignite delivering the Shifters to the Sahara, the Zeta King certainly took me seriously when I asked him to bring help.

There must be two hundred Shifters, most still in human form and dozens of others in their Shifted forms. Lucas, Kai, and his pack are in the center. A massive bear with a scarred blue eye immediately scans the area in a circle. It's Naomi. Other bears, lions and wolves take positions around the perimeter of our allies.

Just as I'm wondering where Medusa is, a final portal flares and she joins us; alone.

Taking a deep breath, Rhea and I look at each other. An understanding of the same thought passing between our bond. Then, without speaking, we look at the sun, seconds away from being kissed by the moon.

Fuck, I wish we had more time.

"I love you. Gods, I love you with every molecule of my being." As the tension between the realms tightens, I'm desperate for one last feel of my mates' lips on mine.

Rhea and I surge into each other, both of us sensing the second we'll be separated rushing toward us.

"I love you." She replies in a breathy response. "And I'm coming back to you."

"You better."

The sound of a large portal flaring on the other side of the crater makes me close my eyes in resignation. My heart sinks as I look across the landscape and see hundreds of soldiers look back at us.

Ares stands at the front line of a massive army.

Fuck.

The God of War is gracing the battlefield himself, today.

Wearing gold armor, Ares' rams' helmet is hanging lazily at his side. The gold armor was an ode to my father, Apollo, the sun god. His sunlight would reflect off Ares' gold armor and become a blazing beam of fiery sunlight.

An homage to my slain father that offends me seeing how Ares is the immortal responsible for his death.

Ares' army wears all-black tactical gear. The Shifters who have come with his are in animal form standing tall above the Elementals.

Rhea tenses and I feel a cold wash of anxiety pour over her through our bond just as the eclipse begins. The first sliver of Gaea's moon begins its path in front of the sun.

The powers of the realms swell, and Rhea's hair begins to lift as if the three moons are pausing to worship the Goddess of the Twelve Realms.

A crackle charges the atmosphere of Gaea and as the sun dims, the auras around us brighten.

Our allies are at our back and enemy is before us.

But all give pause as we soak in the surge the alignment gives us. Every immortal will grow in strength and power for the next seven and a half minutes.

We watch the moon as it kisses the sun. A small crescent of the giant yellow star is blocked, and the countdown has begun.

A dozen meters away, the recognizable flare of sliver starlight bursts into existence. The distant sensation of Rhea's power pulls at us both. My mate and I turn to look, seeing a swirling portal of darkness appear. *The doorway to Tartarus.* Just as Rhea suspected.

She looks at me and my heart breaks, knowing she needs to leave.

The God of War takes a step toward us, then another.

His eyes flick to the doorway and then my mate.

Soot rolls off his shoulders, leaving a trail of smoke behind him that floats away on the gentle breeze as he puts on his ram's helmet.

As much as it pains me, I let go of her hand.

I stroke my finger down Rhea's cheek and she closes her eyes. "Go." I tell her. "Just remember, it will be three days for you but only a few minutes for us. So, take care of yourself. We'll be okay."

"You better be."

I draw my sword and a circular shield of Light blazes in my hand as my heart breaks.

Ares erupts a trail of fire that burns behind him. I see his orange aura expand as he charges himself to strike Rhea.

Calling upon my power, blue starlight expands around me

as I prepare to blast Ares. The God of War lifts his palm, as a wall of fire dancing with orange and black flames surges outward.

Before I release my wave of light, the deep bronze fire of Achilles billows next to me. His wall of fire meets Ares and the Flames battle. Jet streams eject from each of them, and an explosion of fire erupts where their powers collide.

"I've got you covered, brother. Tell your mate goodbye." My oldest friend speaks to me in my mind with a strain in his voice. Ares is the strongest Fire elemental there is but as the currents of the realm blow behind me, I know the Temptress of the Four Winds is coming to fight with her Flame.

Rhea conjures a dark portal and transports herself to the entrance of the silver swirling doorway that waits for her.

Pausing, she looks back at us. Her eyes first going to Achilles and Ares locked in a battle of power. Fifty feet separate them as flames pour from both their hands.

Callie takes several steps toward her mate as the currents swell around her. Like a tide rushing in, the Winds follow her but Callie pauses, looking at Rhea who stands at the opening to Tartarus.

"Be careful over there." Callie says. Squaring her shoulders, Rhea nods. My sister smirks, saying, "Bring me back a souvenir." Rhea smiles and Callie winks.

I know if there were time, the friends would hug and cry, wanting to run into the portal and face whatever is there together. But Callie walks toward her mate and brings the Winds with her. They build and she prepares to send them careening into Achilles' Fire.

Rhea finds me and neither of us want to say the word 'goodbye', so we don't.

As Callie's Winds slam against her mates Fire, they explode. I feel the wall of heat grow and watch as Rhea's face warms with orange and bronze flames reflecting in her honey eyes.

She takes the first step into the silver swirl of her power and then a second. Keeping her eyes on me, she walks into the portal. When she is immersed in the doorway to Tartarus, it closes around her, and she is gone.

I free fall for what feels like minutes but in reality it's only a few seconds. Passing through a tunnel of power connecting the realms is like being stretched through space and time. As if my body was squeezed through a keyhole, the pressure feels as if it will rip me in two.

Panic surges through me as I plummet, my heart pounding in my chest, adrenaline coursing through my veins. With the breath forced out of my body, I gasp for air as I emerge from total darkness and am thrust into crushing sunlight.

I can't help but think of Icarus.

The blaze of this scalding sun sears my skin and I imagine Icarus flew so close, he must have been suffocated by its heat, just as I am. The sun melted his wings and sent him plummeting to the ocean.

In all the depictions of Icarus, his descent looks so elegant and graceful.

But the sudden transition jolts me, disorienting and overwhelming my senses. My arms flail and my legs kick as I drop from the sky.

It's a harrowing fall and I quickly turn my head, trying to glimpse anything to help me but the strong glare of the sun blinds me. I realize it's not a sea I'll be crashing into but an ocean of sand as an endless crimson desert awaits me.

With a grunt of pain, I crash onto a tall sand dune, the impact knocking the wind out of me. I try to brace myself, but the momentum sends me tumbling down the sandy slope, my body bouncing and rolling uncontrollably. My pack slips off my back and slides down with me.

Sand bites my skin, filling my eyes and mouth, choking me as I struggle to breathe. Adrenaline sets in as I feel myself losing control, sliding faster and helpless to slow my descent until I near the bottom, where the dune levels out.

Gasping for breath, heart racing, I lie there for a moment, shaken and but otherwise unscathed. The realization of where I am sinks in, and a surge of fear grips me: *Tartarus.*

I have no idea what awaits me in the realm of eternal sunlight and the final battleground of the Titan's war. There is no moment for me to rest in the ignorant bliss of thinking I'm remotely safe.

With trembling hands, I wipe the sand and grit out of my eyes and mouth. Pushing my aura outward in a large radius, I detect no signs of life. There is not a soul for miles and nothing to see except endless desert.

A cool rush of relief flows through me as I place my hands on my knees and catch my breath.

Everything about my surroundings is a total contrast to Gaea. The very air feels different than the realm I've called home for so many ages, as if it's somehow heavier here. The sky is not blue but a sherbet orange color. The sand that surrounds me for endless miles is rusty red like the color of dried blood.

Coughing and spitting sand from my mouth, I use the sleeve of my brown tactical shirt to wipe my eyes and face before fixing the pack onto my back again. I want to swish some water in my mouth and clear the tiny grains of red sand that are sticking to me everywhere, but I don't. I'm not sure when I'll find more water and need to preserve what I brought as long as I can.

My heart races and I look above me, searching for the doorway that delivered me here. There, suspended high above in the air, is an iridescent swirling disc of silver starlight.

It makes me think of a jellyfish suspended in the ocean, beautiful to look at. Though it doesn't appear to be an open portal, its mere presence offers a sliver of comfort in the vast loneliness of my solitary mission.

Surging my power into it, I try to detect Gaea on the other side. The portal ripples under the force of my aura, but all I sense is a daunting brick wall of nothingness.

Desperation claws at the edges of my mind as I slam my power against the barrier again and again, but it remains impassable.

A gnawing fear whispers chilling possibilities into the dark recesses of my mind. What if this realm becomes my prison, trapping me here for eternity? The thought of never seeing Hermes again, never returning to Gaea, threatens to overwhelm me with dread.

No. I refuse to let myself think of such possibilities. I'm going to do this and return back to my mate, my friends– my family.

Holding on to that flicker of hope, an idea ignites and chases away the thoughts of that dark future.

Maybe this is part of the pathway's construction, and the door remains locked until I've retrieved my powers. A failsafe almost, to make sure nothing from Tartarus escapes into Gaea except my returning powers.

Though it may be a feeble attempt to reassure myself, this explanation offers a semblance of comfort, allowing me to draw a shaky breath.

But I want to let Hermes know that I made it, that I'm okay.

I reach for the bond between us, feeling the reassuring presence within me. Placing my hand over my heart, I tap on my chest three times, a silent plea for connection. And then, holding my breath, I wait.

Relief floods me like a rushing tide as I feel three taps against my heart, a comforting echo of reassurance of my mate's presence. Releasing the pent-up air, I've been holding in my lungs, I lift my head to the sky and close my eyes, allowing myself a moment of respite amidst the turmoil.

It's been several minutes for me here but probably only a second for Hermes.

I have just a little over three days to return to him with my powers and if the Fates are willing, I'm hoping I can do it in a few hours.

Looking at my wrist, the watch I wore is busted and useless. It must have broken when I was rolling down the sand dune like a crash test dummy and I roll my eyes at the ridiculous image that conjures in my mind.

I thought an automatic watch would be helpful for me to keep track of the time difference. The watch would remain wound by my movement, and I could keep myself on time to return before the alignment ends.

Taking it off my wrist, I toss it with irritation to the sand

and stomp on it until I can't see it anymore. I'll have to find another way to monitor my time.

Sending out the ribbons of my power in all directions, I cautiously navigate the desolation of Tartarus, searching for the beacon of my essence that has been calling out to me. Since I don't know what monsters could lurk here, or if there is any life at all, I tread carefully.

Back on Gaea, I felt the pull of Tartarus, a magnetic force drawing me inexorably towards this realm. Now, as I search for my scattered powers, I can sense their presence, a faint echo reverberating through the very fabric of the desert landscape.

My aura is a blanket of silver, traveling low to the ground. Like a curious child skipping and dancing a few inches above the sand, my powers skirt along the realm.

Along the vastness, there is nothing but desert. A sea of dunes gives way to a flat expanse of low rolling hills of crimson sand. Rocky outcrops rise from the depths of the endless grit as a range of giant mountains shoots up, towering over the ocean of sand.

The sharp peaks burn in the bright sunlight and the frigid crevasses hide in the darkness.

Now, as I search for my scattered powers confined within the pendant of a necklace, I can sense their presence, a soft ricochet through the very fabric of the desert landscape.

As I focus on the source of my power, a surge of anticipation, coated with dread, courses through me. But there is another energy, nestled peacefully next to mine.

Amidst the pulsating energy of the mountains, I detect something unexpected—the essence of persistent blue starlight.

Hermes.

Along with my power is that of my mate nestled within the

cave that haunted me. As if protecting the treasure that awaits my discovery, something of Hermes was left behind as well.

The staff of the Herald; Hermes' caduceus.

The realization hits me like a bolt of lightning, igniting a spark of hope within my chest. Could it be that his staff, the final relic holding the power of the twelve realms, is hidden here alongside the pendant I seek?

My heart beats quickly with the prospect of recovering all my remaining power at once. If I'm right, I could return with my Immortality and powers fully restored.

Ares and his allies of hunters would have no power strong enough to fight against me then and we could end this. It could all be over.

This could be the chance for Hermes and me to finally find the peace that has eluded us for so long.

With my course set, I call upon my Darkness to teleport me to the mountains far away, but nothing happens. I try to use my Light or Wind and while my powers answer me, no portals form.

I look back at the orange sky at my hanging spiral of power and the closed doorway that delivered me here.

What if portals are warded here on Tartarus and don't work.

What if I'm trapped here forever?

I push the thought away before it sends me into a panic. Hermes and I have made our way back to each other in every lifetime, including this one. I have to trust that when the time is right, my doorway will open again and deliver me back to Gaea.

Adjusting the pack on my shoulders, I begin walking.

Tartarus' sun is directly above me and it's huge. So much larger than the sun on Gaea and it's incredibly hot.

I'll have to be very careful with the water I brought to ensure I conserve it for my hike to the mountain and back. Raising my hand to cover the sun, I notice something crossing in front of the large orange star and realize it's the tiny moon of Tartarus.

It looks like a mere pebble compared to the giant sun. *Could this be the third moon of the aligned realms?*

I admit my disappointment. I had thought it would be much more imposing like the oversized moon on Avalon and the dappled moon of Gaea.

But this small object crossing in front of Tartarus' sun can perhaps serve as my clock, helping me keep track of time.

I'll need to make it back to my portal before the eclipse is over, when my doorway will vanish, marooning me on Tartarus forever.

As I trudge through the soft sand, each step feels like a battle against the relentless desert. I'm thankful for the protective leather pants and boots that lace up to my knees. The gear is keeping my skin from chafing as I walk through the endless desert. But even as I apply sunscreen for the third time, I can't escape the unyielding sun beating down upon me.

Taking a measured drink of water, I savor every precious drop, knowing that dehydration lurks just beyond the horizon.

I waited as long as possible before taking my first sip. My lips had begun to crack, and my mouth stopped producing saliva about an hour before. Swishing the water around my mouth, I try to alleviate the dryness, but the relief is fleeting.

Drenching a handkerchief and tying it around my neck, I seek relief in the small semblance of coolness it provides. I wish there was a soft breeze to cool the handkerchief but the stagnant air hangs heavy around me.

The Winds are quiet but not just in the fact there are no currents blowing but there is no chatter from the nosey element. Usually, the element of air and wind is like a busy body prattling the latest gossip from one person to the next.

The Winds of Tartarus silent as death itself.

No excitement of a newcomer dropping out of the sherbet sky or amazement of the realms alignment and power pulse it's causing.

It's as if time itself has come to a standstill in this desolate realm, leaving only an ominous feeling hanging in the heavy atmosphere.

It feels like a child, cowering in the back of the closet as parents argue and the fear that trickles down their spine when they hear dads belt buckle unfasten, knowing punishment will soon invade their space.

With each sluggish step, exhaustion bears upon me and my body protests against the relentless march through the shifting sands. My lips sting with every breath, cracked and split from the unyielding assault of the desert. My feet feel numb, lost amidst the sea of blood-red sand that stretches out before me.

Wrapping another handkerchief around my mouth and nose, I struggle to keep the fine grains of sand at bay, each breath a battle against the choking dust.

The pack on my shoulders threatens to crush me beneath its weight, dragging me backward with every faltering step. A dozen times, I've lost my footing and slide down part of the dune, having to start the track up again.

Taking a moment to rest, I sink down onto the unforgiving ground, the exhaustion of the journey weighing heavy on my shoulders. But even as I close my eyes, I know that I cannot afford to linger for long. I have to keep going to beat the ticking clock of the eclipse.

I just need to take a little break.

Unfortunately, there is no place to stop on this side of the dune. It's too steep and nearly a vertical climb. I'm more than halfway up and in the cool shade from the giant blazing sun of Tartarus. At least on this side of the dune it's cooling, and the light is not blaring down on my crisp skin.

I climb and slide, climb some more and slide again. It feels like a step forward and two steps back each attempt, but I keep going.

The fickle sand is almost laughing at me each time I put my footing into the grit, and it scurries down the dune away from me.

My chest tightens with a burning fury, matching the scorching heat of the desert sun. Hot tears of frustration blur my vision, tracing a path down my cheeks. My tears are getting further than I am with climbing over this tall hill.

As I lose my footing and slide down the dune, a primal scream tears from my throat, echoing off the barren landscape, mocking me as it returns to me.

Clenching my fists, tremors course through my arms. The dune beneath me shakes violently as if mimicking me. But as I focus on the trembling grains of sand, a sense of curiosity washes over me, soothing my anger and when I calm, so does the dune.

With deliberate movements, I carve a circle in the air, watching in awe as it materializes in the sand before me.

Drawing upon the depths of my power, I conjure a vortex in my mind, a swirling maelstrom of energy to cut through the towering dune like a hot knife through butter. As the shade dissipates and the sun's relentless rays beat down upon me once more, I open my eyes to behold the circular opening cutting through the dune.

A surge of euphoria floods through me, bubbling up beyond my weariness, as laughter spills from my lips. Happy tears mingle with the sweat and sand on my cheeks, a tangible manifestation of the overwhelming relief that washes over me.

The seemingly invincible mountain of sand that had stood in my way now yields to my will. And as I gaze upon the next dune that awaits me and the one after, a smile of pure exhilaration dances upon my lips.

This just got a lot easier.

Taking a well-deserved drink of water, I relish the cool sensation as it soothes my parched throat, a brief respite from the relentless heat of the desert. With the straps of my pack adjusted and my resolve renewed, I descend into the tunnel I've created, the opening angled like a slide, making for an effortless journey to the other side.

As I emerge from the tunnel, a sense of accomplishment washes over me, boosting my spirits as I prepare to face the next challenge. With a determined stride, I set off towards the looming dune on the horizon, knowing that there is no way around it; only through it.

As I focus on the daunting task ahead, my mind drifts back to the chaotic scene I left behind on Gaea. Seeing Hermes, standing before the rising wall of flames as he watched me walk into the portal is a memory seared into my mind.

With that steadfast glance, he spoke a thousand phrases of concern and love, unwilling to remove his eyes from me until he could see me no more.

I know they are all formidable warriors, but it does nothing to stop the knots that twist in my stomach as I think of the battle I left behind, on the quest to retrieve my powers.

This journey is not just to restore myself, but the realms. The burden of this torment is mine to carry, deemed by the Fates and I must see it through.

So, as I watch my brown boots trudge through the crimson dust, I center myself here and my battle against the brutal landscape of Tartarus. Defeating this adversary sooner will get me back to my family; the sooner the better.

An idea comes to mind as I think about the mortal airports and their moving walkways. A fleeting memory of simpler times as I flew between Atlanta and New York.

I ignore the way my stomach drops when I think of New York, the city that stopped existing only a few days ago.

Calling upon the walkway imagery, I summon the sands beneath my feet to carry me forward, their swift motion propelling me towards the next dune.

Balancing carefully, I glide across the surface of the shifting sands, and exhilaration courses through me as I navigate my makeshift pathway. With each twist and turn, I feel a sense of freedom, the wind whipping through my hair and cooling the wet handkerchief around my neck.

Lifting my arms in triumph, I let out a joyous whoop, a cry of victory echoing across the desert landscape. In a matter of minutes, I've traversed through my tunnel and conquered the next dune in my path.

Sending my aura outward, I make sure I'm traveling in the direction of the mountains that hold my powers. Having scanned the landscape when I arrived, my heart sinks when I realize the small progress I've made, even after all these hours of walking.

I feel like I've spent an entire day in the blazing heat but looking above me at the burning sentinel in the sky, the sun has barely moved on the horizon.

It beats down upon me, its fiery gaze unyielding as it hangs stubbornly in the sky, refusing to dip below the horizon. In this realm of eternal sunlight, Tartarus offers no respite from its scorching embrace.

My burned skin longs for the cool embrace of darkness, for the soothing touch of night that I know will never come in this land. Unlike Avalon, its opposing twin cloaked in perpetual darkness, Tartarus offers no relief from the relentless heat of day.

And Gaea, the realm poised between night and day is a perfect balance of both realms.

But here, the sun reigns supreme, casting its harsh light upon the barren landscape, painting everything in hues of burning reds, yellows, and oranges. Even the promise of the golden hour before sunset brings little solace, for I know that the colors of dusk will only serve to intensify the oppressive heat that surrounds me.

Daylight is an ever-present tormentor, a constant guardian of the harsh realities of this unforgiving realm. I'm not sure which I detest more, the sun or this never-ending sea of sand dunes.

Using the power of Earth to carry me through the desert is working much faster but my legs are aching. Slowing my pace, I draw the sands back until I come to a stop under the shadow of the next gigantic dune.

It's like I'm trapped between two enormous crimson waves in the middle of the ocean, and they are frozen before they crest and fall over.

I let my pack off my shoulders and stretch my sore muscles.

The absence makes my skin burn as I rub the spot the straps have been pressing down upon me.

Laying down with a huff, I rest my head against the dune and close my eyes. Waiting for my heart rate to settle, I block the sunlight with my arm and release large breaths, trying to relax.

As my body settles from the exhaustive walk, I finally feel the first currents of air. They swells near the surface of the sand, a gentle stream of wind coming from the top of the dune and blowing over my head, then down my body.

"Thank the goddess." Relief flows over me with the cool airstream, and I cast my arms out wide, hoping to feel as much of the refreshing element on my body as possible. The breeze dries my sweat and helps to cool me, even though the air is hot.

Within seconds, the wind blows stronger, wafting my hair and adding to a charge in the atmosphere around me. With each gust, I feel the weight of anticipation grow heavier and my senses heighten as I search for an unseen danger that is surely approaching.

Alarmed, I sit up and put my hand on the strap of my pack, readying myself to move should I need to.

Not even a moment later, I'm bracing against the rushing wind that is beating down the dune and hear a single warning spoken by the timid currents of Tartarus.

"Hide."

The urgency of the Wind's message echoes in my mind, insisting I heed its warning and find safety. Not wasting a second to question my instincts, I fling my pack onto my back and run.

But where is there to go amid this endless sea of dunes?

Fighting against the rising panic within me, I focus on securing my refuge.

Creating an opening in the giant dune, I run inside and seal the tunnel behind me, shielding myself from the approaching tempest. In the darkness of the makeshift shelter, I cling to the hope that I am hidden from whatever threat looms outside.

The Wind's howl turns into a scream as a storm rages outside the protection of the dune. Cowering within the confines of my makeshift sanctuary, my mind races with questions and fears, wondering what could provoke such a warning from the Wind.

Sitting inside the dark sand, I expel a sliver of my aura, lighting the space around me. Hugging my knees to my chest, I wait, and I listen. With each passing moment, the tension mounts, leaving me trembling with anticipation, praying that whatever danger lurks beyond remains unaware of my presence.

As I huddle within the protective embrace of the dune, the howling winds outside take on a life of their own, morphing into monstrous growls and screams that echo through the desert. Despite knowing it's only the relentless force of nature, the cacophony adds to the tension that hangs heavy in the air.

Eventually my hunger wins over my anxiety of the sudden storm. I carefully ration my water and savor the meager provisions I brought with me: an apple and some cheese, dried jerky, and nuts. The food lightens the heavy thoughts on my mind, and I save the apple for last. The juices run down my chin so I'm careful as I keep eating it, trying to keep all the liquid I can to help quench some of my unyielding thirst.

I nourish my body, but my mind refuses to rest, haunted by thoughts of the battle I left behind on Gaea that I can't escape.

The fury of Ares, and the unwavering resolve of my mate, replay in my mind like the relentless storm outside, threatening to overwhelm me with worry and doubt.

It does me no good to keep getting distracted with what could be happening on Gaea, so I create a barrier around my imagination. Just like I'm trapped inside this dune, hiding from the winds around me, I trap the thoughts of home in my mind and lock them away.

Closing them inside, I force myself to keep focused on Tartarus and reaching out for the pulse of my power that is resting deep inside a mountain.

The soft sound of sand trickling around me jolts me back to consciousness and I sit up with a gasp. Panic flares within me as I wonder how much time has slipped away while I rested and I instinctively look to my wrist, expecting to see my watch.

Pressing my palms into my eyes, I release an exhale as my heart settles to a steady beat.

Goddess, please let me only have slept for a few minutes.

Hastily, I listen for any sign of danger outside, relieved to find that the winds have subsided, and all is quiet.

Carefully, I peek outside the small tunnel I've created, only to be met with the imposing sight of the enormous dune sea. Stretching out before me, the sands have shifted dramatically in the storm and the terrain shows the signs of the angry tempest and the path it left in its wake.

When I entered the sanctuary of the dune, I was at the base.

Now, I'm poised near the top of the hundred-foot dune, looking over an ocean of sand locked in waves of the Winds rage.

The enormity of the task ahead weighs heavily on my

shoulders along with my backpack. Each dune is a daunting obstacle standing between me and my goal.

It would take days to traverse this endless expanse of sand, and time is a luxury I cannot afford. With each passing moment, the eclipse draws closer to its end, and the window of opportunity narrows.

After the dune sea is a flatter expanse of desert and I'm eager to reach the end of this torturous field of endless rolling sand.

Every muscle in my body is aching and I'm ravaged. My hunger and thirst twisting painfully in my stomach. Before I realize it, I've drunk nearly half of my next bottle of water as I look out over my next set of imposing obstacles.

Even skirting across them, using the sand like a moving sidewalk, it's exhaustive. My legs are screaming at me with the slightest movement. I can't fathom how I'll clear these dunes and leave myself time for the rest of the journey.

I have to make it back before the eclipse ends.

Drawing upon the depths of my powers, I search for a solution, a way to overcome this seemingly insurmountable terrain. And then, like a whisper of inspiration, an idea takes root in my mind.

Recalling the legendary creatures of myth, I envision Athena's mighty Kraken and Medusa astride a sand serpent, and a plan begins to form. With a silent command, I envision a host of snakes.

Behind me, I sense movement and hear the sound of shifting sand in response.

Looking at the opposite end of my tunnel, I nearly fall out of the dune when I see a dozen rust-colored snakes gliding toward me. Solid in color, with no distinguishable face, they slither toward me.

My heart races in my chest and my foot slips down the shifting sand at the tunnel's opening. I pitch backward and free fall for a second before slamming into the dune. Sliding down on my back, I watch the horde of snake's race out of the dune after me.

Increasing their speed, the serpents catch up to me and slither under my body as I slide down the tall dune. Collecting and forming a larger mass, the body of a mighty sand python forms under me.

I'm no longer sliding uncontrollably down the hill rather I'm riding on the back of a thirty-foot snake made from the sands of Tartarus and my power. Pushing myself forward, I brace with my hands to keep myself from falling off.

A sense of exhilaration washes over me and the tightness in my body eases. With a surge of power, I propel us forward, the sand serpent following my mental command as we race across the desert.

A triumphant smile graces my lips as we descend the dune, the wind whipping through my hair as we carve a path through the endless sea of sand. With each passing moment, I draw closer to my destination, fueled by the determination to reclaim what is rightfully mine.

With the third dune, I ride the snake up to the top and raise my hands over my head as I soar down the other side. My stomach leaps into my throat when my bottom comes off the snake as it crests the ridge of the dune and a whip of sand wraps around me, pulling me onto the snakes back.

Picking up more speed, I propel the beast downward.

As the fatigue of my journey settles in, every muscle in my

body protests against the strain of the day's exertion. My back aches, my arms feel heavy, and the constant pressure on my inner thighs adds to my discomfort.

I conjure a makeshift nest atop the serpent's winding form, a small sanctuary where I can rest my weary body. Nestling into the improvised hollow, I allow myself to relax, the weight of exhaustion bearing down upon me.

Using my pack as a makeshift pillow, I take a final sip of water, mindful of rationing my remaining supply. Without a proper sunset, I'm not sure how to distinguish the passing of a day so I need to assume this is still my first day on the realm.

I wish I could see the stars and the rich velvet sky of night. I want my mate with me, laying in our bed with Hermes' arms wrapped around me.

Tapping on my chest three times, I send another pulse down our bond and feel a reply within a few seconds.

Closing my eyes, the rhythmic motion of the sand serpent lulls me into a state of peaceful rest. I imagine the radiant glow of Hermes' power. His blue eyes that pierce me to very core and the way a dimple shows on his cheek when he is up to no good and smirks.

With images of Hermes running through my mind and the lulling rock of the sand snake, I find it impossible to open my eyes again and I let my body melt into sleep.

"**W**ake up, Skyfallen." The voice of a woman, soft and gentle, marries with a gentle shake of my shoulder. My body is screaming with exhaustion and tired muscles.

It takes me a moment to recall why.

Struggling to open my heavy eyelids, I am met with darkness, my vision obscured by the veil of sleep. The sensation of cool water trickling down my forehead and into my parched mouth pulls me slowly out of sleep. It's a cold, sweet drink, dripping into my mouth and as I swallow, I feel it course through my body providing delicious relief and nourishment to my weary form.

My mind is foggy and dripping with confusion. I feel as if I should be alarmed but my brain can't put enough thoughts together to recall where I am or how I got here. I can only think of two things: the overbearing heat and my waning strength to care.

With great effort and a chorus of protests from my fatigued muscles, I manage to sit up, fueled by the promise of relief offered by the refreshing drink. Greedily, I accept the ladle offered by the stranger, allowing the cool liquid to soothe my throat and invigorate my weary body.

Unashamed by the dribble of liquid that escapes down my chin and chest, I drink deeply, savoring every drop of the sweet nectar. As the ladle is refilled and offered to me once more, I accept it gratefully, replenishing my body with the revitalizing elixir.

Sitting up better, I realize I was lying flat on my back on the blood-red sand of the Tartarus desert. My pack was still resting under my head as if the giant sand-snake I summoned dissolved back into the sand sea, leaving me asleep on the surface.

My vision is blurry, acclimating to waking up with the bright sunlight still beaming down overhead.

Behind me is the endless dune sea that I conquered, traversing it on foot and then with my powers. Before me is the low-rolling plains of sand and beyond lay the large stone mountains where my treasure hides.

I must have fallen asleep, and the conjured sand-snake continued to carry me to the end of the dunes.

The woman's hand, offering the ladle, bears the familiar and weathered hue of burnt sand. Her nails, elongated and sharpened to fine points, gleam like polished ivory against her skin. Intricate, swirling patterns, rendered in pale yellow ink, adorn her fingers, hands, and palms. The delicate designs disappear beneath the folds of her woven dress and the cascading fabric of her long headscarf.

But it is her eyes that captivate me the most.

A mesmerizing shade of pale yellow, mirroring the ink markings that adorn her skin, they hold within them a beauty I've not yet experienced in this harsh realm. Cream-colored rivulets converge toward a central golden iris, saturate her gaze with an otherworldly fascination.

Her beauty is undeniable, accentuated by the cascade of long hair that matches the hue of her eyes. Her locks, twisted and adorned with intricate hoops and woven threads of bleached wood, frame her face with a natural elegance. Gilded with rings of gleaming gold and a solitary hoop adorning her nostril, she exudes an aura of grace amidst the rugged expanse of Tartarus.

"What did you call me?" As I raise the ladle to my parched lips once more, my voice emerges from my throat like the creaking of old timber, rough and unsteady. Swallowing the sweet, clear liquid, I take in my surroundings, noticing the presence of more women nearby.

"Skyfallen, drink again." She has a thick and unfamiliar

accent but speaks English, which surprises me. Kneeling next to me, she dips the ladle into a large pot again.

"You speak the same language I do."

"We all speak the common tongue. Drink, Skyfallen. You are very weak." she urges, concern evident in her voice as she offers me the ladle once more.

I empty the ladle again and it's a clear liquid, with a pale pink hue. It makes me think of rosewater but taste like sweet honey.

With each sip, the fog in my mind begins to dissipate, replaced by a newfound clarity and energy. A black banded watch with a busted face takes my attention as I acclimate.

It's my broken watch, discarded at the base of the sand dune where I first landed after falling out of the portal. The realization of the name she's been calling me hits me like a sudden gust of wind.

"You saw me fall out of the sky?"

Taking in the women, they look like a tribe of nomads painted from the beautiful hues of a sunset.

Their silken hair is various shades of rich crimson or sun-bleached pale yellow. Their sand-kissed skin is the color of the desert, and they all have orange or yellow eyes. Their irises are gold, reflecting back at me as they steal glances.

Hunched over large clay pots, they fill them with pink liquid that is pooling in a divot in the sand like an oasis of water. Several pick a delicate flower with pale pink petals that grow from a vine surrounding the oasis.

"Yes, we watched you tumble from the sky as the Savior's Veil began covering the sun."

"What is the Saviors Veil?" Another sip of the refreshing liquid catches in my throat, prompting a brief coughing fit.

"Take your time, Skyfallen. There is plenty more to drink." She takes a small satchel from a leather tie around her waist. Opening it, she retrieves several pieces of dried fruit. Taking one for herself, opening her palm she offers me the rest. "The Savior's Veil." She points to the large sun of Tartarus, and I see a sliver of red is covering one side.

It's the eclipse.

The small object I saw before crossing in front of the big sun was nothing. The alignment of the triple moons causing an eclipse here too. This massive sun must be their moon and as the eclipse on Gaea takes only minutes, it will be days here until the large sun is fully covered in the red veil and will then pass.

"Why do you call it that?" The dried fruit tastes like apricots but looks like a plum. It's a rich purple color with fuchsia center and the chewy sweetness of it is amazing.

"It has been foretold the great alignment of the lost realms will deliver a savior. When the veil lifts, the savior will fall from the sky. And so, we have waited for you, Skyfallen." She smirks as she sits on the sand next to me. "But you are faster than we expected. We nearly lost you in the Dune Sea."

A heavy sigh escapes me at her revelation. I hadn't come here to be anyone's savior, and the weight of their expectations presses down on me like a burden. Guilt washes over me as I realize they had been waiting for me to emerge from my portal, hoping for salvation from something.

Now, with the eclipse looming overhead, I know I must hurry to retrieve my powers and fulfill my own mission, leaving them behind to face whatever trials they were hoping to be saved from.

Gazing up at the orange sky, I rise to my feet with her

assistance, brushing the rust-colored sand from my clothes and hoisting my pack onto my shoulders. It's time to press onward, to the cave where my powers await, leaving behind the expectations and hopes of those who had awaited my arrival.

"My name is Rhea."

"Seraphina." She bows her head in reverence as she introduces herself. "We invite you to join us, Skyfallen and can offer you refuge from the next sand gale, which will be approaching soon."

The sand gale.

That must be the massive sandstorm I hid from.

Behind me is the dune sea. Towering mountains of sand standing in tall peaks. Before me is a flat expanse of desert and then the mountains.

Having crossed the barren dune sea, I can't fathom anyone living there. The dunes seems to shift around on the large storm that apparently circles the realm. If it's approaching again, perhaps these nomads live have shelter along this flat plain of sand, getting me closer to the mountains that conceal my beaconing power.

As I contemplate my options, the sound of powerful wings beating against the air draws my attention upward. Turning, I am stunned to see great winged beasts circling above us, their majestic forms casting shadows over the crimson sand below. With each graceful landing, my awe deepens.

Massive creatures resembling a blend of lion and eagle, their orange fur gleams in the sherbet-colored light of the sky. Watching as the women secure their pots of rosewater nectar to the saddles and mount the beasts, I can hardly believe my eyes.

"Amazing," I breathe, unable to tear my gaze away from the magnificent creatures. "Are those sphinxes?"

Seraphina confirms my suspicions with a nod, her expression proud as one of the sphinx lands beside her.

"Indeed, in the tribe of the Danaides, we call them Sandstriders. They are our faithful companions and formidable warriors." She strokes the head of the animal, and their bond is evident. "This is Phoenixflight." Seraphina introduces me to her sphinx before climbing atop the animal.

Phoenixflight.

The name, reminiscent of the mythological animal associated with me, the great phoenix, strikes me with endearment. As if the Fates have ordained this meeting, the name of this beast is symbiotic of my journey through the cycles of life, death, and rebirth; just like the myth of the great phoenix and of me.

Holding her hand out expectantly, I stare at it a moment before meeting her gaze. As the other tribeswomen take flight on their sphinxes they cast worried glances across the great dune sea.

I take it as a warning of the wonders and dangers that may be waiting for me in this brittle and demanding landscape. Going with them will be an opportunity to learn what I may be up against and request additional provisions. It is an opportunity I can't pass up.

Taking Seraphina's hand, I hoist myself onto the back of her sphinx and hold on as the ground rushes away from us.

The scorching blaze erupting from Ares and Achilles is a solid wall of Fire. The surrounding armies raise their arms to shield themselves from the searing inferno that engulfs the battlefield. Protective shields of elemental powers form barriers, further isolating the troops of fighters from the Flames.

And all I can do is stare at the location where the portal to Tartarus was.

Was.

It's closed; sealed and gone.

Unlike the portal that delivered me to Avalon, which remained open, the gateway to Tartarus swirled shut the second Rhea stepped into it. I expected the portal would wait for her return, just as I'm going to for these seven and a half minutes as the eclipse darkens Gaea.

But as the opening grew smaller, the wards that protect the realm chased after it. The shine of Apollos yellow sunlight and the char of Ares' flames sealed the enclosure.

She won't be able to return to Gaea.

Time slows down and the roar of the flames turns silent as the realization drowns out everything else around me.

Looking across our companions, I'm the only one who noticed. Everyone is watching in awe as Achilles and Ares battle. No one is going to know, the Goddess of the Twelve Realms will become a marooned prisoner on desolate realm of Tartarus, forever.

No one, except one person.

Raising a single eyebrow, Medusa cocks her head to the side, then turns toward the approaching fight.

Did Medusa already know?

The swirling portals to the other realms were constructed of Rhea's power. The silver starlight burned within them both. So, why did this portal close?

What did we miss?

As the two armies hurtle toward each other, racing into the crater where the old library once stood, I can't help but feel a surge of horror gripping my heart.

Rhea is going to be trapped, alone on the realm we thought was destroyed. With only restoring part of her immortal powers, she is still mortal.

She's going to die there, alone.

Looking up, I know the ancient structure of Alexandria looms above us, a silent sentinel waiting for Rhea's return. I pray to the Fates that I am wrong. That she'll reemerge on the bridge of the eclipse with renewed immortality and the key to unlock the ancient wards concealing the library's secrets.

My mind races with desperate hope that whatever lies hidden within those ancient walls will grant Rhea the power she needs to reclaim her lost memories and finally rid herself of her relentless pursuer. Perhaps it holds the key to my own salvation—the ancient Caduceus, and final relic of Nyx's power could be awaiting discovery within.

But as I scan the battlefield, my hopes falter.

Behind Ares, his army hesitates, holding back unnaturally, avoiding the flames with a caution that unnerves me. Among them, Aryana.

Next to her are a dozen Dark Mages. Shadows and obscurities billow from the black cloaks they wear as the mages lift their arms in a synchronized motion.

"Fuck" A curse escapes Hecate's lips as the ground trembles beneath us, fissures splitting open to unleash a horde of shadowy beings. Ares has stolen the Darkness from the Labyrinth and brought the beings of Elysium with him today.

"Shades." Hecate identifies the recent additions to Ares forces. They are terrible and formidable beings.

Shades, twisted remnants of lives extinguished by dark magic, rise from the depths, their formless voids of darkness pulsating with malice. Their hatred for the living is unyielding, their only desire is to consume all life they encounter.

Floating on a wind of darkness, the Shades make their way to us.

But amidst the encroaching darkness, a glimmer of hope rushes over me, before crushing grief sets in. Three gentle taps on the tether of our shared souls—a signal from Rhea. *She made it.*

Relief floods through me as I sense her presence, her resilience undimmed despite the chaos surrounding us. But does she know how dire her situation has become? Does she realize we'll never see each other again in this life?

Closing my eyes, I pull the thousand memories of Rhea that I've collected these past weeks since reuniting with her and I draw strength from them.

I made a promise to her, one that I never confessed but it

burns true in my heart all the same. She'll not be entering the Void alone, this time.

As she crosses through the veil of the realms and enters the dominion of souls, we'll walk hand-in-hand, together.

Returning three taps on my chest, I feel the power of our bond as it carries my reply to the goddess who awaits me on the other end. She'll traverse unfathomable hardships in a solitary quest that will lead to her death. If not now, then soon after as her fragile mortal life comes to an end.

And when the light of Rhea's lifetime fades, so will mine.

The world speeds up and the roar of two armies surges around me.

My senses return to the battle as the pounding of my heart returns to a steady pace.

The eclipse moving across the sun darkens the sky.

I suppose this was the reason for Ares' plan in using the Shades. As the sun is covered by the moon, darkness will befall Gaea. His Dark Mages and Shades will become stronger without the light of the sun.

But I am a son of both of my parents. With the radiant light of my father and the eternal burn of night from my mother, I harness the power of starlight.

Night is my ally as I command the Light that lives in darkness.

Channeling the power of Lumos, I feel the blaze of starlight surge through my veins as my aura crackles with raw energy. With a focused intensity, I unleash a wave of brilliant light, a barrier against the encroaching shadows, shielding my comrades from harm.

The Shades recoil, consumed by the purity of my azure Light, while Ares is thrown back by the force of my power and tumbles. The recognizable ram's helmet of Ares is flung from his head and bounces across the desert ground. The God of War finally gains traction against the force of my hit and slides to a stop.

Seizing the moment, I snatch his discarded helm with my power, calling it to me through a portal.

Ripping one curved horn, with a flick of my wrist, I send it hurtling toward him. The signet of Ares sings through the air with the speed of my throw, and it sticks into the ground only inches away from him, a silent challenge.

Crushing the rest of the helmet with my hands, I lob the bent pile of armor to the ground, and it rolls into the crater created by my mates power ages ago.

Ares's fury knows no bounds. With a primal roar, he incinerates one of his own soldiers, consuming them by the flames of his rage, offended by my actions against him. In a frenzy of anger, he commands his forces to attack, and they surge forward with a relentless determination.

As the clamor of battle draws near, and the pounding footsteps of Ares's army echo across the desert, a surge of determination courses through me. Amidst the chaos, my mind remains clear, focused on the task at hand.

Nervousness swells behind me as our small force readies to meet the might of Ares.

As I steel myself for the coming clash, I refuse any doubts of our victory with a fierce resolve. There is no room for hesitation or uncertainty. My loyalty to Rhea, to our cause, burns brighter than any light, propelling me forward with unwavering determination.

My aura flares and I hope to serve as a beacon of empowerment for the fighters that stand with me and fight for our goddess, and fight for our realm.

With a silent prayer to the Fates, I brace myself to meet the onslaught, knowing that whatever fight lies ahead, I will face them with courage and conviction. For the destiny of my mate, and our world, hangs in the balance, and I will not falter in my duty to protect them.

And when the eclipse ends, and I feel that tether to my mate sever, I will meet her in the Void. But my Immortal life won't be the only one that ends today. Today, the Ferryman will deliver the soul of Ares to darkness, where he will rot as a cursed being of Elysium.

Today, I will die, but Ares will die with me.

The nomadic camp of the Danaides was a twenty-minute flight on the back of Seraphina's sphinx. We traveled at the end of the finery of flying beasts and approaching their homestead, the sphinxes circled a grouping of tents.

Seraphina sits in front of me, holding the reins of her bonded animal and guiding us through the skies. She's strong and sure. Looking back to check on me, she reminds me of Calypso. Especially with the wind blowing in her long hair.

A third of the large sun of Tartarus is covered by its eclipse. If I only have three and a half days, then perhaps I've spent the first one crossing the Dune Sea. My stomach twists in knots as I hope I'm right, but I also chastise myself for letting my exhaustion overtake me so easily.

I'm hoping the Danaides will agree to take me to the desert mountains on their sphinx and help me recover some of the lost time.

The color of crimson like the sands of Tartarus, the Danaides tents blend in with the surrounding landscape and at first, I didn't see it.

I can understand why I didn't notice the nomads when I

arrived through the portal. Everything about the Danaides are made from the same hues of a burning sunset, just like Tartarus and they can easily conceal themselves.

More women come from their tents and stop the chores they are performing around the nomadic base to watch us arrive. There are no men in sight and I'm not sure if that is because they are away or if this is a matriarch.

A woman that looks a lot like an older version Seraphina stands in the center of the camp. The flapping wings of the sphinx blow her long-twisted hair that is the same pale-yellow color, but she stands stoic, a leader among the tribe. Her hands are folded in front of her as she watches us with a warm smile on her face.

"Welcome, Skyfallen," The deep timber of the woman's voice is hospitable and commanding. "it is our honor to host you on this first day of the Saviors Veil."

Relief washes over me that it's still the first day since I arrived. Having fallen asleep twice and trying to measure against the eclipse, I was not sure how much time had passed, and I feared it was slipping away from me like sands through an hourglass.

Stepping to the side, the woman gestures to the large tent in the center of the compound. Before she speaks, the sky darkens and to my left, a stagnant wall of rust-colored sand consumes the entire horizon.

Like any large storm, I know that means it's heading straight for us, and it must be the sand gale that Seraphina warned was approaching soon. The screaming monster I hid from within the tall dunes.

"Let us take rest inside from the storm." The woman turns,

walking toward the tent and Seraphina indicates that I may walk with her.

"My mother and our Chieftainess, Eudora." Seraphina tells me as we enter the crimson tent. Woven together from the delicately crafted fibers, two tall poles in the center support the massive tent.

With a central opening, smoke from a fire in the middle of the tent rises into the sky. Several groupings of women sit in small circles and begin passing food and drink. They speak in hushed tones as some of them look at me, then look away giggling to themselves.

Within the small groups are red clay pots with fires burning in them. Skewers of meat and some kind of sun-bleached vegetable are roasting, and the aroma pulls cries of hunger from my stomach.

The colors of the sunset surround me as the women's golden eyes reflect the flames. There is much beauty here in the harsh desert of Tartarus and I'm glad I listened to my instincts to come here, rather than heed Hermes' beliefs that everything was destroyed.

I'm eager for food and starving for information that will help me.

A metal grate placed over the large central fire holds a thin slab of red meat. Sizzling as the flames and juices kiss each other, the aroma surrounds me, and I nearly groan in anticipation.

Sun-bleached rattan platters are passed around with charred flatbread, and dried fruits. I'm handed a wooden cup filled with a deep burgundy drink that tastes like a mild and slightly bitter table wine.

I want to ask so many questions, learning about the mountains and what is within them, this odd storm and how often it travels the realm. I want to beg them to take me to the mountains as soon as the gale will pass but they expect me to be some kind of savior.

I don't know what expectations they feel I will live up to and I need to be cautious that I keep from offending them. Should I reject their belief in this prophesy, I could find myself in deep trouble.

So, I need to tread carefully and be intentional with my inquiries.

The sandstorm lasted several hours, from what I can tell of the first one I encountered. At a minimum, we're going to have time to eat and rest before it will clear enough to head out on the backs of the sphinxes.

"Will you tell me about Tartarus?" I ask Seraphina, taking a bite from one of the plum-colored fruits. "I'm afraid I don't have a memory of this place, though I believe I've been here before."

The inside of the tent quiets suddenly and the winds outside increase.

Several women make their way around the tent's entrances and close them. Securing the flaps with stakes and ties, it doesn't seem like the tent will withstand the strong gales I heard before, but no one is in a panic, so I conceal mine.

As the last flap closes, the sphinx form a semi-circle around the perimeter of the tribes' tents.

The lions stand on their hindquarters and fan their massive wings. Roaring into the sky, the sounds of their call fades as I watch them turn to stone.

It makes me think of Medusa and her power of petrification. She was a resident of Tartarus, from the tribe of the Gorgons and I'm curious if any survived the Titans battle.

Craning my neck, trying to see what will happen when the sand gale hits, I'm blocked off from observing the spectacle when the tent is fully closed.

"Would you like to watch, Skyfallen?" Seraphina asks, noticing my curiosity.

"Please, call me Rhea."

Seraphina nods once and walks me to the entrance.

Pulling back the flap, I'm able to watch as the rust-colored sand surges toward us. As the storm hits the stone sphinxes the sand is deflected away, like their extended wings provide a shield against the tempest.

The wind rages around the barrier provided by the stone beasts and the sand flies over the Danaides tribe, keeping them safe.

"It's amazing." I exclaim as Seraphina closes the tent again and we return to our spot. Seraphina twists her hand, and the flames respond, dying down so the meat doesn't char too quickly.

Seraphina must be a Flame, able to control the element just as Achilles and Ares. I wonder if the Danaides are also immortal and if they have other powers. A dozen questions fly through my mind that I want to ask that I'm not sure where to begin.

"I wasn't even sure Tartarus would still be here when I came. Can you tell me what happened after the battle of the Titans?" I make sure to ask my question in low tones, in case it's insensitive.

Seraphina motions to her mother and Eudora gives me an

account of the Danaides way of life and what remains of Tartarus as they share their food with me.

The Danaid are a nomadic tribe of hunter gatherers. They mainly search the desert for Lethe Elixir and nectarbloom flowers to trade. It is the pink-tinged water that swelled in the pool surrounded by blush-colored flowers when I first woke up.

The elixir and flowers are rare and contain many healing and rejuvenating properties. The nectarbloom flowers give the elixir its sweet flavor and pink tint and is very valuable when traded.

They are a matriarchy of nomadic women and it's amazing they live in complete isolation, supporting themselves and each other.

Our meal consists of grilled Bloodsand Bison that was hunted earlier today. Crimson spicebush berries, dried and ground, season the bison and added a spicy kick to the meat.

Grilled desert lichen is a pale white fungus that grows in the eternal sunshine of Tartarus and tastes like earthy mushrooms. The dried fruit I've been eating are scarlet sunberries that grow in the shadow of rocks on small bushes. The shade gives them a deep red color that seems almost purple when dried.

Bloodshade berry wine is served with nearly every meal as well as the charred flatbread and I can't get enough of both.

After the battle of the Titans, both Oceanus and Hyperion fell. Chaos fled when King Tantalus, ruler of a walled kingdom called Lydia pledged loyalty to him. The king took over and captured the three surviving cyclopes and the rebel fighters from the Sisyphus tribe.

"Why are they deemed rebels?"

"The cyclopes and Sisyphus fought bravely against the forces of Chaos and the tyrant king. When the Titans fell, they were ravenous, angry, and wanting revenge." Eudora explains and I keep munching on small bites of bison and flatbread. "all the realm would have died in a great war if the fighters were not captured."

"Are they still alive? Where are they?" I ask, taking another cup of bloodshade berry wine.

"The Inferno's Embrace." Seraphina answers. "It is a mine where they extract pyronite ore. The mineral gives elemental control over fire for those not born with the gift as I am."

With a flourish of her hand, Seraphina conjures a Flame in her hand that is as pale yellow as her eyes and hair.

"Did you see the battle of the Titans?" My curiosity is as ravenous as my appetite, wanting to know every detail.

"We are nomads. Our tribe was thankfully on the other side of the realm when the battle took place. We were very lucky." Seraphina traces one of the pale-yellow designs that adorn her finger with a solemn expression on her face.

I don't see any other women of their tribe with similar markings so it must be reserved for the daughter of the Chieftainess.

Eudora asks me about the *lost realms,* and I tell them of Avalon and Gaea. They are surprised to hear the realms survived and are thriving. They believed the realms fell when there had been no contact in so long.

I talk freely of the compulsion I had to come to Tartarus, but I don't share my search for my powers, or my dreams of the cave. Blaming the wine, I put my cup down, fearing I'm being too talkative, but they seem to enjoy hearing about my realm.

A group of three women begin playing a song on primitive hand-hewn instruments.

One plays something akin to a lyre, one beats a drum and another blows into a wooden flute. It's upbeat and sparks a dance to break out in the tent.

I smile and watch the women spin and twirl. Their long flowing skirts billow as they rotate in quick circles around each other. Those of us that watch cheer and clap.

Seraphina joins her tribe, and the ladies form a circle around her.

She's beautiful and graceful as she dances, and the ladies watch her as if they are watching the wonder of a dance for the first time. I admire her as well, until she grabs my hands and pulls me to the center of the tent with her.

My cheeks blazing red, I throw my hands up and dance with them.

The women of the desert, all colors of the sunset, blaze brightly with the strength and power. I admire them and their freedom.

I long to taste this liberty for myself one day; and I will.

Plopping down with a in a fit of laughter, I take large gulps of the sweet wine to cure my thirst.

"What was foretold of the savior?" The tent quiets with my question as I attempt to change the subject and get more information from them about Tartarus. Several Danaid look at me with side-long glances and lean to each other with whispered remarks.

"There is a revered deity among the rebels." Seraphina tells me in a hushed tone. "It is rumored to be a dragon made of pure light."

Cold drips down my spine in shock and the haze of the red

wine immediately clears. My mind surges to Theia, the Titan dragon of Light.

She is the cosmic dragon Hermes and Apollo were both apprentice to and warned the Titans of Chaos by ringing the mighty trumpets of Hel.

The archangels went against her and defeated the Titan, siding with Chaos and helping him steal her power. But what if she was not truly slain and lives still?

My heart races with the prospect and I want to hear more.

"Where is the dragon?"

"Again, there are only rumors. Many have gone in search of the great beast, but none return. It is believed the dragon has immense power and those who go searching for it, wish to slay the dragon."

"How terrible."

"Yes. We Danaids believe only in taking what is needed. Living in excess is against our way. Certainly, the slaughter of such a rare beast would be a tragedy." Seraphina pauses, taking a bite of bison before she continues. "The dragon is said to fiercely guard a valuable treasure which is why no hunter has survived to share the location of the beast."

"Does anyone know where it is?"

"Not for certain, but I once heard a comment in passing when trading in the market at Lydia. A tribe of pastoral nomads worship the beast and leave offerings at the entrance of a cave. It is located in the Blood Spine mountains, marked with the skull of a cyclops at the entrance."

As my heart surges and I fight to keep my eyes from bulging, Eudora interrupts.

"Perhaps you would care to rest, Skyfallen? I'm sure you've had a long and exhausting day." Eudora says and as if she gave a command to the entire tent, the small groups of women stand and begin clearing empty rattan platters.

The wind is still blowing harshly outside. As if her words pull the weariness from me, a wave of drowsiness washes over me. I stretch and release a large yawn that makes my eyes water.

The remaining food is packed away and stored for later. The small pots of fire are smothered with lids and within two minutes, the tribeswomen are unrolling woven mats for sleeping.

Seraphina escorts me to a smaller tent that is divided into three spaces. The central area has a seating space with round floor cushions and a low table. Lanterns burning pale yellow fire hang in the corners and illuminate the inside of the tent.

When the thick outer flaps are shut, it's near dark inside and gives the illusion that nighttime has finally fallen in the realm of eternal daylight.

Eudora enters the room to the right which are her private sleeping quarters. With a smile and a partial bow, she closes the flap, leaving Seraphina and I to ourselves.

"Do you think you could take me to the dragons cave when the storm clears?" I ask in low tones.

"It is forbidden and a very dangerous journey." Seraphina casts a side glance at me, dismissing my request.

The room to the left is Seraphina s private quarters and two mats have been unrolled for us. A wooden cup is sitting on a low table next to my woven mat which is padded with several layers of soft blankets, covering a thick layer of crimson wool and bundle of hay that has been spread over the ground.

"Drink this Lethe Elixir, Skyfallen–apologies, Rhea." Seraphina excuses herself with a bashful smile for calling me Skyfallen again. "You are quite tired from your journey across the Dune Sea and the elixir will not only help you rest but rejuvenate your sore limbs."

With a smile and a nod, Seraphina lays down and the yellow flames dim, casting long shadows in our small, shared room of the tent.

I down the sweet drink in two gulps. It is a thicker syrup this time compared to the diluted water it was when I tasted it.

The strong winds scream loudly outside the tent. A haunting melody that sends a shiver of dread across my skin.

I'm thankful the Danaides found me. Leaving the Dune Sea, and having no place for refuge, I would have been in big trouble when the sand gale arrived.

If only I had spotted them when I first came through the portal, maybe they could have flown me to cave I'm looking for with their sphinx and I would be reunited with my powers already.

As I think about the cave and recall the rumor of the dragon, I realize Seraphina never answered my question about what the savior was foretold to do.

As I'm trying to remind myself to talk to them when I wake up about the cave and the saviors prophesy, the elixir begins to take effect.

My body sinks wonderfully into the mat as if it's the most comfortable bed I've ever encountered. My joints and muscles warm as I feel the elixir spreading within me. Once again, my eyelids are too heavy to stay open a second longer.

As I resign to sleep, I let the thoughts of dragons and storms and quests float away on the strong winds.

40 Rhea

A wailing cry echoes through the desert wind, and I shoot up from my mat, covered in sweat. I dreamt of a great dragon in a cave and like before the large white eyes that pierced me turned to green emeralds.

Seraphina was jolted awake just as I was, having heard the same noise I did.

"It is time to prepare for our day, Skyfallen." Seraphina stands and opens the entrance of her room.

"I need to talk to you about that dragon cave, Seraphina."

"Not now, Skyfallen." Her tone is curt and whispered as if speaking of the cave is a crime.

Several tribeswomen are standing in a line with rattan platters that contain various items of jewelry, deep crimson sandals and other adornments for Seraphina. They give her long, knowing looks that she returns as if they are communicating with their looks.

My head pounds and my limbs feel dense. The friendly hospitality from last night is waning today as a heaviness bears upon us within the tent.

Seraphina's fingers tremble when she reaches for a cluster

of gold rings. Placing them on each digit, her hand is steady by the time she is finished.

Another screech races across the atmosphere like a great vulture is circling high above. The mood is as ominous as the wail. None of the attendants have said a word and aside from Seraphina's initial comments, she has said nothing.

"I'm sorry, what is that sound?" I strain my ears, hearing flapping of a great number of wings. My fingers dance along the hilts of my daggers still strapped to my legs.

"It is the sound of our future, Skyfallen. Taxes are due today."

The attendants file out of the tent and join Eudora who stands relaxed in the center of the compound much like yesterday when I arrived. Seraphina takes a place next to her mother and both ladies clasp their hands in front of them, looking very much like sisters.

I stand next to Seraphina. Leaning closer to her, I keep my voice quiet as my eyes follow the line of their gaze. "Either take me to the cave or give me a sphinx to go on my own, please? The fates of the realms relies on this."

Seraphina gives me a long and pointed look. "Fate has already set this path and abandoned us to walk it alone." Then she turns her head back to the convoy in the sky.

In the distance, a dark swarm of large, winged creatures command the sky. Dozens of sets of wings flap and they bring the wind with them. My hair stirs with each swell of their wings and when the screech races across the sky, a shiver crawls up my spine.

At this distance, it's hard to tell what they are but as they near, my mind has an even harder time processing what I see.

There is no denying the truth as the beasts approach and

circle the compound. My head pivots as they fly overhead. Truly, they look like vultures, circling the camp and scouring for carcasses to scavenge.

"Are those Harpies?"

"That name is forbidden, Skyfallen." Seraphina scolds me harshly in a hushed tone. Averting her eyes to the crimson sand, the bird-like creature's land. "It is law to refer to them as Aves."

They are much larger than I would have expected. Demeter always referred to children as harpies and I suppose I thought that meant they were small.

The lore I know says harpies are small birds with the head of a woman. These large buzzards stand over six feet tall with the long taloned feet of a bird, wearing only an ambrosia-colored cloth around their loins. Their bodies jut forward but take a more humanoid form with two arms that end in a pair of long crimson claws.

Their faces are hideous.

Part vulture, part human, it's difficult to tell where one species ends and the other begins. The shape of their head is human, and they even have hair. With a thick brow bone and beak, the blend of their features makes them look very bizarre.

Two large wings protrude from their backs and as the flock surrounds us, their jerky movements fill me with unease. Feathers cover their back but fade away to rich blue skin.

One of the winged creatures is clearly the leader.

Standing in the center and surrounded by guardians holding long spears, the smallest of the harpies snaps its beaked mouth three times. Lifting its head to the sky, it wails like a banshee, and I cover my ears to the piercing sound.

No one else moved but me and my action caused a stir of

offense. Each of the large birds pierce me with their yellow eyes as if I spit in their face.

In a blink, one of the guards has a whip in their hand and it snaps around my neck. With a strong tug, I'm pulled to the ground and my face slams against the crimson desert floor.

The large, clawed foot of another guard presses hard against my back, forcing the air from my lungs. One of its sharp talons pierces my skin in warning.

The bird in charge walks forward. Bending over, it cocks its head at me, rotating it at odd angles.

"The Savior is weak." The harpy says and defiance makes me squint my eyes.

"Tell your little crony to get their feathered toenails off of me and I'll show you what weak looks like."

The harpy before me smiles with a wide sinister grin. There is nothing but evil lurking behind his yellow eyes.

"You're going to taste delicious when I eat you for dinner." My stomach turns sour at the rancid smell of his breath. It smells like foul meat and blood. When the harpy speaks, I see two rows of thin teeth that look like sharp little razors.

The bird with his whip around my throat approaches. Wrapping it around my neck two more times, the beast pulls up on the leather rope, dragging me to a standing position.

The one I have named, Feather-toes, removes his talons from my back and pulls my hands tight behind me. The whip secures my wrists in a manner that would make me choke myself if I tried to escape. And it's Thaumium metal; a fucking lot of it too. The hallowed feeling of my powers draining from me leaves me barren and cold inside.

A curved blade is pushed against my neck. To let me know they are serious, they break the skin slightly. The short harpy eyes my red blood on the blade with hungry eyes. I think he really intends to eat me.

The central harpy wears a crown of twisted red metal and there are nine red stones fixed within the intricate crown. The crown secretes a red liquid from the stones that have stained the birds head and hair. It gives the illusion the crown is bleeding and adds to the menace of this tyrant.

The crowned harpy looks from me to Seraphina with a different hunger in his eyes and it pisses me off even more. It's a look of ownership and lust.

"My bride?" He asks and Eudora nods once.

"My eldest, your majesty."

What?

The Danaids told me just last night about how the king... did something.

As I try to remember, I can't. I know they mentioned the king when we spoke, but I'm not able to recall anything they said. And as I'm trying to remember, I've even forgotten what I came here for. There is something I was going to search for, but it seems the more I try to remember, the further the thoughts slip away from me.

And I'm thirsty.

So thirsty and I just want more of the delicious elixir. As I think of the sweet pink drink, my mouth nearly salivates for it. I'd almost be willing to choke myself to try and get out of this hold and find some.

"Turn, bride." The harpy's voice is eerie. Deep and melodic, each word is spoke with a sinister undertone.

Seraphina keeps her hands clasped in front of her and turns slowly, allowing the king to inspect her. When she is facing him again, she bows, closing her eyes and I notice the tears she is holding back.

She doesn't want to be wed to him.

I can't blame her. He is disgusting.

"She will be a fine wife." The king says, satisfied with Eudora's selection.

"S-s-she doesn't want to marry you." I interject. My voice slurred and my eyelids long to close again for another long sleep. The king rears back and slaps me across the face. My head shoots to the side and blood lands on the rust-colored sand.

Eudora doesn't even flinch, at the encounter, as she continues the conversation she is having with the king, as if he didn't just slap the shit out of me. "And when she delivers her first daughter, I will receive the child as payment for her dowry."

The king nods once and Eudora bows. The bargain has been struck.

My face is throbbing, and I spit blood. It lands eerily close to Feather-toes. *Why did I even open my mouth to say anything. This isn't my business.*

But what is my business? I can't recall.

I look to this tribe of women and see them differently now. They are sold off for reproduction and paid for by having their babes ripped from them. Delivered back to the tribe that bartered for them, the daughters will never be raised by their true mothers.

It's terrible.

"Let us complete it." The king says.

Seraphina walks beyond the throng. Standing out on her own, she looks to the sherbet sky and whistles. The deep staccato of her sphinx's wings flapping fill the air around us.

Kicking up a crimson cloud of sand, the large animal lands next to its rider and nuzzles her leg with its large head.

Seraphina hugs the neck of the majestic, winged beast but concealed behind her back, she holds a large knife.

Seraphina whispers into the beast's ear before stabbing its chest.

The roar of the animal, writhing in pain pulls tears to my eyes. It collapses to the ground and Seraphina cradles its head, continuing to speak to her companion softly.

"While it's still beating." The king barks at her with impatience.

I watch in horror as Seraphina uses the large knife to open the chest of the animal and while its heart is still beating, she cuts it out. I take a deep breath to scream but the beast behind me pulls down on my wrists, choking me and suffocating my pain.

Walking with her hand covered in red blood, Seraphina holds the heart of the noble animal, walking to her betrothed with the beating organ in her hand.

As the beating slows, the heart turns to stone.

Having reached the king, Seraphina raises the stone to the crown and places the heart of the sphinx in the twists of the crimson crown. It joins the other nine and I realize why they look like they are bleeding stones, because they are.

This must be his tenth bride, which means ten other animals were slain for this disgusting ritual.

With a predatory grin, the king approaches Seraphina. She grips the knife so tightly in her hand, her knuckles turn white.

Just stab him.

But she remains still.

The king tilts his head with a bird-like jerk and opening his beak, he bites her neck with his razor teeth cutting into her soft skin. Seraphina tenses but doesn't scream. Blood runs from the wound and seeing the kings neck muscles moving, I gag.

He's sucking the blood from her wound.

Then I see the movement of his arm and I really want to vomit. He's fucking jacking himself off. This is the most barbaric and disgusting practice I've ever seen. My face heats with anger and Seraphina expressionless eyes flick to mine quickly before she looks away.

I can't believe she is just standing there, allowing this to happen to her. Willingly being attacked and degraded so publicly and to remain emotionless. I can't believe everyone in this tribe is standing here doing nothing.

My body shakes and power thrums inside me. Even against these bindings that suffocate my elemental powers, they swell with my emotions.

The harpies guarding me add a pair of wrist and ankle cuffs that further work to pull my powers away from me.

The fact this realm also has Thaumium metal only adds to my frustration. I suppose in the times before the Titan wars, realms interacted with each other, likely trading and bartering for goods.

The king sucks on her wound and moans when he brings himself to climax on Seraphina's tribal dress. My guards are hissing and fussing with my extra restrains, as. I fight against them.

Looking at me with a sickly blood covered smile, the harpy king is enjoying the reaction this spectacle is causing. My face is in a scowling grimace, partly furious and largely grossed out, but completely ready to kill this asshole.

"My wife and as soon as we return to the palace, my mate." The king smiles with his blood-coated beak.

Seraphina shudders, careful to keep her composure behind the kings back. Perhaps she is opposed to this and has no choice. She said this was a day to pay taxes and now I'm gathering, she is serving as the payment.

Just as nine others have served before her, if my thoughts on the king's bleeding crown is correct.

With his new bride still bleeding, the king wraps both arms around her. Seraphina looks at me with dead eyes, as if she knows she there is no other future for her than this. Beating his wings, the king takes flight.

One of the guards uses a thick rope to secure me to his body and for the second time during my journey to Tartarus, the ground rushes away as we take to the sky.

The shadow of the once magnificent palace envelopes us as we fly in, the flock of harpies circling above announces our arrival to all below. The castle, a relic of Titan craftsmanship, still stands tall despite the ages it has weathered in the desolate expanse of Tartarus. Towering columns, adorned with fading Titan symbols, flank the entrance, a reminder of the structure's former grandeur.

It is evident that in the ages since the Titan of Earth was slain, and the horrid king flying ahead of me took over, the castle has been forcefully altered with sinister additions that mark the king's oppression over the land.

Stone harpies carved into the castle are perched like overseers and watch the sprawling city below. Talons have clawed the stone figures that stood in the time of the Titan, scratching the faces of the once beautiful carvings as the castle's new residents land from their flights.

The tall watchtowers streaked with brown and white, have been turned to nests like ominous sentinels. Guards patrol the towers, ensuring the tyrant kings dominion remains unchallenged. Once vibrant gardens that filled the castle courtyard are nothing more than a twisted heap of thorns. The invasive plant, much like the harpies, suffocating the life of the surrounding inhabitants.

We land in the city center at a fountain erected with a stone figure of the king looking much larger and regal than his actual appearance.

The harpy king's fountain looms menacingly in the center of a darkened square. Its once-grand design twisted and corrupted by the tyrant's influence.

The faint echo of intricate reliefs of natural scenes, now bear crude depictions of the harpy king subjugating his citizens and imposing his will upon them around the fountains base.

Atop the pedestal stands a grotesque statue of the harpy king, his form exaggerated and distorted to emphasize his dominance and cruelty. His wings are spread wide, casting ominous shadows over the plaza below, while his taloned feet crush the broken bodies of those who dared to defy him.

The stone figure of the tyrant holds a scepter forged from bones and from the scepter's tip flows a crimson liquid.

The water cascades down in torrents, churning with dark echoes of suffering and despair. Jagged rocks line the fountain's base, replacing the once-tranquil pools with turbulent whirlpools that promise death should one fall in.

In sharp contrast to the flowing water, surrounding the fountain is a barren wasteland, stripped of life and choked with sand.

The city pauses when the king lands and the citizens watch as he releases his wounded bride. Seraphina stands with her shoulders squared and the newly married couple walk toward the titanic citadel. The king, several steps ahead of his bride, pays no mind to the people.

The citizens scowl at Seraphina, spitting at her as she walks past them with a regal heir of indifference on her face. There are no harpies in the crowd, only people that resemble Seraphina. Yellow, red and umber skinned citizens with golden iris' in their eyes scowl at the king's bride.

My guard removes the rope that bound us together during our flight and I drop onto unsteady feet. With my hands tied behind my back, my shoulders were screaming in pain as we flew here.

During the flight, I felt three taps on my chest and thought of Hermes, back on Gaea.

I need to tell him I'm okay.

As we soared through the hot sky, above the blood-colored desert, my mind struggled to pierce through a dense fog that clouded my thoughts. I recalled leaving Hermes behind, framed against a backdrop of flames. His worried eyes etched into my memory as I stepped through the swirling portal of silver starlight that brought me here.

Yet, despite the clarity of that memory, everything else is a blur. Why had I left Gaea? What had I come here searching for?

The flight and the incessant churn of my thoughts only served to exacerbate my thirst, a relentless gnawing that clawed at my throat. About halfway through our journey, I spotted a small circle of pale pink nectarbloom flowers nestled at the base of a towering dune. I wanted to remove the rope and tumble to the ground below so I could gulp up more of the delicious Lethe Elixir.

And then it hit me: the damned drink Seraphina had given me had clouded my mind. While drinking from the wellspring in the desert had been a rejuvenating experience, the thick syrup she had prepared for me before we slept was different. It was sweeter, more potent—altered or cooked down to enhance its effects.

I'm such a fool.

Blinded by trust, I had stumbled right into the camp of the Danaides, believing them to be allies. I had been impressed by their matriarchal society, seeing in Seraphina a reflection of Callie's strength and resolve. But I had been too trusting, too eager to find allies in this unforgiving land.

They told me of their history, but clearly on the version they wanted me to see. Carefully knitting together the *truth* as they wanted me to believe it.

I should have been more cautious, more vigilant in protecting myself.

My best friend fought her way through the darkness of Ares' depravity, only for Seraphina to keep me subdued and distracted while her allies bound us both in chains.

It was a hard lesson learned—a reminder of the dangers lurking behind even the most welcoming facade. From now on, I will trust no one but myself.

A trio of harpies stand at the top of the citadel, each perched atop one of the three southern-facing watchtowers. Their wings unfurl, revealing a mosaic of primarily brown and black feathers, weathered, and frayed from the relentless onslaught of Tartarus' harsh environment. Even from our vantage point, I can imagine the coarseness of their plumage.

The wings extend out much farther than the height of the harpies, casting ominous shadows on the hot ground as we pass through them on our way to the castle.

With synchronized movements, they flap their immense wings, their beaks lifted skyward as their ear-piercing screeches impale the air. A turbulent wind rises in their wake, birthing the great gale that ravages the realm.

Originating from the king's castle, the great sandstorm will race across the realm, consuming anyone who can't find refuge and locking the realm in a continuous state of shelter.

This city at the base of the citadel seems to be spared from the ravenous windstorm and I suppose that is the design of it. It forces the citizens of Tartarus to live in safety at the base of the king's castle.

For any caught in the great desert, this storm would surely be a death sentence.

But the Danaides have protection from the storm by their sphinxes. I'm curious if the tax they are required to pay is because of their ability to live as nomads. Eudora described them as *very lucky* to have been on the other side of the realm when the Titans fought, but now I believe it was likely the cause of a bargain struck.

One the Danaides are still paying for.

As the powerful gale grows and races away from the castle, all citizens brace against the airstreams. Widening my stance, I drop a shoulder and tuck my chin to my chest until the wind has surged away from us.

Surprisingly, it's not the wind that nearly knocks me off my feet—it's the overpowering stench that assaults my senses. My eyes water, and my stomach churns as I fight against the urge to vomit. It takes a moment for realization to dawn: it smells like shit. Harpy shit, to be exact.

The foul odor emits from the harpies' excrement, splattering against the tall walls of the castle and leaving a repulsive brown and white residue in its wake.

My gaze is drawn upward once more, only to be met with a

sight that chills me to the bone. Swinging rhythmically from the imposing walls of the citadel are dozens of corpses, their bodies suspended by frayed ropes in various stages of decay.

Just as the colors of the sunset fade into dusk, the lifeless forms of the tribespeople deteriorate into nothingness. Eventually, the dry environment will turn them to grit, and the wind will blow away the remnants of their existence.

Hundreds of tattered ropes still hang over the castle walls, swaying in the breeze like a macabre forest of seaweed—a haunting reminder of the lives that once hung in the threads.

This is the cruel reality imposed by the harpy king, ruling through torment alone and using any perceived infraction as justification for torture and murder. It's the only way a tyrant like him can maintain his grip on power.

But the anger in the eyes of the tribespeople speaks volumes, burning with the injustices they have endured for eons. One day, that simmering rage will boil over, and nothing, not even the blazing sun, will escape their retribution.

I hope they find it within themselves to fight back, to taste the sweet air of freedom once more.

Yet, as much as my heart aches for their plight, I cannot waver from my course and be a part of their battle. The battle that is raging on my realm is where my heart is, swinging his swinging of blue starlight and defending the ancient library full of secrets.

I cannot risk being left behind on the waning eclipse and torn from my world.

A solitary tear traces a path down my cheek, its silent journey mirroring the turmoil within me. With my hands still bound behind my back, I struggle to brush the errant strands of hair from my face as the wind whips around us, carrying with it the scent of decay and despair.

A youngling, wobbly on its plump and inexperienced legs gets away from mother, excitedly reaching for the splashing waters of the central fountain.

The king doesn't break his stride or move his course.

Nudging the child with the tip of his wings as he passes, the youngling tumbles into the fountain and disappears within the churn of the dark waters in an instant.

The city stops as people watch with unchanged expressions. It is as if they are forbidden from acknowledging the urgency of the child's situation. My heart misses a beat, then thrums wildly in my chest as I gasp.

I pull, trying to break free of the guard but I'm yanked back by my captors with the whip still fixed in tight coils around my neck.

Even the mother of the child looks at the fountain with a neutral gaze as if merely watching the churning water.

Precious seconds have passed with no sign of the child, and no one has made an attempt to save her. Two harpy guards with long spears, flank the mother on both sides.

"You'll hang for that." One harpy spits as he shouts in the woman's face.

"No one touches the king." The other yells.

Disbelief trickles down my spine in a wave of chills. They mean to hang her from the walls of the castle because the king failed to move out of the way of a babe. Her child is most assuredly drowning because no one dared make a move and this mother is to be punished further by hanging from her feet at the castle walls until her death.

The woman doesn't move but looks a second longer at the bubbling water.

With a blur of activity, she reaches for one of the large, jagged rocks lining the fountain. Swinging it with guttural cry, the woman slams it into the face of one guard and pitches the large rock at the other.

Disoriented and recovering from the surprised attack, the guard doesn't realize the woman has stolen the blade from his belt.

But she doesn't attack them further.

Putting her back to the fountain, she locks eyes with a man across the plaza. He's weeping silently and attempts to remain stoic like the rest of the citizens watching the events unfold.

Running the blade smoothly across her neck, deep purple blood cascades down her clothes. Raising her arms, she drops the knife and falls peacefully into the roiling fountain.

Conceding to death and meeting her daughter at the end of the path where the waters flow, was a better fate for her than the agony of rotting into dust, hung on the walls of the castle.

My overseer slams the back of my head with the handle of his long spear, cawing at me to move. I try to look at each person through the haze of my tears.

I want them to know I share their sorrow and the horror of what was witnessed.

The crowd lining our path watches back in silent sorrow as we approach the castle, but amidst the sea of faces, it's a single pair of emerald eyes that captures my attention.

It can't be her. She can't be here.

My heart lurches in my chest as chills race up my body, and I stumble, the pulse of my heartbeat thundering in my ears.

The green eyes that have haunted my dreams stare back at me from the edge of the crowd, their gaze unwavering.

A second woman joins her, their resemblance strikingly similar, their features mirroring those of someone who should not be here. My eyes dart between them, and suddenly I understand.

With a release of tension in my brow, I crane my neck to keep them in my line of sight as my captors usher me toward the looming castle. The pair of women watch me with perplexed and untrusting expressions as I'm forced toward the citadel.

Medusa's sisters, survived of the battle of the Titans and stand before me.

The Herald of the Realms has balls of steel, but I think his sisters are made from pure Thaumium. Achilles didn't hesitate a second when he charged the God of War, and his flames were as strong and hot as his opponents. Then, exploding her mates Fire with her Wind, the entire crater erupted in flames from Calypso burst of currents.

Gods, they can put on a fucking show.

Hermes' Light has eaten away at the first wave of Shades but rest assured, Ares has more. The Herald of the Realms sends a clear message to Ares as he thrusts his destroyed ram's helmet back at him.

Glaring at the helmets horn impaled in the ground between his legs, Ares erupts in a hailstorm of flames and anger. Achilles meets him, fire on fire and Calypso is relentless in her attacks against the God of War.

The pair of mate's battle Ares with focus, and determination etched into their coordinated moves. It's dangerous to engage a Flame in hand-to-hand combat but the Siren is fearless. After two hits from Achilles, one on each side of Ares' abdomen, he, and Calypso clasp wrists. The Flame spins and releases his mate. She becomes a streak across the crater as her Winds surge behind her.

Both feet strike Ares in the chest and she sends him soaring backwards before he skids to a halt. Still upright, the Flame rubs his injury as his orange eyes narrow in on the Siren and she meets his glare with one of her own.

Ares' Flame Armor intensifies, but Calypso pulls the Winds of the realm away from him, restricting his element. She feeds her mate the realms currents and Achilles' fire becomes a raging inferno of revenge.

Ages ago, it was Ares' hand that threw the wooden spear, impaling their mate, Patroclus. If ever a Flame blew bright and true in this realm, it was him.

He didn't deserve the torment of his last few moments of immortality and his surviving mates are making sure the God of War feels their wrath of that moment.

Slicing Wind cuts against Ares' flames and Callie takes him on with Achilles quickly incoming behind her. Fire and Wind work together against the God of War as the line of Dark Mages break behind their leader.

Walking a steady pace, Aryana and her Mages of Darkness ascend toward us, and we prepare for them.

Ares' army follows the mages. Their dark cloaks billow with shadows that seep out with clawed hands, ready to consume the light of our auras and feed the unending hunger that torments the beings of Elysium.

Hermes centers himself in the middle of those who came to defend the goddess.

Stretching his neck and rotating his shoulders to adjust the scabbard on his back, Hermes waits. Griping the hilt of his sword tightly, he spins the circular shield of starlight in his hand.

His aura pulses like a star on the verge of explosion. With each beat of his heart, his power flares and he watches the mages on their slow approach.

Reaching his hand out, and indicating for us to wait, Hermes steps forward.

My Shifters are restless as they snort and growl around me, but we can't enter the crater with the battle of the Flames within. Soul Fire will consume us all and there will be no one left from either army.

As the Flame and Siren wage war against Ares, his army follows the path of the mages and darkness spreads out from their cloaks. As the dark beings of Elysium take shape, Hermes taps on his chest three times.

Perhaps a ritual before battle; we all have them.

My skin ripples as the beasts within me fight for freedom. They are all savage and hungry for the blood of Ares. At the rate Calypso is fighting, the God of War will not see the end of this day.

Fenrir begs me for release most of all and the wolf that prowls under my skin will have the battlefield today. My beta takes flight. The feathers of the great golden eagle shimmer as Kai's power swells within her.

Her feathers cut like razors and the wind from her wings rustles my hair as it rests on my shoulders. Gathering my locks into a malformed bun at the top of my head, I perform my own ritual as I prepare to release the wolf.

My packs sense my shifting aura as my beast's roar within me.

I shift through the predators contained within my soul and

let each one stretch and bellow inside me. My pack hears the calls of my beasts and roar in response. Transformations take shape around me as Shifters resign their mortal forms, letting their creatures emerge for the approaching battle.

The animals that live within my Shifting ability wash through me like waves of fury. The bear, the serpent, the dark monster that hides in the deepest recesses of my power; the one beast that refuses to come to the surface. They quiver sensing the approaching army and they are starving to consume the blood of my enemies. *And oh, my beasts will feast today.*

The packs distance themselves from me, backing away knowing the space my animals need when they swallow my meager mortal bones and explode out of me.

A swell of darkness deepens within the crater from the Dark Mages and the shadows they command. A sea of Shades rise from the grit like steam and Hermes ignites his starlight.

Behind me, a large portal bursts open and the war cry of hundreds charge forward. Hermes and I look behind us with a synchronized turn of our heads. Ares' forces flank us on both sides.

I quickly look back, locking eyes with the Herald. *We're surrounded.*

"We're going to die today." I tell Hermes through our minds. His eyes begin to glow as celestial light takes over his vision and ribbons of aura sway off him like translucent flames of starlight.

"Probably. But Ares and his army die with us." The Herald's reply is resolute. He nods behind him, where Ares still battles, and half his army ascend closer. *"I got this side; you take that side."*

"See you when it's over." And I hope I do.

Ares strikes Calypso and Achilles with both palms; his flames and strength propel them backward.

Like two flaming comets, they are helpless as they soar through the air. Achilles arms find his mate and he encases her in his protection. Her ribbons of Wind cover them and guide their landing as they slide thirty feet, stopping an arm's length away from me.

The darkness of Elysium swells toward us and I ready my packs for the opposing attack.

Bending at his knees, Hermes braces with his shield covering his body. With his sword ready, starlight pushes him faster than an explosion across the cosmos toward Ares. The Flame conjures a sword of fire and their weapons clash, ringing across the desert.

Erupting from Hermes, a giant dome of Light encases the crater as the Herald separates the two halves of Ares' army. Hermes has encased himself with Ares and the Dark Mages, protecting us from the deadliest half of Ares' army.

Motherfucker.

"Hermes." His sister exclaims under her breath. Standing, she races to the thick shield of her brother's power and beats against it. "HERMES!" She screams at him as tears flow down her face.

Achilles joins his mate and places his hand against the wall of Light separating the warriors on two sides of the same battlefield. "Hermes!" He yells along with his mate, but Hermes ignores them both.

Starlight emits from him and pulsates into the atmosphere, the rains down in a large protective dome of isolation that grows thicker as he pours his power into it.

Shades run into the barrier, sizzling, and disintegrating as the ultra-hot light destroys their dark forms.

We have no chance today against the might of Ares's but if Hermes can survive long enough, we may be able to dispatch the newest arrivals quickly and help him within the crater.

As long as that crazy son of a bitch doesn't die first.

Calm takes over my soul as my wolf growls within in me. My bones crack and twist inside and I close my eyes. My transformation is instant and when I open my eyes again, I see the world through the sharp vision of Fenrir. Lifting my muzzle to the sky, my command rings across the dome of starlight and the battle beneath the library begins.

My whips and cuffs are replaced with a thick collar and forearm coverings that keep my arms locked behind my back. The Thaumium metal starts at my wrists and encases my arms up to my elbows. They lock on to each other, pinning my arms together and making my chest jut out uncomfortably.

Dense chains bind my ankles, trailing behind me as I move, their weight dragging me down with each step.

Gods these chains are heavy.

Thicker and more cumbersome than any restraints I have endured before, they strip away my sense of power and leave me hollow.

The sky darkens and I sense the eclipse looming over me like a clock.

Behind me, a large stained-glass window depicts scenes of the Titan's realm, with towering mountains and lush valleys teeming with life. There is no sign of the endless crimson desert that now dominates Tartarus, leaving me to wonder if this barren wasteland was once a fertile land of green pastures.

Perhaps when Chaos massacred the Titans of Earth and Water their blood rushed the land, evaporating in the scorching heat and turning the realm to a brittle desert. Or perhaps the desert is the doing of the harpy king and his windstorm of torment.

The sun fills the round window perfectly as if it was constructed to capture the radiance of the crimson eclipse. A red haze fills the atmosphere as the eclipse has fully covered the sun. Half of my time here is spent.

With a deep breath to steady myself, I turn my gaze forward, fixing my eyes upon the throne where King Thanatos sits. His attention shifts from the rosette window to me, his head tilting in silent contemplation.

The grandeur of the throne room, once fit for a Titan, now lies in ruins. In its place stands a grotesque testament to King Thanatos' reign—a chair fashioned from the twisted and hollow bones of long-dead harpies, their feathers now adorning the seat in a mockery of authority. It's a stark symbol of the king's obsession with destruction, not only of the tribespeople of the desert but also of his own kind.

The once vibrant hall, where grand celebrations were held, now lies shrouded in darkness, illuminated only by the eerie flicker of torches. The polished floor, once gleaming, is now dulled and worn, obscured by the long shadows cast by twisted statues of harpies that line the chamber.

Some of the statues depict the creatures taking flight, while others are frozen in poses of aggression, their taloned feet poised to snatch up unruly citizens. Still, others cower in fear, their stone faces eternally frozen in terror.

King Thanatos settles into his throne, the crown of bleeding stones adorning his brow, their crimson droplets staining his face as he watches me with keen yellow eyes.

His wounded bride stands at his side, a silent and motionless figure like the statues around us.

The throne room fills with onlookers, their eyes fixed on me, but I refuse to let my gaze waver from the king.

Thanatos runs a thin black tongue along the edge of his beak, nodding once in acknowledgment. My guards jab me in the back with wooden staffs, urging me forward like cattle. I stagger, barely managing to maintain my balance.

With a heated glare, I mark both harpies at my side, one of them squawking in response. The room erupts with the sound of flapping wings and caws as the harpy's cheer on the guards, their unruly enthusiasm echoing off the walls.

The king watches with a satisfied smirk, relishing in the spectacle before him.

"Remove her weapons." The king orders. I look at my daggers still fixed to my thigh holsters. The shields of Light and Dark still woven around the weapons.

Both harpy guards reach for them, and I remain silent. Keeping my eyes fixed on the king, the two guards touch the handles at the same time.

Lightning from Hermes' shield attacks them as my shadows crawl up their arms.

The harpies caw and flap their wings, trying to make the elemental powers cease the barrage of assaults. Smoke from their singed feathers assault my nose but I keep my expression stoic as if nothing is happening around me of any interest.

The harpy king has me locked in a malevolent stare which I return with amusement.

My shadows reach into the guard's mouths and nostrils, filling them with darkness and suffocating them. Hermes light keeps its attack until their hearts stop beating and they fall to the ground next to me.

"I wouldn't touch those if I were you." I raise my voice with confidence, ringing across the great hall of the Titans castle.

The angry king draws out the silence, reveling in the dramatic tension but using the time to calm himself before speaking. Seraphina remains unfazed by the spectacle, refusing to meet my gaze, as the king stretches his vulture-like wings in an attempt to appear imposing. But to me, he only looks like a coward.

"Why have you trespassed upon my realm, Skyfallen?"

If he wants to be difficult and dramatic, then so will I. I let my eyes roam over his thin, wiry form, smaller in stature than the other harpies. I wonder what kind of dark pact he made with Chaos to seize dominion over this realm, and what grip he holds over its citizens to keep them living in such perpetual fear.

When my gaze falls upon his feet, I can't help but notice how absurdly small they are. A snort of laughter escapes me before I can stop it, and the king's blue skin flushes with anger, nearly turning purple. The guard at his right coughs, struggling to conceal his amusement.

In the blink of an eye, the king transforms into a blur of motion. It takes a moment for reality to catch up as I watch the blood ooze from the guard's face, a black feather clutched in the king's hand.

My senses flare with adrenaline as I realize what has just transpired— the king's feather is sharper than any sword, slicing through the guard's head with brutal efficiency, leaving it severed in two with a diagonal cut.

The gruesome scene unfolds before me, the air heavy with the stench of blood and death. The top half of the harpy's head slides down, leaving a trail of black blood in its wake before crashing to the floor with a sickening thud. The body slumps to the ground, a pool of dark fluid spreading beneath it like a morbid offering to the tyrant king.

With a flick of his wrist, the king sends the feather darting across the room, embedding itself in the stone wall with deadly precision, narrowly missing the head of another guard who stands frozen in terror.

"Retrieve his tongue," the king demands, his voice carrying the weight of authority and menace.

The guard complies without hesitation, plucking the feather from the wall and approaching the lifeless body of his comrade. With the top of the head removed, the long tongue of the dead harpy hangs from his mouth. Brain and bone are so cleanly cut by the sharp feather, they appear smooth.

The guard plucks the feather from the stone and approaches the dead body. He kicks the top half of the skull out of his way, and it spins like a top. Coming to a stop, one of the lifeless yellow eyes hangs out of the severed socket and looks at me. The other eye was sliced in half.

My stomach churns with revulsion, threatening to empty its contents as I fight to keep my composure. I force myself to meet the king's gaze as he takes a bite from the severed tongue, blood dripping from his beak with each gruesome chew. It's a chilling display of power and dominance, a stark glimpse into the cruel reality of life under the rule of King Thanatos.

Still chewing, the king repeats his question with a menacing undertone. "I'll ask again, and you'd do better to answer this time. Why have you trespassed upon my realm, Skyfallen?"

"My purpose is not for you to know," I respond, surprised by the steadiness of my voice. Taking a deep, calming breath, I push down my rising disgust and temper. I refuse to give him the satisfaction of seeing me react.

A wicked grin spreads across his beak, but I detect a tremor of anger beneath the surface. "Such arrogance," he retorts. "Why hide your purpose if it is foretold, Crimson Savior?"

"Why ask, if it is foretold, false king?" I counter, eliciting a collective gasp from the onlookers. "My purpose is mine alone, and I'll not answer to you. So, send me to the dungeons. I grow bored of your questions."

Feigning indifference, I scan the throne room, forcing my curiosity to override my nerves. In the back of the crowd, I spot the two Gorgon sisters exchanging whispers before slipping away unnoticed.

The king rises from his throne, feathers rustling in agitation. "Stubborn defiance will not serve you well, Skyfallen," he warns, gesturing to the deceased harpy at his feet. "Take the body to the kitchens."

As the guards drag the lifeless form away, I realize the implications only moments before King Thanatos leans in close, his foul breath assaulting my senses. "Yes, Savior, we will eat my son for dinner," he whispers, sending a shiver down my spine.

"Son?" I echo, incredulous.

"I have many," the king replies with a cruel laugh. "My wives bear me children until they perish, then I take another wife to continue my line. It is their honor to serve their king." He strokes one of Seraphina's long pale-yellow braids as she stares at the floor with lifeless eyes.

"You call yourself a king, yet your throne is built upon the bones of the innocent. How does it feel to rule over a kingdom of fear and despair?"

The kings' yellow eyes narrow with malice "You dare to question my authority, little mortal? You, who stand before me in chains?"

I smirk despite my predicament. Let him keep thinking I am a mere mortal and I'll relish in his shock when he founds out just how wrong he is. "I've been in chains before and left them crumbled on the ground."

The king shakes to settle the raised feathers that are the evidence of his irritation. Twisting his beak into a cruel smile, his head tilts at an unnatural angle. "Ah, courage. A fleeting trait in the face of death. Have you ever looked up the face of death?"

"Once or twice." I let the smugness of my response flow freely. If only he knew how familiar I am to the chilling face of death.

His smile widens as he runs his black tongue over the edges of his razor-sharp beak again. "Let us see if your courage holds when faced with the full extent of my power."

"Your power? Is that what you call it? I see only a coward, too afraid to face the truth of his own insignificance." The crowd gasps again and some of the tribespeople move with quiet steps out of the throne room. Harpies shake their wings and stomp their taloned bird feet against the dull stone floor. My words agitating them.

"Insolence! You will learn the price of defying me, mortal. And it will be paid in blood."

"I'm happy to pay it in your blood, *king*." Every ounce of malice for this hate-filled tyrant oozes into my words as I mock his title. "I hope the people of Tartarus fill the Dune Sea with the corpses of you and your chickens. And when the winds of time blow you away, not even the realm will remember the little tyrant that squawked on a stolen throne."

The kings eye blaze with fury as he slaps me across the cheek. A trickle of blood seeps from a thin slice of his sharp wing.

"History is written by the victors, mortal. And I assure you, victory will be mine. Prepare yourself for the darkness that awaits in the depths of my dungeons." The kings voice drips with venom as he turns and stalks away. "For when we meet next, I'll feast on your screams, and I feast on your body."

Despite the impending doom of an enclosed prison and death at the jaws of this monster, I hold my head high and raise one eyebrow in resentment. "I have faced the darkness of dungeons before, tyrant. Be prepared to meet death, the next time we see each other."

King Thanatos' chilling laugh bounces off the tall ceilings. "We shall see, mortal. We shall see."

44 Rhea

If I knew how badly the dungeons would smell, I would have taken a deep breath of the shitty air **outside the castle.** The smell of rot and stench of raw sewage makes my eyes water and as soon as the guards threw me into the cell, I puked in the corner.

By some miracle it didn't get in my hair.

A decaying harpy in the on the opposite side of my cell is the source of the ghastly smell. The body has burst open and a dark, thick liquid has oozed a puddle in the corner. The squishy little noises of maggots crawling is my only companion in the otherwise empty cell.

As the cell doors slam, I'm left in my uncomfortable cuffs.

That probably means the dungeon is not lined with the elemental metal that suffocates immortal powers. *Good.* When I break out of these bindings, I'm going to tear this dungeon apart on my way out.

Taking a deep breath to steady myself, I look around the cell, searching for something to break my arm covers apart. If I can only bring my arms forward, I'm certain I can free myself from the bindings and gods help this king when I have access to my powers.

Footsteps on the stairwell send a rush of warmth down my body. I know there is no help coming for me and surely whatever is approaching promises pain or torment.

Quick trots slow to more carefully measured steps.

Squinting my eyes to focus on the dark stairwell, I see the obscurity of a form moving in slowly in the darkness. A pair of yellow eyes reflect back at me, a harpy.

Heavy breathing is a faint whisper creeping across the cell floor.

The rhythmic rubbing of fabric on fabric tells me the harpy observing me is pleasuring himself. Perhaps this ritual of masturbation is a form of claiming a mate just as the king did to Seraphina at the camp of the Danaides.

My heart is pounding in my chest so rapidly, I think I could take flight from the speed.

A soft grunt bounces across the darkness as the harpy's pleasure is rising. The bright yellow eyes keep their steady gaze on me, never wavering.

I need to think of something before this bird-human hybrid ejaculates on me and feed on my blood. If this race of beings is a sex deranged as I suspect, I need to fight fire with fire.

The harpy is staring at me, so I raise my eyebrow and part my lips as if curious. My chest is already pushed forward thanks to my arms braced behind my back, so I make a show rubbing myself across one of the bars of my cell.

Taking the bait, the harpy's reflective eyes shift down to my boobs and I know my plan will work.

"What are you doing over there in the dark?" I ask with a breathy voice.

The harpy releases a grunt and takes a shaky breath. "Ye want te see?" He speak with an odd accent the king did not possess.

Since the tyrant king rules by fear, I'm hoping this means the king doesn't spend much time ensuring his soldiers are educated or well trained.

I squeeze my knees together and stick out my ass a little, pretending as if this show is making me aroused. Raking my lip through my teeth, I nod my head as if I'm too bashful to say yes.

Still stroking himself, the harpy steps out of the shadows. Keeping his distance, he stays at the mouth of the stairwell that leads to the castle above.

I release a deep breath for him, as if I enjoy the view he's giving me. "Slower."

He slows down to a languid pace as I flick my eyes to his seductively. The harpy parts his beak and his hooded eyes tell me he's going climax soon if I don't draw this out a little.

"Have you been with a mortal before?" I rub my breasts along the bars again and he releases another groan as he watches me.

Shaking his head, no, he swallows hard before answering. "We not allowed." He huffs. "Only the king."

"Mmmm, so selfish." I look away, then back at him. "I could help you." I look at his penis again and my offer makes him grunt. Squeezing his dick hard, he pauses before resuming his strokes.

"Come on." I turn around, putting my arms through the bars. "It'll be our little secret." I whisper as I look over my shoulder at him.

His eyes move down to my outstretch hand. Licking his beak, he walks up slowly. Before he gets close enough to put his penis in my hand, I pull back slightly.

"Ah, hold on."

He pauses with alarm.

"Will you wet it for me?" I stretch out my palm behind me. The angle I'm holding my arm is painfully uncomfortable, but I can bear it a moment longer.

As the harpy leans down, sticking out his nearly black tongue, I make my move.

Fixing my shackles around his neck, I lurch my body forward and pull with all my might. His hollow bones snap easily, and the weight of his body strains my shoulders.

He falls to the floor in a heap, and I lean against the cell as the rate of my heart and quick breaths are nearly the same pace.

Hot tears prickle at my eyes. The contrast in my conflicting emotions is making me sick to my stomach again.

While I've killed immortals and enemies in other lifetimes, this is the first time in my life as Rhea that I've taken a life with my bare hands.

Moros and the harpy guards above met their ends with my immortal powers. I eased Tritons soul on to the Void with peaceful resignation. But this life was stripped away with the violence of my hands and it's a heavy burden to carry.

Though my own life depended on protecting myself, I hope this is a burden I never get accustomed to feeling.

Allowing myself a moment to calm my emotions, I look to the dead guard. A pair of keys are hanging on his belt and with the position he fell, I can't easily reach them. The keys may unlock my shackles or this cell, so I need to retrieve them.

Working endlessly, I try and fail to get the guard close enough to reach the keys. Hours pass, perhaps half a day and my arms scream at me for relief.

My stomach cries pains of anger and I'm desperate for something to drink and to use the bathroom. Having worked myself into a sweat, I lean against the wall, trying to think of something else that may help me pull the guard toward me.

Footsteps echo from the dark stairwell again, making me freeze as more guards are approaching. From the few words that bounce through the dark hall, they have sinister plans of a carnal nature for me, just like my previous victim had.

Seeing as there is at least two guards coming, and a dead body in front of my cell, I can't bet on using the same tactic as before on my newest arrivals.

"He forbid anyone from touchin' 'er." One harpy says.

"But he didn't say we couldn't make 'er touch us." The other says.

Fucking assholes.

I stand in the center of the cell and ready myself for them. I'm not sure yet what I'll do to defend myself, but I guess I'll find out soon enough.

The guards pause two steps from the bottom, looking at their fallen harpy guard first and at me with starvation in their beady eyes. One is already rubbing his crotch as he sneers are me and the other licks his jagged beak.

They take a step closer and my heart hammers.

It seems as if the body lying on the floor of the dungeon has enflamed their intentions and deepened their sinister plans for me.

If I were unshackled and free to move, I would likely be

trembling. Part of me is afraid but largely I'm getting more pissed off by the second. This race of bird-humanoid creatures are vile but weak.

I'm suffocated by the realms sorrow as I feel the pain of its people flowing around the atmosphere on the giant windstorm.

I can't understand how the people of Tartarus have survived in this realm of terror since the Titans fell. But more so, I can't understand why they don't rise up against the king.

A pair of carnelian eyes narrow on my thighs as the harpy takes in my daggers.

"I wan' those." He says.

"Then let's get on wif' it." The other answers.

Through a dark corridor to the side of the stairs, the sound of a rattlesnake whispers from the darkened passage. It's tail shaking like a wooden rattle full of beads and gets louder as if slithering toward my small, disgusting prison.

The harpies freeze, listening intently. A look of bewilderment covers their face.

"Can it really be a Sunfire Serpent?" The guard on the left licks his beak. A line of slobber leaks from the corner as if the bird is drooling over the prospect of consuming the snake.

"Oh, I 'avent 'ad one in ages." The crotch-rubber says, still massaging his gentiles.

Four yellow and orange ringed snakes slither from the darkness. Three feet in length, they don't appear to be large snakes, but I move backward in my cell away from them.

The harpies nearly erupt into a frenzy, half-bent over and chasing the snakes. Nearing a wall of stone figures, each guard finally gets a snake in their hands, leaving two still wriggling around the dirty ground of the dungeon.

My eyes flick to the snakes on the floor in case they come in my cell. They could be poisonous and I'm not aiming for my life as Rhea to end in a deadly snakebite.

As the harpies lift the reptiles to their mouths, the two snakes on the ground wind up their legs, curling around their bodies and wrap tightly around the birds' necks.

Growing in size, the Sunfire Serpents coil in a vice-like grip, suffocating the harpies.

Opening their beaks and clawing at the snakes, the birds' talons rake along the scaled flesh, and it crumbles to red sand, falling to the ground.

Two pair of green eyes glow from the dark tunnels that flank each side of the stairs leading to the world above. Melting out of the shadows, the near identical copies of Medusa stride up to the suffocating harpies.

The guards attempt to choke out an exclamation, but the snakes tighten around their necks.

I watch as a stone facade creeps over the blue skin and harden the black and brown feathers of the harpies' wings. Just as Medusa would petrify her enemies, her sisters possess the same power.

Before everything on the second harpy is petrified, one of the snakes retrieves the keys that would unlock my cuffs and it slithers to the eldest of the two sisters.

Standing among the alcove of stone figures that adorn the castle at nearly every turn, the guards' bodies join the rock army. My mouth gapes open as I realize, the details of the stone figures and varied poses of birds in flight or landing positions.

They had all been alive at one time.

The castle is littered with the remnants of long-dead

harpies and these two guards make up the most recent additions.

I can imagine a great battle taking place as the harpies took control over Tartarus after the fall of the Titans. The people of this realm must have fought hard but eventually lost.

Their suffering since is nearly unbearable to consider, after my short experience here. I can't imagine living all these ages under the cruel harpy's dark rule.

"How do you know us, Scarlet Savior?" The older of the two sisters ask.

"Get me out of this dungeon first." I cock an eyebrow and speak with too much authority for someone in jail with a partially liquified harpy and my hands bound behind my back. But to my credit, there is a dead harpy lying on the dungeon ground between me and the sisters.

The younger of the two takes half a step but the older sister holds her hand out, halting her. "Tell us, then we may let you out depending on your answer."

Holding each other in a locked gaze of stubbornness, the older sister and I refuse to look away. I hear the seconds tick by with each beat of my heart and feel the oppressing eclipse lighten. How much time has passed on Gaea since I left?

What is the difference of a second here, compared a second there?

I can't see the eclipse of the triple moons here in the darkness of the dungeon and it pulls on my anxiety. I need to move forward and reach the cave that has been haunting me.

But I'm not going to blindly trust anyone like I did the Danaides, so I need to be smart about my response.

With smug satisfaction, I know just the answer that will win my freedom. A sly smile spreads across my face before I deliver their request. I utter the name of the woman who stalks my nightmares; their lost sister, closed off to them when everyone fled from Tartarus and were locked away within the wards of Gaea.

Leaning forward, nearly touching the cell bars, my reply ricochets around the stones that surround us. "Medusa."

The eldest sister reaches through the cell bars, trying to grab for me but I shuffle back. Staying just out of her reach, I hoped she would use her power over earth element to open the cell, but she doesn't.

"How do you know that name?"

"Nope. That wasn't part of the deal."

"We made no deal, Scarlet Savior."

"Then leave me alone so I can break out of here." I stick my foot through the cell and kick at the guards' body, still trying to work him toward me so I can grab the keys on his belt.

I work to control my breathing and hide my frustration as remaining in these godsforsaken cuffs in a cell with a liquified bird-humanoid corpse is about to make me scream.

The sisters debate with loud whispers on the other side of the dungeon. Each of them taking turns looking at me with suspicion. I glance at my cellmate, wondering if the dead harpy is as impatient as I am, waiting on the pair of Gorgons to finish their argument.

One believes I'm only goading them on, so I'll be freed from the cell. The other argues there is no way I would know of their lost sister unless I had met her, making her believe Medusa is still alive.

I thank the Fates when sisters approach the cell and I know the younger of the two has gotten their way. With a reluctant grip on the keys, the young sister conjures a sand snake, and it slithers to the cell.

Wrapping around the lock, the door opens, and I rush out to get far away from the leaking body of the long dead harpy. Turning my back to the sisters, I wait for them to unlock my cuffs, but they don't.

"Tell us how you know Medusa and we will free you from your restraints."

"You sister is alive and trying to kill me."

The eldest ticks her eyebrow as if not surprised by my answer. "So, nothing has changed then, after all this time. That's disappointing." Stepping to me, she unlocks the long cuffs that bind my powers. As soon as the lock is removed, my powers swell within me. A rush of wind swirls in the dungeon and the ground tremors, making dust fall from the rocky ceiling.

The pair of sisters look around, concerned and fearful of the dungeons ceiling caving upon us. Taking steadying breaths, I tamper the emotions of my power.

After a moment, the winds settle and the ground ceases it's quakes.

After exchanging glances, the sisters head toward the dark passageway to the left of the stairs and I tap on my chest three times.

Hermes sent the pulse of his power down our bond so long ago. Hours have passed and I've not been able to return my response. He must be worried sick, even though the time difference is likely only seconds for him, I know he's aware of how much time passes for me.

While I wait for his answer, I look up the dark stairwell, knowing harpies infest the upper levels of the castle. While I feel confident, I could find my way out, I can't risk being seen and having to fight my way to the castle's exit.

With reluctance and caution, and no reply from my fated mate, I follow the sister. Descending deeper beneath the sands of Tartarus, we wind our way deep below the Titans castle.

The air is stale and cool, telling me the hot sun cannot penetrate this far beneath the ground. The tunnels twist and turn like the snakes the sisters conjured but they never slow their steps.

The Gorgon sisters practical and resilient clothing is well suited for navigating the harsh desert environment of Tartarus. They each wear light-weight tunics that sway as we walk the tunnels at a hurried pace.

The earthy browns and muted yellows of their clothing play against their deep umber skin.

Their leather boots lace up their calves, much like mine to keep the sands of Tartarus from chaffing their skin. Each sister wears a pair of forearm guards and a belt with assortment of accessories that clink as we work our way toward the surface.

The elder sister wears her hair in long braids with stone adornments just like Medusa does. The tendrils of hair whip and sway, as if guarding the sister as she leads our path through the tunnels. The younger of the two sisters wears her hair loose at her shoulders. The tight curls reach to the middle of her back, forming a soft halo around her beautiful face.

As we walk the tunnels, my mind races with dark thoughts of what could be keeping Hermes from answering my call down our bond. I know he's alive as I can feel his power, a steady thrum in my chest.

Perhaps the battle is raging too fiercely, and he didn't detect my signal. Or maybe he is held captive, just as I was and unable to answer.

Closing my eyes, I push that idea away from my mind. No, Hermes is a strong fighter and with Callie and Achilles fighting by his side, they will protect each other.

I have faith, they won't allow themselves to be separated on the field of battle and will work together against their attackers until I return.

These thoughts are hard since time is moving so differently for me here. I have the excess time to dwell on the darkest prospects my mind can conjure. I have to keep reminding myself, hours here on Tartarus are merely seconds passing for them.

With a deep breath, I relax the building tension in my shoulders and push my nagging worry to the back of my mind.

Removing a leather flask from her belt, the younger sister offers it to me with a nod. Her striking eyes, the rich color of a pine forest pierce me with the resemblance to Medusa.

Having left my pack at the Danaides camp and having made the mistake of taking sustenance too willingly before, I decline.

"Suit yourself. I am Stheno." She clips the flask back to her belt and returns to the quick pace. "That is Euryale."

"The Scarlet Savior does not require our names." The elder sister barks back. "Hold here." Euryale holds up her fist and we stop. She pulls a thin scarf draped around her shoulders and fixes it over her head. Stheno does the same with a sheer scarf, the color of pale mint.

Light of the tunnels opening ahead is blinding as the warm sun blazes in.

My heart hammers from the long track but also with a pulling need to see how much time I've wasted down here. The alignment is crossing in front of the large burning sun and a pinkish red haze is fills the atmosphere, consuming the orange sherbet sky.

I can sense it. I'm running out of time.

A scurry behind me makes me whip my head around.

My daggers are in my hands and poised to attack but nothing is there.

A dozen orange and yellow ringed snakes slither past me quickly, ushering out into the bright sunlight and spreading in all directions.

"It's clear. Let's go." Euryale sets out of the tunnel without waiting for us to follow.

Casting my hand over my eyes, I thunder out of the darkness with them.

Swallowed in the shadow of a large sculpture, I look up in awe.

Flanking each side of our exit are two large, winged equestrians, carved from rock. One is so tan, it would nearly be blonde and the other is a deep brown, like the bark of an old oak tree. As if captured in time while rearing, both horses are frozen on their hind legs.

Their front legs batting at the air in front of them.

The frozen sway of their manes and tails, even the intricate detail of braided leather saddles is carved into the fine craftsmanship.

But it's the wings of the great horses, stretched to the heavens that I can't stop staring at. They are incredible. Each pair of wings sitting at the horses' shoulders reach outward. A sheen of pearlescent tan and brown glimmers on every long feather as the Tartarus sun shines bright in the sky.

I can almost feel the wind stirred by the movement of the large wings and hear the whinny of the majestic beasts at they would have taken flight.

Like the mighty Pegasus of ancient lore, these winged beasts command attention and inspire the awe of your imagination.

Looking behind me, we are exiting from a jut of rocks that are exposed amid the crimson sand. Like a great mountain has been hidden far beneath the grit of Tartarus and this peak is the only remnant.

The large castle of the once-great titan sits on the horizon.

From this distance, the large structure of oppression seems nothing more than a mirage in the desert. The heat rising off the sands makes the crimson citadel and surrounding city appear to float above the desert.

Looking back at the sculpted flying horse before me, I think of the book I was looking at the day I met Hermes and smile at the memory.

With Winged Grecians tucked into my tote, I nearly plowed through Hermes when I ran out of the bookstore bathroom. A wave of heat ran through me then and it cascades across my skin now.

For the first time since I was coerced by the Danaides, I feel the familiar tug on my powers. The beacon that hailed me to this desolate realm pulses with intensity against my chest.

Tucked away in a great mountain, and I can sense the tendrils of my powers. I feel the darkness that encases a part of my soul and the need to reunite with them nearly steals the breath from my lungs.

I'm much closer now.

The sisters each run a hand of affection down the stone horses. With a gust of hot Tartarus air, the stone veneer blows away, releasing the winged horses from their frozen states.

With a neigh and flapping its mighty wings, the dark brown horse comes back to life and burrows its head into Euryale's side. She fusses with a leather satchel fixed to her belt and retrieves something that looks like a circular almond biscuit.

Holding her hand flat, the horse take the treat from her palm, and she mounts the steed.

Amazing. They must have used their powers to solidify their horses and make them appear as stone carvings while they entered the dungeon through this hidden passage.

Stheno's blonde horse blows a large breath from its nostrils as if complaining about the time they spent in the tunnels. Stheno smiles and pats her horse on its flanks and using the leather saddle, pulls herself onto the horses back.

"Come, Scarlet Savior, we must fly to our tribe first." Stheno calls to me high atop her mount. "We must travel to our tribe before the next leg of our journey."

"My name is Rhea and I'm not going any..."

"You must come with us, Savior." The pleading look in Stheno's eyes almost make me stop and hear her argument. But as if I can feel the crimson veil pull over the sun, my eyes find the large ball of light burning high above us. The first sliver of sun peeks from behind the veil as the eclipse begins to ebb away.

I have just a little over a day left and it will be over.

"I am no savior." My face heats as my irritation grows hotter. "Thank you for freeing me but I'm here to retrieve something. I cannot save your realm."

Euryale dismounts and saunters to me with challenge in her glare. "When the Crimson Veil shrouds the sun's bright light, the Savior shall descend, heralding the onset of night."

She must be reciting the prophesy. I thin my lips and release a frustrated huff. *I don't have time for this shit.* "I'm not your savior."

Euryale pays me no attention and keeps stalking toward me. Taller by several inches, her shadow swallows me and I'm thankful for the cool relief it brings from the harsh sun. Her braids sway about her as her anger rises with my continued argument.

"Upon the back of the Shadowmare, with wings as dark as coal, she'll navigate the heavens, guided by fate's unfolding role."

Backing up to avoid a collision, I hit the rocky wall behind me. Pulling a dagger from my holster, I hold it firm in my grip with the blade running along my forearm, ready for her attack.

"Before the dragon made of light, whose judgment none may sway, the Scarlet Savior must pass, to fulfill her destined way."

My eyes widen at the mention of the dragon and my nightmares flash before my eyes. I try to conceal my memory of the dark cave's entrance that holds the white glowing eyes of a great beast.

Euryale tilts her head to the side and a smirk slides across her face. "So, you're here for the dragon?"

Fuck. I drop my hand and return my dagger to its holder. She's goading me but she's not going to attack me.

"Yes."

Euryale outright grins like a sinister cat. "Good. Savior or not, you'll still need to come with us. The entire realm is hunting you, *Skyfallen*." She draws out the name the Danaides and harpies called me, like a reminder of the bounty that will surely be sitting on my head once they discover I have escaped.

"You'll never make it without the cloak of darkness and with all this sunlight, seems like we're fresh out of shadows." Turning her back, she strides to her great horse and mounts it again with ease.

"And how can you help me with that?"

"Because we keep the only Shadowmare that exists in this realm." Flicking the leather reins in her hands, Euryale kicks her feet. With a click of her tongue, her horse takes several fast strides and flaps its great wings. "Or take your chances with the desert. It looks especially hungry today."

The crimson sand unfurls at the disturbance and the horse takes to the skies. Stheno holds her hand out to me, her blonde horse watches me with knowing eyes.

With a sigh, I take her hand and climb onto the back of another winged animal of ancient mythology. I only hope for a better outcome with these sisters than I fared with the Danaides and their sphinxes.

Trusting Medusa was a mistake and I fear I'm only making another by coming with her sisters.

Flames roar around me as my father clashes with
Hermes. I watch as Hermes casts his protective dome of
Light to shield his tiny army from the might of Ares. With one
hand shoved in my pocket, I stroll across the desert that will
soon turn to a battlefield. My other arm, ending in a stump,
swings at my side.

Looking behind me, I watch the dome feather down to
meet the desert sand. My father's forces fight by his side within
Hermes' forcefield. The other half, newly arrived at the field of
battle, charge the Shifters and Elementals that side with the
goddess.

My goddess.

The acrid smell of my father's flames offend my senses and
I'm glad to be separated from him as the fighting begins. In his
eyes, I'm only a flicker, a Flame weakened by his resentment of
me. But I will show my father I can be great, just like him.

Too bad he won't live long enough to appreciate me the
way he should have.

As I look across the field of battle, Lucas takes the form of
his wolf. The beast rises far above the fray as teeth and fur

collide. The once loyal Shifter-army of Ares that fights behind Lucas combat the newly arrived Elementals.

I know our little gift of the twenty-four women are enflaming their emotions. I'm sure they will fight well today but this rouse doesn't matter in the long run.

My father only plans to distract the Herald and his messengers for the next few minutes, long enough to ensure he keeps the wards around Gaea closed for her return.

Apollo and my father constructed those wards long ago. And only he can take them down, which, of course, he won't.

When the eclipse ends, Hermes and the others will realize their little goddess is stuck forever on Tartarus. She'll waste another lifetime rotting in that eternal desert as the wards that protect Gaea will hold true.

The Titan of Death will be cast out of this realm again.

My father plans to rule this realm and wait her for to return the only way that she can. When she reincarnates to another mortal shell, she will find her mate has been captured and living in the tortured chambers of another Underworld. Ares will finally be able to barter for what he truly wants. *Death*.

Surely she will sacrifice her power to save her mate.

That is my father's plan, but I have another.

I watched Rhea as she entered her portal, just like Hermes did. Both of us, her former mate and me, her new mate, looking after the woman we love as she goes off in search of herself.

I think he knows she won't be able to return.

The way he stared at the closed portal, the loss in his eyes as he turned back to the fight, surely he must know.

That is why he has locked himself in a cage of certain death.

He plans to end himself today, so he doesn't have to live without her.

That just shows me, he is not her true mate anymore.

A real bond would do anything, move any mountain, to make sure she returns safely. And that is just what I plan to do. I'll do anything it takes to bring her back.

And as she opens her portal and returns to Gaea, it will be my open arms that she'll run to.

I scan the clash of power and seek out my prizes among the unfolding battle and quickly find them. My eyes flick over the fighting as immortal ichor stains the Sahara desert and I find my first target of today's battle.

Power radiates from her in arrogant waves and I'm starving to have that strength for myself.

Long ago when she crept around the halls of the Underworld, I watched her wield her elements without discretion and always envied the power of the Gorgon. When she snuck away, welcomed back into the trust of those she was deceiving, I've often dreamt about what it would be like to wield the elements as she does.

I've seen her cast fire and water and wind with ease. But it's her signet power over earth that would be most valuable to me today.

The book of the dead has been such a helpful tool, teaching me how to consume and hold the power of others. Just in the way Chaos devoured the Titans, I'll take my fill of elementals today.

As Medusa is occupied with her fight, I take slow strides toward her.

Dark beings from Elysium bring their fear and terror to the battle. These elementals should have thought better than to lock away so much darkness within the Labyrinth. The Shades are ravaged and starving. Their dark cloaks swaying as they glide over the fighting, consuming the auras of the elementals and feasting upon their fear.

The Dark Mages ensure Ares' forces will not be consumed by the monsters made of shadow and I'm wearing the necklace Michael gave me, but that doesn't mean I trust them to be able to hold the Shades back.

As Medusa faces away from me, her power turns those around her to stone and she grinds their bodies to dust, returning them to the desert. She is fighting adequately enough that her *allies* won't be suspicious of her double-allegiance. But is serves my purpose to distract her against my attack.

With my hand and severed wrist, I conjure a Bow of Flame and Arrow of Fire.

I may only be a flicker, barely seen in the blazing flames of my father. But the embers of my hatred will burn hot enough to snuff out the immortality of Medusa. And as she lays dying on the battlefield, I will devour her power.

Just as Chaos consumed the Titans, I'll consume her.

With the string of my bow pulled tight, I aim. The bronze flames of Achilles steal my attention and I turn my gaze to him. *Such a powerful Flame.*

Swallowing my envy for the power I truly long to consume, I ready myself to strike the Gorgon through the back. I have to stay focused on my plan for this to work.

I cannot take Achilles on as I am. We have trained together for years in Atlanta, and I know he can best me easily.

But with Medusa's power, I can hold Achilles as a stone captive. I will drink the Fire from his soul and steal his power too.

Then I will truly be a son worthy of Ares. I'll finish the work he started at the battle of Troy when he killed Patroclus. Other than Ares, there is no Flame more powerful than Achilles.

But after today, I'll be the strongest Flame alive, and when Hermes hears the screams of his sister, burning under my flames, he'll watch from the other side of his dome, helpless to save her.

Too late to save his friend. And powerless to bring his mate back, he will suffer watching his sister die as well. Then he'll live the rest of his immortality in the Labyrinth, feeling like the failure I've been treated like for all my existence.

Fixing my sights back on Medusa, I pull back on the string of my elemental bow. Holding my breath, I release my arrow.

The two pegasus glide through the warm air, flapping their great wings. My hair blows behind me and the breeze cools the sweat pouring down my back. Euryale leads our parade through the sky and as I look behind us, I realize the harpy guards in their watchtowers can easily spot us.

Stheno's horse lifts its head and bucks in the sky. I hold on tighter to Stheno and the grip the edge of the saddle behind me.

A whinny echoes through the burning sky and the horse flaps it's mighty wings. A swirling portal of clouds forms in front of us. It looks like pink cotton candy, and we fly through it.

It's a portal of clouds and I raise my hand, letting my finger glide across them as we travel through the opening. Looking behind me, the portal closes with a with a fast rotation of the clouds and disappears as if it was never there.

The sight ahead of us makes my jaw drop.

For two long days I've only seen barren desert and felt the harsh grit of Tartarus.

But tucked in a valley surrounded by low rolling hills are lush pastures of deep wine-colored grass that sways with a gentle breeze. Stone dwellings form a large circle around a center boulder garden filled with various sculptures.

On the outskirts of the homes are stables and a large arena with tall stands for spectators. A quartet of flying horses perform maneuvers as a single trainer watches. The rows of seats that circle the arena are elevated, allowing onlookers a height advantage to observe the winged animals in the sky.

The two horses we ride on circle the camp before landing.

Dismounting, I take in more of the facilities and keep a watchful eye on the residents. With my hand firm on the handle of my dagger, I will stay vigilant this time for odd behavior of my *hosts*.

A young girl with similar long braids runs up, taking the reins from the sisters. She gives me a warm smile with eyes the color of the sherbet sky. Saying nothing, she guides the horses toward a stable.

"We need to feed and water the horses." Stheno explains in a gentle voice.

"And I'm fucking starving." Euryale has a temperament much more reminiscent of Medusa. "Those harpies are disgusting. I've not eaten since we left this morning."

Stheno is clearly the softer and youngest sister of the three. Though I can't tell which would be the eldest between Medusa and Euryale. They look too similar for me to distinguish without seeing them together.

"Medusa is the second eldest between us." As if she can read my thoughts, Stheno answers the question I didn't ask while we walk to the large pavilion. Covered and providing shade, with long benches and tables, this is eerily close to the commune at Kenya and makes me think of Hermes and our friends.

Longing tugs at my heart and my powers pull at me from within the cave. Constant tension constricts my chest and heightens my need to reunite with my missing immortality and return to my mate.

Tapping on my chest three times, I wait and again, no response is returned.

Worry blooms in my core and my throat tightens with the prospect of what is happening on Gaea. Twice, Hermes has not returned our signal.

I left them at the start of a battle with my hunter and a traitor in their midst. I thought with grave naivety, that my trip to Tartarus could be achieved within a few hours, at most.

How ridiculous I was only two days ago.

Urgency fuels me to push these sisters for a quicker trip to the dragon's cave. A thought I never believed I would have.

"I need to get to that dragon now." The whinny of a horse and the heat of flames makes me jump.

Raising my hand to shield my eyes from the heat, a remarkable horse grazes on the ashes of the crimson grass.

The coat is deep orange but it's the main and tail made of billowing fire that I can't stop looking at. The horse whinnies again. Fire shoots from its mouth and burns the grass, making more ash for it to consume. As we pass, it lifts its head and fire burns hot behind the sockets where its eyes should be.

"A Flamesteed." Stheno says as we continue to walk. "We need more riders before we fly into the mountains." She adds, answering my demand to leave. "It's too close to the mines and heavily scouted by harpy patrols."

Behind the Flamesteed, a heard of pegasuses gallop by and take flight. The two horses we rode here are among them and leading the heard is a pure white pegasus with gleaming pearlescent wings. Like freshly fallen snow, it's beautiful and the horses coat sparkles in the sun.

"He is Medusa's." Stheno smiles fondly at the winged horse as it leads the herd through the sky before landing again. "But good luck getting close to him. He'll kick the shit out of anyone who tries to get near him." A sadness covers her eyes and makes her smile fade away. "He's waiting for Medusa to return. I think he is the last one holding out hope."

"He's the only one who held out hope for her." Euryale interjects bitterly.

Feeling sorrow for the sister's loss of their sibling, I wish I could deliver better news of Medusa. I look down at my crimson dust coated boots and kick the blades of grass. Small red dandelion seeds flitter into the gentle breeze, and I carefully catch a few of them in the palm of my hand.

Just before I walked into the portal, Callie told me to bring something back for her. I know she was only joking but these small red seeds remind of the promise we made, sitting under a tree, eons ago.

When Callie gifted the sword necklace back to me, it was supposed to serve as a token of our friendship. She was unknowingly returning one of the relics of our forgotten past and these little seeds give me the perfect idea of a gift for her.

Releasing the seeds back into the air, I use my powers to capture two of them in two clear beads. When I get home, I'll fashion these into necklaces for each of us to wear.

Holding the beads up to the light, I inspect the small crimson seeds, frozen perfectly within.

Euryale gives me a sidelong glance as I store the beads in my chest pocket, zipping it closed for safe keeping. "It's for someone back home." I offer her sheepishly.

Hot soup is steaming from a large vat that sits over a fire. A pile of fresh brown bread is delivered by a woman who's long braids have turned white with age.

A big bowl of ripe red melon is cut, and the Gorgons take wooden cups, putting them up to a spicket driven into a hallowed tree stump.

Stheno serves me a large bowl of soup before getting some for herself and we take a seat in the middle of a long table. We're sat away from the other members of the tribe, and I note the mixture of men and women ranging from all ages.

I give the sisters a moment to take several bites of their food before asking my questions. The vegetable soup is hearty and delicious. The oat bread soaks up the thick broth and the refreshing beverage quenches my thirst.

Unlike the mystical elixir that messed with my memories from the Danaides, this pale-yellow beverage calms my thirst and cools my body. The color of lemonade, it taste like honey water.

"I know you are curious about Medusa, but I have to know how she was here, first. I may be in danger from her, and I need to know what she was like before the Titans battled."

Euryale continues to eat her soup at a ravenous pace. Returning for the large bowl of juicy red melons and sitting back down shoving one in her mouth.

Stheno accounts for the time before Chaos arrived. "Medusa was always her father's daughter. Our father, Phorcys was apprentice to the great Titan and Hyperion was a fair guardian of our realm."

Tartarus used to be a realm of vibrant life and vitality under the Titan's protection. The desert is a product of the harpy kings' rule and has suffocated the realm.

"As refugees from the realms flooded Tartarus, Phorcys' views on our Titan began to shift. He spouted very dark thoughts of rebellion, and it caused a rift between our parents. Our mother, Ceto, could not stand to hear such delusions of overthrowing the Titan."

I spear the red melon with my two-pronged wooden fork and roll my eyes at the sweet flavor.

"Medusa stayed with our father and a rebellion was born. Unfortunately, he helped Chaos enter our realm. When Oceanus arrived to help Hyperion, we through the realm would be destroyed. We were nearly crushed under a falling mountain, but our mother sacrificed herself to save us."

"Like a coward, Medusa fled on the last portal that made it out of Tartarus before the portals were destroyed." Euryale adds her only contribution to the story before returning to her food.

"And what of the dragon?" With my second bowl of soup nearly finished, I pick at another piece of crimson melon.

"We found the great cosmic dragon hunting for Sandstalkers in the Wyrmcrest mountains." Stheno explains the Sandstalkers are a large lizard that lives in the mountains and is their main source of meat. The harsh environment of Tartarus doesn't supply much meat, so the Gorgons live largely on vegetables and legumes.

"That's enough." Euryale says pointedly and Stheno returns to her soup. I look between the sisters, and it seems as if they are hiding something about the dragon.

"The cave you found the dragon in, there is a large skull of a cyclops at the entrance." Two pair of green eyes look at me with shock.

"I've dreamt of it and something very important to me is

inside the cave. Something that can help save my realm." Excitement drives me closer to the sisters and I lower my tone. "Medusa is working with someone who is trying to do the same thing to Gaea as what happened here and I'm trying to stop them."

I know my voice is pleading and I can't hold back the desperation in my words. But Hermes has still not answered the thrum down our bond and worry is on the brink of taking over my nerves.

"If you can tell me anything that will help me, I'll try to do what I can here before I leave. But I must return to my realm before the eclipse is over."

The three of us turn our heads at once, looking at the great sun in the Tartarus sky. A quarter of the sun is uncovered by the passing eclipse and a heaviness settles over us.

"The cosmic dragon lets no one enter it's dwelling. It's believed to be guarding a great treasure." Euryale continues the story.

"How did it get there?"

"A falling star arrived during a Crimson Eclipse, just like this alignment. We believed the star delivered the dragon and it hid within the cave. Ages later, night covered the Tartarus sky when a savior arrived during another eclipse. One of the cyclopes were freed and when the savior left, the giant stood watch over the dragons' cave until the savior would return again. And here you are."

The look Euryale gives me is full of unspoken words. Something hangs unspoken and I narrow my eyes at her.

"What is the savior foretold to do? And not the cryptic poem you recited before."

Euryale smirks and Stheno answers. "When Hyperion and

Oceanus fell, Thanatos made a deal with Chaos. He was granted power and Chaos chained the surviving cyclopes to a mine. Thanatos made himself king and each day, his storm searches the realm for rebels."

"The great wind that roams the desert sweeps those it finds into its cyclone and carries them to the king. If they don't pledge loyalty, they go to the mines or they hang on the castle walls. The Danaides bargained with the king long ago, providing him an endless supply of brides in exchange for safety."

"And the kings wind cannot reach you here?" The storm is sent across the realm twice a day. Surely it must sweep here as well.

Euryal answers with firm resolve. "The Gorgons still hold the power of Tartarus within our aura. We shield our compound from his reach and keep him from discovering our haven."

A herd of Pegasus arrive with riders through another portal of clouds. In the center is a finery of sphinxes, just like the very ones the Danaides used, and the one Seraphina slaughtered for her husband.

"The Savior is foretold to free us of the chains that bind the realm to tyranny." Stheno keeps her gentle voice soft but firm. "Some believe that means you will free the cyclops. Other believe you will kill the harpy king. Whatever brought you here, it is tied to our future, and we will help you."

One of the newly arrived tribesman signals Euryal who responds with a nod. "It's time. Let's go." The sisters clear their lunch and with full bellies, we start toward the stables.

When Euryal recited the prophesy, she mentioned a Shadowmare with wings of coal.

Looking at the pastures, the pegasus stretch their wings as Flamesteeds burn and eat the grass. The newly arrived sphinxes mingle with the horses, but I see nothing that resembles a shadow.

Inside the stable, the young girl has cared for the horses and hands each sister the reins to their animal. Like darkness is calling me, my gaze wanders to the darkened corner of a stall. One would assume there is nothing inside but I within the shadows, I feel it.

The obscurity shifts, and a pair of eyes, made from silver starlight open. The animal, its coat the color of the deepest black, stirs from a nap and looks at me.

"Here we go." Euryal mutters under her breath to her sister as they back away.

"Something you would like to share?" I ask with a cautiously low tone.

"Well, Medusa's pegasus will let no other rider mount him, but he at least lets us tend to his hooves and prune his feathers."

"And this horse?"

"The horse just arrived one day and our stable master found it in this stall. He went crazy, saying the shadows whispered to him and when he tried to give the mare food, it opened a portal of darkness and our stable master was sucked into it. He fell from the sky and was killed. The horse just went back to sleep. So, we just leave it alone and it tends to itself."

"Great." I huff out a nervous breath as I wipe my sweaty hands down my pants.

The horse holds me in its gaze and the silver veins that run through its eyes glimmer at me. It's beautiful and deadly still laying in the shadows of the stall.

The sister's trepidation cause my nerves to spike but I sense nothing but peace as I look upon the horse.

My powers whirl within me with familiarity. The obsidian hors stretches out his neck and sniff the air with curiosity. *I know this horse.*

The beast cocks its head at me, as if coming to the same realization that it recognizes it's rider.

My black mist pools from me, meeting the horse as the mare stands, shaking the wine-colored hay from its body. Two large wings of shadow and roiling smoke spread out, overtaking the space within the stall.

Our shadows stretch across the stable and wrap around us, the horse and I walk to each other. Lowering its head, I embrace the mare with tears streaking down my eyes.

She was a gift from Pandora when Hermes and I visited Avalon. We had just secured our bond for the first time and the Queen of Avalon walked a small foal out of the stables of Nightfell castle.

"Nocturna Whisperwing." Pandora's old, blue eyes smiled at me when she handed me the reins made from stardust.

"Whispy" I chuckle as the horse whinnies, shaking its large body and wings, wanting to stretch them with desperation.

"Whispy? That's what you call a mare of darkness? Unbelievable." Euryale throws her hands up, guiding her pegasus out of the stable.

Stheno laughs with me, and we follow Euryale. "Her name is Nocturna Whisperwing. But when she was a foal, I called her Whispy."

In the sunlight, the mare glimmers like a billion diamonds and commands the attention every tribes person. The sphinxes and horses of the pasture even stop, as if the queen of the equestrians has taken the field.

Unfurling her great wings, the Shadowmares span is far larger than those of the pegasus. There is no saddle or reins, but I know when I mount my horse, the shadows will hold me, and starlight will form like ribbons through my hands to guide the horse.

I look with contempt at the eclipsed sun and wish I had more time.

If only I had found the sisters first, I would have been spared so much time and maybe I could have helped them more. But the sooner I get back to Gaea, the sooner I can help my mate and our family with the fight against Ares.

Perhaps when the wards are down and the realms are restored, we can come back here and help the people of Tartarus. I won't fill them with false hope, so I make no such promises today.

The herd of pegasus and their riders that escorted the sphinxes trot to us. The pair of sisters serving as my hosts mount their horses and I climb atop Nocturna. Just as I remembered, a cool band of shimmering stars runs across the horse like a bridle and reins.

Cool bands of shadows wrap around my waist and thighs, and Nocturna rears on her hind legs. Pushing off the ground and flapping her large wings, Tartarus surges away from us. The pegasus gallop across the pasture, flapping their majestic wings and joining us in the sky.

Moving their legs as if they are running on the clouds, the horses gallop across the sky, their wings flapping at a steady pace. Shadows whisper across my mind as Nocturna and I speak a mystical language of darkness. It's not one of words but of obscurity.

She knows exactly where to take me and in an instant our powers meld with each other. Black mist billows from my aura and stretches as far as the horizon extends.

The ground below us is covered in shadow as my power blocks out the great sun of Tartarus and night falls over the realm of sunshine.

The allies that fly with me are protected within our shield of obscurity and a swirl of purple clouds and black shadows forms in the rich sky before us.

The goddess, born in darkness, streaks across the sky, stretching a blanket of night with her. As the portal swallows me and the Gorgon riders, I close my eyes and send a message to my mate that I'll be returning soon.

Worry again fills me as Hermes still doesn't answer my call. Something is wrong.

Something is very wrong.

My aura turns to dozens of projections of Light. My soul transforms into a star and I erupt through Ares and half of his army. Replicas of my immortal essence descend upon his forces with a single goal: Protect this space until my goddess returns and if she doesn't, everyone in this dome, including me, will die today.

I stay with the God of War.

The tormentor that has haunted my mate's existence. The murderer who killed my parents. The mentor who betrayed me.

I keep my attacks focused on him.

Ares was a father to me, training and honing me into a lethal warrior. Then darkness descended across his mind, and he ripped the fabric of our family apart. He challenged Apollo.

Equally matched in strength and power, my father answered the call of Ares.

Once mates, then enemies, the pair clashed in a battle that would take my father's life. Not because Ares overpowered him but because Ares weakened him first. Apollo was poisoned before their battle began and as my father fell, I stepped in front of him, blocking Ares' fatal blow.

With two swords crossed in front of me, I battled my mentor that day.

As the immortal life of my father drifted into the Void, Ares stopped. We watched the sky darken as the sunset with Apollos death and Ares walked away.

But he will have no such luxury today.

Today, Ares' immortal ichor will stain these lands until there is nothing left of him.

Matching my thrusts and parries, my old mentor knows every move he taught me. Ares and I fall into a familiar rhythm as our swords collide, ringing across the battlefield.

But what Ares doesn't realize is I had another mentor who stepped into his vacant space. Where Ares sharpened my speed and power, Atlas sharpened my mind.

Ares is too focused on my attacks that he fails to see the Mirage I'm constructing around him. The projections of my aura that are replicating and taking on his army. As one of his fighters fall, I conceal them. I replicate the image of their fighting forms, battling the projections of myself.

Ares believes his forces are withstanding me. Ares believes he is fighting me.

But moving like a shooting star through his masses, I've hidden myself from view as my Light and sword dispatch his fighters. My projections take their place, and Ares keeps fighting with the confidence that his army remains standing.

I want Ares to bleed across this battlefield today and I want to savor watching the life drain from his eyes. So, I'm saving him for last.

The height of the eclipse has passed, and the moon continues its track passing before the rest of our sun. The Dark

Mages and shadow beings heightened strength is waning as the sky slowly begins to brighten.

I hope with all my immortality that I'll witness Rhea's return soon.

I've taken out half of Ares warriors inside the dome I constructed. Everyone I care about is fighting on the other side of this dome or walking across the dunes of Tartarus. In here, only my fury exists.

I heard Callie and Achilles banging on my shield, begging me to opening it and let them fight by my side. But I can't bring them into the destruction of my implosion that will take place in a few moments, should Rhea fail to return to Gaea.

As I fight, my name whispers across the enclosure constructed of my power.

Sparing a glance, Atlas watches as my Mirages fight his former mate. His eyes carry the promise of tears he's fighting to hold back.

"I hope you know what you're doing." He places his hand on the dome and lowers his head in sorrow. And it's not the ghost of his former mate he is beginning to mourn, but me.

He knows me just as well as Callie or Achilles does. Atlas knows I've come here to fight or die.

"I do. Thank you for everything." I send me message back and watch Atlas' shaky intake of breath.

"Your father would be proud." He gives me a thin-lipped smile and a nod of his head. Now it's my eyes that hold the promise of tears.

Our short goodbye is broken when Callie comes soaring in haphazardly, knocking into our mentor. Atlas helps steady her and projects a shield to block a Shade trying to attack her. They move out of my field of vision, and part of me wishes Callie had looked back.

The rest of me is glad, she didn't.

As the shadows stretch and grow longer as the sun is unveiled by the passing moon, Ariyana discovers my ploy and blasts a wave of Absolute Night across our battlefield. My Light projections dissolve within her shadows. Ares pauses with his sword high overhead, as the Mirage he was fighting fades away.

Flinging the blood of Ares army from my sword, I grab the hilt with both hands and raise my weapon over my shoulder. Ares ignites in anger and a decrepit smile of darkness spreads across Ariyana's face.

Every Shade and Dark Mage left alive focuses on me. Waves of Darkness and fireballs of anger hurl toward me as I feel three taps on my bond from Rhea.

Unable to take my hands from my sword, I close my eyes and release a deep breath. Then I turn to starlight.

I promised to protect this space until my goddess returns; and I will. I will protect this space with my life. And when it's time to forfeit my life, the starlight that burns within me will collapse and no one inside this dome will escape the blackhole that will form of my death.

The mouth of the cyclops cave looks exactly as it did in my dreams. The mouth is gaped open, providing an entrance to the dark recess beyond it. A single hole at the center of the head used to serve as the giant's solitary eye socket. Now, it acts as a skylight, illuminating the space inside.

From this vantage point at the top of the mountains, I can see onward, beyond the range of mountains to the mines. The land levels out and drops down a sheer rock face. Within the deep ravine of Tartarus, the clanging of massive chains echoes into the atmosphere.

The lashing of whips snap into the dry desert air as the shouts of harpies echoes across the canyon. Pushing my aura outward, I scan the horizon beyond the mountains. My powers give me sight, farther than my eyes can see.

The ground quakes as the foot of a giant steps down and I feel the vibrations within me as if I were standing there.

With a heavy load of boulders slung over a scarred shoulder in a sack, a massive cyclops strains with each step as he carries the bundle of rocks up one of the quarry ramps. Another tremor shakes as the giant drops the sack to the ground.

A group of men are waiting to receive the payload and

work together, rolling the large boulders up the next quarry ramp.

Their muscles strain against the weight of the massive rocks and evidence of lashings have left ribbons along their arms and back. Healed, then wounded, then healed again, the pale-pink overlapping scars break up the richness of their deep wine-colored skin.

With rough-spun tunics and worn trousers, each of the men are shackled by their ankles, making it difficult to make long strides.

Deeper within the rock mine, the cyclops returns to the pit and retrieves a large pickax. Joining a second cyclops, they begin pounding away to create more boulders.

Both of them are slaves to the mine with thick collars around their necks and long chains secured into the mountain. Each link is the size of a boulder, and the weight of the chain must be unbearable.

Rhythmic pounding from the top of the quarry shakes the earth as a third cyclops works to pummel the boulders into fine powder. Piles of crimson grit are as tall as the fifty-foot cyclops working on these endless tasks.

"The Sisyphus tribe." Euryale points to the platforms in the middle of the quarry, where the chained men work pushing red boulders up steep hills. "They refused to evacuate when Chaos attacked. They fought bravely and many people escaped Tartarus thanks to them."

"And now they are prisoners?"

Euryale nods once.

"And the cyclops?" I ask, looking back to the mines.

Axes clank against the rock as the two cyclops in the pit excavate the boulders.

As a sack is filled, they take turns walking it up the first ramp where the Sisyphus tribesman wait. The cyclops chain doesn't reach any further, but I see him stretch, trying to place the rocks as close as he can to help to small forms waiting to receive the newest load.

In an exhaustive and endless task, they roll the great stones up the quarry ramp.

At the top of the quarry, the massive fists of a third giant slam down on the delivered boulders, splitting them into a dozen pieces. More tribes' men and women take the smaller rocks and beat them with mallets.

The cyclops keeps pummeling the large stones with his strong callused fists, turning them to pumice.

"The cyclops were the Titans warriors." Stheno, having tended to the horses, joins us as we look over the distant quarry. She smiles fondly but her eyes show the sorrow of her thoughts. "They saved us. Now, only three remain."

The pain of their lives is overwhelming and brings tears to my eyes. Tormented forever to live and die within these pits, it's unbearable.

As another wave of my aura pulses out of me, surveying the land and taking in the scene, the cyclops at the top of the quarry pauses with his fist raised high above his head.

Stopping his work, the cyclops stands.

The gaze of his singular eye lands upon me and I feel the weight of his stare across this great distance.

The two cyclops within the pit stop their work and stand as well. All three of them facing me, their heavy gazes crushing me.

Whips echo across the expanse as their harpy guards lash them for break they are taking.

A single tear drops from my eye and rolls down my cheek.

Then dropping to one knee, the three cyclops kneel in reverence. Bowing their heads, they curl their hands into fists and place their knuckles on the ground. A pose of respect and devotion that I don't deserve.

The harpies lash and whip them, but the cyclops remain unchanged.

Stheno chuckles but it's full of sorrow. "They sense the power of the Earth Titan within you." Stheno pats my shoulder twice.

Then Euryale and Stheno turn and walk away solemnly, heading toward the entrance of the cave. "Let's go, Skyfallen. Time is not your friend, but luckily for you, we are."

A large plume of crimson races across the horizon toward the quarry. The cyclops stand from their reverence.

The lone giant at the top of the quarry covers a mass of Sisyphus tribes' people, forming a shield of protection using his hulking form.

The two cyclops within the pit walk with giant strides up the ramp. The tribes people chained to the first level walk down to meet them. Stretching as far as their confinements will let them, the two cyclops wrap their arms over each other's wide shoulders. Kneeling down, they too provide protection for the smaller slaves from the approaching tempest.

The windstorm screams and growls across the land and I watch from the safety of the mountains that seem to be spared from the storm.

The mounds of newly formed red sand are picked up by the strong gale. It will be dispersed across the realm, adding to the endless desert that chokes the life from Tartarus.

This is the power of the tyrant king. Enslaving those who

fought against Chaos, forcing them to work in these mines and forever suffocating the realm of sunlight with a barren helscape. This entire realm is a prison and everyone, but the harpy king is enslaved to him.

Even the soldiers that fight under his wing have no real freedom from the tormentor that calls himself king.

Following Euryale and Stheno to the cave, I rub my hand on the skull of the cyclops guarding the entrance. I can imagine the great giant of Tartarus standing sentry until his time came to an end.

Now, any that dare enter the cave of the great dragon must forever seek passage through the eternal guard's skull. A monument to the heavy price paid by all realms in this great war of power.

The riders that accompanied us leave in a portal of light and swirling clouds, headed for the mines.

If King Thanatos' guards spot our pegasus while on patrols, the pegasus will communicate with each other. The rebels will cause a disturbance in the mines and hopefully that will buy us time to flee.

Now that I'm standing on the edge of the dark tunnel that haunted my dreams, a heavy sense of dread and foreboding claws at my airway.

Hermes has not answered my calls through our bond and I'm having flashes of my nightmares each time I blink. I hear Teddy's voice echo through the tunnel begging for my help. I see Medusa's green eyes shine at me from the depths of the cave and rush at me in a frenzy to consume my power.

I cannot panic now.

I call my mist to me and with a swirl of cool shadow, I wrap my power around me.

With a deep and steadying breath, I let my power encase me. Releasing the breath and opening my eyes, I replace my power with my resolve. My vow to enter this cave and reclaim my power. This is a promise I will not fail to accomplish.

And once restored, I will return to Gaea with nearly all my immortality. If my earlier thoughts of Hermes caduceus are correct, perhaps all my power resides within this cave. With a look back at Nocturna, and a message of protection passes between us, I know she will watch over the mountain range and protect the pegasus.

Nocturna emits a dark shield that covers nearly half the mountain range in deep shadow. The pegasus are nearly undetectable within her shadows and Nocturna all but vanishes. I'm sure any harpy guards flying overhead would look right past us, unable to see anything within her deep shadows.

Taking a step into the cave, and then another, I let the darkness of the mountain wrap around me as I enter the dragon's lair.

I can't decide if the cool rush of air that swirls along my feet is from the current of the cave or the cool breath of the dragon. Rushing back and forth, the current flows around us as the sisters and I walk through the tunnel.

The similarity to my dream gives me pause when I reach an intersection and look down a passage that ends in darkness. The vision of Teddy and his throat being ripped out by Medusa flashes in my mind. When I blink it's gone.

"We should keep moving, Savior." Euryale urges me onward. Her green eyes darting between the reaching shadows and me as if trying to see what I'm looking at. The alert tendrils of her hair dance like serpents while Stheno holds three stones in the air near her head. They move on a constant rotation around each other, and she is poised to launch them at any threat ahead of us or behind us.

The anxiety I felt at the mouth of the cave grows in magnitude with each step I take. Folding in on me, the aching need to move forward is a pull stronger than my bond to Hermes. The power that lays ahead of me begs for reunion and I long to break out in a run and dash to it.

My only hesitation is the stronger desire to avoid being eaten by a massive dragon.

Hermes shared his memory of becoming the apprentice of Theia, the great carnelian dragon made of cosmic light. As beautiful as she was, looking down the massive jaws of large golden teeth is not something I'm itching to run into headfirst.

Rubbing my chest, my longing for Hermes grows. I'm desperate for his warmth as the cool cave raises chill bumps on my exposed skin. I toy with the hilts of my daggers and sense the threads of Hermes' light laced together with my shadows.

A loud huff in front of us sends a rush of warm air through the tunnel. Rustling my hair, the breath of the dragon brushes against me and tears well in my eyes.

I know this power.

It's as familiar to me as my own and erases the trepidation that slows my pace.

With a gasp, I break out into a run through the dark tunnel. My eyes adjust to the darkness and the shadows guide me as I slide around the corners in my desperation.

Euryale and Stheno call after me in fraught whispers, calling me a fool and warning me of the dragons' wrath. I can't hear them over the thrumming of my heart, and the rushing blood surging through my veins.

The cave widens as I continue to run and my tears flow behind me in my wake.

Before me, the cave is brightening as the light from the great dragon seeps into the darkness and eventually it overtakes everything.

Rounding the corner, I grab hold of the rocky wall and use it to fling myself around.

The cave opens up into a vast cavern and peering directly into my eyes are the large round orbs of the great beast. It's laying down with its long neck stretched across the cave floor, and when I turn the corner, they open, looking directly at me.

Eyes I feel like I've looked into a million times.

The dragon huffs, lifting its large head and rustling enormous wings at my disturbance. A surge of aura fills the cave and I close my eyes, basking in the feeling of it.

Small puddles of water ripple as the beast releases a minuscule thread of power and the mountain quivers.

Visions pass from the dragon to me and in an instant, I know the history of this land. I see the battle that was waged, resulting in this dragon taking refuge inside the cave.

Behind me, I hear the footsteps of my hosts arriving quickly behind me.

The dragon raises its head, and the large eyes shift behind me. A protective snarl forms on its giant mouth, angry at the stranger's arrival.

I rush behind me, casting my arms out wide and blocking them as much as I can with my body.

"Stay back." I call out to them with desperation.

"If you die, who will be our Savior?" Euryale calls back.

Turning behind me, I look into the sapphire eyes of the great cosmic dragon. "He won't hurt me." I chuckle as my tears flow freely down my face. The dragon has passed the truth to me through a bond that ties our souls together.

This is not the yellow aura of Theia.

Long ago, Theia fought hard against the archangels that rose up against her. She lost that battle and with her last breath, she passed along the essence of the Titan to her apprentice. A young boy with eyes the color of the deep ocean.

As Theia died, returning to the cosmos, her successor absorbed her power and Hermes stood, a Titan carried in the body of a small boy.

Apollo knew in an instant, the heavy burden cast into his son's body. Together, Apollo and his mates, along with Hermes' mother worked to protect him. They trained him to be a formidable warrior and kept him out of Chaos' reach. Seeking refuge on the last realm Chaos had yet to consume, Gaea.

And as the war of the Titans was no longer a threat, the war of Ares' took over the realm that was to be their final sanctuary. Hermes was no longer in danger of Chaos, and I became the prey of the God of War.

As Hermes and I fought my hunter, we prepared for the worst.

We hid our powers across the three realms and safeguarded our fated bond within the charms of our necklaces. We protected the things Ares would seek to destroy or consume within us, until we could heal ourselves and finally defeat him.

As I walk to the protective shield that contains the dragon, I place my hand on the barrier. The dragon carefully inches closer. Closing our eyes, we touch our foreheads to the shield that separates us.

This is the first time we've ever come so far in the restoration of ourselves. I'm half immortal, having released my powers from two relics. We restored our fated bond.

And now, as I look at Titan form of my mate, the harness around the great dragon's neck, I see the amber pendent with a swirling galaxy of silver starlight held safely within.

Hope surges through me and I welcome it, letting it flow over me unabashed.

I laugh and cry with happiness, knowing this is going to be the last time Hermes and I will ever have to part. Never again will our hunter succeed in separating us by death.

I will reclaim my immortality. I'll restore Hermes to the full might of his power, bestowed upon him by his dying Titan, so long ago. Then when I return to Gaea, I will reclaim my home, I will take back dominion over my fate and drive down my hunter.

Never again will death come for me. But I promise this, Death will surely come back to Gaea. The hunter will become the hunted and Ares will be striped of everything he has stolen from us.

"**W**hat do you mean the dragon is your mate?**"** It's Stheno asking the question as Euryale stands with her arms crossed in front of her chest, the tendrils of her long braids stroking her arms in comfort as she pulls at her lip with worry.

It's the same actions I watched Medusa do when Callie lay across the beach dying after they returned my powers to me from the chalice. While Medusa cannot be trusted, I can't fault her sisters for the familiarities in their demeanors and the emotions they evoke within me.

Smiling, I can't look away from the dragon formed of starlight. He's beautiful, glimmering like a thousand nebula stars on a constant collision within the universe. The inside cavity containing the dragon reflects the blue radiance and the cave is washed in sapphire starlight.

A wall of my power is barricading the dragon inside the large opening. Shadows and silver aura swirl like oil on water, forming a shield.

It serves to keep the dragon inside but also protects it from threats that may try to enter from the outside.

Placing my hand on the barrier, I pulse my energy inside,

and the dragon absorbs it. He closes his eyes and I watch his large scaly body quiver as it ingests the essence of my aura.

Matching my power, the dragon continues to expel his aura in waves. I feel like he is happy I'm here, though it's hard to say by looking at him. Dragons seem to have two expressions, menacing and downright terrifying.

He doesn't speak, though he seems to understand me. I suppose it's because he is pure Titanic energy. The immortal that owns this great power is fighting my hunter, back on Gaea.

He's truly a giant, taking up all the space of this large amphitheater size cavern within the cave. He's unable to stand or stretch his great wings and I long to see what he looks like outside.

I'm desperate to see the majesty of his aura within the dark cover of night as he soars high in the sky.

Gods, he would be beautiful to behold.

Standing at my full height, I'm the same size as one of the dragons gleaming white fangs. The rest of him is gargantuan.

All I can think of is reuniting my mate with his Titan form. But first, I need to restore my power which is currently hanging on a necklace around the dragon's harness.

I'll need to bring down the mountain to get him out of here. There is no way he can walk through the twists and turns of the cave's tunnels.

The dragon shakes his head and body, trying to stretch within the confined space and I'm sure he's ready to be free of this little cave. The oval pendent of my powers, jingles on the dragon's collar with the movements. The Titan essence of my mate has guarded my immortality like its most precious treasure until I could return for him.

I wonder how many sought out the cave, desiring to slay the dragon and take the power held within the necklace. The dragon's aura can penetrate beyond my shield and I'm curious what became of those who ventured too far into the dragon's lair.

As I stand in contemplation, and hear the sisters discussing what to do next, a whinny fills the cave, bounding toward us as if coming from all sides.

The dragon behind me releases a deep growl and it shakes the cavern where I stand. The clop of horse hooves carries toward us, and I sense Nocturna carefully and hurriedly weaving her way into the depths of the cave.

My breath is stolen from me as fear takes over.

"They're here." I gasp. The Shadowmare communicates with me as she rushes to me. She's terrified to leave me here, trapped within the belly of the hallow mountain as the harpy's approach.

Without thought, I push the two sisters beyond the barrier of my power and thrust them into the chamber of the dragon. They trip and tumble with the force I used to push them through and water splashes as Euryale lands in a puddle, breaking Stheno's fall.

The dragon moves its great front leg and pivots its long neck, covering them with his head and partially shielding them from view. Chortling and agitating his wings, the dragon senses the danger nearing us, and his agitation grows.

If Nocturna can reach me, she'll Shadowstep us to safety. The pegasus were sent away and while a band of harpies chased them into the sky, Nocturna provided them the cover of darkness as they used their portal to flee to safety.

As she rounds the cave, her graceful body reflects the

cerulean shine of Hermes' Titan aura, and the cave explodes in a kaleidoscope starlight.

With her large wings tucked close to her body, her shadows reach out for me, panic set in her wide silver eyes.

But the piercing squeal that emits from the horse, crushes my heart with pain as a crimson steel spear protrudes from her chest.

Rearing on her hind legs, her wings swell out.

In an explosion of obscurity and silver aura, the darkness that makes up the Shadowmares body bursts when King Thanatos pulls the spear out. The echo of her final whinny bouncing out of the cave as the essence of her shadows seep into the darkness.

"No!" The gasp escapes me with an immediate fracture of my heart. I feel the dragon rear back his head and open his great mouth.

Quickly covering my ears, the dragons roar makes the entire realm tremble and swear I feel the great sun of Tartarus shake in fear.

King Thanatos' sharp beak curls into a sinister grin when his yellow eyes settle on the amber pendant secured within the dragon's harness.

He was waiting, knowing the dragon guards my power. And he is here to retrieve it, stealing it for himself.

I can't let the king get my powers, so I push my aura into strengthening the shield that holds the dragon within. My protection is so thick, the dragon's aura can no longer breach the barrier.

The king tries to stab at the wall of my power is his spear shatters. Guards join him in our cavern and its suddenly gets very crowded.

My shadows wrap around the harpies, choking them and pulling their wings off.

Still pushing my powers into the shield, I'm working my abilities at both ends. Another surge of guards rush me and two of them thrash me with their metal and leather whips.

The dragon stomps his large taloned feet and roars again.

Blasting blue starlight against my reinforced barricade of shadow and silver starlight the beast cannot break through and thunders in frustration.

The cave shakes and boulders fall around us.

I have to calm the dragon down or he'll bring the entire mountain down around us. I'm no good to anyone if I die here, buried under a landslide caused by the cosmic power of my mate.

Angry, the king flaps his wings, and his power shoots a hailstorm of Wind projectiles at the dragon. His power is no match for my forcefield, and his attacks are consumed by the undulating power of my shield.

Whatever bargain King Thanatos struck with Chaos made him powerful. But he's nothing more than a weak little bird compared to me. It's doesn't negate the fact that my powers are just beyond my reach, and I cannot let Thanatos get them.

I will be vulnerable as I ingest my immortality back into myself and I can't risk Thanatos stealing the powers from me or killing me as I restore myself.

My heartbeat matches the quick pace of the dragons and we both need to settle down. Closing my eyes, I think Bridget and the warehouse.

"Look at me, goddess. Turn it off." She coached me through my panic to calm down and take control of myself. *"We must attack when the time is right and not a second sooner."*

Our conversation from the warehouse echoes through my mind as I turn my back on the harpy king and stare into the celestial eyes of the raging dragon.

Turn it off.

I recite the mantra and send it to the great dragon with a plan and my hope. *"Please, trust me."* I call out to the dragon through the bond that connects us. *"We can get out of this, but we need to do it together. Keep my powers safe and wait for me."*

I wonder if Hermes can feel this connection back on Gaea. When I tapped on our bond, he didn't answer. Is my nearness to the dragon why I couldn't feel his reply before?

The Titan essence of Hermes, in this astral projected form of a great cosmic dragon, is radiating vast power. I close my eyes as I steady my breathing and calm my racing heart, hoping I'm right and Hermes is okay.

Thanatos sneers at me, realizing my power is feeding the barrier safeguarding the dragon. "Bring her." He snarls at his guards who make quick work of locking me in whips and bindings.

I drop to my knees and raise my hands. Taking steady breaths, I pass my calm resolve to the dragon raging behind me as the mountain tremors under his power. *"Turn it off."*

His large cerulean eyes fixate on me as his great chest puffs heavily with his panting.

"Turn. It. Off."

Like a light dimming with the gradual turn of a dial, the dragons' cosmic light darkens, dipping the cavern into shadow. Lowering his large head, the dragon placates his anger into a deep bellow that emanates from the base of his throat.

Opening my eyes, looking at the king with a dull expression, I stand. "Let's go."

Back in this godsforsaken castle with petrified harpies littering the once-beautiful halls, is not an experience I was eager to repeat. The throne room is setup differently than the first time I was here.

A beaten and bruised Seraphina limps in, standing beside the king as he sits on his throne of hollow harpy bones. Blood soaks her long flowing skirt and I try not to imagine the king's assault on her for their wedding night.

She has more bite marks along her neck and the exposed parts of her skin are littered with cuts and bruises.

Tilting my head, I see her aura, incredibly dim as if her spirit is dying.

She doesn't meet my eye but looks at the dull red ground with a neutral expression. A single tear slips down her cheek and the only movement she makes is a rapid blink of her eyes.

Pity chokes me for the anger I felt at her before. This is not a life anyone would go to willingly. Thinking how Eudora gave up her child to this tyrant, bargaining Seraphina's first-born daughter in exchange. It's terrible and I relinquish a tear too in sorrow for the freedom Seraphina had no choice but to give up.

Though I'm chained in cuffs that bind my powers, I envision sending waves of energy and strength to her. As I feel each beat of my heart, I imagine waves of my aura pulsating to her in encouragement.

Just hold on a little longer.

That is the message I would tell her, if I could speak to her using telepathy. Just a little longer and this oppressor will be no more.

I think I see her shift slightly and then she finally cuts her eyes to me. Even though she may not hear my message or feel the energy I would share with her, I nod my head once and try to convey the words with my eyes.

Seraphina looks away. Perhaps it's my hope but I think I see her aura brighten just a shade.

There are chairs set in rows on three sides for spectators and harpies fill the empty seats. I stand in the center with my guards, heavily wrapped in chains and bindings that suffocate my powers.

Leaning to one side, the king strokes one of his feathers and nods at the guards next to me. Keeping my expression calm, I lock my eyes on his, refusing to look away.

Two guards put a clawed hand on my thigh holders, and one pulls hard, hoping to rip my weapons from me. *Oh, we're doing this again.*

Light and dark tendrils whip out, wrapping around the guards' necks. My shadow shield seeps into their mouths and the light squeezes their windpipes. The protective shields Hermes and I wove holds true.

As the powers flare around me, I grab onto them. Holding light and dark in my palm of my hands, I wrap them around the cuffs that bind me. So minuscule and thin, I work the elements around the cuffs until a small crack forms.

While still muted by the other chains and bindings, I can feel the elements of the realm again.

This time, I do pass a message to Seraphina and the tick of her eyebrows tells me she got it. I send Life power to her for healing. The small bruises and cuts gradually heal and while the dirt and dried blood remain on her, it helps serve as a disguise.

"String her up." The kings order bark across the throne room and I steel myself for what that may mean. "I want those daggers."

Thanatos promised me earlier that I would be tortured before he feasted on my intestines. While I have no intention of watching him chew on any part of my body, I also made a promise to the harpy king of what would become of him at our next meeting.

I fight against my captors to maintain the illusion of my unwilling captivity.

Just survive.

My promise to Callie, made a hundred times over our friendship, rings in my mind and I close my eyes. Hearing the steady and brazen voice of my chosen sister, I take a steadying breaths.

Steeling myself for whatever may come next, I keep my plan running through my mind.

"We will follow you beyond the Void into Oblivion, goddess. When you are ready to extract your vengeance, so will we." Bridget's words from the Shifter-auction run through my mind again and I pray to the Fates the fighters of Tartarus may feel the same.

If not for me, than for their freedom.

While I can't stay to help them fight this battle, I hope I

can leave them with something to help them fight for themselves.

White hot pain surges through me when two large hooks are driven through my shoulders. Stabbing into my back, they protrude through each of my shoulders.

My back bows in pain and I squint my eyes shut holding in the sounds that want to rip out of my throat. I'll not give him the satisfaction of hearing me scream. But more so, I block the sensations from traveling down my bond to Hermes.

Whatever is happening at the battle on Gaea, I don't want to distract him. And I need to keep the dragon form of Hermes' power calm.

Timing is going to be the key at getting out of here with my power and my dragon.

Short, quick breaths race in and out of my nose as my burning flesh calms to an intense throb. Preparing myself, I open my eyes and feels Seraphina's heated gaze locked firmly on mine.

The only movement she made was her grip on the edge of the throne. With her knuckles white, she holds on to the king's chair. I nod once at her. I'm not sure if she cares but I let her know I'm okay.

I'm continuing to control my panic and my power. *I'm okay.*

Thick rusted chains lower from the tall ceiling and the hooks impaling me are fixed within them. A clamp closes down, securing the chains and they begin to retreat toward the ceiling.

Puffing my cheeks out, I ready myself for the pain that is about to bombard my body. As much as I tensed, I was not ready for the pull of the hooks lifting me into the air by the chains.

White static takes over my sight as the throne room disappears from the surging agony.

Blinking and desperate to for my vision to return to me so I can see what's next, my mouth gapes open and I'm unable to breath. Finally, the white begins to fade away and the throne room reappears.

I stare at the tall ceiling and warm tears run down my face.

My chest burns and it's not from my wounds; it's Hermes.

My body is overrun with a thousand sensations as if I'm being pricked by hundreds of needles at once. In the distance, I feel the mountain holding the dragon quake.

"Turn it off." I reassure the dragon, hoping the sensation I'm feeling is the dragon's anger and not my mate being injured on Gaea.

"Just survive." I recite that for myself, for my mate, for the realms that are suffering under this torment. I repeat the phrases over again, waiting and holding out for the right moment. I have to remain composed as I'll have only one opportunity.

Closing my eyes, I push away the pain of the hooks in my shoulders. I block out the thrumming in my chest of Hermes. I focus on that pull of my powers swirling in the center of the small amber pendent.

That small galaxy of silver starlight, held safely inside the pendent and strapped securely to a dragon of starlight is my salvation. After all these days of feeling that power pull at me, I pull on the tether and call the power to me.

The element of Earth is locked inside, ready to explode and

be unleashed on the realm of its origin. I detect the ancient realms heartbeat and feel it falter as I press upon it.

Driving my essence into the center of Tartarus, I work to catch my breath against the sting of molten lava swirling in the realms center.

As if the realm were a living, breathing beast, I envision my heart beating in time with Tartarus. The energy of the realm pulses in a synchronized dance with mine and I feel the sunlight brighten.

The eclipse is waning, and I sense the realm celebrate the return of its sunlight.

Stretching the power of Earth outward, I feel along a billion veins of rock and mineral within the crust of the realms surface. Pulling the powers to the surface, I reach the Dune Sea and the grassy pastures of the Gorgon's camp. I find the ancient rock mines and feel along large chains to the cuffs that imprison the mighty cyclopes.

The cyclops detect the long-lost brush of the Titans' power against their flesh.

Their skin turns to gooseflesh as my aura washes over them, coating the chains that bind them and passing my messages of rebellion to them.

I search for the essence of Light that resides with the Titan aura of my mate. Waiting with fuming anger, the dragon quivers within the mountain. The beasts' steady eyes keep a fixed gaze on the thick shield of my power, praying to me to remove it.

As I run my powers within the vast citadel, a surprise is found. Hiding in dark recesses outside the castle and within the halls, the daughters of the Danaides clutch daggers and sulk closer to the throne room.

They were planning an ambush of their own.

My misjudgment of Seraphina continues to be proven with each passing minute. I suppose she had no intentions of giving into this forced lifestyle and was merely playing along until the right moment also.

I see now, Bridget's lesson of knowing when to strike and not fighting with my emotions is something Seraphina has already mastered.

Thanatos stalks toward me with hunger ringing in his yellow eyes. "Now, *Savior*, let us begin unraveling your secrets, before I unravel your intestines for my meal."

Flaying Wind pierces my abdomen, and the king slices my stomach open with a wide gash. Clenching my teeth together with a force that threatens to break them, I grunt against the pain.

Holding tight to the power I'm coursing through the realm; I creep the claws of my Earth element closer to the king's castle, nearly ready to strike.

I'm certain he'll have wards protecting his kingdom and with my earlier escape, I can bet he extended them.

Like I did at the warehouse of the Shifter-auction, I see the path of my attack, I know the route I'll take, and I can see the outcome.

I only have to make sure I don't miss the closing of the eclipse and I pray to the twelve realms that the dragon is ready to stretch his wings. Because he is going to need to fly faster than he's ever flown before.

My body trembles as I exert everything I have to through the realm. My heart beats harder and faster, pushing silver starlight through the rocky veins of Tartarus. The mountain containing the dragon shudders as rocks tumble from the cavern ceiling. The Gorgon sisters huddled with the dragon, taking refuge under a large wing of his protection.

The chains locked around the necks of the giants of Tartarus and the rebels of the Sisyphus tribe vibrate as my power wraps around them.

The Gorgons take flight on their mighty pegasus, launching off the green pastures and into the sherbet sky when the tendrils of my power seep out of the ground.

The king pushes his flaying wind into me again and this time, I scream.

Letting the pain burn my throat as I project my voice across the burnt sky of Tartarus, the Wyrmcrest mountain range explodes when I release my hold of the barrier containing the dragon.

Igniting the power of Earth around me, Tartarus yields to the might of my power. The chains of the cyclops break and the cuffs around their necks come crashing down.

The three giants that fill the mine with their large bodies lift their mouths to the heavens and bellow. The ground shudders as their heavy footsteps crush against the rock and they make their escape from the quarry that has served as their prison since the fall of the great Titans.

Their flesh turns to stone as they command the power of earth once again. The Sisyphus tribes people use Earthen Levitation to hurl the massive boulders at their harpy wardens. The three cyclops thrust their fists, punching the ground. A rolling wave of Seismic Pulse undulates from their position.

The powerful shockwave rolls through the quarry, bringing down the harpies that attempt to fly out of harm's way and destabilizes the ground.

With powerful tremors, the quarry cracks and a dozen

landslides race into the quarry's center as the prison that confined the giants crumbles.

Within two beats of my heart, I've redirected the desert windstorm and I'm bringing it to the king.

I erode the hooks that were driven into me and drop the cuffs, chaining my powers. As I fall, I open my own swirl of darkness, catching myself in a portal and delivering me safely to the ground below.

My hands are shaking from the immense powers I'm using together but I push harder. As my water element secrets from my body, icy blue waters, like the cerulean sea of the Mediterranean, circle my abdomen and shoulders, healing my wounds.

The harpies around me flap their wings and screech in a frenzy.

Flinging both my arms, my Winds push the harpies against the stone walls of the castle and my currents pin them there.

My eyes fall on the tyrant king as a shadow falls over the castle. The king raises his eyes to the tall windows, but I don't need to look and see what monster is coming for him. I feel the arrival of my bonded mates' power as the dragon crashes through the glass and stone of the citadel.

My chaos reigns upon the king as I withdraw my powers from everywhere I laced them deep under his castle.

The tendrils of earth and wind rip apart the citadel as if I were throwing the blocks aside with my bare hands. The Titan aura of my mate surrounds me. The great winged serpent ejects a deafening cry into the atmosphere of Tartarus.

Euryale and Stheno slide down from the back of the dragon and run out of the castles back door. Their pegasus are nearly here, arriving on a portal of swirling pink clouds.

The pendent encasing my hidden powers thrums at me

only a foot away from me. Grasping the pendent in my hands, I crush it into my chest, the power of the ancient goddess reclaimed.

As if all of Tartarus pauses, the wind of the realm holds for a beat before the very sands of the desert come rushing toward me. Absorbing another wave of my broken immortality and feeling it fuse together with my tattered soul is like being ripped apart and sewn together a million times over.

The king tries to make his way to me. Rising off his throne and grunting against the rush of my power, he works himself one step and then another toward me.

As the great dragon protecting me opens his mouth, it's Seraphina moves first.

Watching me, with tears in her eyes, she wraps her arms around the king and ignites herself. Blazing like a column of pale-yellow fire, she consumes him. "The daughters of the Dainaide will serve as your concubines no more."

Seraphina's warriors enter the castle and battle the harpy guards that are flocking to their king's aid. The dragon burns flocks of them with blue starlight as Seraphina keeps the king locked in the inferno of her hold.

The kings' wings thrash about, slicing her red skin and causing a swell of blood to seep out of her from dozens of wounds.

As the rushing sands and strong winds of Tartarus stream into me, I scream. With my arms cast wide and my hair blowing about, I restore another part of myself while I watch Seraphina sacrifice herself.

Peace settles over her lovely face as she burns white hot.

The rush of her flames and the blast of my winds eat away at the tyrant king until there is nothing left of his body, and he's returned to the sands of Tartarus. And Seraphina, the last bride of the tyrant king, dies with him.

"Savior, the eclipse!" Euryale screams at me from the back of her pegasus.

The castle is obliterated and only a few stones remain. The dragon and I look to the sky and then each other. I see myself reflected in the deep ocean eyes of the dragon and without needing to speak, our souls understand each other.

The great dragon lowers his shoulder and I climb up the scaly body.

Sitting securely in the center of his back, ribbons of light wrap around my legs and waist, constructing a harness to keep me secured.

I feel the realm begin to balance as rebellion surges through the newly freed giants, no longer captive in the rock quarries. With their king dead, the harpies are fleeting the castle, chased away by the Danaides and the Gorgons.

I sense the eclipse slipping away as the alignment threatens to disappear. The moment is soon approaching when I could be marooned on this distant realm forever.

With a firm nod of her head, Euryale doesn't need to speak the words that are blazing in her bright green eyes. If ever I needed to call upon her again, she would be a ready and willing ally.

I can't thank them enough for their help and while I wish I could help them more; but this is not my fight. It's theirs and with the retribution blazing in their resolve, I know they will reclaim their realm.

The cosmic dragon pushes off the ground and leaves my stomach far below as it races to the sky. With several strong pumps of its wings, I bear down, holding on firm to the reins.

The dragon shoots a blast of light ahead, opening a portal that will deliver us to the Dune Sea where I fell out of the sky. Tucking his wings to his body, the dragon shoots through the portal and we race out the other side.

The silver swirl of my doorway back to Gaea, is still suspended in the sherbet sky of Tartarus and I release a breath of relief.

The red veil of the eclipse slips off the sun as the alignment reaches its end. The shimmering doorway sways and grows smaller as it begins to close.

The dragon beneath me becomes a raging missile of speed. Blasting the closing portal of my power with three pulses of blue light, dread clamps over my throat and seals against my heart as the doorway recedes.

We're not going to make it.

As the battle rages around me, the swirling current of the Winds reflect the turmoil on the battlefield. Ares has an endless supply of Shifters and Elementals. But it is the dark creatures of Elysium that are our largest concern.

The Labyrinth has served Gaea well to contain the dark shadows that slip through the thin veil between the realms. But it's weakened us, not having to combat the darkness for so many ages.

My Winds do little against the Shades, aside from blowing them back or deflecting their attacks. It's Achilles cleansing Fire that can destroy them. Fighting by my side, we never leave each other on the battlefield because we are stronger together.

Repelling the obscure creatures with my Wind Shields, I feed the air of the realm to my mate as his Fires destroy the Shades.

As the battle unfolds, my thoughts always drift to Achilles, my steadfast companion and mate. In the midst of chaos, he stands like a beacon of strength and resolve, his valor unmatched by any other warrior on the battlefield.

I cannot help but admire the sheer power and grace with which Achilles wields his weapons, his movements fluid and precise, like a dance upon the winds. In his eyes burns a fire, fierce and unwavering, fueled by a sense of protection and honor that drives him ever forward.

Two Earth Elementals attack me. One hurls large boulders of granite at me. Using my Winds, I take over the path of his projectiles.

Thrusting the boulder high into the air, Achilles heats the rock, and it glows hotter than a comet as it races toward one of our attackers. As I pound the Wind downward, the large rock crushes the man who threw it, creating a divot in the sand where the smoking rock, glowing like a hot ember, is the only thing that can be seen.

Achilles drives his fist through the chest of the other elemental. Taking the man's heart in his hand, a flash of Soul-Fire takes his immortality and consumes it in a fiery blaze.

"That was gruesome." I huff as I deflect the attack of a Shade. Blowing the creating back, into my brothers dome of Light, the Shade is destroyed.

"You love it when I'm a monster on the battlefield." I can feel the grin in his cocky reply and it makes me roll my eyes. But he's right. There are few better views on this earth than watching my warrior unleash his rage against our enemies.

I check on Hermes but there are too many replicas of himself within the dome he created for me to find him.

My eyes dart to each Mirage he's casting as he battles Ares' and the dark mages. Streaks of blue starlight gleam within his protective shield as he destroys the attacks of the Dark Mages and their Shades.

It doesn't seem as if he is making progress, but I know he is unleashing all the fury of an army with his assaults. He is protecting this space just as if Rhea were here and in danger.

He'll not stop until she returns or until he has killed them all.

If he would only let us inside there with him, we could fight together. But he closed himself inside to battle alone. I'm scared for him, and the thought pulls at my heart with heavy dread.

The moon is racing past the sun and the eclipse will end in a matter of a minute. An errant thought streams into my mind. *What if she doesn't return?*

Closing my eyes, I can't let myself get distracted with that right now. She'll make it back. She'll fight just as hard as we are to return here to us, to return to Hermes and the battle against her hunter. She won't give up and neither will we.

A lion-Shifter circles Achilles and lowers his body, preparing to pounce. Achilles is ready with a ball of fire. But a lioness, just behind him, also readies to attack.

As the lion before Achilles lunges, so does the unseen lioness behind him.

Catching her in mid-jump with my currents, I fling her body around. Slamming her into the lion attacking from the front, I keep them in a tangle of my Winds.

"You fucking thought, you bitch." Attacking my mate from behind like a coward? I don't think so. Achilles blazes them both with liquid fire and I give him a flirtatious wink as I slice through another Shifter with Flaying Wind.

"Gods, little siren. You better stop turning me on." Achilles voice wraps around my mind and sends a shiver down my spine.

"Can't stop, won't stop, lover." I throw all the sass I'm capable of into my tone and smirk as I turn back to our approaching enemies.

Achilles is more than my warrior. He is my confidant and my protector. Not just my fated mate but my chosen mate. Our bond has been forged in the crucible of battle and tempered by the trials we have faced together.

But with each passing second, the sky brightens as the eclipse fades away. I spin in a circle, frantic to find the silver doorway that will deliver my best friend back to Gaea. But I can't find it.

Doom settles in the deepest recesses within me and not even Achilles bright flames are strong enough warm the frigid cold realization that washes over me.

Rhea is not returning.

Looking quickly behind me, I watch Hermes as he looks to the sky.

The battle around us pauses for the briefest heartbeat as the entire battlefield comes to the same conclusion.

"No." Atlas' sorrow filled denial of the unfolding events is confirmation we all understand the same thing.

The alignment as passed, and the Goddess of the Twelve Realms is marooned on Tartarus.

Hermes eyes collide with mine, reflecting a pain he's harbored, feeling the death of his mate a thousand times over. We hold our gaze on each other as the horror settles over both of us.

I want to go to him, but the light of his dome is only increasing.

Feeding the pain of know he's going to lose her again; Hermes is channeling the full might of his power into the forcefield.

"Hermes, no!" My cry is a plea across the desert, and it does little to crack the impenetrable armor he is erecting around himself. I know what happens to stars as they die, and I finally understand why he secured himself within an impenetrable dome.

No.

"I love you Cal." His grief-stricken voice crumbles my resolve and tears run in torrents down my face. "Finding out I had a sister, was one of the best days of my life."

"Hermes!" I scream his name in a broken sob as I crash to my knees. Achilles rushes to me, pulling me away from the growing shield and forcing me back to my feet.

The two friends lock eyes and Achilles knows the same thing I do. I feel his pain smash down our fated bond and our souls cling to each other preparing for the agony we know we're going to witness. Hermes is going to sacrifice himself.

The light within dome is becoming blinding and I have to shield my eyes.

"Take care of our girl." Hermes says to Achilles, but my mate can't answer, overcome with emotions.

Turning his back to us, Hermes impales his sword deep into the ground. Two long whips of Light emerge within his hands and strike the surrounding air. Lightning crackles at the ends as he faces Ares and Aryana together.

The ultra-blue light of his power increases, turning pure white. We have to look away from the intense radiance and turning our eyes to the battling armies that still fight.

Beyond the horizon, darkness swells as a raging storm brews from the west. Lightning crashes within the black clouds, bringing a rush of Wind. But it's a familiar warmth caressing my skin that freezes me.

A touch, I've not felt in ages brushes against me as a voice is carried to me on the currents of the four Winds. *"Hello, little siren.* It's nothing more than a faint whisper, but I can't look away from the oncoming storm.

Achilles heard it too. We turn at the same time, looking at the dark swirling mass of storm clouds on the distant horizon behind us.

An Elemental hurls their power in an attack.

Without diverting our attention from the swirling mass of clouds, Achilles and I conjure a shield of our combined powers. My Winds mix with his Flames and protect us with the steady percussion of our auras.

We watch the sky, desperate to hear that voice again.

A clap of lightning is brilliant against the dark storm clouds. The light that shines through the black clouds is a frosted shade of green and my heart drops.

A beautiful seafoam that matches the eyes of our slain mate radiates with each burst of lightning within the storm followed by booming thunder.

"Dance with me."

We hear the voice again and with my brow crumpled, I look at Achilles. He remains fixed on the horizon; a tear rolling down his cheek.

Patroclus.

Thunder grumbles again inside the storm, sounding like someone is knocking on a giant door to the realm, unable to gain entry.

"I don't understand." My voice is nothing more than a whisper because my throat is closing tight with sorrow. I try to say the words, a prayer to the Fates to help us interpret this, but only manage to take in a ragged breath.

He's dead. Slain so along ago by Achilles power, Patroclus' immortal life ended on the battlefield of Troy. Yet, I feel him, just as if he were here again. That voice, one I have only heard in my dreams, wraps around my mind, and coats my soul in a tender embrace.

Another knock, and another burst of green light dances in the atmosphere. As the fingers of light stretch across the sky, the wards of the realm ripple. Yellow sunlight mingles with orange flames before fading away.

"Achilles, watch the light."

With the next knock of lightning, and another growl of thunder, we watch the light that matches our auras flare in the sky.

Long ago, Apollo's golden sunlight and Ares' orange flames wove the impenetrable wards around Gaea, forever protecting us from Chaos. As the thunder booms, we watch those wards flex and wave in the atmosphere, still serving their purpose to protect the realm.

The hair at the nape of my neck raises and goosebumps roll across my skin. Rhea is trapped on the other side of those wards, because she is Chaos; she is Death. And Death cannot return to Gaea.

"She can't get through." The words fly out of my mouth in a panic. "Rhea, she is beating against the wards, trying to return, Achilles." I look at my mate with desperation.

Achilles looks at me, slowly meeting my eyes with the sunset that forever burns in his. Cupping the side of my face with his palm, his steadfast warmth cascades over me and he calms my ragged breaths as he shakes his head in steady understanding.

"We have to destroy the wards." As he says it, I know it's true. *We* have to destroy the wards; he and I.

No two elementals in this realm are powerful enough to

tear them down. Powered by their mated connection, the god of the sun and a living volcano forged these wards. Lasting all these ages to keep us safe, it will take equally incredible power to break through them. Power I feel is unique to my mate and me.

Achilles looks down at my watery eyes as he takes me in. Wrapping an arm around my waist, he pulls me to him. Craning my neck, I hold his stare. Neither of us blink as we understand why we have suffered these ages without our mate by our side.

The Fates are cruel in their patience.

Achilles, Patroclus, and I share a fate braided together by our soul bonds. The Fates severed Pat's line all those ages ago on Troy's battlefield.

We felt every ounce of his death as his bond was pulled from our souls. And each day, we walk unbalanced, forever missing the link to our soul's completion.

But the cruel Fates were only making us wait for the day we would be needed most. But as I look once more at the horizons storm, we have a second or two more, and we'll make the Fates wait on us.

Tilting my head to the side, I give him a sad smile. "Daddy always said I stole a little bit of the sunlight, the day I was born."

Achilles smiles at me. Both of his large hands gently bracketing my face. "I believe it. Since the second you came into my life, I have basked in the warmth of your soul."

I rise on the tips of my toes, and he meets me. Our mouths mold together as a battle rages around us. His tongue sweeps across my lips and I savor the feel of him, the taste of Gaea's greatest warrior, as he softens his touch, just for me.

Breaking our kiss, Achilles gives me a faint smile, rubbing the tip of his nose across mine. His autumn eyes trail down my long blonde hair. He runs his fingers across my scalp, raking them through the long strands. Taking in a deep breath, I lean into him.

Rubbing his thumb and forefingers together, he lets the silky tendrils fall and returns his stare back to mine.

"Are you ready?" He asks me, his eyes weary but gleaming.

We let the shield of our elements fall, revealing the bloodshed behind us.

Death and destruction have flooded the sands of north Africa, but I refuse to sweep my eyes across the mayhem. I can't look to see who is dead and who remains fighting.

I'm only wanting to see my brother, still on the other side of his wall of Light.

"Hermes, the storm; the wards." My plea is enough to pull the last tendril of hope that remains in him. He lets us see inside his fortress of sorrow as Dark weapons soar at him, and he dissipates them all. *"It's Rhea."*

The line of Dark Mages taking him on hold back the rest of Ares' forces, needing to kill the Herald of the realms, so they can continue their attack on the rest of us.

The lighting and thunder boom again behind us and with sweat and soot across his face, Hermes' eyes are tight with his focus on the battle before him. His gaze flicks to mine and I hold him with my stare.

His lips press together in a thin line and sorrow fills his eyes. *He knows what we're going to do.* My chest heaves, suddenly heavy, as I look at him and I think back to the first time I met my brother. I remember the words he said to me on my first night at my strange new home.

"I promise," The tears fall freely down our faces from across the distance of the battlefield. *"I'll always watch over you, alright?"*

"Callie." His broken voice pleas to me.

"Calypso, what are you doing?" Atlas is somewhere nearby, watching Achilles and I say goodbye to Hermes. Selfishly, I can't look at Atlas either. I don't want to see the pain in his eyes as well. *"We'll find another way."* He begs.

"This is the only way." Even in my mind, I can only whisper my response to the man who was like my father. Achilles pulls me closer to his side. His warmth giving me courage.

Achilles nods once at his oldest friend and Hermes takes in a deep breath of resolve. Standing taller and squaring his shoulders, Hermes returns the nod; a final farewell of two men, close as brothers.

"Take care of our girl." I tell him and Hermes releases a choked sob.

"I love you." He answers. *"I love you both, so much."*

Taking him in once more, I see the firm resolve of Daphne and the unwavering strength of Apollo in my brother. Our parents would be proud of him. They would be proud of us both.

Achilles pulls my hand to his lips and kisses my knuckles, holding me in a trance with his eyes. "Dance with me, once more."

I smile widely at my mate and turn into him. Our bodies meld together as my Winds carry us into the clouds for one last dance.

The day Patroclus asked me to dance on the currents of my element, the three of us stumbled into a future together that has been riddled with pain and tremendous loss.

But as my Winds bring us to the clouds and form a funnel of protection, I can only think of my mates and the million memories of happiness I had with them. As Achilles Flames meet my Winds, a raging vortex of our combined powers surround us.

Pushing against the power of the wards, we hold each other in a tight embrace. I place my soul in his loving hold and as he places his in mine, and the sensation of another warmth wraps around us both.

Within our bonded souls, we can feel him reaching through the Void. Patroclus is calling us home.

As we rise higher into the atmosphere and push our powers to the end of our abilities, yellow sunlight and orange flames encapsulate us.

Achilles tightens his hold on me as his Fires grow. My lips meet his as my Winds fan his power into an inferno.

We touch our foreheads together and close our eyes. The voice of our slain mate, dead for so long flows into our minds as our powers consume us.

"I love you," I look into Achilles eyes one last time, reciting the words that reach me from beyond the veil of the realms. "for as long as I draw breath,"

Achilles smiles, finishing the phrase that is spoken into our hearts, "And forever after."

Death never feels the same. The rush of life vacating a body is different every time, I just never imagined it to feel like this. Lying on the desert ground, watching the dark swirl of clouds in the distance, death feels like nothing.

The battle around me is muffled as if the sounds exist somewhere else, too far for me to hear. The eclipse has ended, and sunlight returned but the darkness spread across this battlefield is immense. As the war rages on, the battlefield remains cast in a blanket of shadows.

So long ago, on the emerald sandy beach of Avalon, I forged my vow as the alignment of the triple moons ended. The Goddess of the Twelve Realms forfeit her life that night and I tethered my fate to her destiny.

I didn't realize I also tethered my death to hers.

She did not return. And sorrow pulls my eyes closed as I know she'll suffer an agonizing demise yet again. Still mortal, the harsh reality of her future will grip her, and I'm saddened to know she'll have to die once more. Thrusting the world into another age of forgetting.

But this time, I'll die too and while they will remember my

death, my vow to the goddess will be lost to the sands of this desolate desert that will become my tomb.

The bear-Shifter that attacked me broke my spine over his knee.

While my legs are still attached to my body, it feels as if they are gone. I'm thankful there is no pain, but I am shocked at how numb death feels.

Looking to my left, I find Penelope. Lifeless eyes stare unblinking at Odysseus.

Their bodies are being ravaged by two Shades as the mates lay dead on the battlefield. Their hands are stretch toward each other. As if they tried to reach one another in their final moment; but they didn't make it.

A sob escapes my throat as I know the fate that awaits them in the Darkness of Elysium.

When a soul is killed by a creature of the Dark realm, that soul is destined to an eternity of suffering and damnation.

Penelope and Odysseus will roam Elysium, the realm of Darkness, ravaged by eternal pain and hunger. They will forever search for each other and never will they find peace in the others presence.

Thunderous booms in the clouds feather beautiful lighting across the dark sky and I want to spend my final moments enjoying the spectacle.

A familiar sputtering cough to my right makes me turn my head to see who may lay dying along with me. Perhaps we can enter the Void together.

Never in my ages did I expect to see the powerful Gorgon so vulnerable.

Her braids are splayed along the sand, lifeless. The serpentine tendrils that forever oscillated with the power of the Gorgon lay sleeping on the Sahara.

A trail of blood seeps from the corner of her mouth and her stomach convulses. With her hands covering the gaping wound, I see why. She's nearly been severed in two, sliced open by a Flame.

I can't let her die this way.

The pain finally comes when I push myself onto my side. It's like being dipping in a river of lava. This feels like the death I imagined and as I pull my body along the bloodied desert sand, I prepare to meet the darkness of the Void.

Clutching fists of sand, I drag lifeless legs behind me and make my way to Medusa.

I push a shadow through the flaming arrow that pierced her back and a plume of smoke dances into the air. Her chest heaves as it struggles to breath and the line of blood flows out of the corner of her mouth faster.

I grab her tactical vest and use it to pull myself the rest of the way to her.

Her gargled breaths sound like she's drowning, and blood fills her throat as she tries to speak.

"Shhh." I lay next to her, my own breathing ragged from my journey. "Let's just enjoy the view while we die."

"M—mis," Medusa tries to speak still, and I raise in my elbow to look at her. Eyes the color of a dying forest look at me. "m—mis—take."

Mistake.

I smile at my old friend. "We've all made mistakes, Medusa. It will not do you well to dwell on them in your final moments."

Another boom sounds in the sky and I look to the heavens. The minty green lightning that reaches through the clouds brings a smile to my face.

Achilles and Calypso ascend into the sky, locked in a lovers embrace.

Hermes fights with the might of a dozen warriors as whips of Light assault the Dark Mages he is battling. But he won't be able to fend them off much longer. The Herald of the realms will do well to send one last message to the cosmos and hopefully his lost love will live long enough to hear it.

We're all going to die here today and as the realm collectively resets, and waits for the return of the goddess, a tear falls from my eyes knowing how many of her allies won't be alive to witness her next life.

High in the skies, Calypso and Achilles battle the wards that surround Gaea. They haven't given up hope and their bravery warms me. But the warmth turns frigid when a twisting vortex of wind and flames engulf them.

"They are sacrificing themselves." My breathy acknowledgement relays the events to my companion in case Medusa cannot see the spectacle in the sky.

The wards of the Gaea ripple and quiver under their powerful assault as a pale-green glow fills the atmosphere. It reminds me of Patroclus and the frosted mint color of his eyes.

Three more booms thunder within the dark clouds.

Calypso and Achilles hold each other tight as the green glow surrounds them.

"P–Pat." Medusa gargles the name of her cousin. I lay next to her as the blood that pours from our wounds soaks into the sand.

Radiant yellow and bronze aura blend together as the mates take over the sky.

Their powers grow and build, one fueling the other. They climb to a crescendo until you can longer distinguish the two auras dancing in the clouds. They burn so hot as winds of the realm rush to them, and I watch, unable to look away at the beauty of it all.

Shadows darken inside the dome Hermes has constructed.

Darkness screams from within the protective dome he has encased himself in, and I recognize the angry call of obscurity. At once the mages charge back their powers and blast the Herald of the Realms with their might combined.

Hermes screams against the effort to shield them all and his protective dome quakes and flickers around him. He's losing but he'll hold on as long as he can. Sadly, it won't be enough.

I feel the darkness within Ariyana as she absorbs the powers of the Shades around her. She draws back their dark strength and collects it within her hands. Her veins turns black and tar weeps from her eyes.

It seems there are others willing to sacrifice themselves today.

With a guttural bellow, she surges everything she has at Hermes and her Void Beam hits him directly in his chest.

The impact detonates with his Light and bursts the collective energy around them. Hermes is blast into the sky. His protective dome collapses as if someone snuffed out his Light.

The wards that shield the realm quiver as Achilles and Calypso's powers stream together. With a final pulse of deep thunder, a streaking star, the color of seafoam races across the atmosphere, meeting the pair of mates.

Their dance swells to an eruption of their powers.

"H–he came f–for them." Medusa says but I can't take my eyes off the detonation in the clouds.

It's a beautiful display of sorrow as the wards of the realm are ruptured. Like cracked glass, the shield that kept Chaos at bay crumbles and dissolves into nothing.

Behind the thunderous storm, blue and silver lightning illuminate a great beast prowling beyond the dark clouds. The monster, silhouetted by the shroud of clouds, extends large wings as silver starlight explodes inside the raging storm.

I check on my friend. Medusas evergreen eyes are fixed wide on the sky above. I hear a long gasp escape her throat as the Gorgon's last breath leaves her body.

The realm is overcome by the roar of a great and ancient beast as shimmering silver rainfall pours from the sky above.

Perhaps Gaea is crying with the loss of the Temptress of the Four Winds and her steadfast Flame. Perhaps the realm weeps for the Herald, thrust into the heavens, his body consumed by darkness. Or perhaps Gaea mourns for the great goddess, lost to Tartarus and the eclipse that marooned her on a foreign realm.

Whatever the reason, I'm thankful for the cool rain washing over me. As a heaviness returns to my body, I feel life surging within me.

A silver sheen coats me and brightens as feeling returns to my limbs and my wounds stitch together.

Medusa gasps next to me. Her body also coated in silver moonlight, and she sits upright. Clutching her chest and feeling for injuries, tears streaks down her cheek as she looks at me with wide eyes.

Like a million shooting stars are raining upon us, life, and rejuvenation soaks into the fighters around us and all give pause, looking to the skies.

A looming shadow blocks the sun as a great beast descends upon Gaea.

The Goddess of the Twelve Realms has returned and brought the great cosmic dragon of Hel with her.

"**N**o, it can't end like this. I refuse to let it end like this.**"** Leaning closer to the dragon, the reigns of darkness in my hand, I squeeze my legs holding on tighter as we barrel toward the closed portal. "Let's go!"

The dragon opens his mouth and blasts three pulses of blue starlight. Each one is a detonation against the shields that keep us from returning to Gaea.

Desperation claws at me and I sob into the open sky as we fly in an arc upward and away from the portal that refuses to open.

I'm not going to be stranded on this realm of sunlight, forever taken away from the feeling my mates' power in the night sky. Never to feel the rush of wind against my skin in a reassuring embrace from my best friend.

Destined to feel the burning heat of this intense sun, too similar to the flames my hunter wields until I die another mortal death.

Not this time.

The dragon sets his course again for the portal and we charge our powers together. Hurling our elements at the doorway between the realms, cracks begin to form as if the wards of Gaea are breaking.

Hope burns in me, igniting my resolve.

Pushing more power into the cacophony of our attacks, the dragon and I assault the portals entrance relentlessly.

I feel the misery of our separation crash down my fated bond to Hermes as the barrier blocking the realms is assaulted with our might. With each pulse of my power, the opening weakens. *Gods, please someone help me.*

I release my prayer into the threads that separate the realms and hope it reaches the merciful Fates. Trying to send my resolve through our connection, I push my love and the resilience of my promise down our bond.

The dragon under shoots three more bursts of light from his mouth like a cannon and they rupture against the wards.

Boom!

Boom!

Boom!

It's like knocking on an impassible door. My salvation, just on the other side.

The phantom sensation of a powerful elemental attack slams into my chest. The dragon bows his back and his wings falter. I clutch my tactical vest as the agony steals my ability to breathe and robs me of my voice.

Through the translucent body of the cosmic dragon, I see a circle of darkness on the heart of the dragon.

"Hermes."

Horror takes over my expression as I feel the glowing ribbon of Hermes soul begin to flicker. Traveling down our bond, the tether that links us is being destroyed.

"They are killing him." My whisper is lost on the winds as

the dragon rights his course. With a great roar from the mouth of the beast beneath me, I add my own rage as we scream across the atmosphere of Tartarus.

Pushing both my hands toward the opening, I combine the might of all the twelve Titans and fuse their stolen power within me. A beam of silver starlight strikes the portal, adding to a blazing pulse of energy from the other side.

Someone on Gaea is helping me destroy the wards and the cracks grow as the massive shields weaken. *Thank the goddess.* Hope renews within me and sets my resolve stronger.

The dragon pumps his mighty wings faster and adds a beam of blue light to my silver attack. We are not going to slow down this time or divert away from the portal.

I'm going to break through these barriers and return to my mate.

Hermes is not going to die because I am Death and I refuse to accept his soul into the Void today.

With a final pulse of my power, I blast another bright pulse of silver starlight and feel the rush of Gaea as the wards crumble.

Taking back the reigns in my hand, I snap them against the dragon. Opening my gateway connecting the two realms, the dragon narrows his body and tucks his wings.

My eyes stream constant tears that are snatched away by the raging wind as the dragon flies in a tight spin. My hair billows behind me as we race through the portal, returning to Gaea.

The shift in the realms is instant.

I'm released from the blazing sunlight of Tartarus as I enter the lighter atmosphere of Gaea and its gentler sun.

My senses overwhelm me passing through the veil, but I have no time to stop and orient myself. The dragon beneath me is a seething torpedo of starlight, racing forward to Hermes.

We are both desperate to reunite with him. Me, to save my mate before he perishes. The cosmic dragon, longing to reunite with the immortal whose power he belongs to.

The Winds scream at me. All the currents of the realm are wailing at once with a somber melody and I can't decipher anything. The warm burn of the sun seems to have darkened like all the fire in the realm has been snuffed out, leaving behind glacial darkness.

My chest feels as if it's being cleaved open with Hermes' injury of ultra-cold elemental power, and it turns my body frigid.

Hermes body soars into the air, high above the clouds. His unconscious form has been blasted into the atmosphere by the powerful attack. Darkness is trying to steal his Light and his essence dims. The dragon surges but it's my power that projects ahead of us in a rush of silver.

Gripping the starlight reins tighter, we fly faster, turning into a streak of aura.

Wrapping my mate in my powers I push healing Life and Light into him. I don't care if I expend all my power to save him, I'll release everything I have to keep him alive.

Gods dammit, I'm not going to be too late. I promised him I would return. I promised I'd come back and find him.

My aura pours out of my like rain and falls to the ground below.

The cosmic blue dragon flares his massive wings, slowing himself down. His body pivots upward, releasing the tethers holding me onto the his back.

Hanging, I clutch the thick scales and long ridges of his course armor as hard as I can. But with another flap of his mighty wings, my fingers slip. My body dangles precariously above the clouds and when the dragon beats his wings again, I lose my hold.

Just as I plummeted through the portal of Tartarus, like Icarus falling from sky, I tumble through the atmosphere again. But today, there will be no crash landing.

My hair whips around me. My arms and legs flail upward as I fall.

I watch the Titan dragon made of blue starlight reunite with the body of my mate and a blinding burst of light explodes above me. The power of Hermes' Titan encases our bond, filling in some of the holes missing within us both.

I shield my eyes against the burning light and when I open them again, the dragon is a column of light speeding toward me.

"I'm coming for you, baby." The rumble tethered to Hermes' voice in this state is a caress across my entire being. A smile takes over my face as I turn my body and shoot headfirst toward the ground.

Falling into a dark swirl of my power, I emerge again on the back of my dragon.

My dragon.

Starlight pours from me, covering the bloodied landscape below as we race toward it. With more of my power and immortality returned, my eyes see the realm differently now.

Aura is flowing everywhere. Ribbons of light and power overwhelm me as I watch the waves of magic pulsating around the immortals exerting their elements at each other.

Like sound waves rippling through the air, the colliding

sensations make me dizzy, and I close my eyes against the assault on my senses.

I hear everything and feel too much.

Wind, Light and Life elements all sing to me. Water, Darkness and Sensory bow to me. Now Earth and Sonus, even the faded Shifting power I transferred to Lucas, celebrate my return.

As I restore myself and return the power of the twelve Titans to my immortality, they war within me. Each power collides, wanting to be seen, wanting to be of use to the Titan who commands them.

It's tremendous, almost too much for me to grasp firmly.

The spectators below stop fighting and rush away from the battlefield as the Titan of Light readies to set foot on Gaea for the first time in many ages.

Ares is bloodied but alive and while much of his army has been killed, he retains a lot of fighters. Lucas, transformed into the great wolf Fenrir, backs away and I watch with prideful eyes as Lucas' packs join him. Many are still living. Kai and Naomi, Zara, and Kellan, have all survived.

My mate, transformed to the aura of the great cosmic dragon, flaps his wings, and juts his massive feet forward, readying himself to land. The earth tremors when the great winged beast contacts the ground.

Breathing heavily and flapping his wings in a show of power, Hermes looks over the horizon of fighters. Grumbling, he takes a step or two back but doesn't lower his shoulder for me to dismount.

"Fuck you," Flint's face is red with anger as he looks to Hermes' dragon form. With a bow made of Fire, Flint has nocked an arrow against the string and has it pointed directly at me. "If I can't have her– "

Hermes doesn't allow Flint to finish his threat or give him time to release his weapon against me. With his large dragon paw, Hermes stomps once on Flint, sending a pulse of starlight through his body.

The beam of light thuds with a deep boom into the sand, causing a swell like the detonation of a bomb under water.

Lifting the paw, Hermes growls seeing Flints crumpled form and unmistakable red hair among the mass of twisted limbs stuck to the bottom of his paw.

In irritation, Hermes' dragon form flicks the body from his paw as a severed hand is the only thing that remains behind in the sand. Brushing the small appendage with the beasts' large talons, the extremity flops away from us.

"That's fucking disgusting." The graveling voice of Lucas in shifted form rings within our minds.

My mate and I keep our eyes on Ares.

Hermes finally lowers his large, scaled shoulder and I slide down. Having just left the crimson desert of Tartarus, I'm happy to finally reach the beige sands of Gaea once again.

Ares watches, with flames and soot rolling off his back in a torrent. The returned Goddess of the Realms and her mate, shifted into the form of a massive Titan dragon made of blue starlight, hold the attention of all.

As I walk several steps toward the crater, I work to interpret the many ribbons of light and aura that I see. It's like the strings of a thousand puppets are strung about, all of them twisting together and crossing paths.

I look to Flints crushed body and the sight of him offends me. With the power of Life, I speed up his decomposition until he's nothing more than a withered skeleton. Calling upon the Winds, my power blows his brittle remains away, removing him from my sight, and this realm, for eternity.

There is barely a flicker behind Ares eyes at the loss of his son, his last surviving child. He doesn't even care. It's like he is nothing more than a shell of a being, no longer capable of expressing a shred of feeling.

Ariyana hangs onto life by a glimmer of aura. Her Dark Mages form a protective line, spanning the length of Ares' army. Building their power, they call the Darkness to them.

Reaching the apex of their might, the line of mages fire their Void Beams at once, using Aryana like a conduit. I stay on my path toward Ares. There is no need for me divert my course knowing my mate is behind me.

The ground quakes and we all jostle on our footing when Hermes' power explodes. His anger erupts in a wave of Light and he lifts his head to the skies, roaring a warning to any who would dare attack his goddess.

As the dragon roars, and ground rumbles, his Light and their Darkness erupt. The blast is a shockwave that rolls through us all. And in that second, a heavy Mirage, unknowingly cast over the land falters.

In a fraction of the time, it takes to blink, the truth is revealed.

A hidden veil covers the earth, well disguised and intricately woven. As the dragon's power erupts with the Light of truth, that veil waivers, allowing me to peek through it.

Using my abilities, I stretch that single second into a minute.

The vast army of Ares, and the great God of War himself, look like nothing more than withered skeletons wrapped in skin. As if their immortal forms have been locked away and starved for ages. Unable to die, but not allowed to live, the army is a wailing mass of pain and torment.

This can't be.

The sight of this ghoulish sea of immortals, crying and begging for death, steals my breath and pauses my slow walk through the desert as I stare with my mouth gaping.

The surging wave of their suffering and the cries of their despair nearly knock me to the ground. Each of them are bound by chains of green elemental power. Invisible bindings that keep them locked in a perpetual state of control and misery, just as if they were bound by the thickest Thaumium bands.

"Help us."

"Death, please."

"Death."

"Death."

Their pleading clutches at me and I cover my mouth to stifle my scream.

At the forefront, my eyes lock with those of Ares. The God of War, once strong and mighty is little more than the shriveled carcass of Flint, I just destroyed. His skeletal body tremors. Drool runs down his face as he stands like an immobilized puppet, waiting for his mater to pull on his strings.

"How?"

Everything has slowed to a near stop as I take the scene in.

Hermes is still releasing his roar and the wave of his Light is traveling outward. Aryana has burned out. The combined attacks of the Dark Mages pulsing through her has expended her immortal life and she falls slowly to the ground.

There are no chains on her, and her appearance is not like ghastly prisoners that surround her.

I follow the jade ribbons of power encasing these beings. My eyes shift rapidly from person to person, trying to see where they are tethered. I search to locate the puppeteer controlling my hunter.

As I follow the links of a thousand chains, the true mask my cleaver hunter has worn across the ages of immortals slips when our eyes lock.

The false facade of a friend has vanished, all pretenses are gone. For the first time in a thousand lifetimes, I look upon the monster that consumed the Titans powers. I see the real face of my hunter as deep green eyes peer back at me.

Narrowing my gaze, I ready the combined might of my powers. "Hello, hunter. It's been a long time." My words are laced with contempt.

With a wicked smile and a dark gleam, those haunting eyes hold me. The eyes that filled me with dread and chased me through the dark tunnels of my nightmares. "Only a fool would call me a hunter." Malice oozes from every word. "You can call me..."

To be continued...

In a swirl of portals, the army that battled against us disappears and with them, my hunter.

The weary elementals who fought the most exhausting seven minutes of their lives, release a collective exhale. Confusion, relief, worry, are the emotions that cascade through the desert as survivors look around at the devastation of the battle.

Hermes glows as the Light of the dragon retreats within him and standing before me is my mate. Covered in sweat and sand, we collide.

I jump into his arms and cry.

He holds me, encasing me in his arms and squeezing me as if he knew he would never see me again. For him, it's been minutes since I left. For me, the three days on Tartarus have felt like an eternity.

"Why are you always trying to die when I come back to you?" I sob into him.

Taking my face between his hands, he peppers me with hurried kisses. "I'm just trying to not live without you."

"That is the same thing." The embrace turns to a desperate need to kiss each other. Our tongues battling for control as we fist each other's hair, unable to get close enough. Each of us need the reassurance that we're okay. I need to feel him, in the deepest recesses of my soul, I need to feel the closeness of his aura to know he's okay, and whole and alive.

"There is nothing for me, in any life, if you are not in it." Hermes' deep navy eyes hold me before he kisses me again with desperation.

Breaking our hold with breathlessness, I can't stop the waves of emotions flowing off of me. Everything that happened the past three days rushes out of me and collides into Hermes through our bond.

He sees it all. Conquering the Dune Sea, the betrayal of the Danaides. My imprisonment by the tyrant harpies and how I discovered both of our powers, locked away inside the mountain.

He becomes witness to it all.

The ancient library hanging high above our heads pulls me like all the gravity of the realm is pulling me to it.

I can't stop the flow of visions that keep pouring into Hermes. He watches everything in his mind as I free the Cyclops from their enslavement and the inhabitants of Tartarus rise up against their oppressor king.

"Rhea, I–" Hermes begins but stop him.

Something within the Library of Alexandria is calling me and I won't question it as I did before. "I have to do this first."

Without waiting another second, I raise my hands high above me and peel away the shields concealing Alexandria's ancient library. As my protective wards are stripped away, our surviving army of fighters looks on in amazement as the primordial structure appears.

The Library of Alexandria, the world's largest constructed pyramid, is seen for the first-time ages.

Enormous onyx stones form the pyramids walls, and they climb high with a block of gold gleaming at the top. Using my hands, I guide the building down, replacing it with gentle precision within the crater.

As my silver starlight continues to recede, my careful Mirage dissolving, the massive compound of the ancient Library of Alexandria returns.

The tall palms cast long shadows once again over the hot sands of the Sahara.

Large stone blocks form a wide walkway that leads up to a grand staircase. Two massive doors of polished black metal hold the images of the realm etched within its panels.

A wide smile of accomplishment covers my face as I look to Hermes.

But my happiness fades when darkness still coats his expression. Dread constricts my chest as I tilt my head to the side, wanting to know what plagues him.

"Rhea," His voice cracks and tears well in his eyes and I know something is terribly wrong. My eyes search the sea of immortals and the bodies lying lifeless in the sand.

I look at the faces of those who survived, scanning them for those I call my friends among the strangers that volunteered to give their lives to today's battle.

"Where is Callie?"

As Hermes opens his mouth to answer, the sound of a large door unlocking echoes across the atmosphere. Our attention snaps to the library as one of the large doors opens and it seems as if the world melts away into nothing.

Hermes takes in a sharp breath as he stares with wide eyes at the bright smile that gleams at him. "Hello, son."

Thank you so much for reading. If you enjoyed this story, please leave a review.

Up next up in The Forgotten Goddess series is book four, expected to release fall, 2024. Follow me on social media or sign up for my newsletter to get the latest updates such as the title and cover reveal, release date, and more.

Acknowledgements

Whyyy do acknowledgements have to be so hard?! I can write an entire book without a problem and this little section at the end is the nail in the coffin.

For this one, let's go back to the beginning.

"I spend my birthday, thinking about death."

And it's true, I always do.

When I was making my original plans to release book 1, The Forgotten Goddess, I thought I would have time to release it on my birthday, April 18, 2023.

No one was going to read it anyhow and since my birthday riddled with trauma, I wanted to give myself a good present, for once.

But as #Booktok surprised me and actually took interest in my little story, I knew I needed to give it my all and deliver my best attempt.

So, I revealed the cover of book one on my birthday and delayed the release until August, 2023 and it was totally worth it.

But that nagging little itch in my brain wouldn't stop fixating on that original goal.

Just one year later, so much has changed.

Not only have I released two novels and a novella, but I did another cover reveal and gave myself that birthday present.

Releasing the cover and the surprise novelette on my birthday has brought me full circle and I couldn't be more proud of my story.

Reclaiming the Forgotten Goddess has been my favorite book to write thus far. The journey of trauma recovery is hard.

It fucking sucks sometimes....a lot of the time, actually.... But there is beauty and triumph in there too.

Most days, it feels like I barely have a handle on my notepad, much less my life, but every now and then, I see progress. Occasionally, there is a glimmer of a new person in here.

One who is still having a hard time but is relentless to reclaim herself and forge a new future.

It's very lonely when you look around and realize the people of your past have been left behind. It often feels like an uphill battle, against a fickle sand dune in a massive sea of obstacles, but it's worth it to keep going.

There is value in pushing yourself past new limits and reward in rising victorious.

It's surprising who you find along the way.

The oasis in the desert that shows up when you least expect it.

And it's to all of you, for all of you, that I also write these stories.

The pathway to healing is not solitary one and so, when you find those fellow wanderers, traversing a lonely sea of recovery, don't be afraid to hold out your hand and hold on to each other tight.

When you face those scary things lurking in dark caves, who knows what you will find when you emerge from that darkness. You may just find yourself.

So, to all of you who are coming along on this journey, no matter where you are in that lonely desert or running through a dark cave, keep going. Your dragon awaits you.

First, the kiddos: Thank you for sitting in my office as I work endlessly, each day and night. I hope I'm leaving behind something you can be proud of and that I inspire you to be better.

To Amber: A full moon and a subway sandwich is the weirdest beginning to a friendship but... it tracks. Thank you for listening to my endless ramblings about my story and checking on me when I want to run back inside my dark cave.

To Roxie: You are the delicate flower that survives the hurricane and your gentle power gives me strength. Thank you for randomly braving a TikTok live one night and burrowing into my broken little heart.

To the Inklings: Amber, Roxie, AP, Veronica, Katherine and our Gnome. Our working sessions helped me finish this book and your support helped me keep my sanity... what's left of it.

To my Street Team: The feral late night chats, your unwavering support and camaraderie give me life and help me keep going.

To my readers: Thank you for picking up my stories and I hope you find something in here that helps you feel less alone.

Until tomorrow,

Rebekah Sinclair
Writes

To stay informed on my upcoming releases, book signing events, and more, visit my website and sign up for my newsletter.

www.rebekahsinclairwrites.com

If you'd like to chat with other readers, join the Rebekah Sinclair Writes discord!

Do you want more Mor?
Would you like to know what happens when
a traitor queen faces trial in the fae realm?

Look for more adventures from Orion, The
Morrigan and Hypnos in the next dark
fantasy series from Rebekah Sinclair.

RETURN TO AVALON

2025

REBEKAH SINCLAIR

* 9 7 9 8 9 8 8 1 2 2 5 9 3 *